Lambs to the
Slaughter

Lambs to the Slaughter

A Christopher Worthy/Father Fortis Mystery

<hr />

DAVID CARLSON

coffeetownpress

Kenmore, WA

coffeetownpress

A Coffeetown Press book published by Epicenter Press

Epicenter Press
6524 NE 181st St.
Suite 2
Kenmore, WA 98028

For more information go to:
www.Camelpress.com
www.Coffeetownpress.com
www.Epicenterpress.com
www.davidccarlson.net

Cover watercolor by Kathy Carlson
Interior design by Melissa Vail Coffman

Lambs to the Slaughter
Copyright © 2024 by David Carlson

Library of Congress Control Number: 2024931752

ISBN: 978-1-68492-216-1 (trade paper)
ISBN: 978-1-68492-217-8 (ebook)

One of the themes of Lambs to the Slaughter *is that we do not save ourselves. That theme reminds me of the people who helped me when I most needed help. I dedicate this mystery to John and Ruth Peterson, Bill Bridges, Judy Finn, John Welch, Tim Garner, Taso Gounaris, Margaret Hommell, John Shafer, Ken and Karyn Wilson, and especially Kathy, my wife and friend. Not all of these friends are still living, but all are remembered with fondness and gratitude.*

But I was like a lamb . . . led to the slaughter;
and I knew not that they had devised devices
against me, saying . . . "Let us cut him off from
the land of the living, that his name may be no
longer remembered."

Jeremiah 11: 19 KJV

✝

ACKNOWLEDGMENTS

———◆———

I AM GRATEFUL TO SO MANY WHO have supported my writing efforts. First of all, my wife, Kathy, has been a wonderful first editor of this series and also the artist who paints the covers of the mysteries. I also thank Jennifer McCord of Coffeetown Press and Sara Camilli, my literary agent, for their belief in the series. My sons, Leif and Marten, my daughter-in-law, Mandy, and my grandchildren, Felix and Freya, inspire me with their creativity. Finally, I wish to thank readers who make my day when they ask when Christopher Worthy and Father Fortis will appear again.

CHAPTER ONE

———————◆———————

FATHER NICHOLAS FORTIS THOUGHT THERE WAS nothing more beautiful than autumn in northwest Ohio. Certainly, the number of retreatants to St. Simeon Greek Orthodox Monastery reached its peak in the weeks between late September to early November when the blood red maples and russet oaks were paired with the bluest of skies; Father Nicholas considered no place more beautiful on the monastery's grounds than its small lake.

Not wanting to disturb retreatants who walked the path around the lake, Father Nicholas—Nick—chose the hours of dawn for his own walking meditation. The walk was part of his latest resolution to lose weight. A brisk walk in the morning, unlike visiting the monastery's fitness room, provided a chance to pray without interruption, if one didn't count the cawing crows and the occasional blue heron.

This morning, just as the sun cleared the tree line, he spotted a figure, a woman, he thought, by the bench at the far end of the lake. Immediately, he began to reverse his steps and leave the person to her thoughts and prayers, but when he studied the figure, he could see that she wasn't sitting on the bench but pacing.

He first thought that the woman was trying to ward off the morning chill before he realized that she was agitated. On the chance that the woman needed someone to talk to, Nick picked up his pace. The path, however, meandered from the lake's edge into the woods preventing Nick from maintaining visual contact with the woman until he was nearly at the bench. That was when he saw that the bench was empty, the woman gone.

He initially feared that the woman, in despair, had thrown herself into the water, but he remembered that the lake—more a pond than a lake—was shallow, no more than five feet deep in its center. Yes, Nick knew that a person could drown in less depth, but he speculated that it would take anyone intent on suicide at least five minutes to wade out to even three or four feet of water.

He sat down on the bench for a moment, thinking the woman had more likely taken the path on the other side of the lake to return to the monastery or had chosen one of the paths leading from the lake into the woods. For the rest of the walk, however, Nick met no one. It did no good for him to tell himself to mind his own business. Until he knew otherwise, he would continue to believe that the woman was troubled by something. *I am a priest, after all,* he thought, *even if I am a slow one.*

ST. SIMEON'S REFECTORY

NICK SET HIS BREAKFAST TRAY DOWN on the table next to the young monk. "Brother Pachomius, I need a favor," Nick said.

The young monk looked up from a bowl of muesli and gave Nick a big smile. Not all the monks at St. Simeon's appreciated Nick working with Christopher Worthy, the renowned homicide investigator, but Nick knew from questions that Brother Pachomius had asked him on several occasions that the novice wasn't one of them.

"Ask me anything, Father Nicholas. Really, anything."

Immediately, Nick suspected that he'd made a mistake. St. Simeon's abbot had given Nick permission to help Worthy on cases when a priest would be helpful, but that permission came with a condition. Nick had to be careful that his unusual extracurricular activities didn't disturb the community. There were already too many retreatants and visitors to St. Simeon's who asked about the monastery's somewhat famous detective-monk. He was certain that the abbot would change his mind if Nick developed a following among the younger monks like Brother Pachomius.

"What I need is your computer skills," Nick said. "If you didn't know it before, you might as well know now that technology isn't one of my strengths."

Pachomius leaned toward Nick and whispered, "Are you working on a case, Father?"

Nick shook his head. "No, it's just something I'm curious about."

"Research then?"

"You could put it that way. You monitor the security cameras in the morning, don't you?" When Nick saw Brother Pachomius' eager nod, he realized there was nothing he could do to damper the young monk's hope that Nick was including him in a mystery.

"Is there someone here at St. Simeon's who shouldn't be here?" Pachomius asked.

"Actually, I'm wondering about the opposite. I want to know if a car left the grounds between six-thirty and six-forty-five this morning."

"Someone here on retreat?" Pachomius asked.

"That's what I don't know. But it would be a woman."

The young monk started to rise to his feet before Nick held his arm. "Finish your breakfast, my son. There's no hurry."

Brother Pachomius grinned sheepishly as he sat back down. "Father, have you heard from your friend, Mr. Worthy?"

Nick realized that if he didn't do something to calm the novice monk, he'd have little peace over his own breakfast. He bowed his head and offered a much-longer-than-usual prayer. Yet, Pachomius' question found its way into his prayer. He asked for God's protection and guidance for Worthy, now retired from Detroit's homicide division and running a private detection agency in both Detroit and Rome, Italy, where he lived half of the year with his wife, Lena. That prayer for Worthy's protection was one he offered every day, a request that included an added petition that, as God saw fit, Nick could once again work with Worthy. He had to admit that a part of him wished that Brother Pachomius were right. It had been ten months since he'd worked a case with Worthy, one in Rome that had nearly cost Nick his life. He knew that his close call with death had shaken Worthy more than him, and, over the last ten months, he'd speculated that Worthy was deliberately avoiding asking for his help on other cases. *Then again*, he thought, as he finished his prayer and made the sign of the cross, *maybe Christopher doesn't need me anymore.*

CHAPTER TWO

St. Simeon's Security Office

Nick watched Brother Pachomius' hands fly over the computer keyboard in the monastery's security office. When Nick had first entered the monastery, there'd been little concern for security. The gates were locked at night, and a monk was assigned to sit in the gatehouse during the daytime, but that was more to greet retreatants than look for potential trouble. Back then, the extent of the monastery's security had been a large book in the guesthouse where visitors logged their names and addresses.

The country had changed over the last two decades. First, there seemed to be more untreated mentally ill people who felt drawn to monasteries to find solace or perhaps to act out their delusions. The psychiatric facility in Tifton, along with the police and fire departments, was now on speed dial at St. Simeon's.

Second, monasteries were increasingly being harassed by groups and persons who, following unreliable internet sites, were convinced that bizarre rituals or sexual orgies were taking place within monastery walls. Crude graffiti came not just in the mail but had also been found spray-painted on the walls that surrounded St. Simeon's grounds.

Third, St. Simeon's had been in the news for building bridges with both its Amish neighbors and the growing Muslim community in northwest Ohio. When the largest mosque in Toledo received death threats and experienced vandalism during the rise of ISIS, St. Simeon's had offered one of its larger community rooms for Muslim prayers. TV and newspaper coverage of the gesture had garnered the appreciation of local government officials but had also brought to St. Simeon's something the community hadn't expected—death threats.

"I've cued up the fifteen minutes you asked about, Father," Brother Pachomius said.

"Good. Let's take a look."

Pointing to the two screens, the novice said, "The front gate is covered by this camera, and the other camera is aimed down our access road," Pachomius said.

"You're thinking someone could have parked outside the gate and come onto the grounds?"

The novice nodded. "It wouldn't take much for a fit person to scale the wall."

"Okay, show me what you found, but go back another thirty minutes."

"Ah, I think I get it. You're thinking the woman might have come earlier."

After hitting a few keys, Brother Pachomius brought up the view of the front gate and then the view of the narrow access road that abutted St. Simeon's. "The view of the road is pretty dark because the sun wasn't up yet."

From the first camera covering the front gate, Nick saw nothing unusual, not even a car or pickup truck making deliveries, but at the ten-minute mark on the second camera, he could see a dark sedan pass by slowly. When it was about thirty yards past the gate, the brake lights came on and the car stopped.

"This could be something," Nick said.

After ten seconds, however, the car drove off and disappeared from the screen.

"Rewind it, Brother, and run it slowly."

Nick drew closer to the screen. As soon as the car appeared from the left side of the screen, he said, "Pause it there. Now, can you zoom in on the license plate?"

Pachomius obeyed but then sighed. "It's too dark. All we can tell for sure is that it doesn't look like an Ohio plate."

"Okay. Now pause it once the car stops."

In a moment, Nick saw the car's brake lights light up. "Can you tell if someone gets out of the passenger seat?" he asked.

"Wouldn't the inside light go on if someone opened the door?" Pachomius asked.

"Not necessarily. Someone could have turned it off."

"Sorry, Father. It's too dark to see, given how far the car is down the road, but I don't see anyone outside the car."

Nick sat back. "So, what do we have? We have a car, likely from out-of-state, that drove past our gate this morning. It stops for less than a minute, then drives off. Anything else?"

"Well, there's the woman you saw around the lake about a half-hour later."

"Right. But are the woman and the car connected?"

"I hope so," Pachomius said, before adding, "Sorry, I shouldn't have said that."

"It's all right. I think the fact that we don't see her on the cameras means the woman is here on retreat. If that's the case, I'll look for her in the guest dining room at lunchtime. Anyway, thanks, for trying."

Before Nick got to the door, Pachomius asked, "Do you mind if I take a look by the wall?"

Nick was about to say no, but then asked, "What are you hoping to find?"

"It's just that the road turns at the corner. What if that car turned and stopped back there? Maybe that's where the woman came onto the grounds."

"And maybe that's the way she left our property as well," Nick conceded. "We do nothing until I see if the woman is here on retreat. If I don't see her, let's meet up tomorrow morning at 7:30 before Divine Liturgy?"

Brother Pachomius' face beamed as if Nick had given him a Christmas present.

"Keep in mind, son, that this could all be nothing and will lead to nothing," Nick said.

"Of course, Father," Pachomius replied. "I'll remember that. 'This could be nothing and will lead to nothing.'"

Lowering expectations was almost always sound advice, Nick admitted to himself, though he wasn't good at believing it—such as in this case.

✝

WORTHY'S AND LENA'S APARTMENT, ROME

CHRISTOPHER WORTHY GROANED AS HE LOOKED up from his computer at Lena on the other side of the breakfast table. "I can't believe this. I've been subpoenaed back in Detroit for an appeals case. Homicide division lawyers want me back in four days."

Lena looked up from her croissant and coffee. "Can't they wait? We'll both be in Michigan in a month."

"That's not how the courts work, I'm afraid. One of my homicide cases from over a decade ago," he said, pointing at the screen, "is being appealed, and that kind of case doesn't wait for anyone."

"How long do you think you could be gone?"

"It's impossible to say. Because it was my case, I have to be available until the court makes its decision."

Sighing heavily, Lena said, "I suppose this was bound to happen someday. Maybe we've been lucky that splitting time between Rome and Detroit hasn't posed a problem until now. Will the business here suffer?"

Worthy shook his head. "As you know, the work has been mainly helping English-speaking tourists who've lost their passports or had jewelry stolen from their motel rooms. In other words, low-level stuff. The local police had to handle those complaints before I opened my office."

"But you've spoiled them, Chris. English-speaking victims find working with the police frustrating, but not as frustrating as Rome's police feel working with English speakers. The police will miss you."

"And being missed isn't bad for business, is that what you're saying?"

Lena came around the table, leaned down, and kissed the crown of Worthy's head. "I guess so. But what I haven't said is that I'll miss you. I'll even miss this spot on your head where your hair is thinning."

Worthy reached up and mussed his hair. "You aren't supposed to see that. Anyway, can't you fly back with me now?"

"You know I can't, Chris. Semesters and final exams can't be moved, even with my having tenure. My work and yours are bound to clash sometimes."

Worthy stood and faced Lena. "Well, do not expect me to like being away from you."

Lena hugged Worthy before kissing him. "Same with me. But it's been a while since we've heard from Nick. Will you see him?"

"Of course. I've missed him, even though it's comforting to think of him safe in his monastery. That last case, when Nick was almost killed . . ."

He felt Lena shiver. "I still have nightmares about that, as I know you do. But like you said, he's safe. That's all that counts."

CHAPTER THREE

---◆---

ST. SIMEON'S

RETREATANTS AT ST. SIMEON'S WERE ENCOURAGED to attend an afternoon talk by one of the senior monks, which led Nick to enter the back of the room while Father Constantine was speaking.

St. Simeon's didn't allow more than eight retreatants per weekend, and Nick knew that there were often fewer than that number. From where he was standing, he counted five retreatants in the room before two more entered the room at the last moment. Although three of the first group were women, and one of the latecomers also a female, none of the four was young enough to be the woman whom Nick saw that morning.

After Father Constantine ended his lecture and the retreatants left the room, Nick walked to the guesthouse to talk with Father Ioannis, the Guestmaster.

"Father, can you tell me if there are seven or eight retreatants here this weekend?" Nick asked.

Father Ioannis looked up from a book entitled *New Methods of Winemaking*. "Can I ask why you want to know that?"

Nick was momentarily annoyed at the question. He'd known Father Ioannis for more than a decade and, while the two of them had never been close, he'd never considered Father Ioannis to be one of the monks who resented his absences to help Worthy on cases.

"Is there a problem with me wanting to know that, Father?" Nick asked. "I mean, is there a new rule about protecting the identity of retreatants?"

Father Ioannis' face turned red. "No, no. I wouldn't have asked you except that others have already asked me the same question."

"Others? You mean another monk?"

"Brother Pachomius was here about an hour ago. He wouldn't tell me why he wanted to know that, so I told him that we don't give out that information to novices. But you're hardly that, Father. A novice, I mean." He turned on his computer to a list and turned the screen so that Nick could read it.

"Are you looking for someone in particular?" Father Ioannis asked.

Nick didn't reply as he counted five women's names and three men's names on the list. *So the one retreatant who wasn't at Father Constantine's talk was a female,* he thought. *But is she the woman from the lake?*

"You said 'others' had asked you for the names of retreatants. If Brother Pachomius was one, was there someone else?" Nick asked.

Father Ioannis pointed to the name of one of the other retreatants— Gus Cooper. "He asked to see the list."

"Hmm. Did he say why?"

"He said he was expecting someone he knew to be on retreat this weekend. I asked him to tell me the name, but he said he couldn't remember it. He did think he'd recognize it if he saw it. I know I wasn't very consistent, but I let him look at the list."

"And did he recognize one of the names?" Nick asked.

"I couldn't say, Father. He certainly didn't tell me, but after he looked at the list, he took the key to his room and left."

Nick thought back to the men he'd seen in Father Constantine's session. One man he estimated to be in his early fifties, a bit slumped in posture, wearing a worn flannel shirt, and dangling a prayer cord from his wrist. A second man who entered the room at the last minute looked to be in his forties and wearing khakis and a blue oxford shirt. The third was clearly the oldest, maybe in his late seventies or eighties. One of them, he realized, was Gus Cooper and might have been looking for the woman he'd seen by the lake.

Back in his room, Nick wondered if he had grounds for taking the matter any further. He suspected but had no proof that the woman was at St. Simeon's on retreat, and he certainly had no proof that Gus Cooper had hoped to meet her.

The rule at Simeon's was that retreatants should respect the privacy of the monks. They should approach one of only three monks: the monk who served as confessor while they were on retreat, Father Constantine during one of his sessions, and Father Ioannis, the Guestmaster. The monks at St. Simeon's understood that the opposite—initiating contact with retreatants—was also officially prohibited. That meant that contacting Gus Cooper would be awkward. Besides, what would he say? "Did you come to St. Simeon's hoping to meet a young woman with brown hair pulled back in a ponytail? If you did, I saw her this morning on the other side of the lake."

After Compline and retiring to bed, he lay awake, wondering if anything would be learned the next morning when Brother Pachomius and he inspected the monastery wall. If they found clear evidence that someone—say, the woman—had entered or exited the grounds recently, he'd have no reason to disturb the retreatants. But if there was no evidence, or inconclusive evidence, he felt he had no choice but to find out more about the mystery women.

What Nick couldn't put out of his mind was the woman's agitated movements that morning. *Whoever she is, she was desperate about something,* he thought. *But what?*

✝

OCTOBER 8, 2023,
CHRISTOPHER WORTHY PRIVATE DETECTION
AND INQUIRIES AGENCY, ROME BRANCH

WORTHY NEVER GOT USED TO WALKING the four blocks from his apartment to his office near the Church of St. Maria Sopra Minerva. And his favorite time to do that was early morning when vendors were wheeling carts filled with cheeses, cases of wine, or sides of beef down the cobblestone streets. The strong smell of espressos and pastries wafted out onto the streets from the coffee bars skirting the Pantheon, even as nuns and elderly parishioners passed him as they headed for early Mass at one of the nearby churches.

He remembered the vow he made as a teenager in his first-year Latin class back in Kentucky. Staring at photos of Roman monuments in the textbook, he promised himself that one day he would visit Rome and see those sites for himself. Only six years ago, when a case brought Worthy to Venice, he'd yearned for the chance to visit Rome, but his schedule in Detroit didn't allow even a quick visit. He'd left Italy, wondering if he'd missed his only chance to see Rome.

It was just three years ago that an assassin's attack on the Pope and Ecumenical Patriarch brought Worthy to Rome to work with Nick on the case. As he travelled around the city on that first visit, he found that Rome exceeded his expectations. Falling in love with Lena while on that case had meant that for the next two years, he'd returned to Rome for one, sometimes two, extended stays. But what he could never have imagined—living in Rome—became a reality when Lena and he married a year ago, and he opened a branch office of his detective agency in the city. Working almost solely with English-speaking visitors to the city meant that he lived in Rome from May to mid-November, the high-tourist season, and the other months in Detroit, where he worked the other branch of his business.

Detroit. Twenty-five years ago, Detroit was where he'd entered the police force after college and the police academy. Twenty years ago, Detroit was where he'd become a homicide detective, green and of no more than average ability. Fifteen years ago, Detroit was where he'd developed his own, often considered slow, approach to solving homicides—poring over the hours, days, weeks, and sometimes months of the victim's movements before his or her death, believing that in this systematic work, he'd uncover when, where, and why the victim's life had intersected with a killer's. His methodical approach had been so successful that he became a media favorite, and that meant he'd been resented as much as respected by colleagues.

A case from thirteen years ago was the one being appealed. It was also a case he'd never been able to forget despite trying. The body of a young woman, Renee Vickers, had been found mutilated in Detroit. Because Renee Vickers was African-American, tensions in the city ran high, and charges of police indifference continued even after the case was taken from the first team and given to Worthy.

In his typical fashion, Worthy began by refocusing the case on the victim and, in so doing, he discovered that Renee Vickers hadn't been seen by friends in Detroit for three days before her body was discovered. He also discovered that in the last year of her life, Vickers turned to prostitution to support a deepening drug addiction.

The previous investigation team, which included his nemesis, Phillip Sherrod, had worked the case for seven fruitless months before Worthy took it over. Sherrod's team assumed that Renee Vickers, being new to the street game, had been killed by a pimp. There were no shortages of suspects, but that team could make nothing stick.

Reporting only to his captain and ignoring pressure from the media, Worthy took a different approach. Reviewing the autopsy photos, he concluded that Renee Vickers hadn't been killed carelessly, but cleverly. The body, where it was discovered and the way it had been desecrated, suggested to Worthy that the body had been staged. Gradually, Worthy came to believe that the killer had committed the crime as a challenge to the police.

Five months after being given the case, Worthy arrested William Tremont, a twenty-year-old from Midland, Michigan. The arrest had been front-page news, and Sherrod wasn't the only colleague who viewed Worthy, known for working alone, as a glory hound. But the greater cost of Worthy's success on the Renee Vickers' case what awaited him that night when he returned home. His wife, Susan, demanded a divorce, and five months later, his older daughter, Allyson, a high school junior, ran away. She returned after three months without an explanation, but she'd been clear on why she'd left—her father had ruined her life.

Relations with Allyson, now an FBI agent, had been somewhat repaired, but as he thought about returning to Detroit to defend his handling of the Renee Vickers' case before the appellate court, he felt the past dragging him back to the worst year of his life.

In the official email he'd received from Howard Hullinger, the chief lawyer for the police department, he'd read the basis of the appeal. No, there hadn't been any new evidence in the case; rather, Worthy was accused of bulldozing the interrogation of Tremont to gain a confession, ignoring the possibility that Tremont had been high on Ecstasy when first questioned.

What puzzled Worthy was why the court granted the appeal, given that Tremont had been given a toxicology screening when he was first arrested. Something about the screening, Worthy concluded, must have been found to be questionable. What Worthy remembered about Tremont's confession was that he'd been excited, high even, but on hubris, not drugs, as he bragged about how long it had taken the police to find him.

Worthy assumed that Tremont, with nothing better to do in prison for the past thirteen years than pore over law books, had written the script for the appeal. The clever twenty-year-old was now thirty-three, and, Worthy learned, had earned two Masters degrees while in prison. Tremont had found something, something that had convinced the courts to grant the appeal.

As one of Detroit's most successful homicide detectives, Worthy had interrogated a slew of killers. In nearly every case, he'd faced men and women whose poor choices had led them down a dark path that ended in a nightmare. In Worthy's experience, killers were, in the end, not so much evil as sad.

William Tremont was the exception. Maybe this was Worthy's way of saying that, despite what was shown on TV crime dramas, true psychopaths are rare. Tremont was one of the few killers whom Worthy arrested who'd stalked and then killed another human being without remorse. The murder of Renee Vickers had been a challenge to Tremont, and the appeal suggested that Tremont thought that he'd discovered something that would lead to his exoneration this time.

Another reason Worthy wasn't looking forward to returning to Detroit was that the appeal would force him to reengage with his old homicide division. When he retired the year before, his captain had given him the perfunctory party, but it had seemed lame. When his fellow detectives learned of his retirement plan to open up private detection offices in Detroit and Rome, some of them didn't hide their mixed feelings—happy that Worthy was leaving, resentful that he seemed to be landing on his feet again.

He pictured walking into division headquarters and seeing the faces of ex-colleagues who'd be pleased that one of his most famous cases might be overturned by the courts; leading that parade would be Phillip Sherrod.

The only detective happy to see him would have been Carnell "Hoops" Henderson, his partner on another case that had led to both Worthy and him receiving commendations. Now even that welcome wouldn't happen because Worthy had hired Henderson to manage his private detection office in Detroit.

Worthy's thoughts were focused so much on what was awaiting him in Michigan that he was surprised when he turned the corner and found himself in front of his Rome office. He stood, looking at the door with his name on it, aware that he had a better working relationship with the police in Rome than he did with colleagues in Detroit. *Maybe it's just a matter of time until the Italians get tired of me as well,* he thought.

CHAPTER FOUR

---◆---

St. Simeon's

A s was true of many novices, Brother Pachomius had trouble rising for early morning prayers—but not today. He knew a few of the senior monks would be surprised to see him already in church when they arrived, and he expected his confessor, Father Bessarion, to ask for an explanation.

Brother Pachomius would be the first to admit that his two years at St. Simeon's were challenging. He knew that struggling to adjust to monastic life was normal, as life in the world was almost the polar opposite of life in St. Simeon's. In both high school and college, he'd kept to a schedule of finishing school assignments by nine in the evening so that he could play computer games until one or two o'clock in the morning. Two or three o'clock in the morning at St. Simeon's was approaching the time to rise for the day.

Not having a computer in his cell at St. Simeon's was another adjustment he faced. He knew that some of the senior monks used computers regularly, but novices lived offline twenty-four/seven. His sole contact with a computer came as he sat in St. Simeon's security office.

Another challenge of monastic life for Pachomius was the daily and weekly rhythm of services, which by his second year at St. Simeon's had begun to feel monotonous. Before he entered the monastery, he'd imagined that the numerous prayers services would feel like oases in the day, times when he would have a break from studies and work duties. And, at the beginning, the frequent prayer services had been that for him. Now, however, the repeated services felt like they were carving a groove in his mind. His hope that the feeling would pass, that he could resolve the issue by concentrating, hadn't happened. Instead, the sense of monotony had increased.

Father Nick's request for help had consequently felt like a "get out of jail free" card to Pachomius. He was tempted to ask Father Nicholas if he ever felt the same when Christopher Worthy asked for his help, but Pachomius was sure that Father Nicholas would take his question as proof that he was letting the woman by the lake distract him—so, as hard as it would be, he would pretend that searching the woods with Father Nicholas after breakfast was nothing out of the ordinary—but that would be hard.

✝

The Christopher Worthy Private Detection
and Inquiries Agency, Detroit Branch

Carnell "Hoops" Henderson was watching the last two minutes of the Pistons' game when the phone rang. With the score tied, he was tempted to let the message go to voicemail, but he changed his mind when he saw who was calling.

"Chris, what's up?" he said, muting the audio while still watching the game.

"Just hoping you can pick me up at the airport tonight."

"I thought you weren't coming in for a couple of weeks."

"So did I, but that was before I was subpoenaed on an appeal case. It's an old case and bound to be a headache. I'll fill you in when I get there. And thanks for keeping me up to date on business in Detroit, Hoops. It looks like business is good."

Carnell "Hoops" Henderson found it easy to be with Worthy, but that hadn't always been the case. Their paths had first crossed a decade earlier when, at the lowest point in his career and personal life, Henderson had been partnered with Worthy on the murder of an elderly priest. There was a moment in that case when Henderson's future in the department had been in Worthy's hands, and Worthy, against what Henderson expected, chose to rescue him.

The unlikely partnership included their coming from different worlds—Worthy from rural Kentucky and Henderson from inner-city Detroit. After a rough beginning, however, they found a way to work together, each giving the other space to pursue different approaches on the case.

The crisis that had nearly destroyed Henderson ten years before was still present, though now better understood and better managed. Back in 2015, Henderson's son, Jamie, only ten years old at the time, began to exhibit antisocial behaviors at school and withdrawal at home. Social workers, psychologists, and psychiatrists descended on the family of three: Hoops, his wife, Sulla, and Jamie. For a few months, Hoops and wife were investigated, not for child abuse, but for something far more nebulous and frightening—the possibility that they were somehow schizophrenogenic, parents whose relationship with their child had produced schizophrenia.

Now, ten years later, Jamie's schizophrenia was largely controlled by medication, but another issue—Jamie was also diagnosed on the autism spectrum—had begun to dominate. For the past year, Jamie had made progress, now able to live in a halfway house where his needs—medical, psychological, and material—were met. Jamie had progressed so much that he'd been able to hold down a part-time job repairing radios and stereos for an online company. He also served as a one-man welcome committee at the halfway house for new arrivals. Jamie was also able to come home on weekends, though he'd begun to describe the halfway house as home.

If Jamie had improved, so had Sulla, and so had their understanding of their son's condition. The need to blame someone was over. They were closer to accepting that life had handed them a challenge that could change, but never disappear. With that acceptance, Hoops' life, including work, had improved, leading to his promotion to lieutenant the year before.

His longed-for promotion was what made his decision to join Worthy as a private detective a surprise to his colleagues. For those who knew him, however, his decision made sense. He'd been looking for a new challenge, and the opportunity to work with Worthy on cases not restricted to homicides was enticing. In the months he'd held down the Detroit office while Worthy was in Rome, he'd never regretted his decision.

"Anything new on your end that I should know about, Hoops?" Worthy asked, breaking into his thoughts.

"A bit of good news, Chris, at least potentially. A town board from one of the suburbs is interested in hiring us. They want someone to keep an eye on a company they've hired to build some of those warehouses out by the freeway."

"Do they suspect anything?" Worthy asked.

"I'm not sure. It looks more like due diligence on their part, seeing that they granted the company a tax abatement."

"Ah, I think I get it. If we agree to do the work, will we need to bring in an accountant?"

"You forget that I was a business major in college," Henderson said. "I'm not saying that I won't have to do some homework to keep on top of everything, but I like the challenge. Not only will the town board pay well, but this could bring in more of this sort of work in the future."

"Sounds like you've already decided. You've got my vote, just so long as you know that we can hire temp help if we need to."

"Crunching numbers will be a break from tracking down deadbeat dads, and the job won't start until the new year. But I'm sorry about the appeal, especially given that you'll have to go back to our old home in homicide to look at the case file."

"Worse than that is the fact that the case under appeal is one that I took over from a team that Sherrod was on. He'll be itching to testify about his time on the case and criticize everything I did differently from him and his crew."

"And here we thought we left Sherrod behind when we retired."

"Who was it who said, 'The past is not over; it isn't even past?'"

After the phone call, Henderson sat back and shook his head. Phillip Sherrod was not just Worthy's nemesis, but his as well. It was hard to call someone a racist who was at odds with everyone, no matter what race or gender, and that was Sherrod. It seemed funny to Henderson that he had never thought of Sherrod as married or having kids.

Then, the thought, the razor-sharp one that always popped into his head unbidden, did so again. *Of course, Sherrod would have kids. They might be as nasty as their old man, but they wouldn't be schizophrenic and on the spectrum.*

CHAPTER FIVE

---◆---

St. Simeon's—Searching the Woods

ON A MAP OF THE MONASTERY GROUNDS, Nick showed Brother Pachomius the paths that ran from the lake through the woods to the walls forming the boundaries of St. Simeon's. If the woman whom Nick observed had used one of the paths to enter the grounds, he figured that she would have left the grounds the same way.

When the monastery's bells rang at eight a.m., Nick and Brother Pachomius were walking the road adjacent to the monastery until they came to the place where two paths were closest to the wall. After coming to a place in the wall where a person could climb over, each of them walked slowly along one of the paths toward the lake, looking for anything unusual.

Nick prayed for the mystery woman as he walked. He hoped Pachomius was doing the same, although he sensed their prayers would be different. When he was a novice like Brother Pachomius, he would have prayed for his request to be granted—in this case, that they'd find some evidence of the woman. But now, his prayer was almost the opposite, that the two of them would fail if this were God's will. Yes, Nick believed that for some reason God allowed him to witness the women's distress the previous morning, but only God knew what that reason was.

He thought again about of what novices are told in their first months at St. Simeon's. The one and only goal of the monastic life is to learn how to pray. He noticed that the novices' faces changed from agreement—novices often assumed that prayer would be the easiest part of monastic life—to puzzlement when they were told that their prayer life would go through numerous cycles if they remained at St Simeon's.

From the boredom and then the exaggerated concentration that Nick had seen on Pachomius' face during prayer services, he suspected that Pachomius was experiencing one of the first trials that came with prayer. The two contrasting expressions, boredom and the furrowed brow of exaggerated concentration, formed a spiritual dance that Nick knew every novice contended with. For the first months in the monastery, most novices feel God's nearness in the community's prayer services. They might even feel pride at how quickly they are adjusting to monastic life. But then, without warning, the daily prayer services of the Daily Office start to become a chore.

It is common for novices to try to defeat the boredom by focusing on every word of the prayers. That forced concentration soon becomes exhausting, and the novice inevitably opens his eyes to sneak peeks at the older monks surrounding him, wondering how they are able to recite the same prayers day after day without going out of their minds.

If Pachomius had a genuine monastic vocation, he would discover that the problem wasn't the boredom but the forced concentration. The joy of prayer returned when a novice accepted that all he had to offer God was his boredom, his mental blankness. That was when prayer changed from being something the monk did for God to being something that God gave to the monk. But Pachomius wasn't there yet, and Nick worried that the excitement of the mystery woman would distract Pachomius from advancing in his prayer life.

As Nick approached the place where the path ended by the lake, he prayed, *O Lord, keep me from harming this impressionable soul.* Looking down, he saw something lying on top of the leaves. He knelt down and picked up the two twigs that had been joined with twine to form a cross.

Even though Nick knew that the cross could have been dropped by anyone, he wondered if the woman had dropped it. To his left, he heard Brother Pachomius ask, "Did you find something?"

When Nick handed the cross to the novice, he saw the look of excitement on Pachomius' face. "Do you think it's—?"

Nick cut off the novice. "I assume nothing, other than that the cross was probably dropped by a retreatant. Did you find anything?"

Pachomius shook his head. "Not even a candy wrapper."

"Any evidence of foot traffic?" Nick asked.

"I came across some muddy stretches from the rain two days ago but no footprints."

Nick nodded. "Same with me. So, just this cross."

"Do you think there are fingerprints on it?"

Nick smiled. "It's not a crime to make a cross, Brother. Anyway, I'm sure the only fingerprints on it now are ours."

Looking dejected, Brother Pachomius asked, "So, it means nothing?"

"Of course it means something. Whoever made it probably did so while praying. At noonday prayers today, Brother, let's add our prayers for whoever left this cross. But there's something else we can do. I'll pin the cross on the message board in the guesthouse and leave a note, letting the retreatants know that we found it by the lake. I'll also invite her to contact me if she wants."

"You said 'her' and 'she.' So you do think it could be the woman."

Nick took the cross back. "Just a figure of speech, my son. Just a figure of speech."

He heard nothing the rest of that day, Saturday, but on the way to the church the next morning for Divine Liturgy, he stopped at the guesthouse and saw that someone had retrieved the cross. Knowing that weekend retreatants were required to leave by early evening, he began to doubt that the person who'd made the cross intended to contact him.

Toward the end of the service, he noticed a young woman standing at the back of the church and dabbing her eyes. That was nothing usual, as many retreatants found that the silence of a retreat could lead to tears of thanksgiving or sorrow. What interested Nick, however, was the fact that this woman wasn't one of the female retreatants he'd seen in Father Constantine's lecture the previous day.

Back in his room, he was surprised to find an email from Worthy, which made him temporarily forget the woman. After reading the message, he could tell that Worthy wasn't happy to be called back to Detroit because of an appeal, but Nick was happy to think that he'd likely see his friend in a few days.

He was halfway through replying to Worthy when his cellphone rang. He looked down to see a name on the screen that he didn't recognize—M. Demetrios. Opening the phone, he answered, "This is Father Nicholas."

There was a long silence on the other end before a soft voice replied, "You found my cross out by the lake. Father, I'd like to talk with you."

CHAPTER SIX

---◆---

OCTOBER 9, 2023, DETROIT

As Worthy rode with Henderson from the airport, he glanced over to say, "When I called you yesterday, I forgot to ask about Jamie."

After pausing, Henderson replied, "It says something, doesn't it, when the best thing I can say is that things aren't any worse? Jamie is in his second year at the halfway house, and he also has a part-time job repairing electronics. But he's with us most weekends and sometimes at other times."

The drove in silence until Henderson added, "I know we've always been honest, Chris, so I thought I'd be blunt."

"I wouldn't want it any other way. The question I should have asked is how Jamie feels about the halfway house and the job?"

"That's what Sulla keeps reminding me to do—to see Jamie's world as he sees it. I try, but it's hard. There are others at the halfway house who're being treated for some form of schizophrenia, but most of them are outgoing, almost manicky. Jamie has always been quiet, and so it made a kind of weird sense when we were told that he's also on the autism spectrum. He's smart, really smart in some ways—you wouldn't believe the puzzles he can solve—but when something bothers him, he goes and hides. Literally, he goes somewhere and hides. Maybe it would have been better if Sulla and I had had other kids. But about the time we were thinking about that, Jamie was showing the first signs—the withdrawing, the staring at the TV, the using the eraser on his arms. So we didn't want to risk another kid. We had more than we could handle as it was."

"You must worry about his future," Worthy said.

"You got that right. That's what makes it hard for me to be content when Jamie says he's happy. I mean, Chris, I don't doubt that he's telling the truth. He always tells the truth, but I keep thinking what will happen to him when . . . well, I don't have to spell it out."

"Well, if it's okay with you, I'd like to see him."

"Jamie would like that. I've always thought that was because you've never pitied him, never treated him like . . . like so many others treat him."

"I appreciate that, Hoops, but I can't take credit for that. I saw the damage that pity—at least that kind of pity—can do when I had a summer job back when I was in college. I worked with kids who were labelled 'troubled teenagers,' and I noticed what happened when new staff members pitied them. The kids would react, sometimes acting out, other times just ignoring the newbies. It wasn't the first time that the kids taught me more than some of the staff did."

"I know what you mean by 'that kind of pity.' I see it on people's faces when they find out about Jamie."

"Oh yeah, the look. That kind of pity changes nothing, unless you count the change in the person doing the pitying, and that's not a good change. The bad type of pitiers—if there is such a word—get a kind of buzz. It's like the pleasure some people get by petting a dog."

"Except when the dog doesn't want to be petted and bites back," Henderson said.

"And that only makes the pitier feel more virtuous. 'Look how I'm suffering, and all I did was try to help.' They never stop to think that they deserve getting bit."

Henderson didn't say anything for a moment. It wasn't the first time that Worthy had waded into Henderson's pain and had helped him see things more clearly.

"What you're saying, Chris, is close to what the social worker told us last week. 'Don't be afraid,' she told us, 'to let Jamie teach you what he needs from you.'"

St. Simeon's

WHEN NICK ENTERED THE CHAPEL ALONE—he'd decided not to tell Brother Pachomius about the phone call—he recognized the woman from Divine Liturgy that morning. *So she is the woman who was at the lake,* he thought. She was standing, arms crossed her body, beneath the icon of the Theotokos, the Virgin Mary, as she watched Nick walk down the center aisle.

Nick paused to bow before the altar before approaching the woman. "I'm Father Nicholas. Shall we sit down?"

The woman bowed her head as she replied in a voice little more than a whisper, "I know who you are, Father. I'm Marina Demetrios." After a pause, she added, "I'm from Detroit" before saying, "I don't know why I said that. I guess I'm nervous."

After he sat down next to her, Nick said, "I don't think we've met before, so being nervous is understandable."

Marina Demetrios took a tissue from her purse and dabbed at her eyes. "No, it's me, Father. I'm a mess."

"Take your time, Marina, and please call me Nick if that would help."

"That's my younger brother's name. Nick, I mean, but I think it's better if I call you Father."

"Well, why don't you pretend you're talking to your brother?"

Marina took a deep breath and pointed up at the ceiling. "I want to believe . . . that," she said.

"I'm sorry. What do you want to believe?"

"When I was a child, our priest would point to the icon of Christ in the dome and say, 'Our Lord looks down on us and knows all our troubles.'"

Something told Nick to say nothing. Sitting next to him was the person who'd looked tortured the day before by the lake. She'd made a cross out of twigs and left or dropped it near the site. And that morning in Divine Liturgy, she looked thoroughly beaten down.

"When I found the note you left with my cross, I thought that maybe God did see me, that He sees what I'm carrying. You see, I've read about your work with the detective in Detroit. But this whole weekend,

I couldn't get up the courage to contact you. I read in the pamphlet that retreatants shouldn't bother the monks. So then I thought that my plan to meet you was just selfish."

Nick waited until the woman finished wiping the tears from her face. "When you can, Marina, why don't you tell me about the burden you're carrying. There is no burden that our Lord doesn't want to ease."

Marina Demetrios bent over in the chair and started to sob.

"Yes, go ahead and cry, Marina. Perhaps you've been holding that in for a while."

Marina started to moan, even as she managed to nod. Nick brought out a handkerchief from beneath his robes and placed it in the woman's hand. For a few moments, she continued to sob uncontrollably, but then the crying gradually subsided.

"My mother died two years ago. She was diagnosed with cancer and then, five weeks later to the day, she died. I should tell you that I'm the oldest in the family, Father. Momma's death was hard on Poppa. He did his best by us, but with work and three kids at home, well, he kind of died too. Anyway, I went from being a full-time graduate student to working full-time while taking some courses online. I can't help thinking that if I'd dropped everything . . ."

"You said you were the oldest of three. Tell me about the other children," Nick said.

"Nicky is a year younger than me. After high school, he went into the Army. He's still serving in Germany."

Marina took a deep breath, but didn't say anything as she continued to look down at the floor. Finally, Nick said, "And the youngest?"

"I keep thinking I should have done more, but Father, I tried, I really did."

"I'm sure you did, Marina."

"It's Sophia. She was just eighteen when Momma died. I don't know how it happened. Sophie was always on the quiet side. At first, she started falling behind in her classes at the community college. With Dad and me working, there wasn't always someone home when she got home from class. So, we didn't know that Sophie had dropped her old friends and was hanging out with some other kids until she was arrested for shoplifting. Then she was picked up for possession of pot.

She was in juvenile detention for two months, but she seemed just the same when she came out. We all knew that if Momma were alive, she'd have . . . she'd have done something. But we couldn't get through to Sophia. She was just lost, and then . . ."

Nick sensed that Marina was coming to the most difficult part. After praying that no one would come into the church, he asked, "Where is Sophia now?"

Marina began to moan again, even as her hands were clasped so tightly that the ends of her fingers turned white. "She's in prison, Father. But that's not the worst of it. She was convicted of murder eight months ago. It was a drug deal outside the city, and there was a disagreement over something, probably money. Anyway, a man was shot."

"Oh, I see. What part did Sophia play in the shooting?"

Marina looked up at the icon of Christ in the dome again. "She doesn't remember. She doesn't even remember being in the motel room or the car. But she must have been. The police . . . the police found her fingerprints on the gun."

Nick exhaled, only then realizing how much of Marina's sorrow he had absorbed. From his first glimpse of Marina's anxious pacing by the lake to seeing her tearful that morning in the church, he'd felt something big was coming. But now that Marina had shared her burden, he wondered what he could say to console her.

His first instinct was to ask how convinced the police and the prosecutor were that Sophia had fired the fatal bullet and if Marina believed that her sister had received adequate legal representation. Marina might have come to St. Simeon's specifically to talk with him, but at that moment she needed him more as a priest than a detective.

"Marina, when horrible things happen, there's a part of us that blames ourselves. I would imagine that your father is doing the same."

Marina nodded. "Since Sophie's arrest, Poppa has lost thirty pounds. He traded shifts so he could be in the courtroom every day, but I could see that he was losing hope. Poppa or I go sometimes every week to visit Sophie, and we both come home gutted, but it's hardest on Poppa."

Although Nick knew that it would be painful for Marina to talk about the trial, he also knew that he needed more information if he were to offer more than prayers for her family. In a low voice, he asked, "And Sophia has continued to say that she doesn't remember the shooting?"

"After she'd been there . . . in prison, I mean, for about a month, she said she didn't want to talk about that night anymore. It's too painful, I guess, and she can't see that it makes any difference now that she'd been convicted."

Nick nodded. "I can see how she might say that. If I'm to help you, Marina, I need to know if Sophia testified at her trial."

Marina shook her head. "Her lawyer said it would only harm her case. All she could tell the jury was that she didn't remember anything."

"What I'm asking, Marina, is if Sophia pled guilty or not guilty."

"Oh, Father, that's what's so horrible. Her lawyer said given her age, she'd just turned twenty, that if she pleaded guilty to manslaughter, he could make a deal with the prosecutor for a ten-year sentence. He said with good behavior, Sophia could be out in seven years. But . . ."

"Take your time, Marina."

"The judge made an example of Sophia. I guess because he saw that Sophia was accused of shooting a major drug dealer, he thought that Sophia must be somebody important in the drug world. But Sophia was just a user, Father."

"So her sentence?"

"Thirty years, Father, for second-degree murder. Thirty years."

Nick didn't say anything for a moment before saying, "Marina, I want to visit Sophia."

CHAPTER SEVEN

———— ◆ ————

WHEN HIS PHONE RANG THE NEXT MORNING, Worthy reached over on the bed, expecting to find Lena sleeping next to him. It took him a moment to realize that he was in his Detroit apartment, not in Rome.

Rubbing the sleep from his eyes, he looked at the caller ID on his phone. *Why is Nick calling me?* he asked himself.

"Christopher, I just realized that you're probably still trying to catch up on your sleep. I hope you can forgive me."

"Is everything okay, Nick?"

"With me? Yes, I'm fine. But I wanted to let you know that I'm driving up to Detroit for a pastoral visit. I'm hoping you might be free for dinner tonight."

"Absolutely, Nick, but I don't want you driving back to St. Simeon's. Stay at my apartment tonight."

"I was about to ask if Lena would mind, but then I remembered that she's probably still in Rome."

"Nick, she wouldn't mind even if she were here. We both said that it's been too long since we've seen you."

"Amen, and again I say, amen, my friend."

"What hospital are you going to, Nick?"

"Hospital? Oh, sorry. No, I'm not going to a hospital, but Barminster, the woman's prison. I'll fill you in on that over supper."

"Well, you have me intrigued. Barminster is fifteen miles or so west of the city. Let's meet at that Italian place you like."

"Enzo's? Not just my favorite Italian place, but Lena's as well. And if she likes an Italian restaurant in Detroit, it has to be good."

When the call ended, Worthy lay back down and replayed the conversation with Nick. On the one hand, Nick described his trip as a pastoral call. Having grown up the son of a minister, Worthy knew that much of his father's time during the week was spent visiting the sick, the dying, and anyone called a "shut-in."

On the other hand, Nick's pastoral visit was to Michigan's main women's prison, Barminster. Nick would be visiting a different kind of "shut-in," someone locked behind bars and staring at the walls of a prison cell.

Worthy remembered accompanying Nick to prisons before. Inmates tended to give Worthy dark looks and sometimes spat at him, giving credence to the adage that prison inmates could spot a cop a mile away. Worthy, though, was thinking more of the stunned looks on inmates' faces when they saw Nick. A man standing six feet four inches, weighing close to three hundred pounds, with a heavy black beard, ponytail, and wearing black robes—that usually brought cell blocks to complete silence.

✝

ST. SIMEON'S

SITTING IN THE SECURITY OFFICE OF ST. SIMEON'S, Brother Pachomius struggled with his emotions as he watched Father Nicholas drive out the gate. Father Nicholas had shared that he'd met with the mystery woman, now no longer a mystery, and was driving to Detroit to follow through on a promise that he'd made to her.

Pachomius wouldn't deny that he'd have jumped at the chance to accompany Father Nicholas—and he knew from Father Nicholas' comments that he guessed as much.

"Do you understand why novices aren't allowed to leave the monastery except for reasons of health?" Nicholas had asked him as they ate breakfast together.

"I suppose it's about leaving the world behind," he'd said. What he hadn't added was asking why Father Nicholas didn't have to follow that rule.

Father Nicholas had nodded. "Some of the early heresies preached that the world is evil. We don't believe that. Yes, there is evil in the world, and there is evil in monasteries, even as there are temptations everywhere. And there have surely been as many saints in the world as there are in monasteries. But what the monastic tradition understands is that it's harder to withstand temptation in the world because the world, unlike us, isn't consciously fighting against those temptations."

"You're saying that if I left St. Simeon's, I might succumb?"

"This isn't personal, Pachomius. You're a young monk and your mind and soul are still in formation. What I'm trying to say is that what is taken for normal in the world—ambition, frenetic activity, endless distractions, and yes, even sitting in front of a computer for hours on end—would have a crippling effect on us as monks. Are there people of faith in the world that have found ways to spiritually survive in that climate? Yes, there are, but they're like fish who are swimming every minute against the current."

"But Father, that's like saying monks know that we're weak and easily tempted."

Nick had sat forward and looked across the breakfast table at him. "That's exactly what I'm saying, which is why I need you to pray for me while I'm away. I've been a monk for over twenty years, but even if I'd been a monk for sixty years, the world can still defeat me by drowning out my interior silence."

CHAPTER EIGHT

———— ◆ ————

DETROIT—BARMINSTER WOMAN'S PRISON

LOOKING UP AT THE RAZOR WIRE ATOP the walls surrounding Barminster prison, Nick was reminded of the words of Jesus: "I was in prison and you visited me." *How few times have I done this?* Nick thought.

Marina Demetrios' eyes had brightened when he said he wanted to visit Sophia. But then she apologized, saying she had no right to ask that of him.

"It's no problem, Marina, but has your parish priest visited your sister?" he'd asked.

Marina had looked down before saying that the family had been too ashamed to return to church after Sophia's arrest, and her parish's new priest hadn't reached out to the family. "It's not his fault. Of course, we have friends at St. Michael's, but after the trial, we just didn't go back."

"And yet you came to St. Simeon's on retreat, Marina. That's a good sign."

She had cried again when he'd said that. "I didn't know where else to go," she'd said. "And, as I said, I'd read about you—your helping the detective, I mean."

"I understand, and I'm glad we met. But your family needs the church now more than ever. I know it might feel awkward, but I'm sure that you have friends from your parish who want to support you. Seeing you at church will give them that chance."

"I'll try, Father. And I'll tell the prison officials to add you to Sophia's visitor list."

"Good. Now, I have to ask you something, and I need you to be completely honest with me about. Will Sophia agree to see me?" he'd asked.

"I don't know, but I think she'll do it for Poppa and me. When can you visit?"

"It's Sunday today. I'll ask for permission to drive up to Detroit on Tuesday. Does that give you enough time to make the arrangements?"

On Monday, he'd gotten a phone call from Marina giving the go-ahead for his visit. "I saw Sophia today. She wasn't sure about you visiting, but she said she'd meet with you once and then decide."

Now, as he walked through the prison's first security gate and presented his identification, he realized that Marina hadn't asked if Nick wanted her to accompany him. *Then again,* he thought, *it seems that Sophia hadn't asked for her sister to come with him either.*

In the next room, as he was patted down by one of the guards, he heard the heavily reinforced door close behind him. He offered a prayer asking that he say only what Sophia needed to hear.

He was escorted into a large room with small tables placed apart from one another. As a clergyperson, Nick was permitted to meet an inmate outside normal visiting hours, so he was alone in the room as he waited for Sophia to be escorted by a guard. Not having seen a photo, Nick had imagined that Sophia would resemble her older sister, but he was surprised to see a much shorter and thinner woman than Marina, and Sophia's hair was reddish, not black. The biggest difference was that Sophia, unlike her sister, stared directly at him.

Even before she sat down, Sophia said, "I don't know you."

Nick shook his head. "No, my name is Father Nicholas, or Nick if you'd prefer. I asked Marina if I could visit you."

As he sat down again, he tried to push his chair to give his girth needed room, but then he realized that the chairs were fastened securely to the floor.

"We don't see visitors until the day after tomorrow, but since you're a priest . . ."

"I appreciate you agreeing to see me," Nick said.

"It's not because you're a priest. You're just a change of scenery. Every day is gray in here. It's like a black-and-white world. Our clothes are gray, the walls are gray, the food is gray in its own way. Anything out of the routine, even a priest who's come to save my soul is a break. But then again, maybe souls are gray. At least mine must be."

Based on what Marina had told him, he hadn't expected Sophia to be so talkative.

"How old are you, Sophia?"

"I'm twenty going on eighty."

"Were you nineteen when you were arrested?"

Sophia shook her head. "No, I was arrested a week after I turned twenty."

"So, if you'd been a year younger, you could have been tried as a juvenile?" Nick asked.

"Not in Michigan. Anyway, you sound more like a lawyer than a priest." Sophia continued to hold his gaze as she said, "Or maybe you're one of those who gets off on coming here. Some of us in here get mail from strangers who come across as do-gooders, and then they beg to visit. It's like they're in love with the idea of knowing someone in prison, especially someone in for murder. But I can see you're interested in something else, maybe helping the poor little girl in prison."

Nick didn't respond immediately. Then, he said, "No, it's not pity. The way Marina described your arrest and trial, well, parts of that didn't sit well with me."

"What parts?"

"For starters, the part about you not remembering much about that night, even being in the car. Or maybe since that night you remember things."

"So, if I said I do remember being in the car and if I said I remember shooting Reginald King, you'd be satisfied and leave?"

"No, I wouldn't leave. But it'd change what I might be able to do for you."

"'Do for me?' You can do nothing for me."

"Is that your way of saying that you do remember that night—the car ride and the shooting in the motel room?"

For the first time, Sophia looked away, scanning the empty room before looking down at the table. "I don't think you get it. It's better for me to believe that night went just like they told me. The car ride, the motel room, the gun in my hand, my shooting King. If I believe that, then I can deal with all this." She pursed her lips before looking up at Nick again. "There are worse things than the gray, Father. So, if you've got what you came for, I'll go back to my luxury apartment."

Sophia signaled for the guard, but Nick didn't move.

"What? Not enough?" she asked.

"There's how you've decided to remember that night," Nick said, "and there's how you want your family and people like me to think about that night."

"I have to do what I have to do," she said. Exhaling deeply, she added, "You do what you have to do."

"Agreed. Before I go, I want to give you this," he said, handing her a small paper icon of the Virgin Mary.

"I don't want it, Father," she said, sliding it back toward Nick.

Nick didn't pick it up. "Do me a favor and keep it for twenty-four hours. Then you can do with it what you want."

✝

ARCHIVES, DETROIT HOMICIDE DIVISION

AS HE CHANGED CLOTHES, WORTHY STEELED HIMSELF for his reentry into the homicide division headquarters where he'd worked until the year before. It struck him again that his working relationship with the police in Rome was better than even his best years with the homicide division in Detroit. It was one thing to blame bad chemistry with his colleagues in Detroit, but that didn't explain who was most to blame—his past colleagues or him.

He most dreaded seeing Phillip Sherrod, who had been, for at least the past thirteen years, his nemesis in the department, someone of equal rank who took joy in making Worthy's life as miserable as possible. The animosity began when Worthy took over the case that was now under appeal. Sherrod was a sergeant at the time, and therefore the second officer on that case, but he always took Worthy's success on the case personally.

Ever since then, Sherrod and Worthy had become known in the department as poster representatives for two nearly opposite approaches to homicides. Sherrod was known for speed, Worthy for patience. Sherrod was known for rushing to identify and track down possible suspects; Worthy was known for focusing on the victim's every movement over the days and months prior to the murder. Sherrod was known for leaning hard on suspects, dancing close to the line in intimidation; Worthy known for taking a soft glove approach.

Because homicide cases differed greatly, both men had known success and failure in their careers. But it was Worthy's photo, not Sherrod's, that appeared most often in the media. It was Worthy who was considered Detroit's top homicide detective, and it was Sherrod who resented being left in the shadows.

Part of what annoyed Sherrod and others in the division was not just Worthy's successes, but the fact that he chose to ignore his detractors. Worthy knew himself well enough to admit that he was ambitious, but his ambition was fueled by his need to solve murders as puzzles, not by competing with anyone else. He'd never understood how, in a murder inquiry, the opponent could be anyone else but the killer.

Playing baseball up through high school, he'd felt the same about competition. His focus was solely on the next time at the plate, the challenge of the moment, not the batting averages of other team members.

He felt the same way about homicide cases. Yes, he'd received commendations for success in the past, but those plaques were gathering dust in his closet, and yes, his photo had appeared in Detroit's media, but he kept no scrapbook. For him, it was always the case before him, his next time at bat.

That was what made the appeal so unwelcome. Returning to a thirteen-year-old case was for Worthy like watching a film of a baseball game from high school, but there was more to this particular case than that. This was the case that had brought an entire change to his life. In his public and professional life, this case had put his face and name in headlines. In his personal life, this was the case that triggered his divorce and the loss of so much more.

Worthy knew that he had no choice, however. To prepare for the appeal, he knew that he'd have to meet with the division's legal team and rehash every piece of evidence from the case and every decision he'd made that led to William Tremont's arrest.

He'd thought that by retiring, he would made a final break with the homicide division, but with this appeal, time seemed to be flowing in reverse, and he was, for all legal purposes, once again part of Detroit's homicide division.

Looking in the bathroom mirror that morning, he'd yanked at the necktie that was part of the department's dress code for detectives. *I don't work for them, and I don't have to dress like they do,* he thought as he'd pulled on a crewneck sweater and headed for his car.

He drove slowly from his apartment to the division's headquarters, happy that the afternoon traffic seemed in no more hurry than he was to get to its destinations. When he turned into the department's parking lot, he looked for the visitors lot, for that was what he was—just a visitor.

Inside the building, he saw Lionel DeSmit, an older officer assigned to sit at the reception desk and direct the flow of foot traffic. Sitting in the lobby were a few people who looked like they had appointments with parole officers, others who Worthy thought, judging by their frightened look, had come to make statements, and one guy sitting alone, his head bandaged.

"Lieutenant Worthy, what brings you to the visitors' corral?" DeSmit asked.

Worthy's first thought was that DeSmit was the first of many to rile him, but then he realized that not everyone would remember that he'd retired or knew what had brought him back to the precinct.

"Hi Lionel. I'm here to look at an old case file."

"Ah, you want archives. Through those doors, down a flight of stairs and to your left."

Deciding to play it innocent, Worthy asked, "Is Milburn still in charge of archives?"

"Yup, almost an archive himself. And he's just as ornery as ever, but maybe you'll catch him on a good day."

"Thanks. You take care, Lionel."

"Taking care for sixty-seven more days, then I'm out to pasture."

"Congrats. Any plans?"

"I plan to sleep in until noon, do a bit of fishing, and visit my grand-kids. You'll be there too in ten years or so," DeSmit said with a smile.

Worthy nodded, happy that he didn't have to correct DeSmit.

Entering the departmental archives, he spotted Ben Milburn hunched over as he typed something into a computer. Looking up at Worthy with-out a welcoming smile, he said, "Be with you in a minute."

Worthy took a chair and waited for what turned out to be closer to five minutes. Finally, Milburn rose from his desk. "What are you looking for, Lieutenant."

Again, Worthy realized that people thought he was still with the divi-sion. "I need a copy of the file for State vs. William Tremont, 2010."

Milburn looked puzzled as he caught Worthy's eye. "You too?"

"What do you mean?"

"It's a popular file."

Worthy felt his stomach tighten. "Who else?"

"Let's see. Some hot-shot lawyers from some firm wanted a copy made. I didn't like them all that much. Then there was Howard Hullinger, the department's top lawyer. Maybe one or two more. It looks like the new captain, Captain Walker, has checked the book out. She needs to return it by tomorrow."

"How about Lieutenant Sherrod? Did he check it out?"

Milburn nodded. "I forgot about him. Yeah, he did. You look like that doesn't surprise you."

Worthy nodded. *No, not a bit,* he thought.

CHAPTER NINE

———◆———

Detroit—Enzo's Italian Restaurant

By the time Worthy arrived at Enzo's, Nick was already seated in a booth. As he watched his friend jump up from his seat, Worthy was once again impressed with Nick's agility and quickness. It wasn't every day that a massive middle-aged man, a monk no less, who lived a sedentary life in a monastery, could move so gracefully—but then Worthy remembered that Nick had wrestled in high school.

As was usual, Nick embraced Worthy in a hug that lifted him off the floor.

"Christopher, my friend, you look . . . well, you look younger than ever."

"A monk shouldn't lie, Nick. Lena pointed out where my hair is thinning back here," Worthy said, pointing to his scalp. "But if I'm not mistaken, Nick, you've dropped a few pounds."

"Yes, I've lost almost twenty, but I might gain all that back tonight."

After the waiter took drink orders, Nick said, "So tell me, how is beautiful Lena? I can see that marriage suits you, and I suspect the same is true for her."

"I don't have to tell you, Nick, that I married up when Lena agreed to marry me."

"Nonsense. You're both blessed to have one another."

"Well, all I know is that we're both happy, though being dragged back to Detroit for this appeal is rough on both of us. Of course, Lena sends her love."

"Exactly how I feel. She'll be here in what, two or three weeks?"

"Yes, as soon as her semester and exams are over."

"And your new business in Rome?"

"Business is steady, but my recent cases have been run-of-the-mill. Standard tourist trauma—lost passports, scams, items stolen from motel rooms, and, of course, pickpockets."

"And the branch of the business here in Detroit? As I remember, didn't you hire that partner you had on one of our first cases together? I remember him as a troubled soul."

"That's Carnell Henderson. How do I describe Hoops? You might remember that his son is schizophrenic. That still weighs on Hoops, but he's handling it a lot better."

Nick made the sign of the cross. "I will add his family to my prayer list."

The waiter arrived with their drinks and took their orders. Worthy ordered lasagna and wasn't surprised when Nick ordered cannelloni, his favorite; he hadn't expected Nick to order a tossed salad instead of bread sticks.

After the waiter left, Worthy said, "So, Nick, tell me about your pastoral call to the women's prison."

"What a sad story, my friend, and I don't know if I can do anything more than pray for the family."

"But I can tell that you want to."

"You know me too well." Nick proceeded to describe meeting Marina Demetrios at St. Simeon's and then his visit with her sister, Sophia, that afternoon at the prison.

At the end, Worthy said, "It sounds like the woman doesn't even want your help. Do you think she knows that she's guilty?"

"No, but she made it clear that it'll be easier for her to accept her prison sentence if she believes she did the shooting."

After a moment, Worthy asked, "What would you like me to do, Nick?"

"What? No, I'm not asking—"

"I know you're not, but it'd do me good to have something other than the appeal to think about."

"But you're not with the police anymore."

"Exactly, but the appeal has me spending more time at my old precinct than I'd like, so I'd be happy to poke my nose into something else. The least that I can do is see how strong the police case was against this woman. It's obvious her situation doesn't sit well with you, and we both know your instincts are usually correct."

✝

OCTOBER 10, 2023, ST. SIMEON'S

BROTHER PACHOMIUS' DAYS WERE DIVIDED AMONG services, prayer, study, and manning the security office of St. Simeon's. Because it was a weekday, when retreatants weren't allowed to visit, traffic was light, comprised of a few supply trucks entering and exiting the grounds. Brother Pachomius however, was looking for a specific vehicle—the monastery car that Father Nicholas had borrowed.

By supper time, Pachomius realized that Father Nicholas wouldn't be returning. The young monk felt a pang of jealousy as he imagined Father Nick engrossed in a new and exciting case. Pachomius knew that he had to add that sin to his confession the next morning, even as he realized that he had to be careful about what he revealed of Father Nicholas' activities. He'd heard from others that in the past the abbot had disapproved of Father Nick's extracurricular activity.

In the hope that Father Nicholas would ask him to do something more to help, Pachomius reviewed what had happened the past weekend, from Father Nicholas spotting Marina Demetrios by the lake to his decision to visit the woman's sister in prison. That was when he remembered that one retreatant, Gus Cooper, had asked about another, a woman. Father Nicholas had also told him that the guestmaster, under pressure, had let this Gus Cooper see the list of retreatants.

Pachomius checked himself, knowing he was assuming that Cooper had been asking about Marina Demetrios. What, though, he wondered, would be wrong with his looking into Cooper? The difficulty was that Father Ioannis had rejected his own request to look at the list and would undoubtedly do so again; Pachomius knew that no one manned the reception desk after the evening prayers of Compline.

Dare I do what I'm thinking of doing? he asked himself—but he'd already made his decision. He waited an hour after Compline for the community to settle for the night before walking in stocking feet to the guesthouse. He met no one, if he didn't count the saints looking down at him from the icons in the hallways.

As he hoped, he found the guestbook on the desk. The few lights that remained lit throughout the night were bright enough for him to see by. He turned back to the page for the previous Friday and found the names of Marina Demetrios and Gus Cooper. He ran his finger across the columns to find Detroit addresses for both retreatants followed by St. Anastasia listed as Cooper's parish and St. Michael's for Marina Demetrios'.

After copying the information, Pachomius retraced his steps to his room, his heart racing. He knew he should feel guilty—his action was a willful disregard for the community's rules—but instead, all he felt was excitement.

CHAPTER TEN

---◆---

AFTER BREAKFAST THE NEXT MORNING, NICK and Worthy went their separate ways. The night before, after Nick emailed his abbot to explain that he would be away from St. Simeon's for a few more days, he called Maria Demetrios to arrange meeting with her and her father. When she hesitated, Nick made her promise not to spend a moment cleaning before he came. "I want to spend time with you, Marina, and your father. I won't be judging your house."

As he drove toward Detroit's "Greek town," he thought about a home where the mother had died. No matter if that death occurred a month ago or five years before, it wasn't just the family who remained that mourned. A house also mourned, evidenced by photos and mementos of the deceased that were left on end tables, but also by odd items, a broom in the corner of the wrong room or outdated magazines covered with dust lying askew by the couch, items neglected so long as to become invisible to the grieving survivors.

What Nick most hoped to see at the Demetrios' home was a well-used icon corner, the space in Orthodox homes where icons of Christ, Mary the Theotokos, and a family's favorite saints offered the assurance of God's presence and the hope of the resurrection. No matter what he found, he would not comment, but he was glad that he'd brought an icon of St. Demetrios, the patron saint of the family.

With the help of GPS, Nick found the Demetrios home without difficulty. If he hadn't known that the family lived there, he might have assumed the house was vacant. In contrast to neighboring houses, the Demetrios lawn and sidewalk were covered with autumn leaves and branches. And as he walked toward the house, he noticed that the drapes were drawn across the front-facing windows. *Yes, death has visited this house, and not just physical death,* he thought.

Marina opened the door as soon as he knocked, and, seeing her tear-swollen eyes as she ushered him in, Nick couldn't help but notice how differently grief had affected the two sisters. Marina could hardly raise her gaze from the floor, while Sophia had looked steadily into his eyes. He wondered if Sophia had ever been as grief-stricken as Marina or if the younger sister had turned to stone from the moment their mother had died.

As Marina led him into a musty parlor, Nick noticed that the room seemed dark, despite every lamp in the room being lit. He felt an urge to fling open the curtains and open the windows to let in the October sunlight and its warmth. The feeling passed as he saw a man raise himself from a recliner. Mr. Demetrios bowed and out of respect for Nick's priesthood, kissed his hand and muttered a request for a blessing even as he asked Nick to call him George.

After Nick made the sign of the cross over George and Marina Demetrios, he sat down on the sofa. In front of him on a coffee table was a coffee urn and mugs along with some store-bought cookies. He waited until Marina poured the coffee before speaking.

"Thank you for meeting with me," he said, even as he noticed Marina shaking her head.

"No, Father, it's we who appreciate your coming . . . and for seeing Sophia," Marina said as she passed the plate of cookies. "She did agree to see you then."

"Yes, we visited yesterday. That's why I wanted to see you both, not just to tell you that Sophia allowed the visit but also to ask that you help me understand Sophia better."

Nick looked from Marina to her father and could see the puzzled look on their faces. Finally, George Demetrios said in a soft voice, "Why, Father? Sophia told us that she's accepted her punishment and wants us to do the same."

"But is that the right thing for any of us to do if she doesn't remember what happened that night?"

In little more than a whisper, Mr. Demetrios said, "Father, my hope was that if you visited Sophia, she'd make her confession."

He speaks as softly as if he's at a funeral, Nick thought. He decided to speak boldly. "Would God want Sophia to be locked up for a crime that she doesn't remember committing?"

"But Sophia must have done it. The fingerprints, Father, and what the witness said," Mr. Demetrios said.

"And they found gunshot residue on her hand and sleeve," Marina added.

Nick nodded. "Yes, I know, but can I ask if you were satisfied with Sophia's lawyer? The reason I ask is that there must be lawyers in the parish who'd have taken her case."

Marina looked at her father before returning her gaze to the floor. "We didn't want to ask someone from the parish. So when we were told that the state would provide a lawyer, that's what we did."

They were too ashamed to involve the parish, so they got a public defender, someone probably juggling ten other cases, Nick thought.

"I understand your wish for privacy, but let me ask this. Did it take the jury a long time to return their verdict?"

"Ninety-three minutes," George Demetrios said, and for the first time Nick heard the welcome note of anger.

The room was silent for a moment until Marina asked, "Father, are you saying Sophia could be innocent?"

"I don't know, Marina, I honestly don't know. But I'm troubled that Sophia accepts that she's guilty because the police say she is."

Marina shook her head. "Father, if you're asking us to hire someone to look into Sophia's case, well, we have no money."

"Of course, of course, but I have a friend, a good friend, who was Detroit's best homicide detective. He's now retired, and he's interested in looking into Sophia's case, no charge."

With his eyes closed, George Demetrios shook his head. "I don't think we're strong enough to go through it all again, Father. My health isn't strong, and I . . . well, I want Marina to move on with her life."

Nick reached over and rested his hand on the old man's. "The last thing I want is to put both of you through more grief, but we have to know if Sophia committed this crime. Mr. Demetrios—George—I promise not to bother you unless my friend finds something. Will you agree to that?"

Marina and her father looked at one another. The father finally nodded, which led to Marina nodding to Nick.

"Good, good. I can see your icons on the wall in the next room. Let's go in there to pray before I leave? I'll pray for you both, and we'll all pray for Sophia—and for my friend."

✝

ARCHIVES, DETROIT HOMICIDE DIVISION

WORTHY TOOK A MOMENT TO SIT in the precinct's parking lot and collect his thoughts. It had taken Nick a few moments to realize that he really did welcome the chance to look into Sophia Demetrios' case. If there was one thing that Worthy dreaded more than anything about the appeal, it was being dragged back to that time.

The appeal that had brought him back early to Detroit was not just any case, but one that was tied closely to his failed marriage with Susan. The day he'd arrested William Tremont had led to a media frenzy. His face was on every channel that night, and police and community leaders were praising him for solving a murder that had been close to tearing the city apart.

He didn't get home that night until two a.m., and to his surprise, Susan was waiting up in the kitchen. Later, he realized that Susan had been distant for months before that night, but he'd been too absorbed in the Tremont case to notice. For months, he'd worked sixteen hours a day, seven days a week on the murder of Renee Vickers. Even when he was home, he was either sleeping or preoccupied by the case.

That night, the night when he'd been heralded and toasted across the city, Susan told him that she'd had enough. She wanted a divorce, and no, she didn't want to consider counseling or a trial separation. Somehow, despite moving out a few days later and staying in a motel during the trial, he was able to put on a good face and hold himself together. When the trial ended, however, his life was in freefall.

Now, some thirteen years later, the appeal brought him back to the greatest high of his career and the greatest low of his personal life. That was why he jumped at the chance to help Nick out by looking into the case against Sophia Demetrios. His one hope of not being engulfed by his troubled past was to focus on someone else's troubles.

Back in the divisional archives for a second day, Worthy found that Captain Walker had returned the Vickers-Tremont file as she'd promised. He also checked out the file on Sophia Demetrios and placed the two folders side by side on a desk before opening Sophia's file. He suspected that once he opened the Vickers-Tremont file, he'd have a hard time giving Nick's case the care it deserved.

He studied the mug shots of Sophia Demetrios first. Worthy had looked at hundreds of mug shots over his career, many coming from repeat offenders. Those photos tended to show similar affects—boredom, anger, cockiness, or resignation. Sophia Demetrios' photo showed a young woman who looked sleepy, gazing at the camera as if it could explain where she was.

He turned next to Sophia Demetrios' toxicology screening, hoping that would shed light on the woman's confused expression. Besides the alcohol, Sophia had enough cocaine in her bloodstream to cause someone her size—five foot three, one hundred and four pounds, according to the file—to be high for some time. It was no wonder she couldn't remember what happened that night.

Turning to the forensic report, he read that Sophia's fingerprints had been found on the gun, and gunshot residue on her right hand and sleeve. Leafing back in the file to the transcript of Sophia's initial interview, Worthy found Lieutenant Rebecca Williston's name. Although Worthy had never worked a case with Williston, he knew of her and knew she was respected across the division. She'd braved the longstanding prejudice that homicide was a man's sport. Even as he began to read the transcript of Williston's interviews with Sophia Demetrios, he knew that she would have worked the case thoroughly, letting the evidence speak rather than forcing the evidence to agree with what she wanted to hear.

The transcript of the interview listed the date—March 17, 2023—at the top, followed by the time, 8:44 p.m., and then the list of those present in the interview room: Sophia Demetrios; a public defender, Tricia

Turnquist; Lieutenant Rebecca Williston; and Sergeant Manolo Lopez. It took Worthy a few seconds to make sense of why Lopez, who he knew was DEA, was in the room. Then he remembered that the victim, Reginald King, was a major player in Detroit's drug world.

The transcript of the first interview was only seven pages long, suggesting that the interview hadn't taken more than twenty to thirty minutes. That meant that what Sophia Demetrios divulged or didn't divulge in such a short amount of time had been enough for Williston to make an arrest.

He turned the page and read:

Williston: "Do you know why you're here?" Silence. "For the tape, Sophia Demetrios doesn't answer. I repeat, do you know why you're here?"

Demetrios: "Cuz of the drugs?"

Williston: "Are you asking a question or making a statement?"

Demetrios: "What?"

Williston: "What drugs did you take, Sophie?"

Demetrios: "My name's Sophia."

Williston: "Sophia it is, then. Let's forget about the drugs for now. You're being questioned about a murder."

Demetrios: "Someone got killed?"

Williston: "You know someone did. We have your prints on the gun, Sophia, and we found gunshot residue on you and your sleeve. On top of that, we have a witness that says you shot Reginald King."

Demetrios: (Coughing heard.) "I don't know any Reggie King."

Williston: "But you know he goes by Reggie, Sophia."

Demetrios: "I thought you said Reggie King. Who is he?"

Williston: "You're wasting our time, Sophia."

What followed was in parentheses, a summary of what the police knew about the victim. Worthy read through it quickly, Reginald King having been well known in Detroit for dealing and distributing drugs, although no witnesses had ever testified against him. Several lower-level drug sellers associated with King had been convicted, but none had turned on their boss.

What Worthy was reading was something with which he was all too familiar. The big players were nearly impossible to nail. *So what brought*

Reginald King, one of Detroit's drug kingpins, and Sophia Demetrios, a low-lever user, together that night? Worthy asked himself.

Putting that question aside, Worthy focused on what followed in the transcript. Williston had just described for Sophia what was known in homicide as the "three-legged stool."

Williston: "Sophia, we have your fingerprints, gunshot residue, and witness statements. That means that you're going down for killing Reginald King. But if you confess, well, that's like a fourth leg on a stool. The stool doesn't need it, but you do, Sophia. Your lawyer should agree with me that if you confess, it will go better for you at sentencing. Do you understand?"

Demetrios: "I killed someone?"

Williston: "Is that a confession, Sophia?"

Worthy read that Sophia didn't respond but received at that point instructions from her lawyer. He could guess that a public defender, who'd met Sophia for the first time, had whispered to her—take the deal. But Worthy knew that Sophia's case wouldn't have led to a jury trial if she'd done that. He scanned down the page until Sophia spoke next.

Demetrios: "I don't know how to use a gun."

Williston: "We both know it's not hard. You aimed the gun at Reginald King and you pulled the trigger. Even children can do that."

Demetrios: "I don't . . . I don't remember doing that."

Williston: "All the evidence says you did."

Worthy waded through the back-and-forth, impressed that Sophia, despite whatever the public defender was urging, wasn't confessing. Eventually, Williston tried another tack.

Williston: "Why don't you tell us what you do remember about what happened tonight."

Worthy knew the tactic, having used it himself. Suspects could deny a crime hour after hour only to implicate themselves when they were asked to talk about something tangential.

Demetrios: "I remember lying down in Francine's apartment. I was so tired."

Williston: "That's Francine Nichols?"

Demetrios: "Yeah. Ask her. Francine will tell you I went to sleep on her couch."

That comment provided Williston the opportunity she wanted. She pounced, letting Sophia know that Francine Nichols was the witness who'd implicated Sophia. After that, the transcript stated that Sophia had broken down, sobbing, and repeating the phrase, "Maybe I did shoot someone."

That was when Williston read Sophia her rights before formally arresting her.

Worthy closed the file, wondering what there was in Williston's interview with Sophia that Nick could question. As far as he could tell, there were two words in the interview that made him pause. Sophia said that she might have shot someone. There were no vaguer terms than "might" and "someone." Either Sophia was a great actor, or she didn't remember shooting anyone, much less Reginald King.

The place to begin, he would tell Nick, was with interviewing Francine Nichols and encouraging Sophia Demetrios to remember that night.

Closing the Demetrios file, he turned to the Vickers-Tremont murder book and found the contents, much provided by him thirteen years ago, increasingly familiar as he skimmed through them. From what the department's lawyer, Howard Hullinger, had emailed him, he knew that Tremont was now claiming that he'd been high on Ecstasy when he'd confessed to the crime, but Worthy knew that a toxicology screening would have been ordered as soon as he confessed.

It wasn't until he studied the results of that screening that Worthy spotted what Tremont's lawyers had obviously seized upon. The initial date on the toxicology screening, November 2, 2010, had been crossed out with November 1, the date of Tremont s arrest, written above it.

Mistakes in dating drug screenings were rare and usually had no effect on a case, but Tremont's lawyers obviously saw the mistake as something they could exploit. If Tremont hadn't been given the drug test until November 2, the day after his arrest, any drug in his system, depending on the dosage, might be undetectable. The crossed out and new date could then be interpreted as someone covering up the mistake.

Sitting before the Vickers-Tremont "murder book" and the subsequent court proceedings, Worthy jotted down the questions he needed to answer. The first was, "If the irregularity on the tox screen is part of the basis of the appeal, who first spotted that correction?" While Worthy knew that there might have been law students or journalists working pro bono on murder convictions, he was more inclined to believe that William Tremont had noted the discrepancy as he ruminated on his case in prison. The thought that Tremont, not a legal team, had spotted the irregularity on the tox screening gave him no peace. No one had ever doubted that Tremont, though arrogant, was bright. Worthy knew that many psychopaths had enviable GPAs in school and college.

The next question raised by the file was one he could already answer. "Who administered Tremont's tox screen in 2010?" Although Worthy had worked with various pathologists over his career, he remembered that it had been Dr. Robin Wallace, the most senior in the pathology department, who'd conducted the screenings on Tremont.

Feeling confident, Worthy turned to the end of the case file, looking for the standard "Corrections" page with its three columns. Column one would list the correction and page number of the error in the murder book. Column two would contain the signature of the person making the correction, with column three explaining the reason for the correction. As far at Worthy could see, this page would be the key evidence for the court to consider, and he was confident that Tremont's lawyers would have a hard time chipping away at Doc Wallace's reputation for integrity.

But when Worthy turned to the final page of the Vickers-Tremont murder book, he felt a wave of nausea as he found no corrections page.

But there has to be, Worthy told himself. The correction to the toxicology report would have necessitated all three columns being filled out. He turned the previous pages over, hoping that the corrections page had been misfiled. He tried to push panic down as, turning page after page, he found nothing. There was no corrections page in the entire murder book.

After his head stopped spinning, he tried to think of what to do. When he finally felt strength again in his legs, he brought the murder book up to the archivist, Ben Milburn.

"There should be a corrections page at the end, Ben," he said. "Or have those pages been stored elsewhere?"

Milburn frowned. "Let me see."

After a few moments, in which Worthy watched the archivist repeat what Worthy had done by flipping through every page of the murder book, Milburn shook his head. "And you're sure there was a correction made?"

Worthy flipped back to the toxicology page and pointed to the corrected date.

"I see what you mean," Milburn said. "I'll make a note and have one of my interns hunt for it. It could be that it's been misplaced in another file, maybe another of Doc Wallace's cases that he was involved in about the same time. I saw that happen once."

"But I bet that never happened with one of Wallace's cases," Worthy said.

"No, you're right about that."

"What if I contact Doc Wallace and show him the page. Maybe he remembers why the change was made."

"You don't know?" Milburn asked. "Doc died last year. Some fast-spreading brain tumor. What I heard was that he had trouble focusing in February and was in hospice by the end of May. He was dead before June was out."

The dizziness and nausea returned, forcing Worthy to sit down. Milburn had pulled up a pad of paper and was writing down the name, date, and case number of the Tremont file. When he was done, he looked up at Worthy with a look of "I've done all I can do."

But Worthy wasn't finished. "Ben, remind me who else has asked for the file."

Milburn hit a few keys on his computer. "Like I told you before, lawyers have had copies made, and then there was Captain Walker yesterday. And you asked about Sherrod."

"Walker. Where did she come from?"

"She came over from Cleveland and has been here about three months. It looks like Sherrod checked the file out two weeks before a bunch of lawyers asked for copies, but lawyers don't get to handle the book itself. I do the copying. Before that, nothing since the trial thirteen years ago."

Worthy considered the information. The file had gathered dust for the past thirteen years, but then, after Sherrod checked it out, the file had been popular reading for Sherrod, Tremont's lawyer, the department's lawyers, and finally by Captain Walker.

And what the new captain has heard about me from Sherrod I can only imagine.

CHAPTER ELEVEN

―――――◆―――――

OCTOBER 10, 2023, ST. SIMEON'S

EARLY THE NEXT MORNING, BROTHER PACHOMIUS sat alone in the security office. Opening his email on the office's computer, he hoped to find a message from Father Nicholas explaining when he expected to return to the monastery. Seeing no message, a frustrated Pachomius opened Facebook to see if Gus Cooper had an online presence.

Growing up, Brother Pachomius would have given anything to have a simple name like Gus Cooper. But being born Stavros Mefapoulitis, he'd been teased from kindergarten on, one teacher after another stumbling over his name on the first day of school and never managing to get it right for the entire school year. He'd done his best to offer Stan as his first name, but what could anyone do to tame Mefapoulitis? The only place where his name was pronounced correctly was in the family and at church. It hadn't helped that his grandfather, after whom he'd been named, reminded him that Stavros was the Greek word for "cross," and that every time he had to explain how to pronounce it, he was, to use his grandfather's words, "bearing the cross."

Then, when entering St. Simeon's as a novice, he hadn't been given the recognizable name of an apostle, like Paul or Mark, or a saint like Nicholas, but instead the tongue-twisting name Pachomius.

He sighed as he read on Facebook the list of lucky men who'd been named Gus Cooper and, after fifteen minutes, found two men from the

Detroit area with that name. Even as he realized that there could well be other Gus Coopers in the Detroit area who weren't on social media, he turned to the two sites in the hope that he'd discover something important about the man.

From the photo, Pachomius estimated that the first Gus Cooper from Detroit was in his sixties or seventies. Gus Cooper number one—full name Augustus Cooper—had graduated as a business major from University of Michigan and was now retired, having worked his entire adult life at various branches of an insurance company in the Detroit area. Pachomius accepted that it was certainly possible that this Gus Cooper had come into the Greek Orthodox Church, but looked to see if this man was married to a woman with a Greek maiden name—but no, this Gus Cooper seemed to have been a lifelong bachelor.

The profile of Gus Cooper number two—full name Gustav Cooper with a photo—was significantly different. His hair was almost translucent, suggesting Nordic roots, and had studied sociology and world religions at Wayne State University. Pachomius could see how a religious studies major might visit St. Simeon's out of curiosity or for a class assignment, but the person who'd been at the monastery over the last weekend had been there for more than a retreat. If this was the Gus Cooper who'd been at St. Simeon's, he'd asked about Marina Demetrios specifically.

Just as he wondered what more, if anything, he could find on social media, Brother Pachomius typed in another name on Facebook—Marina Demetrios. *If I'm in luck and she has a profile page,* he thought, *I'll find an overlap between her details and those of one of the Gus Coopers.*

Even if Marina Demetrios had once had a Facebook account, he wouldn't have been surprised if she'd taken her page down, given what Father Nicholas had shared about the mother's death and her sister's incarceration, but Marina did have a page, though her photo, showing a happy face, was clearly outdated.

Nevertheless, he scanned through what Marina had shared on her page. When last she'd posted, she was working for a retail store. She listed her hobbies as singing in several choirs, including the choir at St. Silvanus, genealogy, and watercolor painting. At the bottom of the page, Pachomius found something potentially important. Two years before, Marina Demetrios had been a full-time grad student at Wayne State University.

The younger Gus Cooper and Marina Demetrios had been at the same university, although it wasn't clear if they'd been there at the same time. In addition, Wayne State was huge, making the chances slim that the two knew each other.

He started to close his computer when he felt has mind snag on something. Even as he returned to the notes that he'd made in the guestmaster's office, he knew he was grasping at straws. He typed in St. Anastasia Greek Orthodox Church, Detroit, the parish that Gus Cooper had listed in the guesthouse logbook.

His throat tightened as the words "No Results Found" appeared on the screen. The closest St. Anastasia Orthodox Church, whether Greek, Romanian, Serbian, Antiochan, Bulgarian, or another jurisdiction was not even in Michigan, but in Ohio.

Pachomius accepted that there could be many reasons why Cooper might have made a simple mistake until he asked himself, *Name One*. He couldn't. Gus Cooper, for some reason, had lied about his home parish when he signed in.

Beyond that, Pachomius understood, Gus Cooper had asked Brother Ioannis, the guestmaster, about a fellow retreatant, presumably Marina Demetrios. *Why had Cooper done that,* Pachomius asked, *and did he succeed in meeting with her?*

✝

DETROIT: THE HENDERSON HOME

SULLA HENDERSON LOOKED DOWN AT THE BACON frying on the stove and thought, *Be thankful in all things*. It was a Bible verse from her childhood, one that she'd lost sight of in those terrible first months after Jamie was diagnosed with schizophrenia.

Jamie was home for the day from the halfway house, and, despite no sounds coming from the den, she knew that her husband, Carnell— she never liked his nickname, Hoops—would be in his recliner while Jamie would be next to him in a similar recliner. Together, they would be watching reruns of Jamie's favorite program, the British program *The*

Repair Shop. In each episode, people brought in broken or otherwise ill-used family treasures, which, over the course of the program, would be lovingly transformed by the various professional restorers.

Carnell and Jamie had discovered the program by accident, after Sulla and Carnell noticed that Jamie became anxious when sports of any sort were on TV. It was as if Jamie were naked to the emotions on the screen, overwhelming him until he retreated to his room. Then, one day, Carnell came into the den to find Jamie sitting cross-legged on the floor in front of the TV, a smile on his face as he watched two British women re-padding a well-loved but tattered teddy bear.

That had been the first clue of what brought joy to Jamie. His taking apart faulty radios and stereos and bringing them back to life became his paying part-time job through the halfway house. Although Jaimie never said anything, Sulla knew that Jamie took pride in paying his own room and board.

As she draped the dishtowel over the kitchen faucet, Sulla thought again about the Bible verse: *Be thankful in all things.* In a perfect world, there would be a repair shop for the Jamies of the world, a place where caring restorers would work their magic and make sons, daughters, mothers, and fathers "good as new." But in a perfect world, Sulla reasoned, there'd be nothing to repair and consequently no occasion to be thankful. So she would remind herself, in this imperfect world, to be thankful that Jamie was semi-independent and happy.

She heard Carnell come into the kitchen and felt his arms encircle her waist. She teared up, knowing that she'd give anything if, just once, those arms were Jamie's. At the same time, she believed it was a miracle that Jamie's struggles hadn't destroyed their marriage. Other families whom they'd met with children struggling with mental illnesses had fractured under the weight of helplessness and then hopelessness, and so she believed that it was a miracle that their family, with a child who expressed few feelings but calmly watched rerun after rerun of *The Repair Shop,* had held together.

Captain Walker's Office, Detroit Homicide Division

Walking out of the precinct's archives and knowing that the corrections page in the Vickers-Tremont murder book was missing, Worthy realized that he had to meet Captain Walker. Seeing it was the lunch hour, he left the building and took a walk to calm himself. He knew the chances that Doc Wallace had failed to add a corrections page to the murder file were slim, about the same chance as the corrections page having been accidentally misfiled. Instead, he couldn't stop his brain from returning to the fact that Phillip Sherrod had checked out the murder book.

With Walker being new to the homicide division, Worthy knew he couldn't directly accuse Sherrod. Walker would see him as a retired detective holding a grudge against a past colleague who was still working under her, but with Milburn having established that Captain Walker had requested the file after Sherrod, Worthy was keen to know if she remembered the corrections page being missing.

When an hour later Worthy was admitted into Captain Walker's office, the past seemed to rise up and clutch at his throat. How many times had he been in this office, asking for patience with his approach or defending himself against accusations that he ignored his partners? His captain at the time of Tremont's arrest, Captain Spicer, had pressured Worthy on an almost daily basis to speed up his investigation. The captain after that, Captain Betts, had been better, someone more inclined to trust his approach. This would be his first encounter with Captain Walker, someone who'd never met him but who knew him from the Vickers-Tremont case file. He reasoned that she'd already assessed the appeal's potential damage to her department. If Tremont's conviction was overturned on appeal, lawyers representing others whom Worthy had brought to trial would see their chance to appeal. That meant that Captain Walker would want to see almost anyone but him, an ex-cop who could undermine the reputation of the squad she now led.

Worthy had barely sat down before Captain Walker said, "Mr. Worthy, I looked over the Vickers-Tremont case yesterday, as I'm sure you have, so we both know the grounds for the appeal. The crux seems to be the toxicology report, and by that I mean the date of the tox screening. As bad as that could be, what I need to know from you is if there were any other complications with this case?"

·   He took a moment to study the new captain before answering. She was clearly younger than he, thin, and, given the pack of Nicorette gum on her desk, someone trying to quit smoking. He also noticed that there had been no "It's nice to meet you, Mr. Worthy," or "Would you like some coffee?"

"No, there's nothing else," he said, "and I've never had any second thoughts about Tremont's guilt. When he confessed, he was full of himself. I'd say he was proud that he'd kept us guessing for so long. I never had any sense that he was high on Ecstasy or anything else."

Captain Walker nodded. "I've listened to the interview, and he certainly wasn't in some drugged-out haze. He rambled a bit, but that isn't surprising."

She paused a minute before picking up a small piece of paper off her desk. "Do you know a Kenna McCarty?" she asked.

Worthy felt his throat tighten. "Sorry to say that I do. She's a journalist who tried to intrude on one of my other cases."

"Is that your way of saying that you've butted horns with her?"

"She wanted a scoop on the case and tried to leverage her friendship with the commissioner at the time to force me to let her tag along on the case."

Walker nodded. "So, it wouldn't surprise you that she's taken a more than professional interest in the appeal?"

"Has she? I hadn't noticed, but no, I'm not surprised. It sounds like I'll need to ignore her again."

Frowning, Captain Walker said, "Unfortunately, I don't have that option. You're now a private citizen, so you can do what you like. But I need to play nice. All I ask is that you work with us and our lawyers on this. We're on the same team. Do you understand what I'm saying?"

"You don't have to worry that I intend to blame the department or Doc Wallace. But the correction sheet being missing, well, that's a problem." He tried not to show any emotion when he asked the key question. "Was the corrections page in the murder book when you checked it out?"

"No, and given the grounds for the appeal, I naturally looked for it. Doctor Wallace was dead by the time I arrived, so I was hoping you might have an idea."

"I knew Doc Wallace pretty well. He was a perfectionist, not someone who made mistakes on things like tox screenings. And he certainly wasn't someone who'd forget to fill out a corrections page. So . . . unless it's been misplaced, someone must have removed it."

Captain Walker sat back in her chair. "Be careful, Mr. Worthy, be very careful."

"I'm not naming names," Worthy said, knowing that this was hardly the truth. "But with Doc Wallace being deceased, Tremont's lawyers have been given a gift that they can exploit."

"Then let's both hope that the correction sheet will be found," Captain Walker said, as she rose from her chair and signaled that the conversation was over. "I have us scheduled to meet with the department's legal team tomorrow at eleven. I trust that will work with your schedule."

CHAPTER TWELVE

———————◆———————

St. Simeon's

BROTHER PACHOMIUS TOOK A DEEP BREATH before knocking on the door of his confessor, Father Bessarion. Hearing the expected "Enter," he opened the door and was surprised to see the back of another monk sitting in Father Bessarion's office.

Abbot Lucas stood and turned toward Brother Pachomius. "Come in, my son."

Pachomius bowed before the abbot and kissed his hand. "Bless me, Abba," he said.

The abbot made the sign of the cross over Pachomius and motioned for him to sit in the other chair facing Father Bessarion's desk. With a knot in his stomach, Pachomius sensed that something unusual was about to happen.

"Brother Pachomius, as you know, your time as a novice will determine if you're suited to monastic life," Father Bessarion began. "That determination is ultimately made by the Holy Spirit but through the community and you."

Is that what this is about? Brother Pachomius asked himself. *Has the community already decided that I don't belong?*

"What has been noticed by the community, Brother, is that your movements have recently been somewhat erratic," the abbot added.

"Erratic?" Pachomius asked. "I don't—"

Abbot Lucas raised a hand, and Pachomius fell silent. "You're spending more than your appointed time in the security office as well as coming sometimes early or late to prayers. But more than that, we've noticed that you often look distracted during services."

Brother Pachomius wondered if the expression "the elephant in the room" applied to the present moment. Neither his confessor nor the abbot had mention Father Nicholas, and Pachomius had no intention of blaming Father Nicholas for whatever trouble he was in.

"And there is another matter," Father Bessarion said.

Here it comes, Brother Pachomius thought, but he was wrong.

Abbot Lucas' face looked stern. "Father Ioannis let us know that you asked to see the list of retreatants last weekend. And he was right to refuse your request. The privacy of those who come here on retreat is paramount. Frankly, we're having a hard time understanding why you'd want to see that list."

When he was growing up, Stavros Mefapoulitis had been known for a quick mind and a quick tongue. What his friends said about him was that he could outtalk anyone, especially if he needed to talk his way out of anything. He knew himself well enough to know that under pressure, he had another choice besides fight or flight. He would simply smile, open his mouth, and out of that mouth would come something witty and disarming.

When he entered St. Simeon's, he'd hoped to leave that trait behind, but now, he could feel that familiar wave of adrenalin as his mind picked up speed. Possible responses flooded into his mind. He could say that Father Nicholas had asked him to look at the list, or he could say that he thought he recognized one of the retreatants from his home parish. Both options would be lies, and he knew he'd have to tell more lies to cover those first ones.

He could feel the eyes of the two men, the abbot who was considered the voice of Christ in the community and his confessor, from whom he was to withhold nothing.

Finally, he said, "Reverend Father and Father Bessarion, I confess I was curious. I shouldn't have asked the guestmaster to let me see the list."

Neither man spoke for a moment until Father Bessarion said, "Curious? Curious about what?"

Pachomius shrugged and said nothing.

"Father Ioannis also mentioned that Father Nicholas asked to see the list of retreatants," Father Bessarion said. "Did Father Nicholas ask you to look at the list?"

Pachomius was relieved that he could look his confessor in the face and truthfully say, "No, he never asked me to do that."

Abbot Lucas sighed heavily. "Father Nicholas is away from St. Simeon's right now, but we'll ask him that same question when gets back. But for now . . . for now, I hope we don't need to tell you that behavior like this puts you in a poor light, Brother. Now, can you explain why you've seemed so distracted in community prayers?"

Pachomius realized that the interrogation wasn't over. He took a deep breath, again pushing away a host of reasons—false ones—that sprang to mind. "I admit that morning prayers have been more difficult of late," he said. "My sleep has been uneven, I guess I'd say."

While that was the truth, it was hardly the whole truth. He found assisting Father Nick to be exciting, and excitement wasn't on the emotional menu in a monastery.

"As important as adequate sleep is in our vocation, a restful mind is even more important," the abbot said. "We can sleep less than those in the world because we seek to live intentionally in God's peace. Let me suggest that you avoid strenuous mental activity, even theological study, after the evening meal. And, without breaking the confidentiality afforded the confessional, I have asked Father Bessarion to report to me weekly on how you are doing. Brother Pachomius, we know that the adjustments for novices are many and varied. Please do not feel that you are being singled out."

Then why, Brother Pachomius thought, *do I have the feeling that it's shape up or ship out?*

✝

ENZO'S ITALIAN RESTAURANT

As HE NURSED A BEER AND waited for Nick to arrive, Worthy thought about how much he missed Lena. He'd called Lena after his meeting with Captain Walker and shared that Tremont's appeal was looking more complicated than he first thought.

Lena had listened quietly until she said, "I can hear the fatigue in your voice, Chris. I wish I were there."

"Me too. Rome feels more than four thousand miles away."

"Do you think this man Sherrod would stoop so low as to remove that page from the file? Isn't that tampering with evidence?"

"That's exactly what it is. If Sherrod did that, he's jeopardized his career for what—to get back at me? I'm hoping the sheet was simply misfiled. But the missing page was topic number one at my meeting Captain Walker. She's Sherrod's boss, not mine, which means that she owes me nothing."

"Have you seen Nick?" she'd asked.

"Yes, he drove up to Detroit yesterday for a visit to a woman's prison. We had dinner last night together and will again tonight."

"A woman's prison?"

Worthy shared briefly what he knew of Sophia Demetrios. "I looked at her case file. The girl is barely twenty, and she's been convicted of murder."

"Did you find anything to help Nick?"

"I'm not sure. The evidence against the woman is pretty damning."

"Has Nick met with her?"

"Yes, and I trust his instincts. He feels that something is odd about the case."

As he took another sip of beer, Worthy considered the irony of the two cases that he'd researched that day. In Tremont's appeal, he'd have to prove that he'd done nothing wrong in arresting William Tremont. Nick, however, was facing the opposite challenge. To clear Sophia Demetrios, he'd have to prove that Lieutenant Williston, a respected colleague in homicide, had wrongfully charged Sophia Demetrios with murder.

Of course, he'd be happy to intercede with Williston if that would help Nick, but he knew he'd have to be careful. He needed the department's support for the appeal, so the last thing he could be seen doing was undermining Williston's case.

Worthy's thoughts were interrupted by Nick sliding into the booth. "I hope you haven't been waiting long, my friend."

"Not a problem, Nick. Just licking my wounds from today."

"Hmm. You too? Let's order, and then we can commiserate with each other."

As they ate—Nick having lasagna and breadsticks this time without a salad while Worthy ordered two pizza slices—they avoided mentioning the two cases and instead talked about Rome. Nick wanted to know if Lena was currently researching a modern-day mystic.

After dessert, their conversation turned to Sophia Demetrios, with Worthy sharing what he'd learned from the case file.

"I'm not sure it's all bad news, Nick, but there's no glaring misstep in the file," he said. "The lead on the investigation was Rebecca Williston, who's known for her thoroughness. And the evidence against Sophia looks solid. Williston has Sophia's fingerprints on the weapon, gunshot residue on her hand and clothes, and a witness who named Sophia as the shooter."

Nick sat back in the booth and exhaled slowly. "So, no good news, my friend?"

Worthy shrugged. "I read the transcript of the first interview Williston had with Sophia. That was on the same night as the shooting. Williston already knew she had the three-legged stool, so—"

"The three-legged stool?" Nick asked.

"Sorry. She had what I said before: the fingerprints, gunshot residue, and witness statements. Those are the three legs of the case, enough to make the arrest, but Williston would have been happier if she had the fourth leg of the stool—a confession."

Nick nodded. "When I talked with Sophia, the only thing she could say was that she must have done the shooting, given what the police told her. But she doesn't remember anything about that night, not even being in the car. So, no confession. That doesn't mean she didn't kill the man, but it's something."

"Well, Nick, you've met her. Do you think she killed this drug lord?"

Nick didn't say anything for a moment. "What I know is that Sophia has no hope that she'll ever be cleared. She expects to spend the major-ity of her life in prison. So, I want to prove that she's been framed by someone, but I'm not even sure where to start. And given Tremont's appeal, Christopher, I know you can't accuse Williston of what you're being accused of."

Worthy took a final swig of his beer. "Ah, so you noticed that, did you? But if I'm careful, not be too obvious, I want to help. And don't forget, Henderson will be happy to help. As I remember, the two of you established a good relationship, and he knows the homicide division as well as I do."

"I'd forgotten that Henderson—wasn't his name Carnell?—works for you."

"I prefer to say he works *with* me. He's good, Nick."

"Where would you suggest I . . . or Henderson and I start?"

"Did Sophia mention the name Francine Nichols, Nick?"

"No. Who is she?"

"In Williston's initial interrogation, Sophia said her last memory of that night was being in Francine Nichols' apartment. But before you think Nichols will help you, Nichols testified at trial that she saw Sophia shoot Reginald King."

It wasn't until they returned to Worthy's apartment that Worthy shared his discovery in the archives and his conversation with Captain Walker.

When Worthy finished, Nick asked, "What will happen if the correction page isn't found?"

"I honestly don't know. We both know that there's a lot of anger and suspicion directed at the police right now. Do judges pay attention to that? Maybe not, but the days are gone when police are given the benefit of the doubt."

"But your reputation is solid, my friend, and not just in Detroit."

Worthy shrugged. "You know, I never wanted to be singled out for commendations. Maybe I feared that something like this could happen. Nick, if I lose the appeal, my entire record will be called into question. I can think of a number of colleagues, not just Sherrod, who'll enjoy seeing me face-down in the dirt."

CHAPTER THIRTEEN

BEING BACK AT ST. SIMEON'S FOR LESS THAN AN HOUR, Nick wasn't expecting a knock on his door. He was surprised to see Brother Pachomius' face before thinking that he shouldn't have been surprised.

"Do you have time to talk?" Pachomius asked.

Nick looked at his watch and saw that it was an hour before afternoon prayers. Selfishly, he wanted nothing more than to sit quietly in his cell, to pray, read a bit, and not think about Sophia's and Worthy's cases—but he saw the eagerness on the novice's face and said, "Please, Brother, take a seat."

"Was your trip successful, Father?"

Nick sat in the other chair and thought how best to respond. On the one hand, he wanted some distance from Pachomius, but he also wanted the novice to use his computer skills to find information on Sophia Demetrios.

"My trip was a beginning," he said, "and beginnings don't say much. Helping the Demetrios' family will demand patience. And yes, I do have a task for you, but I need you to wait until I message you."

Brother Pachomius' face turned red as he lowered his eyes. "I don't mean to be bothering you, Father. Sorry."

"I hope you understand that this is for your own good. I don't want you to get into trouble with your confessor." As Nick said this, he saw Brother Pachomius start to respond but then stop.

"What is it, Brother?" he asked.

Pachomius didn't say anything for a moment. "Father Bessarion already talked to me. To be honest, Abbot Lucas was there, too."

"Ah. What did they say?"

"The guestmaster, Father Ioannis, reported on my wanting to look at the guest list of retreatants. And apparently, I look distracted in community prayers."

Nick nodded. "They were right to talk with you about that, and I accept responsibility for pulling you away from what you need to focus on. Perhaps it's best if we don't speak again about the Demetrios matter, and I promise to sort things out with the abbot."

"No, no, Father, please, I want to help. And I can do that, I know I can, without losing my focus."

"Can you, Brother? Can you honestly say that the woman by the lake hasn't taken your mind away from your studies and prayer life?"

Pachomius looked down again. "I don't mean to be presumptuous, Father, but can you honestly say your work with Lieutenant Worthy isn't exciting for you?"

Nick felt a flash of anger but then had to nod. "In a way, you're right, but it wouldn't have been right if I'd asked to work on police cases when I was a novice."

"Just give me a chance, Father. I can be an obedient novice and still help you."

Nick couldn't deny that he needed Brother Pachomius' computer skills, but he had to settle something with the novice before he made his decision.

"Before I agree, I need to know why helping me is so important to you," he said.

Pachomius didn't respond immediately. Nick thought Pachomius might have sensed that his answer would settle the issue one way or another.

"I won't lie to you, Father. At first, helping you gave me a break from the . . . the routine of life here. But I think it's more than that. When I entered St. Simeon, I was told that the novitiate was a time when both the community and I could discern if monastic life is my calling. I'm still trying to figure that out. If I can help you while not shirking my duties and responsibilities, then I'll know . . . and the community will know better if monastic life is for me. You see, Father, I've recognized something over the past few days. God gave me a . . . what I'd call a busy mind. I won't call it a 'restless mind,' but certainly my mind scrolls through a lot of thoughts in a day—no, in an hour. Helping you has given me a taste of the joy that I was hoping to find in monastic life. I'm praying that I can find a way to use the mind that God gave me for the good of St. Simeon's and others. Can I give you an example—in confidence?"

Nick nodded.

"While you were gone, I did something that I haven't told anyone about. I know that Father Bessarion and Abbot Lucas would consider what I did as out of bounds, and in one way it was. Anyway, after Compline the other night, I went to the guesthouse and looked at the list of guests from last weekend. You see, I remembered what you told me, that there was another guest, a man, who asked Father Ioannis to look at the list. You thought he might have been interested in Marina Demetrios."

"Pachomius! I'd never have given you permission to sneak around the monastery. Don't you see that you're not just putting yourself in a bad light? You're jeopardizing my chance to help this family."

"Yes, Father, I can see that now, but can I tell you what I found?"

"I have a feeling you'll tell me anyway."

Pachomius smiled. "I'm sure the man who asked about the other guests was Gus Cooper, someone who listed his parish as St. Anastasia's in Detroit."

"And how does that help us?"

"The next morning when I was on duty in the security office, I looked up the Gus Coopers from Detroit on Facebook. Then I found Marina Demetrios' Facebook page and compared them. They might have been at Wayne State University at the same time."

"You do know that Wayne State University is huge, Brother."

"I do, Father, but that's still a connection."

Nick considered that for a moment, then shook his head. "Even if they know each other, I still don't see how that proves anything. It's not suspicious for friends to arrange to come together on a weekend retreat."

Pachomius flashed an even bigger smile. "But wouldn't she have mentioned him when she talked to you? And there's more. Gus Cooper listed

St. Anastasia's parish in Detroit as his parish, but there is no Orthodox parish by that name, not Greek, Serbian, Romanian, Antiochan, Bulgarian, or Russian. He lied, Father, he lied."

Nick had to admit that if Worthy or he had found this discrepancy, they'd have considered it suspicious, even something worth looking into—but Nick wasn't in the mood to congratulate Brother Pachomius.

"What you found could be important, or it could simply be a mistake, Brother. And even if this Cooper lied, it doesn't mean he has anything to do with Sophia Demetrios, the sister in prison. He might simply have a crush on Marina."

"But couldn't it also mean he's stalking her?" Pachomius asked.

"It could, but if you can't stop yourself from jumping to conclusions, you'll be of no help to me."

"Do you mean I can still be of help—if I don't jump to conclusions?"

Hearing the yearning in Pachomius' voice, Nick could imagine what Abbot Lucas would want him to say. In order to leave the world behind, a novice was meant to focus on his relationship with God. Nick could think of a host of problems, even sins, that Pachomius might fall into by helping him: pride, a sense of specialness, as well as a distracted mind.

"Okay, you can look up something for me on the computer under one condition."

"What is you want me to research?"

Even though Nick noted that Pachomius' focus was on the research rather than the caveat, he said, "Check online for any information on Sophia Demetrios' trial. That should be seven or eight six months ago. Look specifically for the testimony of Francine Nichols at the trial."

"Who is she?" Pachomius asked.

"Someone Sophia Demetrios knew and stayed with a lot. And on the night of the murder, Sophia doesn't remember anything after passing out there in the afternoon in Nichols' apartment. In other words, there are two or three hours that are blank to Sophia, and if anyone can fill in that blank, it'll be Francine Nichols. But before you do that, you have to abide by one condition."

Pachomius sighed and looked down. "Okay, you have my word. What do I have to do?"

"You have to tell the abbot everything you've done and are doing to help me. I'm sure he'll want to talk with me, and I'll explain to him how you can help me with your computer skills. But the decision will be up to him, not me and certainly not you."

Pachomius didn't say anything for a moment. He folded his arms across his chest and glanced up. "So this Francine Nichols is a friend of Sophia Demetrios?"

"Brother, please, focus. Do you promise to meet with the abbot?"

"Yes, Father, I promise. But this Francine Nichols, you think she can help Sophia Demetrios?"

Nick felt like he was pulling on the reins of a stubborn donkey. "Look at me, Pachomius. I'm about this close," he said, showing his finger and thumb about an inch apart, "to never speaking to you again."

"I'm sorry, Father, really I am. "I won't ask anything else."

As Pachomius rose and moved to the door, Nick said, "To answer your question, Francine Nichols isn't someone who wants to help Sophia Demetrios. At the trial, she testified that she saw Sophia pull the trigger."

✝

October 12, 2023,
Christopher Worthy Private Detectio
and Inquiries Agency—Detroit

THE NEXT MORNING, HENDERSON SAT IN HIS OFFICE at the Worthy Private Detective Agency and stared at the headline on the front page of the newspaper. "Decorated Detective's Record Being Questioned." Under the headline was the name of the reporter: Kenna McCarty.

He had no trouble remembering the name. Kenna McCarty had given Worthy fits on Henderson's first case with Worthy. She'd stopped at nothing to inveigle her way into the investigation, even prying into Worthy's divorce. Worthy had reacted in his usual way by resisting her demands and generally ignoring anything that prevented him from focusing completely on the case.

Now Kenna McCarty seemed to be getting her revenge. He read: "Christopher Worthy, recently retired from Detroit's Homicide Division and used to basking in the spotlight as the city's most decorated detective, is now under the scrutiny of a far-less adoring light. Readers might remember the savage murder of Renee Vickers and the arrest of William Tremont thirteen years ago, the case that first showcased Lieutenant Worthy's abilities to solve difficult cases.

"Worthy now finds himself being questioned in the appeal of that case. The basis of Tremont's appeal is unusual. His lawyers claim that the confession Worthy solicited from Tremont was obtained while Tremont was under the influence of the drug Ecstasy.

"Tremont's lawyers also hint that there is further evidence of misconduct on the part of Lieutenant Worthy, and that this other evidence will become public at trial, but not before. Opening arguments in the appeal are scheduled to begin in two days, and, as this reporter has been assigned to follow the case closely, readers will be kept abreast of developments as they unfold."

Henderson cursed the paper even as he wadded it up and threw it across the room. As was his tendency when he felt cornered, he wanted to hit something or someone. He knew that wouldn't be Worthy's reaction, but he wondered how Worthy was taking the news.

What puzzled Henderson was the basis of the appeal. He put aside the teaser of further evidence of Worthy's misconduct and focused on the claim that Tremont was high when he confessed. Certainly, Tremont's tox screening would settle that question.

Something's not right, he thought, even as he heard a car pull up outside. He looked out the window and saw Worthy walking heavily toward the building, a newspaper under his arm.

Just as Worthy entered the building, the business phone rang. Answering it, Henderson heard, "This is channel seven calling. Can I speak with Christopher Worthy, please?"

"He's not here," Henderson lied and hung up.

"Thanks for that," Worthy said as he pulled up a chair and sat down.

"Let me get you a cup of coffee. Milk and a sugar, right?"

Worthy rubbed his face before nodding. "Tremont, then Sherrod, and now McCarty. I have an urge to fly back to Rome."

Henderson didn't say anything until he handed Worthy the coffee. "The Christopher Worthy I know wouldn't do that."

"No, I'm not serious, but I want to tell you something. I've worked three high-profile cases in Rome, and, as far as I can tell, nobody in the police or media there is pissed off at me. But here in Detroit? I can't think of a case I've worked in the last thirteen years that didn't set someone's teeth on edge. And I don't have to tell you that here in Detroit, I was more than once my own worst enemy. Hell, on that first case we worked together, I remember you calling me a prime asshole."

"I actually said that? Well, I wasn't in very good shape, as we both remember. But for this appeal, maybe you should channel a bit of that asshole-ness. McCarty is out to get you."

"I sort of promised Captain Walker—she's new since we left homicide—that I'd play nice this time around."

"Have you met with the department's lawyers?"

"I will later this morning, so I'll be going pretty soon. I expect someone from PR will be there to coach me on how to keep my foot out of my mouth."

"Anything I can do, Chris?"

Worthy sighed. "I can't think of anything even I can do. Until I read McCarthy in the paper this morning, I thought the appeal would be based solely on the tox screening."

"That's what I thought. Ecstasy would have shown up on that, right?"

"Oh, the tox screening shows Tremont was clean. The problem is that the dating of the screening is scratched out and written over. November 2 is replaced by November 1. Doc Wallace signed it, but there's no corrections page in the file."

"Ah, and being dead, Doc Wallace can't be called to explain that."

Worthy took a sip of the coffee and set the cup down near the edge of the desk. "Tremont's lawyers could be bluffing, but I can't imagine what other misconduct on my part they're talking about."

"Then let's hope the department's lawyers know what that means." After a pause, Henderson said, "Chris, do me a favor, will you?"

"I wouldn't fault you if you want me to stay clear of the office for the time being. Better yet, maybe we should change the name of the company."

Henderson shook his head. "No, none of that. Promise me that you'll come to dinner tonight. It's Friday, so Jamie will be home for the weekend. Will you do that?"

"I won't be scintillating company."

"Jamie won't care. He'll just be glad to see you. And Sulla will make her jambalaya, New Orleans style."

Worthy drained the cup of coffee and stood. "Thanks, partner. No matter what the lawyers throw at me today, I'll keep thinking about Sulla's jambalaya."

ST. SIMEON'S

ABBOT LUCAS DIDN'T TAKE LONG TO ASK NICK to come see him. To receive permission to leave the monastery to visit Sophia Demetrios in prison, Nick had already shared with the abbot how he'd met Marina Demetrios and learned about the family's crisis. But he'd given the abbot the impression that his visit to the prison was simply a pastoral call, not that he was looking into Sophia Demetrios' conviction. Brother Pachomius' meeting with the Abbot and Father Bessarion, however, had revealed that.

Until two years before, Nick's abbots had viewed his requests to work with Worthy with suspicion. Monks were allowed to have hobbies, such as beekeeping, iconography, and gardening. But detective work? No, the abbots believed that Nick working with the Worthy would only entangle Nick in the affairs of the world.

Nick had given up trying to convince his abbots, and it had been Worthy who'd been successful. Worthy had argued that Nick wasn't less of a monk when working with him, but more so as Nick ministered to families overwhelmed with worry or sorrow. Yes, Worthy had argued, police departments had chaplains and many families of victims had clergy they could appeal to, but Nick was the rare type of priest who could offer solace to the families while at the same time contribute to solving cases.

Since that meeting, Abbot Lucas had not only stopped resisting Nick's requests to help Worthy, but had also invited the community to pray for Nick while he was away. Now, as he walked to the abbot's office, he feared that Brother Pachomius' eagerness to help had led the abbot to regret his earlier support.

Entering the abbot's office, Nick was reminded of the difference between Abbot Lucas and his predecessor, Abbot Timothy. In Timothy's time as abbot, the office was filled with teetering stacks of books and papers littering the desk. Abbot Lucas' office was neat in every respect. Even the spines of the books on the shelves were set at the same depth, and the desk was empty except for two icons and a laptop.

"Please sit, Father Nicholas. You can probably guess why I've asked to see you, but I want to begin by saying that I don't blame you for anything. And I don't blame Brother Pachomius for his eagerness—no, his over-eagerness—to help you. What I want to discuss is how we can help this young man not lose his way."

Nick felt his shoulders relax. "Helping Brother Pachomius is my wish as well, Reverend Father."

Abbot Lucas smiled. "I assumed that would be your attitude. But perhaps we should first talk about how you hope to help the Demetrios family."

Nick shared how his meeting with the Demetrios' family and his visit to Sophia in prison had led him to question her conviction.

At the end, the abbot nodded. "I suppose the question is, is this a matter for a lawyer or for you, Father?"

"Reverend Father, even if the Demetrios family had the money to hire a good lawyer—which they don't—I'd still want to help. You see, Sophia has no memory of the entire night of the shooting. Even the prosecution conceded that she had no previous experience with guns, yet she was convicted of killing a hard-core drug lord with two shots—one to the head and one to the heart."

After a pause, Abbot Lucas said, "I have no problem with you being involved, Father. Will your friend, Christopher Worthy, be working with you, or is he in Rome?"

Nick shook his head. "He's in Detroit, but he has to be careful. One of his first cases is being appealed, so I know he can't be appear to be questioning Sophia Demetrios' conviction. But he has agreed to help when and where he can."

"Which brings us back to Brother Pachomius," the abbot said. "As he described himself, he's a 'computer nerd,' which, as I take it, is his value to your work. If he weren't a novice and were more established in the disciplines of our life here, I wouldn't be as concerned as I am. But to address the practicalities of the situation, how much time has Brother Pachomius contributed so far?"

"There's more than one way to answer that, Reverend Father. I don't think he's helped me for more than two or three hours, and that has been spread out with thirty minutes here and forty minutes there. But it's obvious that Brother Pachomius has been thinking about the matter for many more hours than that. As he's admitted, he has an active mind."

"Hmm. I appreciate your candor, Father. I've given the situation some thought since he spoke with me, and I can see two different responses. And while the decision is ultimately left to me, I'd appreciate your thoughts."

"Of course."

"The most direct course of action is for you to disengage with Brother Pachomius. His confessor, Father Bessarion, would remind him that he will never achieve interior silence if his mind is tossed to and fro by exterior problems. This is what we would do with every novice, to remove the distractions that stand in the way of inner peace." Abbot Lucas paused before adding, "I have few doubts that Brother Pachomius would comply out of obedience, but I fear that he'd receive this decision as a punishment, a reprimand. Brother Pachomius has no doubt expressed to you what he said to me, that he hopes his active mind can be useful to the community, that I shouldn't equate his active mind with a restless one. In that description, he reminds me of someone else," the abbot said with a smile. "Not every monk is an introvert, is he, Father?"

"No, we're not. You said that there might be another approach to take?"

"Yes, and this approach should be used only in the rarest of occasions. It is based on something that Our Lord spoke to St. Catherine of Siena. Yes, I know St. Catherine is a Western saint, but Our Lord is neither Eastern nor Western, don't you agree?"

"I do, Reverend Father."

"What Our Lord told St. Catherine was that virtues are best developed when they are challenged by vices. It is only when threatened by pride that one develops humility. It is only when tempted to hate that one is given the opportunity to forgive. So, in that understanding, I'm considering that Brother Pachomius' vocation might be better advanced if I allow him to help you, but it has to be for a limited number of hours a day—no more than two, I think."

As Nick listened to the abbot, he saw the great risk that was involved in this approach. It would not be only Brother Pachomius who would be responsible for observing this limitation in good faith. No, Nick knew that he would also bear responsibility.

"If you do decide to take this second approach, I have one suggestion to make, Reverend Father."

"Please share."

"It's based on something that helped me as an easily distracted novice. I was given the honor of joining the older monks at the chanters' stand. Being surrounded by the prayers of the other monks helped in keeping my mind from wandering."

"An excellent idea, Father Nicholas. Well, it seems we're of one mind on the matter. At least until Brother Pachomius proves otherwise, we will allow him to assist you on a limited basis. But I don't have to tell you that we need to pray for Brother Pachomius now more than ever."

CHAPTER FOURTEEN

———— ✦ ————

DETROIT HOMICIDE PRECINCT

WORTHY WOULD HAVE PREFERRED TO MEET with the department's lawyers in a law office, but the meeting was set for one of the department's conference rooms. *We might as well be meeting in one of the interrogation rooms where suspects are grilled*, Worthy thought as he walked into the precinct.

The first person he saw as entered the lobby was Howard Hullinger, the department's chief lawyer. Hullinger's appearance showed how worried the department was about the appeal. Worthy had looked him up on the police department's website and had assumed, from the flattop hairstyle, that the photo was old. But now he realized that Hullinger had kept the flattop, and Worthy wondered if he were retired military.

"Mr. Worthy, I wish I could say it's good to see you, but, well, you know," he said as he led Worthy to an elevator.

I wish I did know, Worthy thought. *I wish I knew what Tremont's lawyers think they know. I wish I knew how Hullinger's team intends to fight the appeal. I wish I knew where the corrections page is.*

As if to punctuate the tension, the first face that Worthy saw when the elevator doors opened was Phillip Sherrod's. Sherrod stared as Worthy walked past him without saying anything, but Worthy suspected that Sherrod standing by the elevator doors wasn't a coincidence.

It had been nearly seven months since Worthy had last seen Sherrod, and Worthy wondered if he'd aged as much over that time as Sherrod had. His nemesis looked as if he'd lost thirty pounds, but his leanness seemed unhealthy to Worthy. Sherrod's complexion had also yellowed and he seemed to stoop. Given the way that Sherrod had stared at him, Worthy concluded that what hadn't changed was Sherrod's hostility toward him.

Following Hullinger into the conference room, Worthy was greeted by Captain Walker who introduced him to the department's PR director, Louisa Hernandez, and a second lawyer, Courtney Ogden.

After they all sat down, Captain Walker said, "This is your team, Mr. Worthy. We're all on the same side, and we all want the same outcome as you —to have this appeal squashed."

Worthy could have predicted that the meeting would begin with a pledge of cooperation, but he also heard the subtext—the "team" was assembled not just to show support to him but to assess the appeal's potential damage to the Department.

"Our goal today is to agree on the steps we need to take before opening statements begin," Hullinger said. "So, let's agree on where we stand today. Courtney, why don't you summarize."

The junior lawyer cleared her throat. "What we know is that the main thrust of the appeal will challenge William Tremont's confession. That confession was the basis of your charging him on November 1, 2010, and his subsequent conviction at trial. Mr. Tremont isn't denying that he confessed—he could hardly do so given the audiotape of the interview—but is now stating that he was under the influence of the drug Ecstasy at the time. Consequently, that part of the appeal will focus on the toxicology screening administered by Dr. Robin Wallace, which revealed that Mr. Tremont was under no influence of drugs on November 1. What Tremont's legal team noted, however, is that the date of November 1 has been written over and slightly above what was originally listed on the report—November 2, 2010. We will argue that the most likely explanation for this correction is that Dr. Wallace, who preferred to work alone even when he was swamped with work, erroneously wrote down November 2 and, perhaps immediately thereafter, corrected his mistake. The ink looks the same."

The young lawyer paused and turned over a page. "Obviously, Dr. Wallace, being deceased, is unavailable to corroborate our assumption. And the recent discovery that the case file contains no correction's page is the crack in the evidence from the initial trial that Mr. Tremont's legal team will focus on. We expect Mr. Tremont's lawyers to impugn the reputation of Dr. Wallace by arguing that on November 1, Mr. Tremont confessed to the murder of Renee Vickers while, in fact, being under the influence of the drug of Ecstasy. They will then argue that the toxicology report, also known as the tox screen, showing no evidence of the drug in Mr. Tremont's system, was, in reality, administered by Dr. Wallace the next day, on November 2."

"Wouldn't that mean that their legal team will point the finger at Dr. Wallace, not Mr. Worthy, Lieutenant Worthy at the time?" Captain Walker asked.

There was an awkward silence in the room. The junior lawyer looked to Hullinger to answer.

"It's logical to assume that Mr. Tremont's legal team also intends to argue that Renee Vickers was killed by someone else. We expect them to point out that a close friend of Mr. Tremont, Kerry Paulsen, recently committed suicide, and we also expect them to suggest that Mr. Paulsen's suicide is an admission of guilt. Paulsen, they will argue, was Renee Vickers' actually killer. Tremont's lawyers will blame Lieutenant Worthy for failing to pursue this possibility."

Captain Walker leaned forward. "But that's surely an argument from silence. Paulsen never mentioned Renee Vickers in the suicide note he left. Unless I'm missing something, it seems that the appeal is based on two persons—Dr. Wallace and Paulsen—who are both inconveniently dead."

Howard Hullinger shook his head. "That was our thinking until we read a recent interview given by the defense lawyers to a local journalist. That interview suggests that you, Mr. Worthy, might be vulnerable on other grounds. That's something we hope you can help us with today. Tremont's lawyers might be bluffing, but we don't think so. What we need from you is your recollection of actions you took on the case that might now be open to question."

Worthy felt his face redden. "It's all in the file—"

"Yes, Mr. Worthy," Hullinger said, interrupting, "but now you need to go over it all again. We'll meet again tomorrow morning, and that's when we'll ask all the questions that we expect Tremont's team to throw at you. So, be prepared for a long day and a rough one."

CARNELL AND SULLA HENDERSON'S HOME

BEFORE DRIVING TO HENDERSON'S HOUSE THAT evening, Worthy called Lena and did his best to minimize the sense of foreboding he felt. If any of his cases were appealed, he'd resent the past rising up to ensnare him, but none more so than this case. Tremont's appeal would force him to return to the darkest days of his life.

That was why on his call to Lena he talked about everything—the Sophia Demetrios case that Nick was working on, the business in Detroit run by Henderson, as well as Lena's last weeks of the semester—except the appeal.

Lena, however, had sensed his evasiveness and asked what worried him most.

"Logically, I know the appeal should be decided on what the pathologist did in 2010, but the lawyers have asked me to go back over them everything on the case, and that's going to be painful."

He'd heard Lena moan. "Because that was when Susan asked for the divorce, right?"

"Yeah. And then Allyson ran away."

"Ooh, I forgot about that. When does the appeal officially start?"

"The day after tomorrow."

"If it weren't for the semester ending, you know I'd be on the first flight out. I hate to think of you having to go through this on your own."

"I have Nick. He's promised to be at the appeal. And Henderson is also here. In fact, I'm having dinner at his house tonight."

"I'm glad you won't be alone. Henderson is your business partner, the one with the son who has schizophrenia, right?"

"Yes, I'll see Jamie tonight. In a way, Jamie will be the easiest one for me to be with. We've always had a good relationship, and I have a present for him. Actually, it's more something I want him to do for me, but he'll take it as a gift. It's an old mantle clock that was handed down to me from my grandfather. The clock hasn't worked for God knows how long, but I'm betting Jamie can fix it."

"If only everything in the past could be fixed," Lena said.

"I'd be satisfied if the past would remain in the past. Anyway, I'll give you a call tomorrow, after my second fun day with the lawyers."

Now, after pulling into Henderson's driveway, he felt exhausted and wondered if he should have cancelled. But he grabbed the box containing the old mantle clock and rang the bell.

Sulla opened the door and gave him a warm hug. "Chris, so good to see you. Jamie has been asking for the past hour when you'd arrive."

"I'm sorry I didn't have a chance to bring wine, Sulla. But I do have something for Jamie."

"Wine we have plenty of, Chris. Carnell is on his way home from the office, but Jamie is in the den."

"I'll go through, then," Worthy said, then stopped. "It's really good to see you, Sulla."

"Me, too. And Lena will be here soon?"

"In three weeks. I know she'll want to see you."

"We'll plan on having a party, celebrating your winning the appeal," Sulla said.

"Let's hope. I'd rather be getting a root canal."

"Carnell said the appeal is one of your cases from before he was promoted to homicide. So over a decade ago, right?"

"Yes. I don't know if 2010 was a good year for wines, but it was the worst year of my life."

"And you had no partner."

"Not really. This was a case that I took over, and they let me work it alone. Looking back, I wish Hoops had been my partner."

Sulla gave Worthy another hug. "Carnell said the same thing just yesterday. Chris, you know that you can call on us for anything."

"Thanks, I do know that. Well, I'm going to go in and see Jamie."

Worthy walked down a hallway and entered the den. He remembered the first time he'd been in the room, when Henderson was hanging onto his career by a thread as Sulla and he were trying to grasp the implications of what the doctors were telling them about Jamie's condition.

Jamie was sitting in a chair, not looking up as he watched an old epi-sode of *The Repair Shop*. But the slight smile on Jamie's face told Worthy that Jamie had recognized that he'd come into the room.

The boy, now a young man, had always reminded Worthy of what Huey P. Newton of the Black Panthers looked like. Worthy wondered if Jamie had any idea how handsome he was. Sitting down on the sofa, Worthy placed the box on the coffee table in front of him. "Jamie, I'm wondering if you'd give me some advice. This is my grandfather's old clock, but it hasn't worked for at least thirty or forty years, maybe longer. Do you happen to know someone who might be able to fix it?"

Without saying anything, Jamie came over, sat down next to Worthy, but didn't touch the box.

"Here, let me show you," Worthy said as he brought out the art-deco mantle clock and handed it to Jamie. After turning the clock over and opening its back, he spoke for the first time.

"It's a Junghans clock from the 1930's, Mr. Worthy. So it's almost a hundred years old. It's from Germany, made before the Second World War. Look on the back, Mr. Worthy. The dials to reset the clock look like a human face."

"You're right, Jamie. And do you remember that you can call me Chris?"

Jamie continued to study the clock, front and back, top and bottom. "The wood is nutwood. Would you like me to repair it, Mr. Worthy?"

"Well, that's what I was hoping. Can I pay you for your trouble?"

"I don't understand. Why is it trouble? I can fix it, and I want to."

"No, you're right, Jamie."

Worthy heard Henderson come into the room.

"That's a cool-looking old clock," he said.

"It's a Junghans clock from the 1930's, Dad."

"Well, Jamie, you would know. It doesn't look like it's working."

"Mr. Worthy is letting me fix it. I'll work on it when I come here. I won't bring it home," Jamie said, glancing at his father even as he took out a small screwdriver set from his shirt pocket and placed it on the coffee table.

"Good plan, Jamie. I promise that Mom and I won't touch it when you're . . . when you're not here."

Jamie said nothing until he'd removed the knobs on the back and begun unscrewing the back plate. He moved slowly and carefully until he'd loosened all but the final screw holding down the back plate. Then, looking up at his father and Worthy, Jamie smiled broadly. "I've never opened a clock this old before."

Worthy scooted over on the couch to make room for Henderson to sit next to Jamie. Jamie rubbed his hands on his thighs as if to warm them. Then with great care, he released the last screw and set it along with the other five on the table.

Worthy looked up to see Sulla watching from the doorway. "We're getting ready for the big reveal," Worthy said.

No one said anything as Jamie positioned his long fingers around the edges of the back plate and slowly twisted. Nothing moved for a moment, and Worthy wondered if the back plate was affixed to the rest of the clock in another way.

Jamie removed his hands and sat back a few inches. "The back plate wants to release, but it's stuck."

"I'm not surprised," Worthy said. "For all I know, no one has opened the back of this clock for forty years or more."

"That was before I was born," Jamie said. "So, when I open the back, the air inside will get out for the first time in all those years. Do you think maybe the air has been waiting for this moment, Mom?"

Sulla nodded. "I do. I think the clock has been waiting for you, Jamie."

Jamie smiled as his hands returned to the clock and his fingernails gripped the edges of the back plate. Worthy watched as Jamie applied pressure to one side and then the other. Finally, they heard a slight clicking sound as the back plate released.

Sulla, Henderson, and Worthy all looked inside the clock to where wheels and gears remained motionless. Jamie, however, sat back on the sofa with the back plate in his hands.

"Look, Dad, here's the initials of the last person to work on the clock along with the date."

"I don't have my bifocals on, Jamie, so you'll have to read what it says."

Jamie brought it closer to his face. "It says, K-O-L-N, followed by 11/46 and the initials W.P." Looking up, he said, "What does that mean, Dad?"

"I think I know, Jamie. When I was in the Army, I was stationed in Germany near the city of Köln, what we call Cologne. I think the marks mean that someone from Cologne with the initials W.P. worked on the clock in November, 1946."

"And from what I know about my grandfather, he served in the southern part of Germany after the war," Worthy said. "He must have bought it in Cologne and brought it home with him. So, Jamie, if you can get the clock working again, I want you to scratch your initials and the date on the back plate."

Jamie continued to stare at the markings on the back plate. After a few moments, Sulla said, "Are we ready for Jambalaya?"

They all stood except Jamie, who remained on the sofa.

"What is it, Jamie?" Henderson asked.

Jamie's hand rubbed the markings on the back plate. "Forty years from now, someone could open the clock and find JH, my initials." He took a breath even as he looked from his parents to Worthy. "They will know . . . they will know that I lived."

CHAPTER FIFTEEN

---◆---

Barminster Prison

Sophia's second cellmate, Deidra, an African-American from Detroit, had spoken openly about why she was in Barminster.

"My no-good husband almost killed me five times, but I'm the one serving time for dealing coke," she'd shared the first night she was assigned to Sophia's cell.

Sophia had been too numb to be afraid of Deidra at first, and Deidra had seemed to sense that.

"Listen, girl, they're saying you're in here for killing Reggie King, and from what I heard, you did the world a favor. So, I'm not going to let anyone hit on you. That's not because you're going to be my bitch, but because I can see you don't have the strength to protect yourself. Not yet, anyway. All I ask is that when the lights go out, you let me sleep. I don't want any late night talks; I just want my beauty sleep."

That arrangement was fine with Sophia. She was happy to be left alone, especially after lights out when other inmates, sick of one another after a day in each other's space, went at each other. That was when the guards would open the cell and drag one of them off to solitary.

In the rec yard, Sophia noticed the other inmates who looked like they were sleepwalking through their sentences and thought she must look the same. Not thinking, not feeling, not reacting to the guards or other inmates when they pushed or tripped her made it easier to deal with the gray world as she described it to the priest who'd visited her. It struck her that prison life was its own kind of drug, one that numbed a person both physically and mentally unless you fought it, and Sophia had no desire to do that.

The priest's visit had been only a slight break from her routine, not that different from visits from her father or sister. The priest had seemed to want to give her something—hope, she imagined—but he also wanted something from her. It took her a while to guess what that something was. The priest, like Marina, wanted her to snap out of her numbness for even a few seconds, anything to convince them that their visit had been worth it.

But the visit had done nothing for her. She looked at the icon of the Virgin Mary that the priest had given her before he left. That too, she realized, was something he'd done so that he'd feel better on his drive back to Detroit. It was like his promise to look into the case against her. What good could a priest do? No, he'd said that to get a response from her, some sense of gratitude or hope.

She thought about tearing the icon up; after all, it was only a piece of paper, and she would have done so if Deidra hadn't noticed it and told Sophia to tape it to the wall. "Maybe she'll bring us good luck," Deidra had said.

If there were any minutes in prison when the numbness seemed to lighten, it was at night after Deidra turned off her flashlight. Sophia would think back to the last time she'd been happy, which was before her mother was diagnosed with cancer. Because Sophia had rheumatic fever when she was young, she was never an active child. While other kids were outside playing, she was more likely inside with her mother. Because they'd spent so much time together, her mother's diagnosis, together with the wearying chemo treatments, had hit Sophia hardest. Her mother became increasingly silent as death gradually took up residence in the house.

After her mother's funeral, death stuck around as her sister, Marina, buried herself in her classes and work, and her brother went off to boot camp. When she came home from school, she was alone for hours, with nothing to do until her father arrived from work, and when her father was home, he sat in the dark, drowning in his grief. For the first time in her life, she realized she'd have to make her way outside the family.

School wasn't the answer. As her future more and more darkened, her community college classes seemed increasingly pointless. The only class that interested her was an astronomy elective. After that class was over, she pretended to go to campus, while instead walking aimlessly around one of the city's malls. When her absence went unnoticed by the college authorities for nearly a month, she realized that she was as good as invisible. She didn't blame the school officials; she was in community college, not high school. Even her closest school friends stopped calling after a few weeks.

Several months after her mother died, she was walking around one of the malls when she spotted a woman sitting on a bench. As she walked by, the woman said, "Hey, why don't you sit and do nothing with me?" Sophia stood for a moment without moving, surprised to be noticed. That was when she met Francine Nichols, a woman a few years older. They began to meet daily, and in addition to people-watching—more like people-judging—they stood outside the mall to smoke. After a week of this, Francine invited Sophia to her apartment. It wasn't long before Sophia was spending more time in Francine's apartment than at home, and that apartment was where Sophia started sampling Francine's ample supply of drugs.

What most surprised Sophia was that her family didn't notice. She knew that her mother would have spotted something wrong immediately, and the fact that neither her father nor her sister noticed her slurring speech convinced her that they didn't care. Her initial feeling of freedom was replaced by the realization that she was invisible to them as well, which meant there was no reason to stop hanging out with Francine or stop experimenting with drugs.

Eventually, the community college sent a letter home, saying she'd been officially withdrawn. Her father hadn't said anything, but Marina had come down on her. "Can't you see how you're hurting Poppa?" she'd screamed. Sophia understood the message. Her only importance in the family was as someone who could make life harder for others. No one cared about how hard life was for her.

The one person who seemed to notice her was Francine, and together they roamed the mall until that felt as dull a routine as sitting in class. Life became more exciting when Francine asked her to distract store clerks while Francine shoplifted—but then the day came when an alert security guard spotted the two of them in action. Francine managed to escape, but Sophia was caught and turned over to the police.

At the beginning of her stay in juvenile detention, the police tried to convince her to name her accomplice, but Sophia played dumb and said she didn't know what they were talking about. She was learning the value of being numb. She had no way of knowing that her stonewalling about the shoplifting would be brought up at her murder trial, when her claim of not remember shooting Reginald King was described by the prosecution as, once again, her standard ploy of playing dumb.

If her two months in detention was meant to convince her that Francine was a toxic association, those months achieved the opposite. Her one worry while being locked up was that Francine would want nothing to do with her when she was released. But if Francine hadn't thanked her for not giving up her name to the police, she had contacted Sophia two days after her release and invited her back to her apartment.

The one difference in their relationship after Sophia was released was the presence of another woman nearer to Francine's age. Other than looking coolly at Sophia for the first couple of days, the girl named Connie mainly ignored her. When they drove around in Francine's car, Connie rode shotgun, with Sophia, relegated to the back seat, left out of the running conversations between the two women in the front—invisible once again.

From what Sophia gathered, Connie had arrived recently in Detroit after living for a time in Baltimore with a grandmother and in Alabama with her mother—when her mother was sober. Connie laughed with she told stories of how easy it was to rob from her mother's purse after her mother passed out, and Sophia got the impression, from other stories, that Connie had also spent time in juvenile detention.

The odd thing about Connie, Sophia remembered, was that her only drug was weed. She never joined in when Francine and Sophia would do lines of coke; instead, she'd sit by herself and laugh at the two of them.

Sophia was thinking about Connie the night after the priest's visit when Deidra did something she'd never done before. As they lay quietly in their bunkbeds after lights out, Deidra had broken her vow of total silence at night by whispering, "Sophie, I heard a rumor out in the yard at rec time. I suppose you shouldn't be surprised that a number of our sisters here in Barminster knew Reggie King. It turns out they were some of his customers. So, the gist is that you should watch your back."

Sophia didn't say anything, not sure if what Deidra told her mattered. More than once since arriving at Barminster, she'd thought that death wouldn't be so bad. She knew of other inmates who'd fashioned sharps that they used to try to kill themselves. One had recently succeeded. She'd heard others talk about playing the red-letter "get out of jail" card, a euphemism for suicide.

But now it seemed likely that someone else, another inmate, might play that card for her. She turned over and looked at the icon of the Virgin Mary on the wall but could think of nothing to say.

✝

OCTOBER 13, 2023, DETROIT HOMICIDE DIVISION
—CONFERENCE ROOM

AS WORTHY WAITED FOR HULLINGER AND his team to arrive for the morning meeting, he looked down at the notes that he'd written the night before. After Jamie finished dinner and returned to the den to begin work on the clock, Carnell, Sulla, and he had said little about the appeal, and Worthy was happy to pretend that he wasn't overly worried.

Looking at his notes, which listed the steps he'd taken on the case, he looked for anything that he might have missed at the time. But as he read and reread his notes, he could spot nothing procedural that he'd neglected. *So what do Tremont's lawyers think they have on me?* he asked himself.

The door to the conference room opened with Captain Walker entering the room followed by Howard Hullinger and Courtney Ogden, the junior lawyer. None of them smiled, and Worthy had the feeling that they'd come from an earlier meeting in which he was the main topic.

Hullinger spoke first. "Good morning, Mr. Worthy. A warning as we begin. Our words and tone today will likely sound adversarial. That's only because we believe those issues will be ones that the defense lawyers will exploit. Understand?"

Worthy nodded as he looked over to see the junior lawyer turn on a small tape recorder.

"When you were first given the case, what did you conclude had been the previous team's mistakes to that point?" Hullinger asked.

"That's not the way I ever approached a takeover case. If I'm looking for someone else's mistake, I'd still be caught in that team's approach. My approach is to look at all the evidence as if I'm the original investigator."

"You probably think that will sell well in the appeal, but doesn't that approach run the risk of your repeating the false steps taken by the first team?"

Worthy glanced at Captain Walker. "I think my captain at the time, Captain Spicer, gave me the case because he knew that I'd take a different approach."

"So you didn't see yourself in competition with the other team or out to embarrass them?"

Worthy bristled. "Certainly not."

"Moving on, it took you another five months to arrest William Tremont. Might you have solved the case sooner if you'd found what was valuable in the other team's work?"

"What's all this about? Are you saying Tremont's lawyers are going to criticize me for not being more collegial?" Worthy replied. "Anyway, I think it will be obvious to the court—or any thinking person—that I wouldn't have known what elements of the other team's approach were potentially helpful or were a waste of time until the case was solved."

If Hullinger understood that Worthy had taken a swipe at him, he didn't show it.

"You admit not being collegial. Why were you working the case alone? The previous team had two other detectives assisting, including Sergeant Sherrod. Doesn't your approach of going it alone assume that you'd succeed where others—teams of others—would fail?"

So they're thinking Tremont's team will make me out to be a narcissist, Worthy realized. *Well, let them.*

"My record will show that I've worked with partners on a number of cases. In the Tremont case, the partner assigned to me asked to be relieved."

"What was the reason?" Hullinger asked.

"It's a long time ago, but as I remember, he thought I was moving too slowly."

"Actually, the file records that he felt excluded by you. He called you a 'lone wolf.'"

Worthy glanced again at Captain Walker but realized she had no obligation to support him.

"As the lead on the case, I decided to split the tasks between us. It seems a waste of resources on a case when the lead and the second on the case are together on every step."

"But wouldn't a partner check the excesses of the other, spot when the other perhaps missed a clue?"

"Is that what you think Tremont's lawyers are going to argue, that I missed a clue?"

Hullinger's eyebrows arched. "You can count on it. They'll argue that you fixated on William Tremont and ignored the possibility that Tremont's friend, Kerry Paulsen, could be the killer."

"I didn't fixate on Tremont. All the evidence pointed to Tremont, not Paulsen. Paulsen met Renee Vickers once, and that was through Tremont. Paulsen admitted having sex with her, but in terms of murder, no, it wasn't Paulsen. And the case file shows clearly that we interviewed Paulsen three times."

"You say 'we interviewed Paulsen.' But there was no 'we' in any real sense, was there? Okay, Captain Spicer sat in on the separate interviews with Paulsen and Tremont, but Tremont's lawyers will come back to this central point, Mr. Worthy. You worked the case alone, just as you have on numerous other cases. The defense is going to portray you as the very definition of a lone wolf."

CHAPTER SIXTEEN

— ◆ —

St. Simeon's Library

Nick waited until he was alone in the library with Brother Pachomius before passing him a sheet of paper with the abbot's decision about the novice's future work for Nick. Brother Pachomius' frown revealed his reaction to the abbot's ruling.

"What we know as monks, Pachomius, is that the hardest vow to honor isn't the vow of chastity or poverty, but the vow of obedience," Nick said. "A monk doesn't have to agree in his mind and heart with what the abbot dictates, but he has promised before God to be obedient."

"So the abbot doesn't trust me, is that it?"

"You need to take yourself out of the equation, my son, and see that the abbot's ruling is based on his considerable knowledge of the human heart and human nature. I hope you can see, given the excesses that you've already shown in helping me, that Abbot Lucas could have denied your helping me. He could have transferred you away from the security office and its computer. The fact that he's allowing you to help at all demonstrates his belief that you can accept discipline."

"But two hours a day, Father? Is that fair to Marina Demetrios and her family?"

Nick sighed, and not for the first time wondered if the arrangement would ever work.

"The one task of every monk is to 'put on Christ' every day," he said.

"And that means letting go our own desires, even those we think are our greatest contributions to others. Neither you nor anyone at St. Simeon's is here to become compassionate social workers, or successful detectives, or anything else but Christ-filled men. And, as our Lord prayed in the Garden of Gethsemane, that means 'not my will, but thine be done.' Can you accept that, Brother, I mean truly accept that?"

Brother Pachomius didn't answer immediately, which Nick took as a good sign. The novice had to know that merely by thinking about Marina and Sophia Demetrios beyond the limit of two hours a day, he would be missing the ruling's intention.

"Okay, I agree," he said, "but why has the abbot assigned me to serve at the chanters' stand?"

"That was my suggestion. You have to know, Brother, that I see a bit of myself in you. My brain tends to churn faster than is often good for me . . . and others. When I was a novice, my confessor recognized that and wisely suggested that I join the senior monks at the chanter's stand. My hope is that what I experienced will have the same effect on you."

"It slowed you down?"

"That's one way of describing it. What I know is that my mind, instead of being distracted, was better able to focus on being in the presence of God. I'm convinced that the brother monks who surrounded me were praying for me."

For the first time, Brother Pachomius smiled. "I'm glad that you think we're alike . . . at least, somewhat alike, Father."

Nick stood. "That's enough for now, Brother. I'll let you know when we'll meet again."

Pachomius didn't rise. Instead, he asked, "Would it be okay if my two hours started now? I'd like to tell you what I discovered online about what happened at Sophia Demetrios' trial."

✠

October 14, 2023, Rome—Lena and Worthy's Apartment

Rain had fallen in Rome that entire afternoon, the dreary sky contributing to Lena's sense of helplessness. Tremont's appeal was centered on what had happened a decade before she met Worthy, and, from

Worthy's comments, he'd been a different person from the man she'd fallen in love with and married. The appeal was forcing Worthy, the man she loved, to return to a time of loneliness and vulnerability.

More than anything, Lena wanted to fly to Detroit, but she knew the appeal wasn't sufficient reason for her to be allowed to leave this close to the end of the semester.

And so I sit here worrying, which helps nothing, she thought. But to fight that sense of helplessness, she sent Worthy an email: "Chris, I love you, and I'll love you even more tomorrow." Then, just as she was about to close her computer, she thought of something else she could do. She typed in the words "Detroit, USA, Renee Vickers Murder Case, 2010" and opened the first site, an article from one of Detroit's main newspapers.

She expected to see photos of the victim, Renee Vickers, and the accused, William Tremont, but she was surprised to see Worthy's photo as well. Before reading the newspaper account, she studied Worthy's photo. The man she'd come to love looked more than thirteen years younger in the picture, showing none of the lines around his eyes that she suspected had come not only from age but also from the pain he'd experienced over the intervening years. She couldn't help wishing that she had been in his life when everything fell apart.

After nearly an hour of reading newspaper updates on the arrest of William Tremont and the subsequent trial, Lena googled Chris' name and started reviewing the newspaper coverage of his later cases. She felt odd, as if she were disturbing his privacy. There was a series of cases after Tremont's arrest and conviction that had garnered little press attention, Chris' name appearing in small print, before she came to his first case with Nick. Nick had told her the main elements of the case before, but she read again how Chris, while searching for a missing student on a Spring Break college trip to New Mexico, had solved a murder even as he'd failed to find the missing woman. Lena smiled, as Nick had told her what the press would never know.

But she felt her face burn when she read an account of Chris' next big case, the murder of an elderly priest in the city. The name of the reporter, Kenna McCarty, was familiar to her, and it was clear from McCarty's coverage that she had it in for Chris as well as Henderson, Chris' partner on the case. Even when the case was solved, McCarty had lauded Nick's contribution more than Chris' and Henderson's. *Not that Chris minded being overlooked*, she thought, *remembering how his successes had alienated him from colleagues in his homicide division.*

After scanning the media coverage of his later cases, cases which solidified Chris' reputation as Detroit's top homicide detective, she came to an article about Tremont's upcoming appeal and was shocked to see Kenna McCarty's name again. Any hope Lena had that McCarty had viewed Chris in a fairer light over the years was dashed with the headline: "Decorated Detective's Record Being Questioned."

The article was completely one-sided, reading like a press release on behalf of William Tremont's defense. "Worthy now finds himself being the one questioned, as Tremont's lawyers have appealed the case." McCarty clearly gave credence to the defense's contention that Tremont had confessed while under the influence of a drug, but the climax to the article was a teaser left by McCarty. She hinted that the defense planned to offer evidence of additional misconduct by Worthy.

Looking at McCarty's photo next to the headline, Lena understood something that she was sure Worthy had missed. McCarty was attractive and Chris, by refusing her request to shadow him back in 2016, had wounded her vanity. She knew what Chris would say, that his refusal to accommodate McCarty's request was based on his need to preserve the case's integrity. Lena also knew that Chris would have missed the fact that he was a good-looking recent divorcee at the time. McCarty had made a play for him, and he'd dismissed her—no, he'd scorned her.

Lena looked out at the falling rain outside her apartment and muttered, "Oh, Chris, my love, you are so clueless."

Closing her computer, Lena sat with her head in her hands. Worthy had told her that he'd been treated better by the police and media in Rome than he'd ever been treated by their counterparts in Detroit, but until now she hadn't fully grasped what he meant. The plan of Tremont's lawyers and the goal of the journalist Kenna McCarty was to pull Chris off the pedestal he'd never wanted to be on in the first place.

For a moment, Lena wished that Chris had refused to return to Detroit, that he'd made up some excuse about being entangled in cases here in Rome. She wished he'd told the court that it would have to be satisfied with his testimony online. Then, at least, he'd have had some distance from people in Detroit who longed for his downfall, and she would have been with him to offer support.

Lena knew, however, that Chris would never have seriously considered that option. She knew that what drew Worthy back to Detroit wasn't a desire to protect his reputation. No, the reason that he'd had flown back to Detroit was the same reason why he'd sacrificed so much on the original case thirteen years before. Renee Vickers might have been a young prostitute who mattered little to anyone but the few who knew and loved her, but, as Chris would insist, she didn't deserve to be murdered. What Renee Vickers deserved thirteen years before in the original trial was what she deserved in the appeal—justice.

CHAPTER SEVENTEEN

---◆---

St. Simeon's

OVER HIS FIRST CUP OF COFFEE OF THE DAY, Nick looked over what Brother Pachomius had sent about Sophia Demetrios' trial. The trial had garnered extensive media coverage because of Reginald King's notoriety as one of Detroit' major drug lords. Sophia Demetrios' name was hardly mentioned, as if the media found her a poor choice to play a central role in the drama. King deserved to die in a drive-by shooting, or by a spray of bullets from an assassin sent by one of the Mexican cartels, or in a coup staged by one of King's lieutenants. Instead, Reginald King had died from two bullets fired by a young girl who had no memory of firing them.

On a separate sheet of paper, Nick made a note of the prosecution's witnesses. The main witness, Francine Nichols, testified that she'd driven with Sophia Demetrios to the motel room where Reginald King had been killed. The two police officers who arrived at the site less than twenty minutes after the shooting testified that they found the murder weapon in Sophia Demetrios' backpack. There were no other fingerprints in the room besides Sophia's, Nichols', and King's. The officers who interviewed Sophia at the site found her incoherent, unable to deny or confirm that she shot King.

By far the most damning testimony came from Francine Nichols, who testified that she witnessed Sophia shooting King. Nichols described the meeting as one called by King, who wanted to discuss the intrusion of Mexican cartel dealers in what he considered his territory. Nichols said Sophia Demetrios had tagged along for no particular reason—"She was always just hanging around"—and Sophia had lain down on a couch as soon as they entered the motel room. Nichols testified further that while King and she were looking at a map of Detroit, Sophia had come up behind them, taking a gun from King's coat draped over the back of the chair, and then, when King turned around, had shot him twice.

In the aftermath of the shooting, Nichols said that she pushed Sophia to the floor, screaming, "Are you out of your mind? This is all on you, Sophia This is all on you."

When the prosecution asked what Sophia Demetrios had said in response, Nichols testified that she said, "What just happened?"

The motel manager testified that he called the police as soon as other residents heard the shots and called the desk. The two police officers testified that when they arrived Sophia was sitting on the floor. "She looked higher than a kite," one of them had testified. Reginald King was lying six feet from her, one shot to the head and one to the chest.

"And what did the accused say to you when you arrived?" the prosecutor asked the lead officer.

"She didn't say anything. I'm not sure she knew where she was."

"And was Ms. Nichols checked for gunshot residue?" the prosecutor had asked.

"Yes, she was. There was none."

Nick sat back and exhaled. He'd hoped to spot a misstep by the police, but none was obvious. If what happened in the motel room was as Francine Nichols had described, then Sophia Demetrios was guilty of murder.

Nick thought about Worthy's image of the three-legged stool, the three elements that supported the state's case against Sophia. There was Francine Nichol's testimony, Sophia's failure to deny that she committed the crime, and the forensic evidence of Sophia's fingerprints on the gun and gunshot residue on her hand and sleeve.

Yet, what struck Nick was the oddness of the scenario. Reginald King, one of Detroit's drug royalty, a hardened criminal who had lived as long as he had by protecting himself and rarely going anywhere without a bodyguard, had come alone to a motel room where a minor drug user with no prior experience with firearms had shot him expertly.

The prosecution had offered an explanation for the oddity. Sophia's two shots, either of which would have been fatal, had been effective because she'd fired at such close range; the thornier issue of Sophia's motive for shooting King had been sidestepped by the prosecution's claim, substantiated by Sophia's toxicology screening, that Sophia was likely hallucinating when she'd shot King.

Nick looked up the icon of the Virgin Mary and Christ child on the wall above his desk and asked, "What do I do first?" Someone had to locate and talk with Francine Nichols, and he thought that would be either Henderson or he. Someone also needed to talk with Lieutenant Rebecca Williston, the lead on King's murder—and thirdly, someone needed to investigate Gus Cooper. If that were the man's true name, Cooper had been at St. Simeon's the same weekend as Marina and may have been looking for her. He'd also lied about his home parish.

What, Nick asked himself, *does this Gus Cooper have to do with Sophia Demetrios?* Was there a link between Cooper and Sophia, or was the connection only in his head?

He remembered a warm summer night from his childhood, when he'd lain in the backyard with his brother and gazed up at the stars. Andreas had a keener interest in astronomy, and Nick had listened as his brother used his finger to outline the constellations overhead.

"I see the stars, Andreas, but I don't see the lines," he'd said.

"What lines?" Andreas had asked.

"The lines connecting the stars, like the ones making Orion's belt."

"The lines are in your head, stupid," Andreas had said. "Like the man in the moon. There's no face there until we think we see a face."

That was what Nick was wondering about now. Sophia sitting in Barminster prison was one star, one point of light barely flickering. Gus Cooper, or someone using that name, had been at St. Simeon's the same weekend as Marina. He was a second point of light…and wasn't Marina a third star? If there was a line linking Sophia Demetrios and Gus Cooper, that line ran through Marina. Then another thought struck him. *Is Francine Nichols another star, one further complicating this constellation?*

OCTOBER 15, 2023, DETROIT POLICE STATION, HOMICIDE DIVISION

OVER BREAKFAST THE NEXT MORNING, WORTHY managed to eat only a piece of toast with his coffee. He dreaded his next meeting with Howard Hullinger, the police department's chief lawyer. He knew that Hullinger's goal was the same as his goal—to have the appeal dismissed—but a person had to be dense to miss the lawyer's frustration with him as a client.

Being a "lone wolf" was Worthy's main problem. If he'd had a partner tagging along on his every movement in the Vickers-Tremont case, that partner would now be able to corroborate Worthy's actions.

He could imagine how much Kenna McCarty would enjoy the appeal once Tremont's lawyers started their attack. Once before, she'd portrayed him as a lone wolf, arrogant and intent on grabbing all the glory. McCarty also would have undoubtedly discovered that the Tremont case wasn't the only one that he'd worked alone.

Sitting in the conference room and waiting for the lawyers, he shook his head as he thought of the irony of the media's perception of him. The truth was that he never wanted the accolades, the attention, or being labelled Detroit's finest homicide detective. If he solved cases alone, that was sometimes his choice, but not always. Several of the partners he'd been given over the years had demanded to be reassigned. They described him as moving too slowly but, worse than that, they believed that he deliberately held things back from them.

Worthy's father was a Baptist minister, a man who moved from church to church, town to town, nearly every five years. It seemed that just when Worthy managed to make a close friend or two, his father would announce that God was calling him to take a new church in a different town. Once again, he became the new kid forced to start all over in making friends, and that became harder with each move. Could he be blamed if, after the cycle repeated itself, he began to doubt if making friends was worth the effort?

His thoughts were interrupted by Hullinger and Ogden, his junior, entering the room. He wondered what kind of omen it was that Captain Walker wasn't with them for the afternoon session.

After opening his laptop, Hullinger said, "I hope you haven't been waiting long. We spent last evening watching your interviews with Kerry Paulsen, the one Tremont's lawyers will suggest was Renee Vickers' real killer. They'll present Paulsen's suicide as proof of his guilt. I assume nothing I've said surprises you."

Worthy shook his head. "No, but don't forget that Paulsen killed himself thirteen years after Renee Vickers' death and said nothing about Renee Vickers in his suicide note."

Hullinger turned and nodded at Ogden. "Granted, but we'd like you to walk us through several parts of your interrogations of Kerry Paulsen." He swiveled his computer so that Worthy could see the screen. "This first excerpt comes toward the beginning of your first interview with Paulsen, after he's admitted being Tremont's friend."

Hullinger hit a key, and Worthy saw an earlier version of himself sitting with his superior at the time, Captain Spicer, and across from Paulsen and his lawyer. Paulsen looked exactly as Worthy remembered him—shell-shocked and terrified.

"Mr. Paulsen, tell us in your own words how you first met Renee Vickers," he asked.

Even though Paulsen's hands were folded and resting on the table, they were clearly shaking. "I'd never done anything like that before," he said.

"Never done anything like what before?"

Paulsen looked down at the table and shook his head. "I'd never been with a prostitute before."

"How did you know Ms. Vickers was a prostitute?"

"William told me. He'd already had sex with her, and then, after I . . . after I had sex with her, I paid her."

"For the record, by William you mean William Tremont?"

"Sorry, yes."

"What was the date of your having intercourse with Renee Vickers?"

Paulsen could be seen wiping tears from his cheeks. "It was the Friday after Thanksgiving."

"So you had sex with Renee Vickers on November 27, 2009."

"I guess so."

"You said that William Tremont told you that he had intercourse with Renee Vickers before that. Do you know exactly when that was?"

"Not really, but it couldn't have been too long before that."

"Why do you say that?"

"He was excited about doing it, you know. He made it sound as if they'd just done it." Paulsen said. "He was bragging about it, and he told me that I should have sex with her too."

"Was that usual for Mr. Tremont, to brag?"

"I guess it was. We were in scouting together, and he'd brag about the merit badges he got and how much faster he earned the badges than the rest of us."

There was a pause on the tape. Worthy watched as his younger self turned a few pages.

"Where did intercourse with Renee Vickers take place?"

"William's uncle had given him an old panel truck. He had a mattress and sleeping bags in the back."

"Can you describe the truck?"

"White, but lots of rust. I think it was a Dodge."

"Okay. Where was the truck parked when you met with Ms. Vickers?"

"It was down a dead-end country road not far from the truck stop out on Highway 10."

"And what time did your interaction with Ms. Vickers occur?"

A chill seemed to pass through Paulsen's body. "It was at night, maybe nine o'clock."

"Where was Mr. Tremont when you were having intercourse with Ms. Vickers?"

"He took a walk. He came back after about thirty or forty minutes."

"What happened then? Did he take Ms. Vickers back to the truck stop?"

Paulsen sighed as he lowered his head. "No. He told me to take a walk so he could . . . so he could do it with her again."

"You know for certain that William Tremont had intercourse with Ms. Vickers after you did on November 27, 2009?"

"I think so. I mean, yeah, I'm sure. She was putting on her jeans when I got back to the truck."

"Okay. Describe how Mr. Tremont and Ms. Vickers related to one another."

"What do you mean? Oh, you mean besides the sex."

"Tell us how they talked with each other. Were they friendly?"

"Friendly? No, I wouldn't say that."

"What would you say?"

Paulsen rubbed his face with both hands. "She was giving him a hard time. She was needling him about . . . well, to be honest, she was teasing him about the size of his . . . you know, his penis. She said, well, she said mine was . . . bigger."

"And how did Mr. Tremont react?"

"He called her a couple of names, about her being Black and being a prostitute, I mean."

"So, would you say he was angry?"

"Well, what guy would want to hear that?"

"Had you seen Mr. Tremont angry before?"

"A few times. William doesn't like to lose."

"What have you seen him do when he's angry?"

"He's good at hitting back, with words, I mean. If he's mad at you, he'll humiliate you."

Hullinger hit a key on his computer and the excerpt stopped. "After seeing that, do you wish that you'd conducted the interview any differently?"

Worthy felt the first signs of a headache coming on. "You wouldn't be asking me that if you didn't think I'd made some mistake. So tell me what you think I missed or did wrong."

"It's not what I think you did wrong, Mr. Worthy, but what the defense will do with an excerpt like this. The exchange came at the beginning of the first interview you had with Mr. Paulsen. You couldn't have known at that point that he hadn't killed Ms. Vickers or at least hadn't been an accomplice to her murder, could you?"

Hullinger didn't wait for Worthy to answer. "And yet, in this first interview, it doesn't take you more than four or five minutes to shift from asking Mr. Paulsen about his relationship with Ms. Vickers to focusing on William Tremont's relationship. Do you see my point?"

"You're forgetting the context. I'd already interrogated Tremont twice, and, he'd not only confessed to killing Vickers but had also said that Paulsen had nothing to do with it."

"But think about it from the defense's perspective. We know that they plan to argue that he wasn't in his right mind when he confessed, that he was high on Ecstasy. With the toxicology report posing a problem, the judges will have to entertain the possibility that Mr. Tremont was, in fact, high. Consequently, both his confession and his statement that Mr. Paulsen had no part in Vickers' death are questionable. Can't you see that the excerpt shows that you've already determined that Tremont killed Vickers and Mr. Paulsen had nothing to do with her death? In short, you treat Mr. Paulsen in this interview as a witness, not a suspect."

Worthy felt his throat tighten. He felt caught in the age-old animosity that existed between police and lawyers. They were both part of law enforcement, but if anyone scratched the surface, that person would realize that police often feel that lawyers exist to twist their words even as lawyers feel that police are too often careless in following proper procedure.

"Anyone who listens to the rest of my interviews with Paulsen will realize that I did push on him, trying to determine if he had any part in Renee Vickers' death."

Hullinger nodded. "I'm glad you point that out. The next excerpt is from a later interaction with Mr. Paulsen, one where you say you pushed him." The lawyer hit another key and turned the screen back around.

In this video, Kerry Paulsen looked calmer, his hands resting quietly on the table. The other difference was that the chair next to Worthy was no longer occupied by Captain Spicer, but by another detective, one whose name Worthy had forgotten—but he was clearly young.

In the excerpt he heard himself say, "Tell us how and when you heard that Renee Vickers had been murdered, Mr. Paulsen."

"I saw it in the newspaper that she was killed in Detroit."

"Let's be more specific, Mr. Paulsen. Did the newspaper article say that she'd been killed in Detroit or that her body had been found in Detroit."

Paulsen seemed confused for a moment. "I think it said her body was found in Detroit."

"So, she could have been killed elsewhere, in Midland, for example, and someone then drove her body to Detroit and dumped it."

"What? Well, hmm . . . I guess that could have been what happened."

"Mr. Paulsen, now isn't the time to hold anything back from us. I can guarantee you that we will find out everything that happened on November 27, 2009. This is your chance to do yourself some good."

Paulsen could be seen glancing at his lawyer before looking back at Worthy. "I don't know what you mean. I've told you the truth."

"Well, the truth has to be supported by facts, Mr. Paulsen. One undisputed fact is that Renee Vickers' blood was found in the back of Mr. Tremont's white van, which proves to us that Mr. Tremont's van was used to transport her body from Midland to Detroit. A second fact is that, despite our forensically analyzing the van almost a year after Renee Vickers' murder, we managed to identify fingerprints from three persons in that van. Most of them are William Tremont's fingerprints, which isn't surprising. It was his van. But we also found several fingerprints that match Renee Vickers' and two other prints that are yours. That raises the possibility that you were in the van when someone drove that vehicle to Detroit to dispose of Renee Vickers' body."

"Wait a minute—"

Worthy ignored Paulsen's interruption to finish his point. "Your prints could also mean that you joined William Tremont in killing Renee Vickers."

Hullinger hit a key on the computer and the screen went dark.

"And thoughts, Mr. Worthy?"

"Well, I think that shows that I wasn't giving Paulsen a pass, even though Tremont had already confessed and cleared him."

The room was deathly quiet until Hullinger said, "You don't see it, do you?"

"What I see, or should I say remember, is that right after the part you showed, Paulsen fell apart, sobbing. After he gained some control, his lawyer asked if the police knew from highway and street cameras when Tremont's van had been spotted in Detroit. We had camera evidence showing Tremont's van near the dump site in Detroit at noon on November twenty-ninth. And the same van left by the same route later that same day. Paulsen's lawyer then offered proof that Paulsen had worked a double shift as a cook at a hamburger joint on the twenty-ninth—all day."

Hullinger shook his head. "That's all well and good, but let me remind you of what you said to Mr. Paulsen about his prints. You said his prints proved that he could have joined Tremont in killing Renee Vickers. Good Lord, Mr. Worthy, you never once considered the possibility that

Paulsen killed Renee Vickers on November twenty-eighth or early on twenty-ninth, and Paulsen got William Tremont to drive the body to Detroit. You were so convinced that Tremont was the sole killer that the best you could do was consider that Paulsen might have been an accomplice. Your bias is all over the place."

Worthy sat for a moment, feeling a bit dizzy at he considered Paulsen being the alpha male and Tremont the follower, but then his head cleared. "I did what any homicide detective would have done. I followed the evidence. So, let me take you through that. Two facts were almost immediately known. One, it was clear from the lack of blood on her body that Renee Vickers had been killed elsewhere and dumped in the city. Two, her friends told us that Renee Vickers had recently gotten into prostitution to fund her drug habit and that she was known, because she was new to the game, to take some chances. From those two bits of evidence, I pursued the possibility that she had been a 'lizard' at truck stops—you know, a prostitute who makes her rounds when drivers are crashing for the night. I circulated her photo at all the truck stops with rest areas within a hundred and fifty miles of Detroit. Her photo was recognized by a trucker, a born-again Christian who described how he'd witnessed to her at the Midland Gas n' Go on Highway 10. My first thought was that Vickers was killed by a trucker, which I point out to show that I wasn't even looking for someone like Tremont."

Worthy waited for some acknowledgment, and after a pause Hullinger said, "Go on."

"And it's not true that I worked the case on my own. Once we had a list of all the truckers who'd bought fuel at the Midland truck stop between November fifteen and December fourth, I had colleagues work through that list. That was slow going, but after all our interviews, we were convinced that none of them was the killer. That's when I interviewed the wait staff in the restaurant at that truck stop. A number of them remembered seeing Renee Vickers, but two waitresses remembered seeing an older teen drinking cups of coffee for hours in the café as if he were waiting for someone or watching someone. Each of waitresses worked separately with a composite artist—those sketches were very similar, by the way—and that gave us a person of interest."

"No cameras?" Hullinger asked.

"I'm coming to that. First, we hoped that whoever this older teen was he'd paid with a credit card, but the receipts we found from November twenty-fourth through the thirtieth for coffee alone had been paid with cash. The cameras at the truck stop were either looking from the store and restaurant to the pumps, or they were outside the bathrooms. My crew looked through hours of video, but we were left with as many questions as answers. First of all, the videos were poor quality. Second, from watching the videos we were able to isolate someone who could have been a teenager gassing up a white van, an older Dodge, but he wore a kind of bucket hat, low over his brow and ears. And no, we couldn't make out the license plate other than it was a Michigan plate."

Hullinger jotted a note down before looking up. "I assume your next point is that the artist's sketch bore a strong resemblance to William Tremont but not Kelly Paulsen."

"I won't lie," Worthy said. "We were looking for the older teen in the video and the sketch, but that's not bias. That's just standard procedure. Of course, it was much too early to assume the kid was the killer. But he'd spent hours in the same truck stop where Renee Vickers had been. At bare minimum, we hoped he'd seen something that could help us find her killer."

Hullinger was about to say something, but he turned to his assistant instead. "Courtney, why don't you ask Mr. Worthy your question."

The assistant cleared her throat. "If I read the case file correctly, you seemed stuck at this point. You had the sketch, a few grainy video images, and the white van down as an ten- to twelve-year-old Dodge. But that didn't give you much. The two waitresses thought that the video image might be the teenager who'd ordered coffee, but they couldn't be sure. You reinterviewed the truckers from your list, but none remembered seeing the teenager. But you decided not to publish the sketch or the video image in the local paper, thinking it could spook the teenager if he were from the Midland area. So, as I said, you were stuck until one of the waitresses called you, saying that the same teenager had been at the truck stop that day. Not only that, but the waitress had had the presence of mind to ask one of the dishwashers to go outside and copy down the license plate of the white Dodge van. Is that about right?"

"Yes, that's right. What's the problem with that?"

"It just seems . . . it just seems so convenient. It's almost in the cat-egory of a miracle. Just as you were stumped, the killer goes back to the scene of the crime."

Worthy looked down at his hands, his fingers stretched out to their maximum width on the table. "We didn't know at the time if he were the killer or not," he said, speaking very slowly and methodically. "If he'd been at the truck stop for innocent reasons, why shouldn't he go back? But then I put myself in his place and asked why, if I were the killer, I'd risk going back. First, I thought it was hubris. He went back to the truck stop to celebrate how he'd fooled everyone. But after we tracked Tremont down through the license plate, another possibility presented itself. We discovered that he'd been president of nearly every extra-curricular organization that had to do with academics—debate team, Latin club, Student Mensa, and National Honor Society. Then there was his being the top Eagle Scout in the Midland region.

"All of that led me to size Tremont up as someone who believed he would always be the smartest guy in the room. So, why would a super-smart guy who'd killed a young woman risk going back to the truck stop? Sure, hubris fit, but so did another possibility. The waitress who called, the one who was sure she'd seen the person matching the sketch, made that call on October 21, 2010. That was ten days after I'd brought the sketch and the video image around again, asking the waitresses if seeing it jogged their memories. In other words, she had that image and sketch in her mind just days before this older teen returned. That's when it dawned on me that this kid, if he were the killer, could have come back to the same truck stop not just once, but regularly, maybe as much as every week or two after the murder. That would be through the seven months when Renee Vickers' murder was being investigated as a local crime here in Detroit and then through the months I had the case. And when we checked the videos at the truck stop over those months, we found I was right. William Tremont had come back every Thursday, like clockwork."

"I still don't follow," Courtney said. "Why would Tremont risk re-turning at all?"

"You have to understand a guy like Tremont. It wasn't enough that he killed a prostitute and got away with murder by dumping her body in Detroit. He wanted more; he wanted to get into the minds of any possible witnesses from back in November, like those waitresses. He was sure that he could control how they remembered him. He counted on witnesses who would view the truck stop's security videos looking for someone suspicious. Tremont counted on those witnesses not fingering him because he wasn't suspicious. He was always there, a regular customer. In a way, he was hiding in plain sight, Thursday after Thursday, week after week. And like I said, that's what we found when we checked security videos from November, 2009 to September, 2010. Tremont was too smart to return with the white van, but his face was all over the place."

"Then why was he caught?" Courtney asked.

Worthy looked over and saw Hullinger smile. Worthy relaxed, feeling that Hullinger might be starting to respect him.

Hullinger closed the computer. "Finish the story, Mr. Worthy."

"Tremont was caught because, like other killers who see themselves as geniuses, he overthought the situation. He convinced himself that he could control what witnesses remembered about those few days in November of 2009. But what Tremont didn't grasp was how waitresses and truckers think. When Tremont met someone like Renee Vickers or a waitress, a long-distance hauler, or a sycophant like Kerry Paulsen, he saw them as beneath him."

Worthy paused before continuing. "Look, I know you're here to coach me on how I should respond when Tremont's lawyers grill me. I get that. But I think I'm one of the few people who can say he knows William Tremont. So, if we can turn the tables for a minute or two, let me ask you a question. How do you plan to cross-examine Tremont when he takes the stand?"

Hullinger nodded. "Fair enough. In an appeal like this, when the defense's strategy is to twist the evidence, I expose what they're doing for what it is, an attempt to confuse the judges. I return to the facts established in the first case and explain how the jury's decision in 2010-11 was the right one. To do that, I destroy the credibility of people like Tremont, and, honestly, I quite enjoy doing that."

Worthy shook his head. "No, no. Tremont has had thirteen years to do nothing but go over every moment of his first trial—every witness that was called, every piece of evidence provided by the prosecution, every mistake he believes his lawyers made, and every instruction the judge gave the jury. So, the question is, how does Tremont plan to win his appeal? Is there new evidence? Not really, at least, not incontrovertible evidence. What Tremont plans to do, if I'm right, is convince everyone in the courtroom, from the reporters to the witnesses, to the lawyers—his and mine—and the judges that he's still the smartest person in the room."

Worthy clapped his hands together, and he saw Ogden jump. "Tremont's testimony will be a performance, one that he's orchestrated from beginning to end, and one he's waited thirteen years to give. You say you plan to poke holes in his performance. I'm telling you that he's thought of everything you'll say. Instead of embarrassing him, he's more likely to embarrass you. He's that good."

"Let's say I agree," Hullinger said. "So, what's a better approach?"

Worthy was exhausted. He'd had nothing to eat since toast at breakfast, and everything he just said about William Tremont was what he'd learned at a great cost. Thirteen years before, he'd been forced to go deeply into himself to that place where he could understand the kind of person who would kill someone like Renee Vickers without remorse. Through that descent, he'd realized that the killer would likely be a loner. Renee Vickers' killer was likely a damaged version of himself—another loner. Yes, he'd found Tremont by going into himself, but in the process, Tremont had robbed him of his marriage and family.

He took a couple of deep breaths, then continued. "You want a better approach? Instead of trying to take Tremont apart in cross-examination, I suggest that you feed his ego. He's been a loner his whole life, a misfit, and the way Tremont has coped is by looking down on everyone. I doubt that he's made one friend in prison, and I wouldn't be surprised if Paulsen killed himself because of something Tremont said to him. Tremont has been isolated in prison for thirteen years, and this appeal is his chance to prove that his isolation is because he's a genius in a world of mediocrity. What he doesn't understand, and what you have to exploit, is the fact that he's his own worst enemy. Give Tremont the chance and he'll self-destruct, another Icarus flying too close to the sun."

CHAPTER EIGHTEEN

OCTOBER 16, 2023, BARMINSTER WOMEN'S PRISON

NICK SAT IN THE PARKING LOT, AWARE AT HOW MUCH of his routine had changed in the last twenty-four hours. The jolt of energy that he'd felt when he realized his next step would be to locate Francine Nichols and Gus Cooper had evaporated. Finding either of them would be difficult, and it was obvious that he could find neither one from inside St. Simeon's. He had to move to Detroit, and that meant getting Abbot Lucas' permission.

Resolving that difficulty proved easier than he'd thought. When he approached the abbot, he hadn't hesitated to agree, seeing this as another way to limit Brother Pachomius' assistance to Nick.

"Seeing you every day in the sanctuary is likely distracting Brother Pachomius," Abbot Lucas said. "All I ask is that you keep me informed of what you're discovering. I know you wouldn't abuse my permission to be away from St. Simeon's, but in case some of our community start grumbling, I'll know that their grumbling is without merit."

The other problem, by what authority he could inquire about Francine Nichols and Gus Cooper, was settled almost as quickly. Over dinner the night before, he'd considered asking Worthy to help him, but he'd changed his mind after Worthy described the grilling he'd received from the department's legal team.

"Do you feel betrayed, Christopher?" he'd asked.

"Betrayed? Yes, maybe a bit. I became defensive when the lawyers told me that Tremont's legal team would be attacking my integrity. But I got over that, and then I was able to be some help. I explained how arrogant Tremont was in his first trial and how unlikely it was that that he'd gained any humility over the past thirteen years. I reminded Hullinger, the senior lawyer for the department, that Tremont had all that time to write the script for what's going to happen next week. I suggested that they let Tremont try to wow everyone in the courtroom, rather than dispute everything he says. That will be his downfall because I know that he is his own worst enemy."

Nick had smiled at his friend. "I hear the old Worthy in your voice, my friend. When you first arrived from Rome, I could see that you'd have preferred to be anywhere but here."

"No, you're right. I didn't want to be here, and I certainly didn't want to return to the pain from back then. I still don't. But this afternoon with my lawyers, I realized that what convinced the jury in the Tremont's first trial was keeping the focus on the evidence. I'm counting on the evidence doing that again. Now, enough about that. Tell me where you are with the Demetrios family."

After Nick told Worthy what Brother Pachomius had learned about Gus Cooper and Francine Nichols, Worthy repeated his offer for Nick to use the spare room in his apartment. "And Henderson will be happy to help. He's a genius at tracking people down. You might remember that about him from the case back in 2015."

That was why Carnell Henderson was now sitting next to Nick in the parking lot of Barminster prison. Nick remembered that Henderson tended to swear like a sailor, but that didn't bother him. Nick had grown up in Baltimore, his immigrant uncles picking up the strong language of other longshoremen who worked the docks; he appreciated that Henderson had never treated him differently because he was a priest. Furthermore, Nick had never considered his role as a priest and monk to be a language censor.

"Nick, I understand that this is a 'meet and greet' for Sophia Demetrios and me, but is there anything I should know before we go in?" Henderson asked.

"There is something, but it's more about me than Sophia. I met Sophia through her sister, Marina. That means that I'm likely to see Sophia through her sister's grief, which means I'm biased. After we meet with Sophia today, I'd appreciate your candid assessment. Does her claim to remember nothing about the night that Reginald King was killed seem genuine? It's possible that she's using her blankness as a dodge, something to help her and her family live with her sentence."

"Nick, I can tell you right now that ninety-nine out of a hundred inmates in prisons claim they're innocent."

Nick nodded. "But Sophia isn't claiming her innocence. When she says she can't remember, it's more like she's admitting that she could have shot Reginald King."

"Well, I'll tell you one thing, Nick. If she did shoot King, there are a lot of cops who'd want to thank her. King won't be missed."

"Hmm. That's . . ."

"Go on. What were you going to say?"

Nick wondered how best to explain his misgivings. "What you said about Reginald King not being missed is part of what bothers me. What I've learned is that King was a major figure in the city's drug scene. On the other hand, Sophia Demetrios was just a low-level user."

"I see your point, but if you're thinking that she's a convenient scapegoat, you'd better be careful. That's as much as saying that the police took King out and then managed to pin the murder on this girl."

"And you're saying that's not likely."

"Nothing to do with drug dealers is impossible, Nick, but if someone in the police took King out, they'd have found a better scapegoat than this girl."

"I'm not sure I understand."

"Think of scapegoats this way. The best scapegoat is a believable one. In this case, someone from one of the Mexican drug cartels moving into Detroit, for example."

Nick thought for a moment. "Does that mean that framing Sophia would be wasting a golden opportunity?"

"Exactly. If they could pin the murder on another drug dealer, they could use King's death to take down another major player in the drug scene. All the more reason to find Francine Nichols."

Nick opened the car door. "Maybe Sophia can help with that."

Twenty minutes later, after being searched, Nick and Henderson sat in the empty visitor's area and waited for Sophia. Nick wasn't certain that she would agree to meet again, so he was relieved to see her escorted into the room even though her eyes were looking at the floor.

"Is it necessary for her to be handcuffed?" he asked the guard.

"That's policy, no exceptions, and no physical contact," the guard replied as she walked to the rear of the room.

Nick remembered visiting another prisoner five years before when he was working a case in New Mexico. This room, like that one, had the same sense of sterility, the feeling that it had been washed of every ounce of kindness. From the bars on the windows to the chairs and tables being secured to the floor, everything conveyed the same message—inmates don't deserve better treatment.

Sophia didn't say anything until Nick introduced Henderson as a private detective. Then, glancing briefly at him, she said in a low voice, "You're dreaming if you think my family can afford this."

"I'm a friend of Father Nick's, so there's no charge. We just want to make sure you ought to be here."

Sophia looked from the two of them to a far corner of the room and didn't say anything.

Nick broke the silence by saying, "We're wondering if you remember anything more about the night you were arrested."

She sighed. "Marina asks me the same question every time she comes. Don't you think I'd say so, if I did?"

Henderson leaned forward. "Okay, let me ask you a question. What do you remember from that night? Start at Francine Nichol's apartment. How many times had you been there?"

"I don't know. Lots of times."

"And you stayed there, not just dropping in?"

"I slept on her couch a lot."

"Who else was there?"

"A bunch of others. Why does that matter?"

Henderson jotted down a note. "Were they there to score drugs?"

Sophia shrugged, then nodded.

"Think carefully, Sophia. Who brought the drugs? Who'd you pay? Was it Francine?"

When Sophia managed, despite the handcuffs, to rub her right hand, Nick could see that her fingernails were bitten down to the quick.

"There was a guy who showed up," she said. "Didn't stay long. But when I had money, I paid Francine."

"What happened when you didn't have money?"

"Francine paid for it."

"Okay. Was your understanding that Francine Nichols had a business relationship with this guy. Was that guy Reginald King?"

"You mean the guy they say I killed? No, it wasn't him, but I got the impression he worked for King. The guy was Asian."

Nick could see that Henderson jotted down Sophia's responses almost as fast as she spoke. "How many times did you see this other guy?"

"Twice, maybe three times."

"Did Francine Nichols ever introduce you to him? Did you ever see him looking at you in particular?"

Sophia shook her head. "Why are you asking all these questions?"

"Because we're planning on tracking Francine Nichols down and speaking with her. Now, tell us about Francine's habit. What did you see her using?"

"Coke, mainly coke."

"Not heroin? No fentanyl?"

"I don't know. Maybe."

It seemed to Nick that Henderson was speeding up his questions, not allowing Sophia time to think before responding.

"Sophia, on the night you were arrested, did Francine drive?"

"I already told the cops. I don't remember anything about that night."

"Right. Were you ever in her car when she was driving?"

"Yeah. A few times."

"Where did you usually sit?"

"Ah, always in the back."

"Someone else rode in the front passenger seat?"

"Yeah, I guess so."

"Tell me who that was."

Nick noticed that Henderson was no longer asking questions but giving Sophia orders.

"It was a Black woman. Connie somebody."

"Connie somebody. Her last name?"

"I don't know. I never did."

"Okay. So Connie sat in the passenger seat while Francine drove. Did the police ask you about Connie?"

Sophia paused. Her hands were no longer fidgeting. "No."

"Sophia, describe Connie."

"I already told you. She's Black." When Henderson didn't say anything, Sophia looked down. "Okay, okay. She doesn't eat pork, and she's tall, skinny. I thought she must have played volleyball or basketball. My guess is that you played too."

Nick didn't miss the moment. This was the first time Sophia had done anything other than respond.

"My nickname was 'Hoops,' so you guessed right," Henderson said. "Was Connie on something?"

"She smoked weed. Why?"

"Well, here's the thing, Sophia. No one named Connie and no Black woman testified at your trial. So, we need to find her. Anything else you can tell us about her? Did she ever stay over at Francine's? What kind of clothes did she wear?"

"Clothes? I don't know. Wait a minute. She wore this yellow sweatshirt."

"A yellow sweatshirt. Anything written on it?"

Sophia exhaled, looking exhausted. "I don't remember."

"Yes, you do, Sophia. What was written on it?"

After a long pause, she said, "I think it was the name of some school."

"What, like Michigan, Michigan State, Wayne State?"

Sophia shook her head. "No, I think it was a high school in the city."

"Why do you say that?"

"It had a cross on it."

"Good. A parochial school then."

After a long pause, Sophia said, "How do you know I'm not bullshitting you? Maybe I made all that up."

Henderson closed his notebook and stood. "We're done here for now, Nick. Thanks for speaking with us, Sophia. We'll be back."

Sophia didn't move. "I asked how you know I'm not bullshitting you."

Henderson leaned down and drew closer to Sophia. "Because this is what I do for a living. I interview people and I study their eyes, their tone of voice, their body language. You weren't bullshitting me."

As he walked with Henderson toward the exit, Nick glanced over his shoulder. Sophia looked five years younger than when she first sat down. He knew that Henderson had accomplished that, not by saying he believed in her innocence, but by treating her as if she could be innocent. *And, thank God, she looks like she wanted to believe him,* Nick thought.

OCTOBER 17, 2023, ST. SIMEON'S

BROTHER PACHOMIUS WAITED AT THE CHANTER'S STAND in the monastery's candlelit church for afternoon prayers to begin. Father Nick had been right. He'd been less distracted by thoughts of the Demetrios family by chanting with older monks. When he devoted his daily two hours on research for Father Nick, he'd felt less guilty about neglecting his duties as a novice monk.

Every day since Father Nick had left for Detroit, he emailed him an assignment related to Francine Nichols. On the first day, Father Nick asked him to scan newspaper accounts online for anything about Francine Nichols. Pachomius was disappointed to find her name linked solely with her testimony at Sophia Demetrios' trial.

On the second day, Father Nick asked him to tap into internet sites that provided the public records on any person. There, Pachomius found that Francine Nichols was twenty-six years old, had been born in Detroit, had been arrested twice for possession of class A narcotics, and had served two stints in juvenile detention when a teenager. Since then, Nichols had no other convictions.

This morning, day three, Father Nick gave Pachomius more assignments. One was to locate Nichols. The second was to find out what he could about a friend of Nichols named Connie. "Without a last name, I know it's a long shot that you'll find out anything about her," Father Nick had written, "but try anyway. Finally, look for the address of anyone named Gus Cooper in Detroit."

As tempting as it was to let his mind wander from his prayers to Father Nick's most recent assignment, Brother Pachomius was determined to focus on the service. As he read the scriptures for that service, he felt a jolt pass through him. The scripture was one of Jesus' best-known parables, the one where God is compared to a good shepherd in search of one lost sheep.

It struck him that this was what Father Nick was doing, trying to rescue Sophia Demetrios, the lost sheep. Wasn't he, himself, also helping to find that lost sheep? He made the sign of the cross, aware for the first time that his research for Father Nicholas could be part of his vocation as a monk.

CHAPTER NINETEEN

———— ✦ ————

DRUG ENFORCEMENT AGENCY DETROIT OFFICE

SAMIYAH AISHA HAD WORKED UNDERCOVER BEFORE in her first year with the DEA, usually portraying a desperate user looking to score. Apparently, as a lean African-American who could imitate jitters, she was convincing as a junkie.

After that first year, she'd felt that she was ready for a more consequential case but had been passed over three times. She wondered if being Muslim and having a Middle Eastern name had contributed to being ignored. Then her luck changed. Ronald Fithian, one of the senior agents with an impressive arrest record, had emailed, telling her to meet him at a downtown coffee shop. There, he gave Samiyah her next assignment, to infiltrate a circle of drug users headed up by a middleman—in this case, a middlewoman. Samiyah was to cozy up to Francine Nichols, an up-and-coming figure in the city's drug scene, and uncover whom she worked under and who worked under her. Fithian shared the rumor that he'd heard, that someone in law enforcement was tied into drug trafficking in Detroit.

Samiyah had eagerly agreed, knowing that impressing Fithian could lead to other high- profile cases.

When she used her initiative and asked if Fithian thought the culprit could be someone within the DEA, he shook his head. "We don't think so. That would be much too risky, but on the off-chance that's true, you're to talk to no one besides me about your assignment. The two names that you should listen for are Henry Streeter and Lamar Wilson. Streeter's in vice; Wilson's in homicide."

If there were one lesson that had been reinforced in working undercover within Nichol's circle, it was that life in the DEA was murky. The secretive world of drug dealers and users was mirrored in the agency itself, where the familiar adage was borne out that the right hand didn't always know what the left hand was doing.

In the fight against Detroit's lucrative drug trade, staying squeaky clean as an agent wasn't an option. The best undercover agents had to know their own limits with drugs, and that usually had to be learned under the suspicious gaze of drug dealers. In her first meeting with Ronald Fithian, he made it clear that he knew she was Muslim and asked if she were willing to use drugs in the presence of the target. It was a difficult decision, but she agreed to use marijuana in moderation, but nothing stronger.

How about money? Posing as a hopped-up user, Samiyah had been given just enough money to buy drugs on the streets, but working undercover within Nichols' circle of users meant that she'd see more money in a day than she'd make in a lifetime in the DEA. She thought the same could be true for those working vice or investigating illegal financial dealings in the corporate world.

What was a dirty agent? She couldn't say what a dirty agent was for other branches of law enforcement, but she thought she knew what a dirty agent was in the DEA. A top-level dirty DEA agent would work as a double agent, taking down some dealers while protecting others who would pay him or her handsomely. In contrast, a low-level dirty agent was one who skimmed small amounts off the ever-present money. However, there was a parallel between drugs and money. If agents had to know how many lines of coke to snort or joints to smoke to be believable, they had to know how much money to accept and spend to be convincing. That would be especially true in the drug world. Samiyah was certain that not every dollar passing through an undercover agent's hands was turned over to the DEA. The more effective the agents, the less the DEA asked them to account for every penny when they brought down those dealers.

Samiyah was positive that few police recruits imagined that they would one day pocket even a fifty dollar bill, but to work undercover, that person had to get used to a new understanding of money. In her first week working undercover in Nichols' circle, she learned that a hundred dollar bill in the drug world had less value than a quarter in regular life. The first time Nichols entrusted Samiyah with a packet of money to be dropped off to another dealer, she'd counted the money on the way and found that she had a hundred and fifty thousand dollars in her hand. Even though the bills were bone fide U.S. currency, they felt like play money.

Given her strong grounding in Islam, Samiyah was certain that she'd never be tempted to pocket any of the outrageous amounts of money in the drug trade. Then everything changed when her father's diabetes worsened to the point where his right leg had to be amputated. Overnight, he had to give up his janitorial job at the local Islamic school and begin to live on disability. Even with Samiyah's salary, the family struggled to pay their bills. Thinking about their struggles, the money in her hand became real.

In the months before Reginald King was killed, when Samiyah was worming her way deeper and deeper into Francine Nichols' circle, she met with Ronald Fithian at a safe site to update him on what she was learning about Nichols' drug connections. Despite her learning little yet about who Nichols worked under in the drug world, Fithian seemed satisfied. "The keys to undercover work are being patient and keeping your ears and eyes open," he told her more than once.

It wasn't until her fourth month undercover that she first heard Nichols talk to someone named "Reggie." She'd pretended to be asleep in Nichols' recliner, wasted from smoking a joint, when Nichols was on the phone in the kitchen.

"You don't have to worry, Reggie. Connie's cool." After a pause, Nichols had added, "Because I've checked her out. She's on the level, just moved here from Alabama."

Samiyah had listened intently as Nichols added, "Of course I've checked her out. Listen, Reggie, you don't have to worry about my people. Who's asking, by the way?" Nichols had asked.

Samiyah had held her breath, hoping to hear Henry Streeter's or Lamar Wilson's name. Instead, Nichols didn't say anything for several moments, apparently listening to King before whispering, "Are you kidding me, Reggie? It's someone in the DEA?"

Fithian was clearly doubtful when she passed on what she'd learned. "The rumor I heard was about Wilson and Streeter. You're sure you heard right, that it's someone in the agency?"

"Positive, and I've thought of a plan. I'll tell Francine that I want to be a bigger player in her operation and that I want to meet King."

"You'll have to be extra careful, Samiyah. Proceed slowly. Don't force the issue, or you'll arouse suspicion. But assuming Nichols agrees to introduce you to King, let me know as soon as that happens. Understood?"

"Of course."

Just before the two parted, Fithian said, "Is there a lot of money flowing through Nichols?"

Samiyah hoped that her face hadn't given away her panic. With her father still waiting for his first disability check, they'd been short another three hundred dollars on rent and hospital bills. She'd told herself that she'd only skimmed off that amount from the thousands that Nichols entrusted with her as a loan, just like the money she'd taken after her father's leg was amputated. For the next two weeks, she'd been on pins and needles, waiting for someone in the agency to uncover what she'd done.

When nothing happened, she'd taken solace in the fact that Fithian was trying to find a dirty agent who was high up in the agency. She was safe for the time being and promised herself that she'd stop skimming money, but with additional medical bills, she wasn't sure she could keep that promise.

After King was killed, Samiyah wasn't surprised when Fithian called her into his office and told her that her undercover work was over. "Whoever was over King will have gone to ground," he'd said, meaning that the dirty agent will have descended deeper into the shadows. She'd been returned to the pool of agents who worked undercover as street buyers. But Samiyah had secretly committed herself to finding the agent who was above King. That commitment had nothing to do with ego, but rather for deeper and darker reasons that she told no one else about.

OCTOBER 18, 2023, APPELLATE COURT

As A HOMICIDE DETECTIVE, WORTHY WAS FAMILIAR WITH courtrooms and being called to testify. Most often it was his testimony, his methodical presentation of the evidence, that doomed the accused.

In an appellate court, Worthy's role was reversed. On trial was not Tremont but every step that he'd taken thirteen years ago to achieve a conviction. Just by granting the appeal, the court conceded that significant errors might have occurred in the first trial, which sent an innocent man to prison.

Worthy could feel the tension in the room on this, the first day of the appeal as everyone sitting in the gallery waited for William Tremont to appear. It wasn't hard for Worthy to imagine what Tremont was feeling as he waited in a holding cell below the courtroom. Tremont would be in handcuffs, but Worthy expected Tremont to enter the room like a boxer climbing through the ropes for a return match. He would exude confidence.

Seated in the gallery was Kenna McCarty, the journalist who clearly hadn't forgotten his slight of her years before. Sitting next to McCarty was Phillip Sherrod, his nemesis in homicide. He too hadn't forgotten or forgiven Worthy for making him look bad.

Worthy looked around at the others filling the courtroom, not surprised to see a few of Renee Vickers' family attending. He had to give them credit for being willing to be dragged through their loved one's murder a second time. Sitting closer to the front were Tremont's mother and younger sister. He knew that they'd never accepted the verdict from the first trial, that their son and brother was not just a killer, but also a psychopath.

Like many single parents, Mrs. Tremont had worked two shifts, leaving her two children on their own much of the time. Even though Tremont had picked up odd jobs as a young teenager, none seemed to lead to friendships with others his own age. He'd made his one friend, Kerry Paulsen, through scouting. Although Tremont and Paulsen were the same age, their relationship was hardly that of equals. Paulsen, with a high quavering voice, had been pushed by his father into scouting, but had been teased there as he'd been in school. Only Tremont, who'd been aloof and resented by the rest of the troop, had befriended him—or perhaps, as the police psychologist said, it was truer to say that Tremont adopted Paulsen.

The previous day, in Worthy's walkthrough with his lawyers, Hullinger had asked what Worthy remembered about Paulsen.

"If you mean besides the videos of our interviews with him," Worthy had said, "I can't tell you much. He was the kid who was always picked on in school. When we questioned him, he was overweight, wore T-shirts a size too small, and spoke barely above a whisper."

"Courtney did some research and found that Paulsen worked in one of those big box stores," Hullinger shared. "Not a job with much future, but he stayed there for the last twelve years and lived alone. His family shunned him once it came out in Tremont's trial that he'd had sex with Renee Vickers. Paulsen's father was a lay minister at some small church, which might have caused the break."

"As far as I could find out," Courtney said, "Paulsen's family didn't even attend his funeral."

"Sounds like another life that Tremont stole," Worthy said.

Hullinger nodded. "You've said that before. Here's an interesting fact. In addition to visiting Tremont, Paulsen also wrote him twice a month. What's uncertain is if Tremont ever wrote back."

"None of Tremont's letters were found in Paulsen's apartment?" Worthy asked.

"No, but we have copies of the ones that Paulsen sent to Tremont," Hullinger said. "Courtney has looked through them, and on the whole they're pretty innocuous. Paulsen writes about what's happening in Midland, how he hates his job, that sort of thing. It seems that Tremont remained Paulsen's only friend. About the only thing that's interesting in Paulsen's letters is how he always ended them. Every letter ends with 'I wish I could do more to help.'"

"'More?' What did he mean by that?" Worthy asked.

"Without Tremont's letters to Paulsen, it's impossible to say."

As Worthy waited for Tremont to enter the courtroom, he texted Nick and asked if his computer friend in the monastery could look into Paulsen's activities over the past thirteen years—where he traveled, what books he took out of the library, and what websites he frequented. He shared that Paulsen had written Tremont regularly in prison and had frequently expressed a hope that he could help Tremont.

Just as he turned off his phone, Worthy heard a stirring in the room. He looked up to see the door opening, the door that would produce William Tremont.

CHAPTER TWENTY

---◆---

WORTHY'S PRIVATE DETECTION AND INQUIRIES AGENCY, DETROIT BRANCH

Henderson arrived at the office that morning still thinking about his son, Jamie. As usual, Jamie spent the past weekend with them, but their time together this time was different. Jamie spent almost the whole weekend working on Worthy's mantle clock, and Henderson and Sulla watched as their son reassembled the clock from a table full of scattered pieces. Without any plans before him, Jamie worked from memory, putting together the clock that he'd taken apart the weekend before.

As Henderson watched in silence, he felt a lump in his throat as he realized that Jamie's hands were no longer those of a boy, but a man's. He also noticed Sulla turning away to hide her tears when Jamie, after solving some problem with the clock, had sat back from the table and given his parents a smile.

That night as the got into bed, Sulla turned to him and said, "I'll never forget how I felt when we watched Jamie work on that clock. I know you were proud of him too."

"I am, and I think he knows how we felt. If only . . ."

"Shh," Sulla had said. "There are no 'if onlys,' Carnell. We had today, and it was wonderful. And next weekend, think how Jamie will feel when he gives the clock back to Chris."

In the office, Henderson opened the file he'd begun on Sophia Demetrios. The first two names that appeared on the first page were Gus Cooper's and Connie's. He was disturbed that Connie hadn't been called to testify at Sophia's trial. He remembered Worthy vouching for Lieutenant Williston, the lead on Reginald King's murder. Williston would certainly have interviewed Connie if she'd known about her. That left Henderson with one other likely explanation. Connie was someone in law enforcement who, working undercover, managed to worm her way into Nichols' circle—and the agency most likely to plant an agent undercover would be the DEA.

If he were still an active homicide detective, Henderson might expect cooperation from the DEA, but they owned him nothing now that he was retired. As a rule, police didn't like private detectives, and they liked even less detectives who'd turned in their badges to work the private side of the street.

The one clue to Connie's identity was the yellow sweatshirt with a cross on it that Sophia remembered. Henderson knew that the sweatshirt could mean nothing or, at best, something Connie wore to throw off Francine Nichols, but with no other lead to follow up, Henderson had no choice but to pursue the sweatshirt.

Detroit and its suburbs, as was true of most major U.S. cities, had numerous parochial high schools. Using the internet, he was able to find Detroit schools selling yellow sweatshirts with crosses. Three were Catholic high schools, one was a Catholic junior college, and another was a Protestant college. He made copies of the images to show Sophia the next time he visited.

Compared to Connie, Francine Nichols was easy to locate. Nick's friend in the monastery had found the address of her apartment, but when Henderson dropped by, he found junk mail and flyers jammed into the mailbox. Though Nichols' parole officer, he discovered that she'd been granted immunity to testify against Sophia, but had managed to stay out of trouble for only six months. What puzzled Henderson was that, despite her previous troubles with the authorities, Francine hadn't been sent to jail for dealing cocaine but instead had landed in a rehab center in rural Ohio.

Now, who's paying for that? Henderson wondered as he jotted down the name of the facility and considered the various challenges facing him. If Connie were DEA, why and where was she hiding? Second, how was it that Francine Nichols, a known drug dealer who'd been present at the death of Reginald King, was in a private rehab clinic in Ohio? Third, how had Kerry Paulsen, before his death, tried to help Tremont?

He hated to think of Sophia Demetrios spending even one day more in prison if she were innocent, yet, if he were to prioritize the three challenges, he knew he had to start with Paulsen, as whatever he found there might help Worthy in the appeal.

Henderson knew that his best bet to finding out more about Paulsen was to follow what Worthy had taught him years before. Worthy's dictum was that the killer and the killer's motive would most likely be found hidden in the thoughts, actions, and decisions of the victim in the days, weeks, and months before he or she died. As a suicide, Paulsen was both killer and victim, which meant that the reason he'd killed himself would be found in what he'd been thinking and doing in his last days and weeks. Henderson knew that those thoughts and actions might have nothing to do with Tremont's appeal, but if there were the smallest connection, then Worthy needed to know it.

By accessing public records, Henderson found Paulsen's address and, within the hour, was driving to Detroit's Northside. Given that the apartment had likely been rented out again, Henderson didn't expect to find possessions that Paulsen had left behind, but he did hope to talk with the neighbors and landlord.

Paulsen's apartment was in an older brick building built in the nineteen-thirties or forties. To his surprise, he found the nameplate on what had been Paulsen's apartment blank, and he could see advertising circulars stuck in the mail slot. When he thought about it, however, he realized that renting an apartment where the last resident had killed himself might take some time.

He knocked at the apartment adjacent to Paulsen's and heard a dog yipping inside. In a moment, the door was opened a few inches, only as far as the chain would allow. The face of a woman in her seventies or maybe eighties peered out at him. As he gave his name, he showed her his outdated police ID.

"I don't mean to bother you, ma'am, but I'm working on a court case that involves finding out all I can about Mr. Kerry Paulsen, who lived next door to you. Can I come in and ask you a few questions?"

"He's dead," the woman said, doing nothing to remove the chain. Her reaction didn't surprise him, given that the woman wasn't the first to see him as a six-foot-four-inch black stranger.

"How many years was Kerry Paulsen your neighbor?"

The woman told her dog to shush, then looked back and up at Henderson. "I already told the police. He moved in about twelve years ago."

"Did Mr. Paulsen have many visitors?"

"Visitors? No, most of us live alone here. My hearing is good, and I never heard anyone next door, other than Kerry."

"But you knew him as Kerry, then. Was he friendly?"

"His name was Kerry. Friendly? Well, he kept to himself. Very quiet, as I said."

"I suspect you have resident meetings. Did Kerry come to those?"

"Of course, he did. He always stood in the back."

"Did he ever tell you where he worked?"

"No, and I never asked him."

"It looks like his apartment is still empty."

"What do you expect? He hanged himself in there."

Henderson suspected that the woman's patience was wearing thin. "I'd like to talk to the landlord. Can you give me his name and contact information, please?"

"Contact information? It's Leon. He lives with his wife, Mildred, in the first floor apartment."

Henderson thanked the woman even as the door was closing. Before he headed for the landlord, he knocked at the apartment on the other side of Paulsen's. This time, a man at least as old as the woman answered, and Henderson realized that Kerry Paulsen had lived surrounded by people old enough to be his grandparents.

"Paulsen? Yes, I knew him. He was my neighbor. Damn fool, ruined the entire building by hanging himself."

"Did Mr. Paulsen seem different in the days before he died?" Henderson asked.

"Different? He was always different. He lived alone in there, never a sound. If he had a girl in there, I'd never have known it. Hell, I don't even know if he had a TV."

"Did the two of you speak?"

"Of course, not that he said much more than a 'yes' or 'no.'"

"He never asked to borrow anything?" Henderson asked.

"Like what? You thinking sugar? No, nothing. Wait a minute, he did ask me for stamps once."

"Stamps? When was that?"

"Let me see. It was a week or so before he . . . you know," he said, making the gesture of pulling a rope tightly around his neck. "Anyway, he knocked and asked if I had two dollars and forty cents worth of stamps. I said, 'What you sending—a package?' He just repeated that he needed two dollars and forty cents worth of stamps. He seemed excited about it."

Because Paulsen's routine was normally so private, Henderson wondered if the stamps for a package could be important. Tremont seemed to be Paulsen's only known friend, but Henderson knew that if Paulsen had sent a package to Tremont in prison, the prison authorities would have opened it and logged its contents. What, then, was in the package, and where had Paulsen sent it?

Henderson's final stop in the building was to the landlord's apartment on the first floor. On the door were posted the names Leon and Mildred Lockwood along with emergency numbers. He knocked several times before the door was opened by a woman holding a glass of what looked like scotch.

"You here about the apartment?" she asked in a slurred voice before Henderson could identify himself.

"The one on the third floor? In a way, I am."

"What do you mean 'in a way.' You either want to see the apartment, or you don't."

For a brief moment, Henderson thought about playing along, to pretend he was apartment-hunting but decided to explain who he was.

Looking disappointed, the woman said, "Police have already been here. Ask them your questions."

Henderson decided to push through the roadblock. "As his landlord, you must have known Mr. Paulsen better than most people. What was he like?" He could see that she was weighing closing the door or taking the opportunity to talk about Paulsen.

"He paid his rent on time. Never a complaint about noise. No pets. Wish they were all like him . . . other than stringing himself up."

"I imagine you were inside his apartment, for inspections, that sort of thing. What was it like?"

"I'm not nosy, but yes, when the exterminators show up, I open the apartments if the residents are at their jobs. I saw Paulsen's a couple of times. He kept it neat, I'll say that for him."

"You didn't see anything unusual?"

Mildred Lockwood paused for a moment, before responding. "It's a two-bedroom. And with him being single, he slept in only one of them. The other room was locked when the exterminator came last time. But I had a key, of course. So, I opened it and looked. Nothing in there but newspaper clippings taped to a wall."

"Did you see what the clippings were about? Sports or movies, maybe?" Henderson asked.

"Not sports, not movies. There were headlines and photos. Some of them looked old, yellowed, if you know what I mean."

Henderson pictured a wall of newspaper clippings related to Tremont's arrest and trial. He did his best to hide his interest in how the landlord would answer his next question. "Just one more thing, Mrs. Lockwood. What happened to Mr. Paulsen's things after his body was found?"

"Thank God we didn't have to clean the place out. I mean, what were we supposed to do with his clothes and his books? Maybe we could have sold the computer, but we were happy when the police sent a company that handles that sort of thing. When they left, the place was as bare as a baby's bottom."

Henderson nodded as he counted to five. "Do you happen to know the name of the removal company?"

Mildred Lockwood took a sip of her drink and held up her index finger. "Hold on a second." She disappeared for a moment before returning. "Here," she said, handing him a business card.

Henderson read the card. "A to Z Removers. 24 Hour Service" in bold red letters with an address and telephone number below.

"Can I keep this?" he asked.

"It's yours. And if you know anybody looking for a two-bedroom, let them know, will you?"

✟

APPELLATE COURT

WHEN TREMONT WAS ESCORTED INTO THE COURTROOM, Worthy noted that he took a moment to gaze around the gallery. Wearing a suit and tie, Tremont raised his hands, even though handcuffed, to signal and smile at his mother and sister.

It had been thirteen years since Worthy had last seen Tremont, and in 2010, Tremont had just turned twenty. Given that a person had to be over seventeen in Michigan to be tried as an adult, there was no ambiguity about Tremont being charged as an adult with first-degree murder. But that wouldn't prevent his lawyers arguing on appeal that the sentence had been too severe for a first-time offender who'd killed on youthful impulse.

But Worthy suspected that Tremont wouldn't allow his appeal to end in a reduced sentence. Tremont would want nothing less than for everyone to see him as someone wrongfully arrested, questioned, and convicted because of misconduct by the police—by Worthy. Tremont didn't simply want to be released; he wanted to win.

From where Worthy was seated, he could study Tremont's face in profile. Tremont had the pasty complexion and soft features of inmates who avoided the prison's rec yard, preferring their cells or the library that held the law books. New to Worthy were Tremont's wire-rim glasses and a small goatee.

Tremont stared straight ahead as his legal team opened the appeal proceedings by outlining their defense. Worthy had sat in enough courtrooms to view Tremont's presenting lawyer, Janine Reeves, a Black female, as a deliberate choice to offset Renee Vickers also being Black and female.

"Your honors," she said, addressing the three judges, "you have our brief, and we welcome this opportunity to present our client's case. As an overview, we intend to establish that William Tremont received inadequate legal counsel in 2010. Specifically, his lawyer failed to challenge evidence submitted by the prosecution that was, in fact, questionable, if not false. These errors were committed in not one, but in numerous ways by the Detroit Police Department, chiefly by the arresting officer, Lieutenant Christopher Worthy, and the departmental pathologist, Dr. Robin Wallace. In addition, we assert that the judge in the 2010 case failed in her judicial responsibilities by refusing to allow significant evidence to be admitted. We will delineate these errors and miscarriages of justice and are convinced that the court will agree that Mr. Tremont's conviction should be overturned."

So there it is, Worthy thought. *Tremont and his team aren't questioning just me, but Dr. Wallace, Tremont's legal team back then, and the judge in the case.* Worthy knew, though, that he would be the main target.

He watched as Howard Hullinger stood and prepared to address the judges. In something of a dramatic gesture, he turned and stared for a moment at Tremont as he removed a handkerchief and wiped his glasses. Worthy thought the symbolism effective, suggesting to the judges and those in the courtroom that the defense had only blurred the picture.

"Your honors, I want to begin by reminding everyone in the courtroom, particularly the members of the media, that an appeal is ordinarily restricted to what was presented in the initial trial. The general rule is that no new evidence can be presented. What the defense contends is that the interpretation of that evidence was flawed; it is our contention that the original judge, legal counsels, and jury performed their duties fairly and wisely. The accused in that case receives what the law promises and guarantees—a fair and unbiased trial."

Hullinger sat down and the courtroom was quiet until the senior judge of the three, seated in the middle, directed comments to the lawyers. "We have received your briefs, learned counsels, and our ruling is that this appeal should allow additional testimony if we agree that the judge in the first trial prohibited some testimony that could have affected the trial's outcome."

Worthy wasn't surprised to see Kenna McCarty smile. The judges had left the door open for witnesses from the initial trial to offer new evidence. Tremont turned his head and offered a smile, signaling to the gallery that he'd won round one.

DEA HEADQUARTERS

SAMIYAH LOOKED AROUND THE ROOM, TRYING TO PICTURE one of her colleagues as the dirty agent. She thought it likely that some of them had had the same experience as she, having thousands of dollars in drug profits and payoffs passing through their hands. That meant that a percentage of them had done what she had, skimmed money for themselves.

She remembered an instructor at the police academy who'd warned that recruits would be fooling themselves if they assumed that they'd never be tempted to cross a line from legal to illegal. Officers in vice would be surrounded by sex workers all too willing to trade sex for looking the other way. Those investigating corporate greed would be offered secret bank accounts, while officers looking into protection rackets would be offered a lucrative cut for turning a blind eye. Even traffic cops would have hundred dollar bills handed to them along with driver licenses. "You will be tempted by what is closest to you," he'd said.

Looking around at her fellow agents, she thought of possible motives leading an agent to cross that line. There might be some whose family, like hers, had unexpected medical or other expenses. Some might have aging parents for whom they were responsible. Younger agents might be living a lifestyle beyond their means. Others might have a gambling problem.

The simpler motive was just the allure of the money. It wouldn't be hard to justify taking a cut by thinking you were robbing from drug lords, but Samiyah knew that the agent Fithian was hoping she'd find wasn't a reluctant skimmer. This agent had carved out a niche in the drug pipeline, a position that would bring him both hundreds of thousands of dollars and power. She thought this agent was long past regretting his or her actions, a cynic who might view the drug trade like the city's garbage. The government could pick up trash on Tuesday, but the garbage would be back by Thursday.

Samiyah knew that flushing out the dirty agent would be the greatest challenge she'd faced so far. Whoever the culprit was, he must have smiled through gritted teeth when everyone learned of Reginald King's death. The flow of money from petty dealers like Francine Nichols to King and to those above had been interrupted. Yes, King would have been replaced, but the world of the dirty agent was less secure.

CHAPTER TWENTY-ONE

———— ◆ ————

BARMINSTER WOMEN'S PRISON

SOPHIA SAT ON END OF HER BED AND LOOKED OUT at the falling rain. The prison cells didn't have windows as much as narrow slits through which inmates could see a thin slice of the world they were no longer a part of. Even Barminster's exercise yard had high walls that offered a view of only the sky.

In the months that she'd been in Barminster, Sophia might as well have been in solitary confinement where there weren't even the narrow slits of light. She was one of the inmates who didn't need solitary confinement to be imposed by prison authorities. She imposed it on herself.

Barminster had no need for a bell or morning alarm to wake its inmates. Each wing of the prison had inmates who awakened the others with their screams and curses as another day dawned. From her first days in prison, Sophia had established a morning ritual where, as soon as she was conscious, she shut her mind to all thoughts and feelings. It was as if she intuited that the greatest threats to her sanity would be dwelling on memories of her childhood or hoping for the day when she might be released. As the guard who'd unlocked her cell the first day had said, "Welcome to the gulag."

But that morning, the moment of her coming to consciousness hadn't been followed by the usual numbness. Instead, she felt that some thought was trying to surface. As she looked again at the rain outside, she debated about what to do. Part of her wanted to remain one of the walking dead in Barminster. But another part waited for the thought to explain itself. Finally, in no more than a whisper she heard the question, "What really did happen that night, the night they say I killed a man?"

She realized that she hadn't heard that voice since her mother died. After that, the only voices she heard were from people outside herself, telling her what to do. From Marina and her father, she heard that she needed to return to the community college or get a job. From her friends at the time, she heard that she was acting weird and that she needed to snap out of it. And then from Francine Nichols, she heard that she'd feel better than ever before if she tried cocaine.

She thought of one of the posters in Barminster's art therapy room. *Are You Living or Reacting?* But she knew it wasn't this poster that forced to the surface the question of what had happened the night she was arrested. No, it was the tall Black man, Father Nick's friend, the ex-cop who'd peppered her with questions. He was the one who'd broken through the fog and awakened a small part of her brain.

✝

WORTHY'S APARTMENT

NICK HAD PLANNED TO ACCOMPANY WORTHY to the courtroom, but Worthy told him that the first day would be devoted to preliminaries. Nick hadn't pushed the issue and had remained in Worthy's apartment, offering prayers for his friend as well as pondering what steps Henderson and he should take to help Sophia Demetrios.

The two of them had agreed that progress on Sophia's case depended on their breaking through a series of barriers or difficulties. The first barrier would be the easiest to overcome, that being for someone to meet with Lieutenant Williston, the lead on the murder of Reginald King. Nick remembered Worthy saying that she was a capable detective as well as someone who would level with them.

The second barrier would be getting Francine Nichols, the prosecution's key witness to Reginald King's murder, to talk. Nichols had traded her testimony for immunity, despite Nichols being responsible for Sophia being in the motel room the night that King was killed.

The third difficulty would be finding Connie, if that were even her real name. Sophia remembered Connie being close to Francine, though Connie, oddly, hadn't been called to testify at the trial. The final difficulty would be breaking through Sophia's blankness about the night of the shooting. Her inability to confess her guilt or profess her innocence at her trial had been, Nick knew, the deciding factor in her sentence.

Just as Nick had finished praying to St. Phanourios, the Orthodox equivalent of St. Jude, the Saint of Lost Causes, his phone rang.

"Nick, I'm tracking down some developments that might help Chris," Henderson said. "Care to come along?"

"Absolutely. I'm ready whenever you are."

"I'll be there in twenty minutes. Keep a positive thought, Nick."

In the car, Henderson explained their destination. "It's a removal company that emptied Kerry Paulsen's apartment."

"Ah, the young man who killed himself. Christopher probably told you that Paulsen wrote to Tremont regularly in prison."

"Yeah, he did. I talked with Paulsen's neighbors in his apartment building, and one of them told me that just before he died, he wanted to send a package to somebody. If he sent that to Tremont, the prison authorities would have opened it. But there's no record of a package. That's why we're headed to the removal company."

"You think this company might still have that package?"

"There's a chance. Paulsen was estranged from his family, and Tremont remained his only friend."

Nick waited until Henderson passed a truck before saying, "Any progress on Sophia's case?"

"Not much more than what we talked about yesterday. What is clearer is that Francine Nichols is all over the case. She's the one who got Sophia hooked on cocaine. Her apartment is where Sophia spent a lot of time and where she slept off and on. And she ended up being granted immunity for agreeing to be the prosecutor's chief witness."

"Given her drug history, I've wondered if she told the truth at Sophia's trial."

"Ah, that's what I'm getting to. Since the trial, Nichols has been in and out of trouble. She was picked up again for dealing coke, and she should have been slapped with a stiff sentence. Hell, she should be in a cell at Barminster. But instead, she's in a rehab center."

"Huh, that is odd. I wonder who's paying for that," Nick asked

"Exactly. And there's something else. Do you remember Sophia talking about Connie?"

"Of course. I got the impression that she was closer to Nichols than Sophia was."

"But her name never came up in the trial. Okay, so she wasn't in the motel room when Reginald King was killed, but she should have been called for background. If Sophia knew this Connie person, then Connie knew Sophia."

Nick exhaled slowly. 'So, Francine Nichols is granted immunity and ends up at a rehabilitation facility, and Connie—whatever her last name is—is never called to testify in the trial. You must have a theory."

"I do. What makes sense is that Connie is in law enforcement and was undercover, someone who infiltrated Nichols' group hoping to find intel on drug lords like Reginald King. If Connie is in the Drug Enforcement Agency, she didn't testify because that would expose her real identity."

"Let me see if I understand. Connie could be the name of a cop inside Francine Nichols' circle. But then King is killed, and Nichols is not only given immunity but, after that, is given another break by the police."

Henderson pounded the steering wheel like a drum. "That didn't happen because the police are generous. Nichols must know something—something important—that gives her some leverage."

CHAPTER TWENTY-TWO

◆

APPELLATE COURT

WORTHY WASN'T SURPRISED THAT THE FIRST WITNESS called by Tremont's team was Phillip Sherrod. Sherrod had been second officer on the original investigation into Renee Vickers' murder and had, in Tremont's first trial, provided the evidence that his team had collected—and, as Worthy remembered, Sherrod's failure to make progress on the case had also been noted in the first trial.

If Worthy expected Sherrod to view the appeal as an opportunity to redeem his reputation, he didn't have long to wait. After Tremont's lead lawyer introduced Sherrod as a senior homicide detective with a solid reputation, she said, "Let's return to the discovery of Renee Vickers' body in Detroit. What struck you about the body, Lieutenant Sherrod?"

"I didn't allow anyone to touch the body before the coroner and my forensic team arrived, but it was obvious from the marks on her neck that she'd been strangled as well as stabbed. The coroner gave a preliminary estimation that the victim had died two to three days before we found her body. His post-mortem confirmed that."

"Being a homicide detective, Lieutenant, did this case resemble others that you've investigated?"

"It did. From associates of the deceased, we learned that the victim had recently taken up prostitution to support a drug habit. Renee

Vickers is one of numerous women with a similar profile who ends up being killed in Detroit."

"So, sadly, her death was not uncommon."

"As you said, sadly," Sherrod said.

"And that would be supported by the estimate you gave in the initial trial, when you stated that only twenty to twenty-five percent of murders of women involved in both drugs and prostitution are ever solved. Now, no one is suggesting that the police don't give maximum effort in solving such cases, but would you answer that question any differently today?"

"No, that still seems about right."

"There was little then about the case that surprised you. Her work as a prostitute, her drug habit, and then her murder."

"That's right."

Yet after you worked the case for seven months, the case was transferred to Lieutenant Christopher Worthy. Why did you think that happened?'

Sherrod shot Worthy a glance and without pausing said, "Politics."

"Would you elaborate, Lieutenant?"

"Renee Vickers was Black. Certain political elements in the city decided that my team wasn't taking her death seriously. Which was bullshit."

"So, is it fair to say that you believed that there was nothing about your handling of the case that justified the case being transferred to Lieutenant Worthy? Rather, the cause was the racial tensions between various communities and the police."

"I still believe that."

"But certainly Lieutenant Worthy faced the same racial tensions when he led the investigation?"

"That doesn't mean he responded the same way I did."

"No, Lieutenant, I'm not saying that. What I'm asking you, as the second officer on the initial investigation, is if whoever led the investigation would have felt pressure from the media and, as you say, the political leaders, to solve the case."

Sherrod initially looked confused, then seemed to understand. "Yeah, there was a helluva lot of pressure." Glancing at Worthy again, he added, "But a good police detective would never bow to that pressure."

"Because?" Janine Reeves asked.

"Because it clouds your judgment. It gets in the way. Or worse."

"How worse, Lieutenant?"

"A cop who can't stand the pressure will arrest someone just to please the powers that be. Everyone is happy, except the poor sap who gets charged."

"Thank you, Lieutenant Sherrod. That's all the questions I have."

The center judge looked at Howard Hullinger. "Your turn, counsellor."

Hullinger paused for a moment before standing and gazing at Sherrod. Sherrod stared back.

"Lieutenant Sherrod, how long did your team lead Renee Vickers' murder case before it was transferred to Lieutenant Worthy?"

"Haven't you read the file? Seven months."

"And how long did Lieutenant Worthy lead it before arresting William Tremont?"

"I don't remember."

"Then I will remind you and set the record straight. As you say, you had the case seven months. Lieutenant Worthy was lead on the case for just short of five months. You imply that he rushed the investigation because he couldn't deal with the pressure. But on another case that was transferred from you to Lieutenant Worthy, didn't you tell a newspaper reporter that Worthy had a bad habit of moving too slowly and methodically on cases?"

Sherrod shrugged. "Everyone in our division knew that Worthy had a case of the slows."

"The 'slows.' I think I understand. But let me repeat my question. If Lieutenant Worthy had a reputation for being . . . you say slow, I would prefer 'thorough,' he could hardly be accused of bowing to public pressure in this case, could he?"

Worthy noticed Sherrod's face begin to redden. "Why not?" Sherrod asked. "Maybe he twiddled his thumbs for four months and then, when he realized the case was going to be yanked, he rushed to make an arrest."

"If it please the court, I'd like to refer Lieutenant Sherrod to the case file."

The three judges deliberated for a moment before the chief judge replied. "As the case file was a key piece of evidence in the first trial, you may proceed."

"Thank you, your honor. Now, Lieutenant Sherrod, the case file quite clearly describes Lieutenant Worthy's disciplined and pragmatic strategy over those five months, a strategy that, it must be admitted, succeeded where you failed."

"And who do you think wrote those entries in the file? Worthy did."

"Ah. If I understand, you're now accusing Lieutenant Worthy, in addition to bowing to public pressure, of falsifying police records." Hullinger paused. "Your honor, as this witness seems intent on attacking the character of Lieutenant Worthy, can I pursue the relationship that existed between the two men from 2010 onwards."

"You may."

"Thank you, your honor. Lieutenant Sherrod, how many of your cases were eventually handed over to Lieutenant Worthy?"

"I can't remember. Maybe two or three," he said in a tight voice.

"It was actually four. And how many of Lieutenant Worthy's cases have you taken over?"

"Look, he's had his failures. Just check the record."

"Oh, I have, Lieutenant Sherrod. The answer is that not one of his cases was ever transferred to you. I have no further questions for this witness."

✝

DEA HEADQUARTERS, DETROIT

INSIDE DEA HEADQUARTERS, AGENT RONALD FITHIAN reread the homicide report on Reginald King for the fifth time. Again, his mind balked at what he was reading. Reginald King, one of the city's most notorious and successful drug lords, had died at the hands of Sophia Demetrios, a twenty-year-old nobody in the city's drug scene.

He knew that Reginald King had survived as a drug lord by being cautious, rarely going anywhere without a bodyguard. Yet, a hopped-up kid with only one prior conviction for shoplifting and with no known knowledge of guns, managed to wrest King's gun from him and shoot him expertly in the chest and head from four feet away.

That's what all the evidence pointed to, and furthermore, Sophia Demetrios at trial hadn't denied shooting King, although she hadn't admitted doing it either. The jury had been out for less than two hours before they returned a verdict of guilty, giving Lieutenant Rebecca Williston her first major conviction.

According to the case file, the only other person present at the shooting beside Sophia Demetrios and Reginald King was Francine Nichols. Had King been shot by Nichols, he would have been able to swallow the court's verdict. Dealers like Nichols might have any number of brain-addled reasons to shoot their suppliers. Had King been shot by someone from one of the Mexican cartels rumored to be moving into Detroit, that too would have made sense.

The second bothersome issue for Fithian about King's murder was the absence at the scene of his agent, Samiyah. From regular briefings with her, he knew that she'd succeeded in infiltrating Francine Nichols' ring. She'd established that Nichols was one of King's dealers as well as learning that the dirty agent was someone in the DEA, but she'd never witnessed a meeting between Nichols and King.

Samiyah should have been there when Demetrios shot King, he thought, but when he'd asked her why she wasn't there, she'd said it had been bad luck. She'd been called that evening to the hospital where her father, whose leg had recently been amputated, had been rushed with a blood clot.

On the one hand, the death of Reginald King was a boon for the DEA. Somehow Sophia Demetrios in few seconds had taken King off the map, something the drug squad had been trying to do for years. How had a waif like Demetrios accomplished that?

Samiyah's claim hadn't stopped Fithian from checking on the date of her father being admitted to the Emergency Ward. Her father had, in fact, been admitted that same evening for treatment of a blood clot, and the nurse on duty remembered his daughter being there with him.

In the wake of King's death, Fithian had gone several steps further. He had to consider the possibility that Sophia Demetrius wasn't an in-experienced druggie at all. It was possible, he'd thought at first, that she killed King because she was on the payroll of one of the Mexican cartels moving into the city. In that scenario, she was fully alert the night she killed King and only acted the part of a "stoner" in hopes that she'd received a reduced sentence. Even though that had backfired with the

judge's harsh sentence, she might have traded her silence for money for
her family. But Marina's and George Demetrios' bank accounts had revealed nothing suspicious, and that led Fithian to conclude that maybe
Sophia Demetrios didn't, in fact, remember what happened that night.

The transcript of the trial revealed that the only witness called by the
defense was Sophia's sister, Marina. Marina said that she knew little of
Sophia's relationship with Francine Nichols, much less Reginald King,
but what was clear from her testimony was that the two sisters were close.
Fithian concluded that if Sophia's memory of that night would ever clear,
the first person she'd share what she remembered would be Marina.

That was why he began tracking Marina's movements, especially in
the days after her visits to her sister in Barminster. He'd followed her to
St. Simeon's monastery, his first clue that Marina might be doing more
than grieving her sister's downfall. A quick search for St. Simeon's on
the internet brought up articles about one monk, Father Nicholas Fortis,
who'd assisted Christopher Worthy, one of Detroit's most honored detectives on several homicide cases. Fithian wasn't sure what plan Sophia
and Marina Demetrios were hatching, but he understood that she'd chosen wisely by including Father Fortis. If there was any chance that their
plan would embarrass the DEA, he needed to do whatever he could to
prevent that.

Fithian had gone undercover on numerous cases, but he'd never
pretended to be a religious person who'd go to a monastery on retreat.
Borrowing his uncle's name, Gus Cooper, he'd done his best to keep
Marina Demetrios in his sights over that weekend, waiting to see if she'd
contact Father Fortis. From Saturday morning until late Sunday afternoon, Marina had done nothing but walk the grounds of the monastery
or sit alone in the church. The reward for his efforts came late on Sunday,
when he followed her to the church again, but this time to meet a monk
he recognized from photos to be Father Fortis. He was unable to overhear their conversation, but he left St. Simeon's that night convinced
that he'd discovered something important. He knew that Sophia, even
if she remembered what happened the night King was killed, would tell
him nothing if he visited her in Barminster. Keeping tabs on Marina
and Father Fortis would be his next best option. *I won't be caught nap-
ping,* he thought.

A to Z Removal Service

As Henderson drove through the gates of A to Z Removal Service and passed along the long rows of storage units, he said, "Nick, I think of these places as cemeteries for things no one wants anymore."

"That's a good description. At least four storage companies have sprung up in the last few years within five miles of the monastery."

"They're everywhere," Henderson said. "Let's hope they haven't disposed of Paulsen's stuff."

Entering the building marked "Office," they found a woman and a man arguing.

Looking up from a desk, the woman said, "The bill is overdue, Mike. You want them to shut off our electricity?"

The man looked over her shoulder at a document. "Stop your worrying. Wait until they send a second notice. Jeez, Linda, we can't have them thinking they can threaten us."

"Except they can," the woman replied, even as she set the bill aside.

"Can I help you gentlemen . . . er, Father?"

Henderson flashed his old police ID. "We understand you removed what was left in Kerry Paulsen's apartment."

The man named Mike stepped forward. "Whoa, let's start at the beginning," he said. "We organize by date and location. What date are we talking about, and where is this apartment?"

Henderson thought for a moment. "I can only give you a ballpark figure on the date—sometimes in early July, but here's the address."

The landlord handed the slip of paper to his wife. "Look that up, will you, Linda? If it was June and no one has claimed it, you're out of luck. Everything unclaimed gets trashed after two months."

Linda looked up from her computer screen. "It's flagged."

"What does that mean?" Henderson asked.

"It means the state paid for the removal," Linda answered. "For the state, we're required to hold the contents for an extra five months in case the contents contain evidence of a crime. It says here that we did notify a Rev. Nils Paulsen, but he hasn't gotten back to us. Right now, it's in my rights to sell the unit to anyone who's interested."

Henderson looked at Nick. "Let me get this straight. You still have what was found in Paulsen's apartment?"

"That's right."

"And you'd be willing to sell it?"

"The contents, yes, but under some conditions. I open the unit, and you can take your time to look through what's in there. But if you want something, you have to show that to me. I put a price on it, and you can take it or leave it. Sound fair?"

Fifteen minutes later, Henderson and Nick were inside a small storage unit that was only a quarter full of boxes along with a recliner, two other chairs, and a kitchen table.

"At least Paulsen wasn't a hoarder," Henderson said.

"I take it we have no interest in his clothes," Nick added.

"No, we're looking for papers and that package he didn't get around to sending."

Ninety minutes later, Nick looked up from one of the last boxes to be checked. "How about his computer?"

"We definitely take the computer. Check out the keypad. Any chance his password is on a post-it note?"

"Aha! Yes, indeed. And get this. The password is 'FreeTree #10.' Is that what I think it is?"

"Free Tremont with 2010 being the date of his arrest. That's a nice bonus for our efforts. So, we buy this box full of papers and, if I'm not mistaken, a package. And we buy the computer. You don't happen to know a computer wizard, do you, Nick?"

Nick smiled. "In fact, I do."

On the way back to Detroit, Henderson suggested they drive by one of the addresses for a Gus Cooper that Brother Pachomius found on the internet.

"This Cooper is our mystery man, assuming that's his real name, Nick."

"I agree. If he listed a non-existent church in St. Simeon's guestbook, he might have invented his name as well."

In little more than a half-hour, Henderson pulled up across the street from the house that was listed as belonging to Gustaf Cooper. It was an older bungalow from the thirties or forties in one of Detroit's middle-class neighborhoods.

"What's the plan?" Nick asked.

"Well, standard police practice is to be patient, watch the house for a bit, in case the owner comes out. If that doesn't happen, we'll need to get creative."

After a hour of waiting, Henderson turned to Nick. "Do you mind if my creative suggestion isn't exactly legal?"

"It suppose that depends. What do you have in mind?"

Henderson smiled. "Better if you just stand behind me and don't say a thing. That way you can't be arrested—like I could be. All you have to do, Nick, is get a good look at the guy and tell me if you recognize him from the weekend Marina Demetrios was at St. Simeon's."

Nick followed Henderson across the street to where this G. Cooper had a mailbox. Looking both ways, Henderson opened the mailbox and took out a travel magazine. In a moment, he was at the door ringing the bell as Nick stood behind him.

They heard a dog barking loudly and then the even louder sound of a man's voice telling the dog to be quiet. Then, the door opened. Facing them was a man easily in his eighties, bald and standing with the help of a walker.

"Sorry to bother you, sir," Henderson said, "but we found this piece of mail on the sidewalk. We read the address and thought it might belong to you, assuming you are Gus Cooper."

The man accepted the magazine. "That's very kind of you. Yes, I'm Gus. And I do love travel magazines. I can't travel much at my age, but the magazines bring back good memories."

"Then I hope you enjoy the magazine," Henderson said.

Back in the car, Nick sighed. "Well, we tried."

"Look, I'm not a detective for nothing. Did you see the car parked behind the van with the wheelchair bracket?"

"No, where was that?"

"At the end of the driveway. It was a Ford Taurus Interceptor."

"I still don't understand," Nick confessed.

"It's a cop car. You can find the odd civilian who fancies it, but that car is standard issue for police departments. Fast and furious, as the saying goes, and it had the telltale trunk antenna to boot. I can't see that old man driving a car like that."

"Are you saying that someone in law enforcement lives there with him?"

Henderson flashed a smile. "It makes a kind of weird sense. What if the guy who followed Marina Demetrios to St. Simeon's is a cop and picked a name he was familiar with—like the other guy who lives here? That might mean—I say 'might'—that we now have two cops who figure in Sophia's case. We have this Connie person as possibly undercover DEA inside Francine Nichols' ring, and now the guy using Gus Cooper's name is also a cop. Sophia's case is getting more and more interesting."

CHAPTER TWENTY-THREE

BROTHER PACHOMIUS COULDN'T HELP BUT BE EXCITED when he read Father Nick's email the next morning. In the first paragraph, Father Nick updated him on a possible link between the person going by the name of Connie and another person using the name of Gus Cooper. In a second paragraph, Father Nicholas wrote: "I also want you to help out with an appeal case that my friend Christopher Worthy is involved in. Please find out all you can about Kerry Paulsen. I've attached folders from Paulsen's computer, and I'd like you to look for anything that has to do with these names: Renee Vickers, William Tremont, and Christopher Worthy. Brother Pachomius, I know you'll be tempted to violate the two-hour-a-day limit, but I urge you to resist."

Pachomius knew that Father Nick was right. Had Father Nick not reminded him of the abbot's limitation, he would have rationalized the added work as permission to spend four hours on the computer.

Before opening the files that Father Nick had sent, Pachomius did an online search for Kerry Paulsen. Within ten minutes, he'd read the sad details of the young man's short life. A brief obituary reported the thirty-one year old's untimely death, which led him to wonder how Paulsen had died. A second entry, from 2010, listed Kerry Paulsen as a witness in the murder trial of William Tremont.

If Paulsen's online presence was minimal, William Tremont was the subject of numerous articles, all related to his trial in 2010. A long account in the *Detroit News* provided details of the murder of Renee Vickers, William Tremont's arrest and conviction for her death, and Christopher Worthy's role as arresting officer. A recent article reported the appeal of Tremont's conviction, with the writer hinting that Tremont's chances of winning the appeal looked good.

Pachomius looked at his watch. His research had absorbed all but fifteen minutes of his allotted time, but he knew it was time well spent. He might be miles away from Detroit, living in peace and safety behind monastery walls, but Father Nick's email had dropped him into the middle of two murder cases. *Lucky, lucky me,* he thought.

OCTOBER 20, 2023, PRECINCT #7 DETROIT

SAMIYAH HAD ALWAYS KNOWN THAT HER QUEST to uncover the dirty agent depended on her finding out everything that Francine Nichols knew. That chance came unexpectedly, when just six weeks after Sophia Demetrius was sentenced, a desk sergeant from Detroit precinct seven called her at work.

"Someone here is asking to see you," he said. "You know a Francine Nichols?"

Samiyah felt her heart race. "Has Francine been picked up for something?"

"Yep, caught dealing cocaine. She says she knows you."

At least the precinct cop didn't say 'She says you owe her,' Samiyah thought.

"I'll be there in thirty minutes."

"No hurry. She's not going anywhere."

After Samiyah arrived and showed her ID, a young uniform officer escorted Francine into an interview room. When he acted as if he would stay, Samiyah said, "I need to talk to her on my own."

The officer had hardly left the room before Francine said, "Look, Samiyah, I can't go down for this. I was set up. The bitch approached me, said she wanted to score some coke. I told her to go to hell, but she said she'd been told that I was the person to go to. That has to be entrapment. Thank God you still owe me."

"Owe you, Francine? Really? I'm the reason you didn't go down with Sophia."

Francine pointed her index finger at Samiyah. "That was then, but now is now. You have to pull some strings, get me into rehab. Otherwise—"

Samiyah leaned over the table and whispered, "No threats, Francine. If I help you a second time, you need to give me more."

Francine seemed to be weighing the comment. "What do you have in mind?"

"I need to know who King reported to."

"And this will get me rehab instead of jail?"

"I'll do what I can. But you have to tell me everything you know," Samiyah said.

"Look, when I gave you money to take to King, you saw who hung around him. What makes you think I know more than that?"

"All I saw was King's hangers-on, Francine. I'm still looking for who was above King."

"You think Reggie told me that?"

"What I'm saying is that you had to wonder about who that person was."

Francine shook her head. "It's not safe to be too nosy. You of all people should know that."

"Stop stalling. You want rehab again? Then tell me what you know."

Francine didn't say anything for a moment, then muttered, "It's nothing I know for sure. It's more something from things I overheard."

"What?"

"Reggie liked to act like he was top dog. He'd say 'my name is Reginald King, but you can call me King Reggie.' Very full of himself. But one time when I was at his place, he got a phone call. I heard him say 'sir' and 'I'll do my best.' I mean, whoever he was talking to really scared him. I realized Reggie was just middle management."

"You said there were things, that's plural, Francine. What else do you know?"

"There was this time Reggie stopped by my place, and we ended up smoking hash. It was just that once, and I thought maybe he realized afterwards that he'd told me too much."

"Francine, the cops are going to march in here any minute and cut me off. What did he tell you?"

"I asked him if he'd heard about rival Mexican cartels moving into Detroit. I asked what he'd do if it came to a street war. I thought he'd do that King Reggie posturing thing, but he just looked at me and smiled. 'I got protection.' I said, 'I know you do. I've seen the muscle that you run with.' He said, 'No, I mean real protection. I got a 'get out of jail free card.' I laughed. 'Are you telling me you've got a cop in your pocket?' I said. He shook his head. 'More like I'm in his pocket.' And then he said, 'And so are you, Francine.'"

Samiyah had never told Francine that she'd overheard her on a phone call saying the dirty cop was DEA.

"That's not news to me, Francine. I need more."

"You think King let me meet this guy?"

"You tell me. All I know is that I need more."

"Look, it's just a feeling I got."

"What was? Come on, Francine."

"I think he's an older dude, someone who's been a cop for a while. I mean, Reggie was scared of him, right?"

Samiyah put together what she knew. The dirty agent was one of the higher-ups in the DEA, someone with some years of service that gave him—Reggie described the person as a male—some cover. But she still wasn't any closer to identifying him.

She heard the key turn in the lock. "You're running out of time. I need it all, Francine, and now."

"Look," Francine said, "why don't you ask one of Reggie's bodyguards?"

"Quick, which one."

"Loften, but he goes by the name of Lofty," Francine whispered. "I've heard he's taking Reggie's place."

Samiyah bent over the table. "If I get you into rehab, we're still not even. Expect to see me again."

As the door opened and the guard came in, Samiyah rose. "I need to talk with your captain right away. And this woman wants a lawyer."

✝

LENA'S APARTMENT IN ROME

LENA THOUGHT WORTHY SOUNDED COMPLETELY SPENT when he called after the first day of the appeal.

"I know it's late Rome-time, but I knew you'd be wondering how things went in court today."

"Not to worry. It's Friday night, so I can sleep in tomorrow. Plus, I'm up grading papers and was hoping you'd call. Was today bad?"

"I've had better days. Tremont's lawyers showed their hand by calling Sherrod as their first witness."

"Oh, no. He's the guy who hated you."

"He still hates me. I took over the case from his team, so he took some shots at me. Only Sherrod could claim that I moved too slowly on the case but also rushed it."

"Won't the judges see through that?"

"Let's hope so." After a pause, Worthy said, "Tell me something wonderful about your day in Rome. Anything."

Lena felt a pang of sorrow. *He's really low, and this is only the first day of the appeal,* she thought.

"Someone from the police called, wondering when you'd be back. You see, I'm not the only one who misses you. On a happier note, I spent some time in the antique market near Porta Portese. I bought a Christmas present for you, but that's all I'm going to say."

"I'd love to be at a street market right now." She'd heard a sigh before he said, "So, how many days until you can join me?"

"Less than two weeks, my love. I wish I could be there now, but you know that. Have you thought about spending the weekend at your summer cabin?"

"It's crossed my mind, but the cabin is four hours from here, and my lawyers want me available. So, I'm stuck in Detroit."

"Chris, is there anything I can do to help you from here?"

"If you can perform some magic, kindly find the missing corrections page from the case file. I've been warned that Tremont's lawyers are going to portray me as a lone wolf and glory hound, but I still believe the final decision will come down to the pathologist's report."

"And that's a problem because your pathologist friend died last year?"

"I don't know if I'd call Doc Wallace a friend. Come to think of it, I don't know anyone who'd claim they were his friend. But yes, his death and the missing page in the case file give Tremont's lawyers an opening to exploit."

"What about your lawyers, Chris? Do you have confidence in them?"

"They seem solid. By the time Hullinger, my head lawyer, was through cross-examining Sherrod, he looked like someone obsessed with me."

"Was Nick in the courtroom with you?"

"He wanted to be, but I told him opening day would be mostly procedural and rehashing. Plus, he's tied up with another case. I'll see him tonight. We're having dinner again at Henderson's."

After the phone call, Lena found she couldn't concentrate on student essays. Instead, she pictured Worthy, the man she loved, alone in the courtroom while Tremont's lawyers attacked. If the appeal had been delayed two weeks, she'd have been with him in court every day. But being stuck in Rome, she could of nothing more helpful than calling Nick. No matter what Nick was working on, she knew he would also sense the toll the appeal was taking—and would take—on Worthy.

HENDERSON'S HOME

NICK SAT WITH SULLA AT HER KITCHEN TABLE, sipping spiced tea as they waited for Henderson to return with Jamie for the weekend and for Worthy to arrive. Sulla was one of those persons whom Nick felt he'd known for years, not minutes.

"I'm sure Chris has told you about Jamie."

"He has. How's he doing?"

Sulla didn't answer immediately, instead looked out a window to a back garden. "Jamie is happy. Nine years ago, when he was first diagnosed, I didn't know if I'd ever say that again. And that meant that I wasn't sure Carnell and I would ever be happy again."

"Christopher said that Jamie lives in a halfway house in the city."

Sulla nodded. "The house is a big part of Jamie being happy. He has a part-time job and pays his own rent. And he's become the one-man welcoming committee to the house." Exhaling slowing, she added, "I've had to learn to look at Jamie's life through his eyes, not anyone else's."

Nick could imagine the looks of shock, then pity, that Sulla and Henderson faced whenever someone learned of Jamie's condition, but Sulla had found a way to change her focus. Her son wasn't a tragedy, someone without a life or a future. Jamie was her son, someone she could see was happy.

The front door swung open and a young man came running into the kitchen ahead of Carnell Henderson. Not seeming to notice Nick, Jamie hugged his mother even as he said, "Is he here?"

"Not yet, Jamie, but Mr. Worthy should be here any minute."

Rubbing his hands together, Jamie said, "I can't wait. I can't wait."

Sulla reached out and held her son's hands. "Jaimie, this is Nick, a friend of your dad and Mr. Worthy."

Before Nick could say anything, Jamie glanced at him briefly before saying, "You have a black beard. And a ponytail."

Nick smiled. "That I do, Jamie. Some people think I look like Hagrid."

Jamie looked at Nick more intently. "You do. You look just like Hagrid. Do you know that Hagrid died?"

Nick wasn't sure if Jamie was talking about Hagrid's fate in the Harry Potter series or the death of the actor who played Hagrid. Either way, Jamie was right.

"I did hear that, Jamie."

Sulla poured a glass of chocolate milk. "We start every week with chocolate milk, don't we, Jamie?"

Jamie, still standing, shuffled from one foot to the other as he drank the milk. "I fixed Mr. Worthy's clock," he said. "I'm going to give it back to him."

"That couldn't have been easy."

Jamie shook his head. "It was fun. I like to fix things." Looking over his shoulder at his father standing at the entrance to the kitchen, he said, "Don't I, Dad?"

"Yes, you do, son. Tell Nick what your favorite TV program is."

"*The Repair Shop*. It's from England. Have you seen it?"

"No, I haven't. It sounds like I'm missing something."

Before Jamie could answer, the doorbell rang.

"It's Mr. Worthy!" Jamie said, running from the room.

The three adults were silent as Jamie opened the door and pulled Worthy into the house.

"I beat you here, Mr. Worthy. And I have something for you. Do you want to see it?"

Nick was relieved to see Worthy's face brighten as he let Jamie lead him from the kitchen to the den. Lena's phone call had left him concerned. Today was only the first day of the appeal, but from Lena's perspective the trial had already wounded Worthy.

Henderson sat down at the kitchen table. "Nick, I've done a quick look-through of Paulsen's papers. Not surprisingly, most of them have nothing to do with Tremont. I put those in one pile, and, in a second pile, I have the newspaper clippings about Tremont's trial. He wrote in the margin on some of those, but his handwriting is a mess. I thought you, Chris, and I would go through them later tonight."

"Any letters from Tremont to Paulsen?" Nick asked.

"Not yet. I opened the package, by the way. It was a Star Trek DVD. Maybe he intended on sending it to Tremont, but the package hadn't been addressed yet."

Jamie stood in the doorway. "Everybody, come see."

Henderson, Sulla, and Nick rose from the table and followed Jamie into the den. Jamie sat down next to Worthy, who was holding an object. Across the room was a table holding stacks of papers—Kerry Paulsen's, Nick reasoned.

"Show them, Mr. Worthy."

Worthy turned the object around so everyone could see the clock face. "I brought this old clock last weekend hoping Jamie could fix it. I don't think it's been working for thirty or forty years or more. But listen."

With one hand, Worthy opened the glass protecting the hands of the clock and with the other turned the minute hand until it was one minute to the hour. The room was quiet until a soft chime rang.

"I'd forgotten there was a chime. I haven't heard that since I was a boy. It's wonderful, Jamie. I still can't believe you fixed it."

Jamie looked down at the floor. "It's like *The Repair Shop*. The clock gives you your past back, Mr. Worthy."

Nick could see that Worthy was moved, and Nick half expected Worthy to give Jamie a hug. Instead, Worthy put his hand out for Jamie to shake. "You did a wonderful job, Jamie. I can't think of another person who could have fixed this old clock. But it's not really old anymore, is it? You made it new. Now, Jamie, is there anything I can give you to show how grateful I am?"

Nick saw Sulla wipe tears from her cheeks, even as Henderson cleared his throat. Jamie sat in silence for a moment, before glancing at Worthy with a sly smile. "Can you give me another clock to fix?"

Worthy laughed. "Maybe I can find one. I'll keep my eye open for one."

After dinner, during which they all agreed not to talk about either case, Jamie sat with Sulla watching episodes of *The Repair Shop* while the men sat around the table at the other end of the room to look through Kerry Paulsen's papers.

Nick thought that Worthy's mood had brightened since arriving at the Henderson's home, though he was sure that the pain of the first day in court lingered. Lena and he had talked about Phillip Sherrod, Worthy's nemesis, offering the opening salvo of the appeal. From what Worthy had told him, Nick knew what would come next. Tremont would have the chance to give his own version of his arrest and conviction, his claim that he was under the influence of Ecstasy when he confessed.

Not for the first time, Nick thought about Worthy's claim that Paulsen's death would benefit Tremont. If Paulsen were alive, he'd surely be subpoenaed in the appeal, and under oath he'd have nothing more to contribute than what he said at the first trial: that he'd had sex with Renee Vickers at the invitation of Tremont but had no knowledge of Vickers' death nor of Tremont driving her body down to Detroit. None of that would help Tremont.

A second benefit from Paulsen's death was that Tremont's lawyers could plant the seed that Paulsen killed himself because he'd killed Renee Vickers and couldn't live with the guilt.

Now as Nick, along with Worthy and Henderson, began looking through Paulsen's newspapers clippings related to Tremont's first trial, he wondered if Paulsen's comments in the margin would shed any more light on his suicide.

Henderson had put the clippings in order, from oldest to newest, with most coming from the time of the first trial. The rest of the clippings showed how the media lost interest in William Tremont except on the first, fifth, and tenth anniversaries of Renee Vickers' death. The most recent newspaper clipping showed a photo of Tremont's lawyers as they went public on their petition to appeal the conviction.

"Look at this," Henderson said, showing Nick and Worthy a clipping that included a photo of Tremont and Paulsen from their days in Boy Scouts.

Nick squinted at the faded scribblings in the side margin. "It's clear that Kerry Paulsen didn't win any penmanship awards in school. Can you make out what he's written?"

Worthy and Henderson both studied the scribbles but could decipher only a word or two. From behind them, Jamie asked, "Can I see?"

Henderson glanced at Nick and Worthy. "Jamie is a whiz at solving puzzles. Here, son, sit by me."

Looking down at the first clipping, Jamie traced the scribbles with his finger. "This is not a nice person. He's calling Mr. Worthy a bad name."

"He wrote something about Christopher next to a column about his scouting? What does it say, Jamie?" Nick asked.

"I don't want to say it, but it starts with a b."

"Now I see it," Worthy said. "Trust me, Jamie, I've been called worse."

"Not by nice people," Jamie said. "Do you have another?"

Worthy handed Jamie a second clipping, this one under the headline, "Tremont Shows No Remorse." After tracing the words in the margin again, Jamie pushed the clipping away. "He likes to use bad words. I don't like this person."

"You can whisper what he wrote to me, Jamie," Henderson said.

Jamie put his hand over the side of his mouth as he whispered in his Dad's ear.

"Paulsen wrote, 'Remorse? She was a whore!'" Henderson shared.

Worthy picked up a third clipping with tiny words written in the margin. The headline to this one was "Tremont Sentenced to Forty Years." Jamie took a moment to study the scribblings in the margin before saying. "He wrote 'So unfair.' Then, 'Unproven' and after that 'Stay Strong.'"

"A true believer," Worthy said. "Maybe that's what he had to be, given that Tremont might have been his only friend."

For the next hour, Jamie translated Paulsen's margin markings, most conforming to the same three topics: Worthy being the enemy; Renee Vickers being a whore who deserved what happened to her; and Tremont being innocent despite his recorded confession.

At the end, Worthy said, "What can I say, Jamie? First, you fix my clock and now you solve these puzzles. You've been a big help, like a real detective."

Jamie rose and retreated to the sofa, but he was smiling broadly. "Except for the bad words, it was fun," he said to his mother.

Still at the table, Nick looked at Worthy and Henderson. "I've been glancing through the newspaper clippings that have nothing to do with Tremont's first trial or appeal. There's something disturbing about them, something that might be important."

Handing one to Worthy and another to Henderson, he said. "Read these and tell me what jumps out at you."

After a few minutes, Henderson said, "Mine's about a homicide in 2011, the murder of a clerk at a Dollar General."

"Mine is about the murder of Father Spiro, the case that you and I worked together, Hoops," Worthy said.

Nick handed a short article to Henderson. "If you look toward the bottom of this one, Carnell, you'll see Christopher's name."

"That wasn't a case I solved, though. Nick, are you saying that all these other clippings are about cases I worked?" Worthy asked.

Nick nodded. "I think he was obsessed with you, Christopher."

Worthy put his head back and stared at the ceiling. "After what Sherrod said in court today, I'd say, 'Join the queue.'"

"Anything we can do to help, Christopher?" Nick asked.

"You know what would help the most right now? Tell me something about the Demetrios case."

Henderson looked at Nick and shrugged. "You're sure?" he asked.

"I can't tell you how exhausting it is to be dragged back thirteen years and have that mess dredged up again. Does Sophia remember anything more about that night?"

"Not much so far," Nick said. "But that could change. I think she's finally waking up—at least, I pray that's the case."

"We do have a working theory," Henderson added. "It goes back to Francine Nichols."

"Nichols was the one who testified against Sophia, right?"

"Yeah, but now we know from Sophia that another woman was a regular in Francine Nichols' circle," Henderson said. "Someone who called herself Connie."

"Hmm, 'called herself.' You have doubts?"

Henderson nodded. "We do, especially as she wasn't called to testify at Sophia's trial, not even to offer background information on Nichols' ring. We're now thinking she could have been undercover, probably DEA."

"Carnell is being modest," Nick said. "He's the one who figured that out."

Worthy thought about that for a moment. "That would explain why she wasn't called to testify. They didn't want to blow her cover for other investigations."

"That's what we're thinking, but there's more," Nick said. "Do you remember me telling you about Gus Cooper, the guy who came to St. Simeon's the same weekend as Sophia's sister, Marina?"

"Of course. That's what got you interested in Sophia in the first place. You found him?"

Nick shook his head. "Not in person, but we stopped off at a house in the city that belongs to a Gustaf 'Gus' Cooper. When an old man answered the door and said he was Gus Cooper, I was sure we'd struck out. But that's why I'm so glad Carnell was with me. He noticed something, so he should be the one to tell you."

"Parked behind a van in the driveway was a Ford Interceptor with an antenna on the trunk. Not the car of an old guy on a cane."

"A cop car?" Worthy said. After pausing, he added, "You know I don't believe in coincidences, so what do you make of all that, Hoops?"

"No proof yet, but red flags go off for me when I think Connie might have been an undercover DEA agent and then another cop, living in Cooper's house and using his name, could be the guy who followed Marina to the monastery. It begins to smell like there's something fishy about Sophia's conviction."

Nick could see the look in Worthy's eyes had brightened.

Sitting forward, Worthy said, "You might have figured out why the guy using Cooper's name came to St. Simeon's the same weekend as Marina. He's worried that Sophia might be remembering what really happened the night King was murdered, and she'd shared something embarrassing to the police with her sister. Marina didn't show up at just any monastery, Nick. She came to St. Simeon's, where a monk with a reputation for working with the police happens to reside."

"So, Chris," Henderson said, "if you were in our shoes, what would you do next?"

Worthy looked over at Jamie sitting with Sulla. "Jamie and I are alike. We both like puzzles. But anything I might suggest you've probably already thought of."

"You're too modest, my friend. What are you thinking?" Nick asked.

"Okay. My first suggestion is that you shouldn't share any of this with Sophia or Marina at this point. Granted, if you're right, it raises the odds that there's something problematic about Sophia's conviction. But given the forensic evidence, Sophia still looks guilty. My second suggestion is that someone needs to talk with Rebecca Williston. I hope you'll let me do that. Nick, I think having you come with me might be less intimidating than if I show up with you, Hoops."

Henderson nodded. "No, you're right, but are you sure you want to do this, given the appeal?"

"Look, you're both my friends, and I know you'd do anything to help with Tremont's appeal, but that case was long before I met either of you. Letting me help with your case is the best thing you could do for me. Tremont's appeal is shaping up to be a massive pit of quicksand intent on sucking me down. Helping you when and where I can on your case, well, it gives me some solid ground to stand on."

CHAPTER TWENTY-FOUR

The next morning, Saturday, Brother Pachomius was at his post in the monastery's security office. In the second hour of research the previous day, he'd done a quick review of the folders saved in Kerry Paulsen's computer. Some of the files, such as Paulsen's financial records, showed that he worked for the same company for twelve years and never earned more than thirty-eight thousand dollars a year. Pachomius remembered enough of his own expenses from the two years between college and coming to St. Simeon's to know that thirty-eight thousand wasn't much to live on.

Pachomius had looked to see if there were any expenses that showed Paulsen took vacations, but there were none. Instead, even on his meager salary, Paulsen saved twelve hundred dollars a year, his bank account showing a balance of eleven thousand dollars when he died. Saving money seemed to suggest to Pachomius that Paulsen had a future in mind. Yet something, Pachomius realized, had changed Paulsen's mind and led him to end his life.

In a second folder, Pachomius found photo after photo of train engines, suggesting that he'd stumbled onto Paulsen's hobby. But when he came upon selfies of Paulsen smiling with trains in the background, he had to stop. Until that moment, he'd felt buoyant, feeling privileged to help Father Nicholas on not one, but two cases. Now, with each of

Paulsen's photos, he realized that that he was looking at another human being, someone nearly his own age.

That morning, after a rough night of sleep, he wasn't paying much attention to the security office's computer screen when a car approached the monastery gate. It didn't surprise him, given that retreatants who were unable to arrive on Friday night would arrive early on Saturday morning. Consequently, he saw nothing unusual when the driver reached out to punch in the combination on the gate keypad. Then, for some reason, Pachomius zoomed in on the driver's face and felt his heart jump. Unless he was mistaken, the person driving into the monastery was Marina Demetrios.

LENA'S APARTMENT IN ROME

FROM WORTHY'S PHONE CALL, LENA REALIZED that the missing corrections page would likely determine Worthy's fate. Not being someone who could abide feeling helpless, she called her cousin, Maria, a pediatrician in Rome.

After explaining Worthy's predicament, she said, "Maria, I know you work with children, but I'm hoping you have experience with toxicology screenings."

"I wish I didn't know anything about them, but I've treated children as young at eight who've taken drugs. Sometimes, they gotten into their parents' drugs by mistake; other times, they experimented on a dare. What do you want to know?"

"I need to know when a screening is usually done."

"Lena, I've only ordered screenings in a hospital, and I do that as soon as I suspect a child has taken drugs, deliberately or accidentally. I can't speak for how toxicology screenings are done in police stations, especially in the US, but I assume they're also done as soon as possible."

"That's what I thought. Now tell me how a screening is done."

"It's quite straight forward. A pathologist takes a blood sample, enough to run through the tests to determine what drug has been taken, the dosage, and when the drug was likely ingested."

Lena thought back on what Worthy had told her about Tremont's appeal. "Okay, Maria, this is my biggest question. If a pathologist wrote down one date for a toxicology screening and then changed that date, what would you think?"

"In a hospital setting, there'd be no problem because I, being the one to order the screening, would have recorded the date of the screening in my records. But in terms of the police in the US, I don't know their procedures."

"From what Chris told me, he orders the screening as the arresting officer. The pathologist is the one who records when the screening takes place and the results. If there is a correction made, the pathologist is required to list that on a corrections page. But here's Chris' problem. That page is missing."

"What about the pathologist who administered the screening?"

"He's dead."

"*Dio mio.* I'm so sorry, Lena. Did the screening show that the man had drugs in his system or not?"

"The screening showed no sign of drugs. But the man's lawyers are now claiming that he was high on Ecstasy and didn't know what he was saying. That's why the change of date on the form is so important. The lawyers will claim that the screening was administered a day later when the Ecstasy was out of his system. Because that pathologist is dead, Chris is pretty sure that they'll go for him."

Lena heard Maria gasp. "They'll say Chris forced the pathologist to change the date?"

"Chris hasn't said that, but I'm sure that's what he's thinking."

"Lena, I so wish I could help."

"I feel the same way. That's why I called. He has friends with him, but no one who was with him thirteen years ago when he arrested the man."

There was silence on the other end of the line. "Something you just said, Lena, about him being alone. This might mean nothing, but a pathologist in Italy rarely works alone. She'd have an assistant, maybe a student, under her, and there could be others in the lab at the same time. As I said, I don't know how things work in the States, but Chris should find out if the pathologist on the case had an assistant."

ST. SIMEON'S

BROTHER PACHOMIUS SAT IN THE SECURITY OFFICE drumming his fingers on the desk as he waited for Father Nick to return his email. He'd told Nick that Marina Demetrios had arrived for a weekend retreat and asked if Nick wanted him to communicate with her. He hoped that Nick would ask him to serve as an intermediary, which would mean the abbot's two-hour-a-day limit to help Nick would likely be relaxed.

He'd heard nothing by the noontime prayer service and had stolen glances from the chanter stand to confirm that the woman he'd spotted was Marina Demetrios. The service was nearly half over before he saw her enter the church and kneel in prayer.

What a weight she must be carrying, Pachomius thought, as he dedicated his prayers to her and her family. That didn't stop him from hoping he'd be able to lighten Marina's burdens.

Reflecting on what he done for Father Nick, he could see that he'd devoted more time to Kerry Paulsen than Sophia Demetrios. The only significant success he'd had on Sophia's case was finding the Detroit address of Gus Cooper, the man who'd tailed Marina Demetrios to St. Simeon's two weeks before. He'd had less to show for his searches for Francine Nichols and someone named Connie.

The computer beeped, and Pachomius opened the email from Father Nick. "Be on the lookout for anyone who might have followed Marina to St. Simeon's before. That person could be the man who tailed her last time or it could be the woman going by the name of Connie. Brother Pachomius, please remember that Marina is at St. Simeon's to pray. DO NOT DISTURB HER. I'll contact her Sunday night, once she's back in Detroit. You can do the most good by remembering that you are a monk. Pray for Marina and Sophia, and please also pray for Christopher Worthy, Carnell Henderson, and me."

That was hardly the response that Brother Pachomius had hoped for. It wasn't that he felt used. In fact, he felt unused, but he knew that Father Nick would disagree. The clearest definition of a monk is someone who prays and who is obedient.

The question that Pachomius couldn't answer was "Is prayer enough for me?" It was that question that led him to be standing outside the guesthouse after Compline, the last service of the evening. In the end, he'd decided that he, as the one person at St. Simeon's who knew the burden Marina was carrying, could console her.

He took it as a good sign that the other retreatants, three women and an older man, walked from the church across the courtyard ahead of Marina. A few minutes later, Marina could be seen leaving the church with her head down and her arms crossed.

As Brother Pachomius stepped from the shadows, he said, "My name is Brother Pachomius, and I'm helping Father Nicholas with your sister's case."

Marina stepped back. "What? Has something happened to Father Nick?"

"No, he's in Detroit, but he asked me to keep an eye on you." Even as he said it, Brother Pachomius felt a pang of guilt at the lie.

"But I didn't tell him I was coming."

"I know, but I work at the security gate, and I saw you drive in this morning. I emailed Father Nick, and he told me to keep an eye on you." Repeating the lie came easier this time. "And, I have a message to you from Father Nick. He's going to phone you tomorrow night."

Marina looked confused. "Why?"

Beyond making contact with Marina, Brother Pachomius hadn't thought about what he would say. Now it seemed impossible to stop the words from pouring out of him. "He thinks there's someone following you, someone who goes by the name of Gus Cooper."

"Gus Cooper? I don't know any Gus Cooper."

"He was here on retreat the same time you were here before. And he lied about who he was. We think he's following you," he repeated.

"But why—Oh God, you think he's following me because of Sophia?"

"We're not sure, but Father Nick thinks so."

Despite the warmth of the evening, Marina shivered. "I can't take all this in. I really can't. I'm sorry, Father, but I didn't know he'd asked anyone else to help me."

"Well, I'm not a Father. I'm a novice . . . just a Brother. And I'm helping Father Nicholas mostly on the computer." *And by lying*, he thought.

"Is there anything else Father Nick wants me to know?"

"No, I don't think so, other than to be careful."

"Okay." As she opened the door to the guesthouse, she said, "I guess I should say thank you, Brother."

As Brother Pachomius turned to walk to the dormitory, he regretted everything that had happened in the last two minutes. What he'd done wasn't for Marina Demetrios and certainly not for Father Nicholas, but for himself. He'd not only wanted to feel important but also be seen by Marina to be important. Instead, he'd accomplished nothing other than jeopardizing his relationship with Father Nick. When Marina talked with Father Nick Sunday night, she'd surely tell him about their meeting. Pachomius could imagine Father Nick's disappointment, and he knew that Father Nick would understand that he could no longer trust him.

Castigating himself further with every step, he heard nothing behind him until a hand clamped down on his shoulder. He had the bizarre feeling that the hand was Father Nick's or his guardian angel's, but then the hand swung him around and he looked at a figure in a hooded sweatshirt. He couldn't see the features clearly in the darkness, but was certain it was the face of someone who wasn't supposed to be at St. Simeon's.

CHAPTER TWENTY-FIVE

WORTHY WONDERED IF THERE WAS ANYTHING WORSE than telling someone you love that her offer to help wasn't a solution at all. That was what he'd done to Lena when she woke him at six on Sunday morning, her voice excited, as she shared her cousin Maria's thought that Doctor Wallace probably had an assistant working with him.

The momentary flush of adrenalin, brought on by Lena's excitement, faded quickly as he remembered that Dr. Wallace was old-school and stubborn. He worked alone. Wallace had been forced by state law to have someone assist on post-mortems, but not on toxicology screenings.

As he heard Lena moan when he shared the bad news, he felt anger at Wallace—anger that he died, anger that he might have neglected to report the correction in the case file, and, in the end, anger that Wallace had been so much like him— a lone wolf.

By the end of the phone call, he could hear Lena sniffling, and that made him feel worse than he'd felt sitting in the courtroom. Not only could the appeal destroy his reputation and cast doubt on other cases that he'd worked alone, but he could see that the appeal could take down those closest to him—Lena, Nick, and Henderson.

Awake now with no hope of going back to sleep, he got out of bed and looked out at the rain. He could think of few lousier ways to begin the day.

ST. SIMEON'S

BROTHER PACHOMIUS HAD SLEPT POORLY, THE incident outside the guesthouse the night before waking him over and over again.

The man hadn't immediately said anything, and Pachomius would have tried to run away if the man hadn't still held him so tightly by the shoulder.

Finally, the man had spoken in a raspy voice. "Meeting women at night, huh? Is that something monks are allowed?"

Not knowing what would happen to him, Pachomius decided to play dumb.

"I have permission," he'd replied, telling yet another lie. His next thought had been that he wouldn't be facing the man in the dark if he'd obeyed Father Nick's order not to contact Marina Demetrios, but then he thought that if he'd obeyed, the man might have done something to Marina.

"If you're here on retreat, you should be in your room after Compline," Brother Pachomius had said, as if being stopped and grabbed by a retreatant was a regular occurrence.

The man grunted. "You know who I am."

Even though Pachomius knew it was a statement, not a question, he said, "How would I know that?"

"Because I heard you mention my name when you were talking with Mar—with that woman, and I want to know why."

Pachomius, known for thinking quickly under pressure, now found his mind blank. What he was sure of was that Gus Cooper hadn't driven through St. Simeon's gate. He pictured the man scaling the monastery's wall and taking one of the paths that Father Nick and he had found.

He felt the man's hand tighten on his shoulder but still said nothing.

"Son, I want answers. Are you working for Fortis? Is that why you met with the woman? Tell me what Fortis knows."

Pachomius' mind cleared enough for him to look at his watch. "At nine, the prior will be checking to see if I'm in my room. They'll start a search, and that means that they'll find you. We both know you have no business being here, and that means they'll call the police."

Instead of a worried look on the man's face, he saw a slight smile.

"You think— " the man began, then stopped. Letting go of Pachomius' shoulder, he muttered, "I'll find out what Fortis knows anyway."

With those words, the man had trotted in the direction of the lake and the paths leading into the woods.

Now, he wondered if his life or Marina's had ever really been in danger. The man could have done anything to him in the dark, and his body wouldn't have been found until morning. The man's goal hadn't been to harm him but to find out if Marina had spoken to Father Nick.

Brother Pachomius wondered who he should tell about the altercation. His first thought was to confide in the abbot, but he then realized that Abbot Lucas would ask what he'd been doing outside the guesthouse at that late hour. Before he could even tell them about the man he thought must be Gus Cooper, the abbot might think that Pachomius was the stalker. As he groggily rose from bed, he decided to talk with Marina again, to warn her of possible danger.

He had a hard time concentrating during morning prayers until he saw Marina enter the church late and kneel in the back. After the benediction, he hurried from the church and saw Marina nearing the parking lot. He quickened his steps, approaching Marina as she opened her car door.

Seeing her startled expression, he said, "Please, I need to talk to you. It's important."

"What is it? I need to get back to my father."

Trying to settle his breathing, he said, "After I talked with you last night, I was stopped by a man on my way back to my room."

"I don't understand. What man?"

"I'm sure it was Gus Cooper, the man I told you about."

"But I told you. I don't know any Gus Cooper."

"But he knows you."

If Marina hadn't been leaning against her car, he thought she might faint.

"Here, sit in your car," Pachomius said.

After she did, she said, "You said he was here on retreat the same time I was. And now you say he was here again?"

"But he wasn't here on retreat. He was on the grounds without permission."

"To spy on me," she said in little more than a whisper. "Are you going to tell the police?"

"I want to talk with Father Nick first."

"You think this Cooper has something to do with Sophia?"

"Father Nick thinks so."

Marina wiped tears away. "It makes no sense. Sophia is in prison for thirty years. Why would anyone be following me?"

"We're not sure. But until Father Nick figures it out, you need to be careful."

Marina looked straight ahead through her windscreen and said nothing for a moment. Finally, she looked up at him. "What does he look like?"

"It was dark and he was wearing a hoodie, so I didn't get a good look at him. We don't even know if Gus Cooper is his real name. I'll email Father Nick and let him know everything that happened last night. And remember, he plans to call you tonight."

Marina nodded slowly, then started her car. She gave Brother Pachomius one more glance as she said, "Please pray for me and my sister."

Pachomius nodded. "I already am."

CHAPTER TWENTY-SIX

N ICK HAD TO DECIDE WHAT TO DO ABOUT PACHOMIUS' email informing him that he'd been stopped by the man he was sure was Gus Cooper. The email was vague, not only about the circumstances of the encounter but also about what the man looked like. He had a suspicion that Pachomius had disobeyed his instructions and had met with Marina, but he would deal with that later. The most that Pachomius could say was that the man was tall and, based on his grip on Pachomius' shoulder, muscular. Nick toyed with the idea of going with Henderson back to Gus Cooper's address to see if the person who drove the Ford Interceptor would show himself.

In the end, he decided to accompany Worthy to court, wanting to support his friend but also wanting to be present when Tremont took the stand.

Nick knew he'd made the right choice when, sitting next to Worthy before procedures started, Worthy turned to him and whispered, "Feel free to pray, Nick." As recently as two years ago, Nick would have been surprised by the request. When Worthy and Nick first met and began working together, Worthy had made it clear that his faith had left him at the same time his wife demanded a divorce and then only three months later his older daughter, Allyson, ran away. That unexpected collapse of Worthy's family began the same day Worthy had made headlines for arresting Tremont for Renee Vickers' murder.

Out of the corner of his eye, Nick noticed the stoic look on Worthy—his friend glanced neither to the right nor the left—as spectators began filling the seats around them. The first face that Nick recognized was Kenna McCarty's. Of the newspaper clippings that Kerry Paulsen had saved about Tremont or Worthy, McCarty had written quite a few. And he remembered that her most recent article about the appeal revealed her glee that Worthy was getting his comeuppance.

Sitting behind McCarty was a second person he recognized, though he had to study the face before he was certain that he was looking at Phillip Sherrod. Nick hadn't seen Sherrod for ten years, but the changes to the man's face seemed to be caused by something more than aging. Sherrod's face had a pallor that Nick associated with cancer. Sherrod had already testified in the appeal, and yet here he was in court again. *Christopher is like Daniel in the lion's den,* Nick realized.

There was a nervous twittering in the courtroom as a side door opened, and Tremont was escorted to where his lawyers were seated. Nick had seen his photo in the newspaper clippings, but those were from thirteen years before. In a suit and tie and wearing black horned-rimmed glasses, Tremont looked like an accountant. He was thin and pale, but he seemed to lack self-consciousness despite everyone looking at him. He was the picture of calmness as he took a moment while standing to unbutton his suitcoat and straighten his tie before sitting down and whispering something to the lawyer next to him.

In working with Worthy in the past, Nick had taken a stance toward killers that, he hoped and prayed, squared with his calling as both a monk and a priest. While he knew that evil was real, he also knew that no one grew up with the intention of committing a murder. The journey of almost every killer whom he'd met had begun with a poor choice, often under desperate circumstances, a choice that led to other choices which, in turn, led to the person committing the apex of crime—murder.

Nick wanted to see Tremont in that light, even though Worthy had described the young Tremont as a psychopath who'd enjoyed killing, then fooling the police. The person taking the witness stand was now a grown man with an odd smile on his face, as if he knew a secret.

"Does he always look like that?" Nick whispered to Worthy.

"That smile? He was like that thirteen years ago, even on the day he was sentenced."

"It's his mask, then."

Worthy shrugged. "Perhaps, but if it is, I don't want to see who's behind it."

Their interchange was interrupted by Janine Reeves, one of Tremont's lawyers. "Mr. Tremont, this is your chance to tell your side of what happened thirteen years ago. Let me start by asking what you were most proud about before your arrest for Renee Vickers' murder."

Tremont looked calm as he glanced around the courtroom. "I'm the youngest person to become an Eagle Scout in the history of central Michigan."

"And can you remind us of the oath you took as a Boy Scout?"

"Of course, I say it to myself every day. 'On my honor, I will to do my best to do my duty to God and my country and to obey the scout law; to help other people at all times; to keep myself physically strong; to be mentally awake and morally straight.'"

"You say this daily despite being incarcerated?"

Tremont nodded. "A person has to have a code to live by. This has been my code since I joined the scouts when I was eleven."

"But it can't be easy to keep yourself mentally awake and morally straight in prison."

Tremont's smile left him, replaced by a frown. "A lot of inmates give up, but I've reorganized the library and designed a reading program that helps fellow inmates understand their legal rights."

"And how many years are left in your sentence?"

"Twenty-seven years, four months, and twelve days, unless I am paroled for good behavior. My parole is possible in nine years."

"Twenty-seven years is a long time."

"Even a week is a long time, given that I am innocent."

Nick felt Worthy stiffen in his chair, as Reeves paused, letting Tremont's claim echo in the courtroom.

"You have always maintained your innocence, isn't that right, Mr. Tremont?"

"Always. I wonder if all of you who sit in this room can imagine how humiliating it is to be here, being labelled a murderer and having to defend my innocence."

The murmurs that Nick heard around him suggested that Tremont had achieved his purpose, to shift from answering Reeves' questions to speaking directly to the gallery.

"I'm asking you to think back on your arrest thirteen years ago by Lieutenant Christopher Worthy. As we all know, Lieutenant Worthy was a highly respected homicide detective, perhaps the most well-known police officer in Detroit. You do realize, Mr. Tremont, that your claim of innocence is a direct attack on Mr. Worthy's reputation."

Tremont pointed at Worthy and when he did so, Nick noticed the other spectators looking at Worthy as well. "The two people in this room who know that I'm innocent are me and Mr. Worthy."

"But you confessed, Mr. Tremont. The videotape of your interrogation with Lieutenant Worthy shows not only that you confessed to killing Renee Vickers, but that you also seemed proud of it."

"The truth is that I don't remember being interrogated at all. I was high on Ecstasy, completely out of it. A person isn't normally proud of killing someone, and my oath, my code, was to help people at all times. I would never, never have even thought of killing another human being."

"You have no memory of being questioned by Lieutenant Worthy?"

"The first time I remember meeting Lieutenant Worthy was the next day, when he played the videotape."

"What was your reaction? Did you state your innocence at that time?"

"I was in shock. I had what scientists call an out-of-body experience. It was like I was looking down on a stranger, someone who'd just been told that he'd killed somebody."

"So, you don't remember saying anything at that time?"

"It's clear from the videotape of that second day that I said nothing. Shock, pure shock. My mind froze, and I kept waiting for someone to tell me that this was a joke or a mistake by the police—by Lieutenant Worthy."

Reeves turned to the judges. "I remind the court that Mr. Tremont never repeated his confession after the first interrogation when he was under the influence of a mind-altering drug."

Hullinger rose. "Objection, your honors. The record should not state that Mr. Tremont was under the influence of any drug during his initial interview. Instead, the record should state that Mr. Tremont claims that to be the case."

"Objection sustained," the head judge said. "Be more careful, Ms. Reeves."

"My apologies, your honors." Turning back to Tremont, she said, "A toxicology screening is standard procedure when someone is arrested. You stated a moment ago that you don't remember your first interrogation by Lieutenant Worthy when you confessed to killing Renee Vickers. Isn't it possible that the screening was done that first night and you were too much under the influence of the drug to remember?"

Tremont shook his head. "No. You see, I remember having blood drawn but it was on the second day. Until a few months ago, I was under the erroneous impression that a screening of my blood was administered on both that first day and the second."

"What changed you mind?"

"That was when I was informed that there is a discrepancy in the police records of my case. There was only one blood draw, and it looks like that test was done the second day. But then someone crossed that date out and wrote in the previous date, November first."

"Where did this information, this startling information, come from?"

"It came from Kerry Paulsen."

"Will you please tell the court who Kerry Paulsen is, or was?"

Tremont paused, letting the silence fill the room. "Kerry Paulsen was, I'm quite sure, the person who killed Renee Vickers."

OUTSIDE GUS COOPER'S HOUSE

HENDERSON SAT FARTHER DOWN THE STREET from Gus Cooper's home to be less conspicuous. He had a camera with telephoto lens, a thermos of coffee, and his computer. He'd toyed with the idea of sneaking down the back alley to photograph the Ford Interceptor's license plate but decided that was too risky. Henderson knew that Gus Cooper might be elderly, but that didn't prevent him from keeping an eye on his property. Furthermore, if their theory was correct, the Ford would be registered to the city's police department, not to an individual.

Henderson thought about Nick sitting with Worthy as Tremont took the stand. From what Worthy had told him, Tremont's version of what happened thirteen years before would be a command performance, mixing lies and sowing doubts. Henderson wondered how calm he would be in Worthy's shoes, especially as he knew that if Worthy showed a reaction to what Tremont was saying, that could work against him. *Thank God it's not a jury trial,* he thought. *The judges will know that Tremont has nothing to lose by twisting the truth.*

His thoughts were interrupted by Gus Cooper, with the aid of a walker, walking slowly down his front steps to get into his van. It took the elderly man a few minutes to balance himself, open the driver's side door, and pull himself into the vehicle.

Henderson waited, ready to slide down into his seat should Cooper drive in his direction, but after backing out, Cooper headed off in the other direction. Henderson weighed his options and rejected his first instinct, that being to knock on Cooper's door in hopes of confronting the man he was certain was a cop.

Patience, Hoops, he told himself. Patience was a trait he'd never been accused of, but he'd learned its value on stakeouts. Twenty minutes of nothing happening this time was followed by what he'd been waiting for. The Ford Interceptor pulled out of the driveway and drove directly at him. He leaned down in the seat, even as he prepared for what he'd do next. After a count to five, he sat up, started the car, and completed a U-turn, even as he saw the Ford Interceptor already two blocks ahead of him.

That the car was going above the speed limit didn't surprise him. All cops knew that they'd never be charged with speeding unless alcohol was involved, but Henderson also knew, despite his need to keep the Ford in sight, that the same wouldn't be true for him.

Henderson also knew that while he suspected this man was law enforcement, he couldn't be sure. There were police stations all over the city, and, in addition, the driver could be heading for a grocery store, pharmacy, or gas station.

Once the Ford took the on-ramp to the freeway, Henderson breathed more easily. Morning traffic would prevent the Ford from speeding, making it easier to follow without being obvious.

Finally, at the second of the downtown exits, the Ford exited with Henderson three cars behind. Knowing inner city Detroit well,

Henderson felt a jolt of adrenalin when he realized the car was headed in the direction of DEA headquarters.

When the Ford Interceptor pulled into the DEA parking lot, Henderson took a chance. He pulled in and stopped illegally in a fire lane close to the building's entrance. He readied the camera and angled the rear-view mirror so he could see whoever was entering the building. It would be tricky, shooting photos in in the rear-view mirror, but it was something he'd done before.

His plan was almost thwarted by a group of men and women exiting the building and stopping to talk in front of the entrance, but just before a man entered the frame from the direction of the parking lot, the group dispersed. He took one photo after another of the man as a security guard approached his car.

"You better have a good reason to be blocking the fire lane, buddy," the guard said.

Henderson pulled out his old police ID and flashed it quickly, hoping the guard wouldn't see that it had expired. "Just leaving. Have a nice day."

Henderson pulled around the block and parked in front of a used car lot. He opened his camera and studied the man in the photos he'd taken. The man, Caucasian, was on the tall side, though not as tall as Henderson, was well-built, and moved quickly. He was relieved that in none of the photos the man was looking in his direction.

He opened his computer, loaded the photos, and sent them in a message to Nick. "I think this is our guy. See if these photos match the man your friend at St. Simeon's met last night at the monastery."

He smiled as he thought, *Connie, or whatever your name is, you're next.*

CHAPTER TWENTY-SEVEN

----◆----

DEA HEADQUARTERS

INSIDE THE BUILDING, SAMIYAH WAS USING a protected search engine to access the arrest record of Eldridge Loften, aka Lofty, one of Reggie King's lieutenants. Loften's mug shots showed a heavy-set African-American sporting a vintage-style afro. His deadpan expression suggested that he'd been processed before, which Samiyah confirmed by reading his rap sheet—Loften had been in and out of jail since being a teenager, once for assault and later for possession with intent to distribute. Now twenty-six, Loften had achieved what was considered middle-age for drug dealers. If Lofty made it to thirty, he'd be considered an elder.

She thought it likely that Loften, being part of Reggie King's inner circle, knew the identity of the dirty agent. But that was the kind of information that Loften would guard with his life—if he valued his life.

The one advantage Samiyah had was that King's death would have shaken matters up in Loften's and the dirty agent's world. The rival Mexican cartels that were moving into the city would view the death of King as an opportunity to gain territory. That would mean that Loften's and the dirty agent's attention would be turned outward, looking for signs that a drug war was imminent. Samiyah's one chance would be to take advantage of Loften's preoccupation and trick him into revealing the identity of the dirty agent.

As soon as Samiyah put her plan together, she realized that once again Francine Nichols would play a key role. Samiyah had managed to convince Francine Nichols' parole officer to agree to rehab instead of jail. For four more weeks, Francine would be staying in Northwest Ohio for a course of treatment. Samiyah's plan was for Francine to contact Eldridge Loften and tell him that Samiyah was her replacement until she was released. From that point on, it would up to Samiyah to get Loften to reveal whom he reported to.

The risks of the plan were obvious to her. She would be working two jobs, and that meant she'd have to find some help for her father. That could be managed, but the trickiest part of being Francine's replacement was the expectation that she'd funnel drugs to Francine's customers. This was not just a moral dilemma for Samiyah. She could do what she could to steer Francine's customers to other street dealers, but if she provided drugs to even one of Francine's regular customers and were caught, she risked arrest and jail time. She'd have no support from the DEA, as she couldn't risk anyone in the agency knowing her plan. She had no idea how much of the day-to-day operations of the agency was known to the dirty agent.

Not for the first time, Samiyah realized how much simpler her life would be if she'd followed Fithian's order and forgotten about the dirty agent. She could convince herself that, with King's death and her being reassigned to more routine assignments, uncovering the culprit was no longer her responsibility.

To walk away, though, would let a traitor to the agency carry on with his lucrative game, leading people to commit crimes and die from overdoses. But Samiyah had a darker reason for continuing the search, a wound she'd inflicted and yet one she carried. For herself and others, she had no choice but to risk everything to find the dirty agent.

✝

APPELLATE COURT

WHEN TREMONT ACCUSED KERRY PAULSEN of the murder of Renee Vickers, Worthy suspected that he was the least surprised person in the room. It made sense for Tremont to take advantage of Paulsen's suicide.

Janine Reeves waited for one of the judges to silence the gallery before continuing. "Before we talk further about Mr. Paulsen, let's return to your interrogation by Lieutenant Worthy. I'm sure you've reviewed the transcripts of the nine interrogations that Lieutenant Worthy had with you."

"Of course. There's little in prison to interest someone with an active mind, especially if that person knows he's innocent. I'm sure I know the details of those interrogations better than Mr. Worthy." Again, Worthy sat stoically with eyes forward even as he could feel the eyes of those in the gallery centered on him.

"In those nine meetings with Lieutenant Worthy, who else was present?"

"There didn't seem to be any one particular police officer. I think I remember three or four others who sat next to him and took notes."

"Did they contribute anything besides taking notes?"

Tremont smiled. "I just remember how bored they looked. If one of them asked me a question or made a comment, I don't remember. It all seemed a one-man show, all Lieutenant Worthy."

"What was your impression of Lieutenant Worthy?"

"Oh, I had a lot of impressions."

"Such as?"

"He was methodical. Each interrogation had a different focus, like he was following some script. One session was about my van; another centered on the truck stop outside Midland; another time he wanted me to say how many times I had sex with Renee Vickers. Then it got weirder."

"How do you mean?"

"There was one time, it must have lasted two hours, he wanted me to describe my time in scouting. Why I'd joined, how long it took me to earn Eagle Scout rank, how I got along with the other boys. Another time, he wanted to know if I had good relations with my mother and sister. But what really topped things off was the time he'd tracked down my biological father. He wanted to know what I'd say to my father if he let him meet me."

Worthy understood that Tremont was blending accurate memories with sheer fantasy. He had quizzed Tremont on his scouting experience, but he never thought of tracking down Tremont's father. What he did remember asking Tremont was about his feelings concerning his absent father, but Tremont's invention at that point was clever, making him, not Tremont, look at fault.

"Did you think that Lieutenant Worthy was obsessed with you?"

"You'd have to ask him, but I know he was obsessed with my being found guilty. I had the feeling that Renee Vickers was his first big case."

"Would you go so far as to say it was 'win at all costs' for Lieutenant Worthy?"

Hullinger rose. "Counsel is leading the witness, your honor, putting words in his mouth."

"Overruled. The witness can deny or amend the suggestion."

"Thank you, your honor," Reeves said. "I'll repeat the question. Did it seem that Renee Vickers' murder was a case that Lieutenant Worthy had to win at all costs?"

Tremont offered another smile as he glanced around the room. "Isn't that why we're here—because he had to win regardless of my rights and my innocence?"

"Now, Mr. Tremont, let's address the issue of Mr. Kerry Paulsen. It's clear from your first trial that Paulsen and you were friends. In fact, you both had sex with Renee Vickers, isn't that right?"

Looking down for a moment, Tremont nodded. "It's not something that I'm proud of. In fact, I have a hard time understanding how I got talked into doing that."

"'Got talked into doing that.' What do you mean?"

Tremont looked up at the ceiling. "It was a moment of weakness— several moments, actually, ones that I've gone over and over in my mind. I keep asking myself, 'Why didn't I just say no?'"

"Say no to whom?"

"Oh, sorry. To Kerry Paulsen. I met Kerry years before in scouting, and, as you said, we became friends. It didn't take me long to realize that Kerry wasn't the person others thought he was."

"In what way, Mr. Tremont?"

"Kerry came across as shy, but when it was just the two of us, he had . . . he had ideas. And he was devious."

"What kind of ideas?"

"Kerry thought Midland was boring. He said nothing ever happened there, and then he'd describe things he'd like us to do, things that would be exciting."

"Can you give us an example?"

"Sure. One time, we were hiking in a forest preserve. We'd been there before with the scout troop, but this time it was just the two of us. All of a sudden, he stopped by this dead tree and said it would be cool to set it on fire. It was just so crazy, and that's what I told him. I mean, we were in scouting, and here he wanted to do something that scouts would never do."

"But Kerry Paulsen wasn't very successful in scouting, was he, Mr. Tremont?"

"No. At first, I thought that was because he wasn't committed. I tried to encourage him, set an example, but then, when he lit the tree on fire—"

"So, he actually lit the tree on fire?"

"Yes, but thankfully there'd been a lot of rain, so all it did was smolder. That's when I should have stopped seeing him, but he kept coming around."

"Would you say he was attracted to danger?"

"Undoubtedly. He told me there'd been a cat in his neighborhood that pooped on his folk's lawn. He said he'd caught it and drowned it in a pond, then buried it. When the lady who owned the cat asked if he'd seen it, he said he'd seen some Black kids teasing it."

"Some Black kids. Did Kerry Paulsen have a problem with Blacks?"

Tremont shrugged. "I don't know if he had a problem with them, but he'd make jokes about them sometimes."

"What kind of jokes?"

"About sex, mostly, how they liked a lot of sex."

Worthy pictured Tremont lying in his cell at night and constructing this fiction about Kerry Paulsen by projecting his own traits onto Paulsen. If there were a search for the tree in the forest preserve that had been burned, Worthy thought it would be found—but it was Tremont, not Paulsen, who Worthy knew set it afire. It would have been Tremont, not the timid Paulsen, who'd drowned the neighbor's cat. The racist remarks about Blacks that Tremont's lawyers would now, Worthy was convinced, parlay into accusing Paulsen of killing Renee Vickers, a Black teenager turned prostitute, but those remarks had come from Tremont, not Paulsen.

After Janine Reeves sat down, Howard Hullinger rose to begin his cross-examination. Hullinger looked at Paulsen for a moment before saying, "Mr. Tremont, how would you rate your I.Q.?"

Worthy realized that Hullinger had accepted his warning, that Tremont would have anticipated how Hullinger, as the police department's head lawyer, would attack him. He was glad to see that Hullinger had taken Tremont off-guard.

"My I.Q.? I'm sure I don't know."

"Then let me refresh your memory. From school records, based on the tests you took at the beginning of your senior year, your intelligence quota, your I.Q., is 145. The median is 100, by the way. Assuming all of us present in this courtroom averaged our I.Q. scores together, we'd probably be in the 100 to 110 range, if that. Does that make life difficult for you?"

"Difficult? How do you mean?"

"Being top of the class, at least on test scores. Top of the Boy Scouts, earning Eagle Scout rank at an earlier age than anyone else in your county. Can you remember another student your age who scored higher than you on tests?"

"Do I remember anyone? No, but there might have been."

"Were you competing against anyone in earning badges is scouting, or were you pretty much competing against yourself?"

"It's not a crime to be smart," Tremont said.

"Of course not. I'm just thinking it might be lonely to be so bright. By the way, would you like to guess Kerry Paulsen's I.Q.?"

"I'm sure I don't have the expertise to do that."

"If the median is 100 and your I.Q. is 145, where would you place Kerry Paulsen? I'm just asking you to guess, and, as you said, it's no crime for you to be so smart."

Worthy understood that Hullinger was playing on what he'd said, that Tremont would want to convince the courtroom that he was the smartest person there, but Tremont would have preferred to leave that as a subtle impression. Hullinger was making him explicitly state it.

"I'd say Kerry was 100."

"Good guess. I have Kerry Paulsen's I.Q. based on his score from his senior year of high school. It was 89. That's quite a gap, 145 to 89. Now, let's think about Lieutenant Worthy. You stated that he met with you nine times. You also stated that he seemed to be following a script, one topic for every interview or interrogation and that the only police officer in the room looked bored at times. Do you remember saying that?"

"Of course, I do. I said it just fifteen minutes ago."

"Very true, and very accurate, by the way." Hullinger looked at his wristwatch. "It was, in fact, fifteen minutes, almost to the second."

"What would be your estimate of Lieutenant Worthy's I.Q. based on those nine meetings? Just an estimate."

"I don't know. We didn't talk about intellectual matters," Tremont said with a slight smirk.

"Did he bore you at times?"

"He was accusing me of murder. Of course, I wasn't bored."

"Exasperated, then?"

"How do you mean?"

"For example, did he ask you the same questions over and over again?"

Tremont paused before saying, "Yes, but I think that's pretty much standard procedure for the police, isn't it?"

Hullinger gave a short laugh. "I would agree, Mr. Tremont. I deal with the police all the time, and you're absolutely right. They do tend to repeat themselves. Why do you think they do that?"

"I assume they hope that someone in my position will contradict himself and thereby incriminate himself."

"Ah. I'm a lawyer, and I couldn't have put it better than what you said. Lieutenant Worthy hoped that you would contradict yourself and thereby incriminate yourself. Did that happen in your nine meetings with Lieutenant Worthy?"

"No."

"So you saw through it," Hullinger said. "After that initial interrogation when we have you on videotape confessing to Renee Vickers' murder, you never again admitted guilt. Isn't that a fact?"

"Yes, it's a fact, because—"

"A 'yes' is sufficient. Now, let's talk about Kerry Paulsen. How often did Mr. Paulsen visit you in prison?"

"I don't remember exactly, but I'm sure you have the prison records."

"I do. On average, he came once a week for the past thirteen years. And in that time, did he confess to killing Renee Vickers?"

As Tremont paused, Worthy could guess what he was thinking. Prison officials were prohibited from audiotaping conferences between inmates and lawyers, but not between inmates and visitors if their suspicions were aroused. Tremont couldn't be sure that Paulsen's visits weren't on record somewhere.

"No explicitly, no. But why else did he come so often? He felt guilty for killing her."

"Renee Vickers, you mean."

"Yes, Renee Vickers."

"But in our research into Kerry Paulsen, we found that he stayed in a low-paying job, had no real friends at work, and, according to neighbors in adjoining apartments, never had people coming to see him. In fact, the only friend he seemed to have in his life was you. Now, you described him as devious? But don't we normally think of devious people as being clever?"

Tremont's face seemed to brighten. "Maybe highly devious people are secretly clever."

"Ah, that helps, Mr. Tremont. I bow to your insight. Perhaps it would take someone with an I.Q. of 145 to spot something like that. And, of course, in addition to Mr. Paulsen visiting you, the two of you also communicated by email. Now, I'm sure you know that prison officials can do what's called 'spot monitoring' of both email exchanges and visits. Do you think that they missed some clever hints that Mr. Paulsen conveyed in his emails and visits that would point to his being Renee Vickers' killer?"

"I didn't say that he left clues. I just said—"

"I can repeat what you said exactly. You said, 'but why else did he come so often?'"

Over the last five minutes, Worthy had noticed red streaks rising from Tremont's collar to his ears.

"You're ignoring the fact that he killed himself. Certainly, that's means something."

"Of course it does, Mr. Tremont, but what does it mean? He didn't commit suicide after Renee Vickers' death. He didn't commit suicide after you were found guilty. He didn't commit suicide after a year, or five years, or ten years after Renee Vickers' suicide, but only a few months ago. And it was not long after he visited you."

Worthy was surprised that Reeves had let this back-and-forth continue uninterrupted, but she rose now.

"Counsel is suggesting that there is some correlation between Mr. Paulsen's death and his last visit to my client. If he has evidence of this, he should present it. If not, it's supposition that is detrimental to my client."

"Sustained," the judge ruled. "The linking of Mr. Paulsen's suicide with his last visit to Mr. Tremont will be struck from the record."

Hullinger nodded, then continued. "You describe Kerry Paulsen, a boy with an I.Q. of 89, who lagged behind you and almost everyone else in school and scouting, as devious and even clever. Now, records show that Mr. Paulsen was never before or not since been charged with any crime or misdemeanor. His work record shows nothing inappropriate. He didn't even have a parking ticket. Yet, it's your opinion that he was the one who killed Renee Vickers and fooled the police not just thirteen years ago but ever since."

Tremont looked down and shook his head for a moment before looking up at Hullinger. "Maybe you should consider that the police were just too dense to see Kerry Paulsen for who he was. Kerry Paulsen might not have been the smartest person in Midland—"

"No, that would be you," Hullinger interjected.

"Let me finish! Kerry didn't have to be the smartest person in the world, but he was smarter and cleverer than the police."

"Smarter than Lieutenant Worthy, then."

"Yes, dammit, smarter than Worthy."

CHAPTER TWENTY-EIGHT

———— ◆ ————

St. Simeon's

Feeling guilty for disobeying Father Nick's instruction to avoid contacting Marina Demetrios, Brother Pachomius had the energy of the repentant sinner as he began to look through Kerry Paulsen's computer files for anything there that might bear on William Tremont's appeal.

Immediately, however, he ran into a brick wall. To protect his files, Paulsen had assigned them nonsense names. The earliest saved file was labelled "Sunrise in the Upper Peninsula," but, when opening it, he discovered that it contained a collection of barbecue recipes. Another file which he thought might be related to the appeal, though dated months later, was under the heading "Favorite Summer Foods." Instead of that file being about food, it contained a list of his colleagues from Shummer's, the big lot store where he worked. Scrolling down, he spotted another file labeled "Fellow Slaves Revolt."

The hair on the back of Brother Pachomius' neck began to tingle by the end of his first hour of work, as he realized that the files weren't randomly named and organized. Instead, Paulsen had linked the files by a kind of clever sequencing, a way to fool someone who managed to access the files. The earliest file, "Sunrise in the Upper Peninsula," had led to "Favorite Summer Foods," which, in turn, with its list of work colleagues had led to the file, "Fellow Slaves Revolt." Opening that file, Pachomius found a list of Detroit's police stations.

Bingo, he thought, as he scrolled down through the list of other files, looking for one that would be connected in some way with Detroit police stations. He was right in thinking that "Cop" would be too obvious, but "Jail" and "Arrest" also failed to produce a result. Finally, remembering the slur "Pig" for the police, he spotted a file labeled "Bacon Gone Rancid." Opening the file, he was frustrated to find newspaper articles centered on various cities in Lower Michigan that had received environmental awards. He was about to close the file when he saw the name of one of the cities, "Midland."

Just as his watch beeped, letting him know his two-hour time limit was over, he sat back and took a deep breath. Midland was where Paulsen and Tremont had grown up.

"I'm onto you, Paulsen," he whispered to his computer screen. *Lord, forgive me and please help me,* he prayed as he looked for another file that might connect with "Midland," "environment," or "award." Fifteen fruitless minutes later, just as he was about to close his computer, his eye stopped on a file labelled "Middle-Earth." He knew that "Middle-Earth" might connect with Tolkien's fictional world, but he was also struck with the possibility that "Middle-Earth" could relate to "Midland."

He breathed a prayer of thanksgiving as he opened the file. But his excitement dissolved into disappointment when he realized what he was looking at. It was the public records of divorces granted in Wayne County, Detroit's county, from the month of January, 2011. Hundreds of names were listed in print so small that Pachomius could hardly read them. He despaired of finding anything that would take him to the next file.

But then, with a jolt, he spotted among all the names one that was familiar. "On January 12th, the marriage between Susan N. Worthy, nee Hart, and Christopher H. Worthy was dissolved in Wayne County Family and Divorce Court number seven."

✝

LIEUTENANT WILLISTON'S OFFICE

NICK TRIED TO DISCOURAGE WORTHY FROM driving with him from the courtroom to meet with Lieutenant Rebecca Williston, but Worthy insisted.

"Honestly, Nick, this has nothing to do with my putting on a brave face. I need to focus on something other than the appeal, and after Hullinger let Tremont expose himself as a narcissistic liar, I'm feeling better about my lawyers. Besides, if Sophia Demetrios is sitting in prison because her conviction was flawed, she deserves to be the priority."

Nick realized that his questions about Tremont's testimony would have to wait. Worthy was right. He needed something to take his mind off of the appeal, and Sophia's case was the kind of puzzle that offered Worthy that diversion.

As they entered the homicide division of Detroit, Nick followed Worthy to an elevator. Entering and pushing a number, Worthy said, "So far, so good."

"What do you mean?"

"I'm happy to meet with Williston, but I'm not anxious for the word to get around that I'm here."

"Are you thinking of Lieutenant Sherrod?"

"Phil? No, he's probably commiserating with Kenna McCarty after Tremont's comedown today. I'm thinking more about Captain Walker. If she finds out I'm here to talk with Williston about Sophia's case, she'll throw me out. Which is another way of saying I have to play it cool with Williston."

"You said before that you respect her. Does she know that?" Nick asked.

Worthy didn't answer for a moment. "I think you've just hit on my Achilles' heel, Nick, or at least one of them. I don't always let people know things like that."

"Maybe not in so many words, but I bet she knows."

The elevator door opened. "We'll see, won't we?"

After knocking on Williston's door and hearing her invitation to enter, Worthy looked in and said, "Do you have a few minutes, Rebecca?"

"Lieutenant—Mr. Worthy, sure, come in."

After Worthy introduced Nick and they took chairs facing Williston's desk, she said, "I want you to know that I hope the appeal is squashed. Everything I've read about Tremont suggests he's a psychopath."

"Thanks. This is my first rodeo in terms of appeals, so I'm finding that it's a bit like a bad déjà vu experience."

"I get that. And the case is from at least ten years ago?"

"Thirteen to be exact. But I brought Father Nicholas along because he's working with, or maybe I should say he's ministering to, the Demetrios family. Sophia Demetrios' family, that is."

"Ah, yes. If there was ever a case where I wanted the evidence to point in another direction, that was the case. But the poor girl didn't even put up a defense." Looking at Nick, she said, "Father Fortis, I've heard about you, And I'm actually glad that someone is working with the family. Dare I ask how they're holding up?"

Nick was relieved that Lieutenant Williston didn't seem defensive or on her guard. "They're crushed. First the mother died, and now Sophia is in prison. But please know, I'm not here to dispute how you handled the case. Christopher and I both agree that the evidence is pretty much all against Sophia. But there are some strange things that have cropped up since her sentencing that I'd like to ask you about."

"Ask away. But first I want to ask you a question. I assume you've talked with Sophia. Has she remembered anything more about the night King was killed?"

"Very little, I'm afraid. She has mentioned that there was another person who hung around Francine Nichols a lot. Someone who went by the name of Connie. Did she come up in your investigation?"

"Let me check," Williston said, moving to a filing cabinet. Pulling out a file, she returned to her desk and began looking through the file's papers. "I can't let you see this, but I'll let you know that it's a list of the people whom Francine Nichols gave us. It's the names of those she sold drugs to." After a moment, she looked up for the list. "There's no one named Connie on the list. And, I'm positive that Sophia never mentioned anyone by that name in our interviews. Did Sophia describe this person?"

"She's said she is Black, someone who only smoked weed, and who never ate pork. Perhaps she was Jewish or Muslim," Nick said.

"Wow, that's pretty specific, but like I said, there's no Connie mentioned in the file. What's your instinct, Mr. Worthy?"

"Please call me Chris, and I want you to know that I'm not looking into the Demetrios case at all. But Carnell Henderson has visited Sophia with Father Nick."

"Hoops? Doesn't he work for you?"

"He does, but, like I said, he's not looking into this for me. He's doing Father Nick a favor."

"Not to mention the Demetrios family. But let me ask my question another way. What's Hoops' instinct?"

"Father Nick and he are wondering if Connie could have been DEA undercover. Could she have infiltrated Francine Nichols' circle?"

Williston's eyebrows shot up. "That's some instinct. Does DEA always level with us? We both know the answer to that, Chris, but, honest to God, we never got a whiff of anyone from DEA being involved. Certainly not on the night King was killed. According to Nichols' testimony and the forensic evidence from the scene, it was just the three of them in the room: Nichols, Sophia, and King. And, as you know, Sophia never claimed that anyone else was there that night. So, if DEA had someone undercover earlier, looking into Francine Nichols selling drugs, we don't have any record of that. Of course, you could always ask DEA."

"I think we both know how they protect their undercover agents."

"You said Hoops has an instinct about this Connie being a DEA agent. It there anything more than that?"

"Maybe there is," Nick said. "Do you remember Marina Demetrios, Sophia's sister?"

"Yes, I remember her feeling guilty. She blamed herself for Sophia's problems after their mother died."

"I think that's another way of saying she is the closest in the family to Sophia since her mother died." Pausing, Nick added, "She came to see me at my monastery. I was happy to listen, but what we discovered afterwards is that a man followed her there. Marina came back to St. Simeon's just two days ago—I was in Detroit, so I didn't see her—but another monk ran into the same man again."

"Could he be a stalker?" Williston asked.

"He gave a false name in the guestbook, but Carnell Henderson was able to track him down. I won't go into the details of how he did that, but Henderson tailed him and confirmed that he too is DEA."

Williston frowned. "I understand your curiosity. Sophia has already been convicted and is in prison."

"That's the big question," Worthy said. "It might suggest—we just say 'might'—that someone in DEA is worried what Sophia is remembering about that night."

Williston looked down at her notes and shook her head. "It's bizarre, to say the least, but I'm not sure what I can do about it."

"I agree," Worthy said. "There's probably nothing you can do about it now. To be frank, we were hoping you'd tell us if you had doubts during the investigation if King's murder."

"Doubts about what?"

Nick looked at Worthy and nodded. "First about King," Worthy said. "Wouldn't a drug lord like King have brought a bodyguard with him? But mainly, it's the doubts about Sophia Demetrios. Her sister said there's never been a gun in the house, yet Sophia managed to take King's gun from his coat pocket and shot him like a professional. Two shots, one through the heart, the other to his head."

"I don't know why King was alone, but that's what the evidence and Nichols' testimony say. And Sophia never contradicted that. And on the gun? Forensics confirm what Nichols told us. It might have just been lucky shots."

Worthy nodded in agreement. "It was certainly bad luck for both King and Sophia, but was it bad luck for the DEA? And are they now worried that Sophia might remember what really happened that night?"

Williston's raised her hands as if to push the suggestion away. "Look, Chris, do you really want to go down that rabbit hole? You're as much as accusing DEA for what you're being accused of—a law enforcement cover-up."

Seeing Worthy wince, Nick sat forward. "Okay, let's take that possibility off the table for now. It's clear that you care about Sophia Demetrios and had no joy in convicting her."

"I don't deny that. I'd have preferred arresting Francine Nichols. But the evidence doesn't lie."

"We understand, but we're just trying to make sense of why Marina Demetrios is being followed by someone in the DEA," Nick said. "Maybe there's a legitimate reason, and perhaps that's something you, better than us, could look into."

No one said anything for a few moments. "I'll ask around, but as we both know, Chris, DEA lives in its own universe. I'll have to tread carefully, but I'll try. There are some cases you hope you were wrong about, and this is one of them."

CHAPTER TWENTY-NINE

◆

LENA'S AND WORTHY'S APARTMENT—ROME

LENA'S FIRST THOUGHT WAS TO IGNORE THE DOORBELL. She was working through a pile of student papers, trying to concentrate despite her worries about Worthy, but when she pushed the button and heard her cousin Maria's voice, she was glad for the distraction.

After the women embraced, Maria said, "I've brought a bottle of wine that I need help with. And I want to know what you've heard from Chris."

Lena brought two glasses into the living room and sat with her cousin on the sofa. "I need a break from my students' papers. We're only days until the semester is over, and you'd think that students would be trying to raise their grades. But I'm not exaggerating when I tell you that the pandemic might be over, but students haven't fully recovered."

"Let me guess," Maria said. "They're on their computers or phones, even in class."

"How'd you know?"

"I can't tell you the number of calls I get from parents. Because I'm a pediatrician, they want me to prescribe pills to help their kids concentrate. They can hardly get their kids to put down their phones for dinner."

Lena took a sip of the wine and shook her head. "It used to be that students waiting in the hallway before class would talk to one another. The sound was like insects buzzing, and I loved it. But now? The hallways are still filled with students, but it's as quiet as a morgue. They're all looking down at their phones as if the secret to life will pop up any moment."

Maria laughed. "We sound like grumpy old maids. Anyway, what do you hear from your dreamy husband?"

"Dreamy? Well, I see Chris that way. We haven't talked today, but I know he's going through a nightmare. And where am I? I'm stuck here grading these God-awful papers."

"I take it that my idea about the pathologist working with an assistant didn't help."

Lena sighed. "From what Chris tells me, this pathologist was old-school. He allowed an assistant when he conducted a post-mortem, but he did all the toxicology screenings on his own."

"And now the old-school guy is dead. And what was it you said about corrections?"

"According to Chris, the last page of every file should be the corrections page. But there's none in this case. So that page has either been misplaced, or it's been removed."

"How is he holding up?" Maria asked.

"It's clear to Nick that the case is taking him down. And today the man convicted of the killing had his say in court. I'm still waiting for Chris to call and fill me in, which makes my being four thousand miles away seem like I'm on Mars." Lena paused and shook her head.

"Nick is the monk who spoke at your wedding?"

Lena nodded. "Yes. Thank God, Nick has been going with Chris to the appeal, but I should be there."

"And there's nothing I can do, Lena?"

Lena wiped tears from her cheeks. "Until the semester ends, I don't see anything that I can do. And by the time I get to Detroit, the trial could be over. If the verdict goes against Chris . . . well, I dread thinking how it will affect him."

✝

October 24, 2023, New Life Rehabilitation Facility

Samiyah sat with Francine Nichols out on the tree-shaded grounds of the rehab center. The facility looked more like a college campus than a health-care facility, and Samiyah hoped Francine was making good use of the state's money to get clean for good this time. Francine certainly looked healthier, having gained weight and some color to her face. With Francine's chestnut hair washed and brushed instead of being stringy, Samiyah realized that she was attractive.

Samiyah had travelled to northwest Ohio to convince Francine to help her flush out the dirty agent. "I need you to call Loften and introduce me as your business partner, your replacement until you get out of here."

Francine stared at Samiyah, her eyebrows raised. "It sounds like you're assuming I'm going back to dealing."

"No, just pretend—one last time."

"One last time? Where have I heard that before?"

"Look around, Francine. This place is better than a four-star motel."

"Easy for you to say. You don't have to sit through group sessions when we all pretend that we've turned our backs on our past."

"Seriously, Francine, don't blow this chance. There won't be another one."

"And yet you want me to pretend I'm still in the game."

"All I'm asking for is one phone call."

Francine looked around the manicured grounds before replying. "What is it I have to say?"

"Begin by explaining why you haven't communicated. Tell him you're in rehab."

Francine laughed. "You don't think he already knows that?"

"Even if he does, start with that. Tell him that you'll be out in four or five weeks and will be back in business. Until them, you've turned decisions over to me. And give him this number to call."

Looking down at the slip of paper, Francine asked, "Are you still going by the name of Connie?"

"No, I'm using the name Savreen."

"What kind of name is that?"

"It's a Muslim name."

"Oh, yeah, I forgot, you're Muslim. A Muslim narc. Go figure."

"So, I can count on you to make the call?" Samiyah asked.

"You do realize that if this all goes south, whoever it is above Lofty will come after me too. So this is the last time I do anything for you, got that?"

Samiyah breathed deeply. "Right, the last time."

WORTHY'S APARTMENT IN DETROIT

AFTER RETURNING FROM THE COURTROOM WITH WORTHY the previous day, Nick called Marina and heard what he'd feared, that Brother Pachomius had disobeyed his order by contacting her when she was at St. Simeon's. Worse yet was Pachomius frightening her with the news that a man going by the name of Gus Cooper was following her.

After doing what he could to calm Marina, he knew, despite a headache coming on, that he had to confront Pachomius. "I'm not sure where to begin," he said when the novice answered his phone. "When you told me that Marina Demetrios had returned to St. Simeon's, I gave specific instructions for you to keep your distance from her. Do you have anything to say in your defense?"

"Father, if you'll give me the chance to tell you what I've found out, maybe you'll forgive me."

"So you admit that you disobeyed my instructions and needlessly frightened Marina."

Nick heard Pachomius groan. "I didn't mean that to happen."

"That's exactly what happened. Instead of my telling her that the man following her is likely in law enforcement and is no threat to her, she's now so terrified that she's afraid to leave her house."

Pachomius was silent before saying in a low voice, "I have no excuse, Father, and you'd be right if you didn't trust me anymore. But I beg you to let me finish what I've figured out about Kerry Paulsen's computer files. I think it's important to your friend Christopher Worthy." After pausing, he added, "When I've finished telling you what I've discovered, if you want to tell me that I can't help out any more, I'll accept that. But please let me finish."

After pausing a few moments, Nick said, "You've done everything you can to destroy my trust in you, so I intended to end our relationship, no matter what you've discovered. But . . . go ahead. Just know that this might be our last conversation."

"Fair enough, Father," he said, and Nick could hear the relief in the novice's voice. "To organize his computer files, Paulsen devised a code, a nonsense code, but it turns it's not actually nonsense. I mean, I've started to crack it."

"What kind of code?" Nick asked.

"It'd take too long to explain how it works, but the name he gave one file led to another, and that one to another, on and on until I opened a file that contained the public records listing of divorces for Wayne County, that's Detroit, back in January of 2011. I thought that Paulsen had sent me down a blind alley until I spotted two names—Susan and Christopher Worthy. Father Nick, he saved the notice of Mr. Worthy's divorce."

Nick thought for a moment, remembering Paulsen's marginal notes on the newspaper clippings. Most of those comments were crude and nasty ones about Worthy.

"Is that all, or is there more?" he asked.

"I'm sure there is. I wasn't surprised that the names 'Worthy' and 'Tremont' would be too obvious as file labels, so I tried 'Susan' and 'Decree.' Still no luck. But then I found a file labelled 'Suomynona.' That doesn't make sense, right? I opened the file, hoping it would leading me to something anyway, but Paulsen's message was 'Not so fast. You go no further on that bastard Worthy until you figure out suomynona.' So this was a game to Paulsen, and I have to solve what suomynona means before I can go on."

Nick felt his headache throb as he wondered if Paulsen were doing just that, luring Pachomius into a pointless game.

But Pachomius wasn't finished. "I first thought that suomynona could be an East-Asian word, but after running the word through Japanese, Chinese, Korean, and Pacific Island word lists, I got nothing. But I've prayed about it, and I'm sure it's important."

Nick could hear the conviction in Pachomius' voice, but was at a loss to know how to respond. Finally, he said, "Just stay on the line. I know someone who's good at puzzles."

Dialing Henderson's home phone, he heard Sulla's voice.

"Sulla, it's Father Nick. I have a favor to ask. Actually, it's a favor I need to ask Jamie. There's a puzzle that might contain something that could be helpful to Christopher's appeal, but a friend of mine at the monastery is stuck. I was hoping you might give me the phone number of Jamie's halfway house."

"I can do better than that, Nick. Jamie is here for my birthday. I'll get him."

Nick offered a silent prayer of thanks before Jamie said, "Yes?"

"Jamie, do you remember me, Father Nick?"

"You're Mr. Worthy's friend with the ponytail."

"That's right. We have a puzzle he can't solve, so I thought of you. Would you help us?"

"A puzzle? What kind of puzzle?"

"It a word we don't understand. Can I spell it for you?"

"Mom, would you hand me a piece of paper and a pencil?" After a moment, Jamie said, "I'm ready."

"Here are the letters, Jamie. S-u-o-m-y-n-o-n-a."

Nick heard Jamie repeat the letters and then there was silence.

After no more than two minutes, Jamie said. "It's the word 'anonymous' spelled backwards."

"Oh, my Lord, you're right, Jamie. Did you hear that, Pachomius?"

"I did. I never thought of reversing the letters. Jamie, you don't know me, but you opened a locked door for me."

"It wasn't hard," Jamie said in a soft voice.

"Well, it stumped me. At evening prayers tonight, I'm going to thank God for sending you our way."

"Okay. Bye."

Sulla came back on the line. "Nick, I can tell that Jamie was very happy to help. You gave him a gift."

"He's the gift, Sulla. And speaking of gifts, happy birthday to you. I hope we didn't interfere with a party."

"Not at all. You said this could help Chris?"

"That's my hope and prayer." After ending the call with Sulla, Nick said, "Pachomius, are you still on the line?"

"I am. So, Father, can I continue at least until I find out what else is in Paulsen's files?"

Nick realized that his headache had lessened. "Before I answer that, what about the photos that I sent you of the guy we think is going by Gus Cooper? Could this be the man who grabbed you the other night?"

"I can't say for certain, but it's possible. He was hooded, and it was dark. I have a better memory of his voice than what he looked like." After a pause, he added, "Father Nick, will you give me the chance to rebuild your trust in me?"

Nick smiled. "I wouldn't be a very good monk if I weren't ready to forgive. But you're right about the need to rebuild my trust. Pray that you can do that."

CHAPTER THIRTY

❖

ENZO'S ITALIAN RESTAURANT

THAT EVENING, HENDERSON, NICK, AND WORTHY SAT in a booth at Enzo's to review what had occurred that day. After Worthy summarized for Henderson how Tremont had hurt his own case in court, he asked again that they talk instead about Sophia Demetrios.

Henderson's confirmation that the man posing as Gus Cooper was DEA was just the beginning. Nick had received a phone call from Marina Demetrios as he was on his way to the restaurant. His first thought was that this was a follow-up to their talk earlier that afternoon, but Marina's frantic tone convinced him otherwise. She had just learned that Sophia had been attacked that afternoon in the prison, her rescue coming not from the guards but from Sophia's cellmate. Sophia was in the prison's hospital wing with a concussion and bruises to her face as well as defensive wounds on her arms.

Nick promised to visit Sophia the next day as soon as Worthy's appeal case rested, but the shock of Sophia being attacked left the men uneasy.

"I remember your caution about jumping to conclusions, Chris, but it looks to me that the puzzle pieces are starting to fit together," Henderson said. "Sophia Demetrios is convicted of murdering Reginald King, a major drug dealer. She doesn't remember a thing, but the forensic evidence and the testimony of Nichols put her away for thirty years. That should be case closed. But just as we find out that a DEA agent has been following Marina, Sophia is beaten up in prison."

Nick nodded, as he'd come to the same conclusion. "And don't forget that the Connie person could also be DEA."

Worthy nodded. "Let me play devil's advocate for a minute. People get beaten up in prison all the time. And it's only a theory that this Connie person is undercover DEA. The only solid fact you have is that the man calling himself Gus Cooper and following Marina is DEA."

"You think these developments are just coincidences?" Henderson asked.

Worthy held up his hands in surrender. "I'm not saying there aren't new leads to follow up. If I weren't tied up with the appeal, I'd help out full-time. And that's why you should forget about coming to court tomorrow, Nick, and work with Hoops on Sophia's case."

"No, Christopher, it's fine. I've already told Marina that I'll visit Sophia after court tomorrow." Turning to Henderson, Nick added, "If you'll come with me, I think Sophia might tell us more."

"Happy to do that, but while you two are in court, what's my assignment?" Henderson asked, looking at Worthy.

"My advice is that you find some way to break through DEA's wall of secrecy. Start with the agent posing as Gus Cooper. If you're right, he'll lead you to this Connie."

✝

OCTOBER 25, 2023, APPELLATE COURT

THE NEXT MORNING, WORTHY SAT NEXT to Nick in the courtroom, waiting in silence to testify. Hullinger had phoned late the night before, asking if he were ready.

"Ready as I can be, though neither of us knows how Tremont's lawyer will attack me," he'd said. "I still believe the appeal is going to come down to the missing corrections page."

"That's logical, but they might mimic the approach we took with Tremont yesterday and try to goad you," Hullinger had said. "My advice is that you keep your cool, no matter what they throw at you."

Hullinger's warning had led to a poor night of sleep for Worthy, and even after two cups of strong coffee, he still felt foggy.

He watched as Tremont was escorted in from a side door to take his seat beside Reeves, his lead lawyer. Tremont's smile was gone, and Worthy wondered if Reeves had told him how badly he'd damaged his case by falling for Hullinger's I.Q. trap. Worthy also noticed that while Kenna McCarty was sitting with others in the media, Phillip Sherrod wasn't with her.

After the head judge used a gavel to assert control, she offered a preview of the day's proceedings.

"The record of the first trial includes Lieutenant Worthy's statement under oath that he followed standard procedures when he took William Tremont into custody. That included requesting an immediate toxicology screening. That would have been on November 1, 2010. The results of that screening, which confirmed that Mr. Tremont was not under the influence of any intoxicants or drugs, was entered as evidence at the initial trial. It must be stated that Mr. Tremont's legal representation did not object to the toxicology screening, although Mr. Tremont's current legal representation is arguing that the failure to note the discrepancy in the dating of the toxicology screening is proof that Mr. Tremont was poorly represented at his initial trial."

Worthy listened not just to the judge's words but for any hint of how the judges were leaning after Sherrod's and Tremont's own testimonies.

"The key basis for this appeal, consequently, is the question of possible tampering with the toxicology screening, specifically the dating of the pathologist's report. Clearly, the date of the screening was changed by someone, from November 1 to November 2, although the change was not, as we would expect, recorded on a correction page in the case file. Based on the amended date on the toxicology screening, Mr. Tremont's legal representation is claiming that this test was administered as much at twenty-four hours later. If that were the case, then Mr. Tremont could have been under the influence of a chemical substance when he confessed. At this later date, the court cannot determine if the error occurred in the administration of the toxicology screening or in the contradictory dates given by the attending pathologist. However, the court must weigh the possibility that a procedural error sufficiently serious to raise doubts about Mr. Tremont's conviction could have occurred."

Worthy felt Nick's hand on his arm. Turning slightly, he whispered, "It's okay, Nick. That's what they have to say."

The judge continued. "Now, before we proceed to hear Mr. Worthy's testimony, I ask both legal representatives to confirm that this is a fair summary of the basis of the appeal."

Howard Hullinger, the department's chief lawyer, rose. "We agree, your honor."

Janine Reeves, Tremont's chief lawyer, started to stand when Tremont reached over and laid his hand on her arm.

"A moment, your honor," Reeves said, as she turned toward Tremont. There was a short whispered discussion before she nodded and stood. "Your honors, we wish to point out for the record that our doubt about the dating of the toxicology screening relates not solely to the patholo-gist, now deceased, but to another party."

Worthy felt his body stiffen as if he realized what was coming.

When the chief judge asked Reeves to clarify, she said, "For the re-cord, your honor, we have only the word of Lieutenant Worthy that he did, in fact, request the toxicology screening on November 1, 2010, when my client was arrested."

Out of the corner of his eye, Worthy saw Tremont's smile return.

The judge nodded. "Counsel does know, from the videotape of your client's arrest and initial interview, that a second officer was in the room. Are you suggesting that both officers conspired to falsify the record?"

"Your honor, our response is twofold. First, your honor will have noted that there is no mention in that initial interview about a toxicol-ogy screening. Yes, we recognize that this isn't unusual, as the admin-istration of the screening is routine whenever a suspect is taken into custody. In other words, the screening would normally be administered close to the time of the first interview. However, this is precisely what the change in the dating of the screening puts into doubt. And second, the second officer in the room, Sergeant Pinckney, was in his rookie year on the force at the time. Lieutenant Worthy was in his sixteenth year at the time. We believe there is a strong possibility that Sergeant Pinckney assumed, whether rightfully or not, that the screening had been ordered by Lieutenant Worthy and administered at the proper time. We think it also likely that a rookie police officer, even if he had doubts that the toxicology screening had been done when required, would have hesitated to question Lieutenant Worthy as his superior officer."

Howard Hullinger rose. "May I address the court, your honor?"

"You may, although I believe we can guess your concern."

"I'm sure the court does, for defense council has offered noting but suppositions. Not able to confront the pathologist on the case, the defendant's legal team has decided to attack Lieutenant Worthy and suggest criminal activity on his part without evidence."

The middle justice nodded. "We understand your concern, but the court believes that Sergeant Pinckney should be called to testify. We note that he testified for the prosecution in the initial trial, which means that Mr. Tremont's legal team deserves the chance to question him concerning the new issues that have arisen."

Just as Nick whispered to Worthy that it looked like he wouldn't be testifying that day, Reeves rose. "If it please the court, Sergeant Pinckney has emigrated to New Zealand. We can, of course, have him testify by ZOOM, but we request that Sergeant Pinckney's testimony be postponed until after Mr. Worthy testifies. We think Sergeant Pinckney's testimony might be unnecessary."

CHAPTER THIRTY-ONE

---◆---

HENDERSON'S CAR

CARNELL HENDERSON WAS DRIVING TO HIS OFFICE when his phone rang. When he recognized the halfway house's number, he pulled over to the curb. Hearing his son breathing quickly, he asked, "What is it, son?"

He heard Jamie moan before he said, "I'm worried about Mr. Worthy."

Henderson took a deep breath, picturing Jamie pulling on a hank of hair. "Okay, Jamie, what are you worried about?"

"That man that wrote all those bad things about Mr. Worthy."

This wasn't the first time that Jamie had become fixated, and Henderson remembered the advice of the halfway house's social worker. "Don't try to change the subject when Jamie is upset. Let Jamie tell you what he's worried about."

"Yes, that man wrote some bad things, Jamie."

"But Mr. Worthy is a nice man. He's my friend."

"Yes, he is, and it's hard when someone says something bad about a friend."

"I shouldn't have told Mr. Worthy what that man wrote," Jamie whispered.

"It's okay. Mr. Worthy needed to know what the man had written." When Jamie didn't respond, Henderson said, "Would you like to do something for Mr. Worthy?"

"Yes."

"What would you like to do?"

"I want to fix something for him. I want to fix something that's broken."

Henderson felt a lump in his throat. He was happy to work with Nick on Sophia's case, as Worthy had asked, but he realized that Jamie, by deciphering Paulsen's annotated newspaper clippings, had helped Worthy more than he had.

"Are you okay, Dad?" Jamie asked.

"Yes, I am, Jamie, but I realize that I want the same thing that you do. I want to help Mr. Worthy." He did a U-turn and headed away from DEA headquarters toward Detroit's homicide division where he intended to confront Phillip Sherrod.

Henderson had squared off with Sherrod only once, nine years before on another case that was shifted from Sherrod to Worthy and him. That case was centered on the death of an elderly priest and, if Tremont's arrest had been the low point in Worthy's personal life, the investigation into Father Spiro's death had been Henderson's low point. Sulla and he had been told, just a week before Henderson was paired with Worthy, that Jamie was schizophrenic as well as being on the autism spectrum. The future that Sulla and he had looked forward to for their son and for themselves had dissolved in a nightmare of meetings with psychiatrists and psychologists.

Henderson's life had gone into a tailspin, with violent outbursts at work nearly leading to his dismissal. Sherrod wouldn't have known the personal background to Henderson's troubles at the time, but Henderson remembered Sherrod being one of those who was happy for anything that made Worthy's life difficult.

Once, Henderson had asked Worthy if Sherrod hated him because Worthy was a college graduate while Sherrod had worked his way up from street duty.

"That could be part of it," Worthy had replied, "but I think there are other reasons he hates me. You know my approach on a case, Hoops. I focus on the victims, what they did and who they met in the days and weeks before their murders."

"That's because you think the killer will be found somewhere in that," Henderson had said.

"Exactly. But there's another reason, and to be honest I agree with Sherrod about this. The media decided early on to make me their favorite. When I did my best to avoid the media's attention, that only added to what Nick calls 'my mystique.' Sherrod wasn't the only one who resented me, but two of my bigger successes were cases that he'd failed to solve. And the press didn't help, making Sherrod look bad in both cases."

As Henderson walked into Detroit's homicide division, he thought of another reason for Sherrod's obsession with Worthy. In Henderson's experience, some people needed someone to hate. If their nemesis were having a bad day, that was a good day for them. If their nemesis were receiving attention and accolades, such as Worthy attracted, these people were convinced the thorns in their sides had manipulated the situation to push them into the shadows.

Knocking on Sherrod's door, he heard a loud, "Yeah, come on in." Stepping into the room, Henderson was struck with Sherrod's gaunt and jaundiced look. Worthy had told him that Sherrod didn't look well, but Sherrod didn't just look unwell; he looked like someone battling cancer.

But if Henderson expected what Sherrod was battling would mellow him, Sherrod robbed him of that hope with his first words.

"What's this about, Sergeant—oh, wait a minute, you're not on the force anymore. So what do you want, Henderson?"

"Actually, I was a lieutenant like you when I retired."

"Don't kid yourself. You were never like me," Sherrod said.

And I totally agree with that, but not for the reasons you think, Henderson thought.

"You checked out the Vickers-Tremont file two months ago. Why was that?"

"Ah, so Worthy sent you here. I should have known. Well, the answer is simple. A little birdy told me that Tremont was spending a lot of time on the computer in prison looking into how his conviction could be appealed. As Vickers' murder was initially my case, I naturally wanted to know if he had a beef with me."

"Naturally," Henderson said. "And who was this little birdy, Phil?"

Sherrod sat back and seemed to be pondering the question. "You know, I don't remember, but it turns out the little birdy was right."

"What did you think about Tremont's chances when you read over the file?"

"Geez, such a long time ago. I guess I agreed with what Tremont's lawyers apparently concluded when they studied the case. Everything rests on Tremont's confession. Did he offer that freely, or was he coked up when he gave that?"

"It wasn't coke, but Ecstasy."

"Whatever."

"I assume you listened to the tape of the confession," Henderson said.

"The kid sounded high to me, if that's what you're asking."

"And being a good homicide detective, you would have checked the tox report."

Sherrod paused, and Henderson noticed again that Sherrod's breathing seemed uneven.

"Like I said, it was a long time ago. But yes, as a good homicide detective, I'm sure I looked at it."

"Do you remember seeing the date being crossed out and corrected?"

"No, I can't say that I do."

"So you'd have had no reason to see if there were a corrections page at the back of the file."

Sherrod sneered. "Nope, no reason at all. But, from what I can tell—you see, I've been following the appeal—it sure seems that Worthy's ass is in a sling. About time, but I will say that I'm glad I'm not in his shoes. Who knows, maybe he's grabbing a flight back to Italy as we speak."

"You do know, Phil, that if someone tampered with the file, that's the same as destroying evidence."

The sneer disappeared, Sherrod's face turning red. "Watch it, Henderson. I've always known where the lines are." After pausing to catch his breath, Sherrod added, "When I retire, there'll be no appeals of my cases."

Henderson thought he caught something in Sherrod's last comment. "You planning to retire, Phil?"

"I could be, but I'm too interested in Tremont's appeal to leave now. After that, well . . ."

"Why wait until then? As you said, it's not your case."

Sweat was forming on Sherrod's forehead. "It was my case. Vickers's murder was my case, mine. Worthy took it over, and now we're finding out how badly he blew it. Vickers wasn't the only time he took over a case of mine and hogged all the glory."

Henderson looked down at Sherrod. "Ah, now it's clear. You gave Tremont's lawyers all that shit about Worthy's personal life back then."

Sherrod shrugged. "I'd say 'prove it,' but what if I did help them out a bit? Everybody deserves justice, and that includes Tremont."

Henderson held Sherrod's gaze. "You know, you don't look well, Phil. It might be better for your health if you just let this appeal go."

"What are you, a doctor now?"

"Just someone looking at a man who looks damn sick."

Sherrod turned away from Henderson's gaze and glanced over at the windowsill in his office. Henderson followed his gaze and saw the medicine vials stacked side by side.

"I've got a message for your buddy," Sherrod said. "Tell Worthy that Tremont's appeal is Christmas come early for me."

✝

APPELLATE COURT

EVEN THOUGH COURT HAD BEEN IN SESSION for only thirty minutes, Worthy's legs felt like lead as he walked to the witness stand and took the oath. He looked at Hullinger and no one else in the room, especially Tremont.

"Now, Mr. Worthy," Hullinger began, "Let's discuss William Tremont's initial trial. Do you still maintain that you followed official procedure in that initial interrogation, including ordering a toxicology screening?"

"Yes, that's what I did."

"And that initial interrogation took place on November 1, 2010?"

"That's right."

"Then, how do you explain the striking out the words November 2, 2010, and replacing it with November 1 on the pathologist's report?"

"I can't explain it. Arresting officers have nothing to do with those forms."

"But Doctor Wallace certainly would have shown you the results."

"Yes, I saw the report by the end of the day."

"Were you still interrogating William Tremont at that point or were you finished?"

"He was being held the interview room. I was waiting to see the results before arresting him."

"So, you're stating under oath that on November 1, 2010, you saw the results of the toxicology screening, which were that Doctor Wallace had found no evidence of Ecstasy in Mr. Tremont's blood."

"Yes, that's right."

"We know that Sergeant Pinckney was sitting in on the initial interrogation with William Tremont. Would he have seen the toxicology report at the same time?"

"At the time? Probably not. He sat in on the initial interrogation, but I was the one who went back into the room to formally arrest Mr. Tremont. I suspect that Pinckney looked the file over before we went to trial."

"Of course, if Doctor Wallace were alive and able to give testimony, we'd have no reason to doubt your answer."

Reeves rose. "Objection, your honor. Because Doctor Wallace is in fact deceased, we don't know what he would have said under oath."

"Sustained. Stick with the facts of the case, Mr. Hullinger."

"Of course, your honor. Now, let's talk about Kerry Paulsen. Were you surprised when William Tremont testified that Mr. Paulsen was the dominant partner in their friendship and was Renee Vickers' killer?"

"In one sense, I was surprised, but not in another way."

"What do you mean?"

"We interviewed Kerry Paulsen several times before we arrested Mr. Tremont and several times afterwards. Once Mr. Paulsen admitted having sex with the victim, of course we considered him a suspect in her death. However, the more we interviewed Mr. Paulsen, the more we determined that he wasn't involved in any way with Renee Vickers' murder."

"Can you share what brought you to that conclusion?"

"The hard evidence was that Paulsen had an alibi for the time parameters given by the pathologist for Renee Vickers' death. We also had traffic camera footage from Midland to Detroit, showing William Tremont's van with William Tremont driving alone on November 30, 2009. And, of course, we had Mr. Tremont's confession. In addition to that, it was obvious from interviews with those who knew both Tremont and Paulsen that William Tremont was the dominant one. Everything that William Tremont said in his testimony about Kerry Paulsen's devious deeds were, I'm convinced, done by William Tremont."

Reeves rose. "Again, your honor, suppositions here are being presented as facts. It is not pertinent how Mr. Worthy interpreted our client's recent testimony."

After consulting with the other two judges, the chief justice said, "Overruled, but qualified. Mr. Worthy, as investigating and arresting officer, is entitled to interpret testimony from your client."

"But doubts about Mr. Worthy's credibility and honesty are at the heart of the appeal, your honor."

"And that is why we say that our judgment is qualified. We have not lost sight of your concern."

Hullinger again addressed Worthy. "Did you ever, in the intervening years, doubt that Mr. Tremont was guilty of Renee Vickers' murder?"

"No, never."

"But you said you weren't surprised completely by Mr. Tremont's testimony about Kerry Paulsen. What do you mean by that?"

"Kerry Paulsen is dead by his own hand and can't testify. He cannot appear here. It's sad but not surprising that Mr. Tremont would try to throw the blame onto Kerry Paulsen."

"That's all, your honor."

Worthy took a deep breath. *That's my half of the first inning. Now it's Tremont's lawyer's turn to take her swings,* Worthy thought. If he'd scored some runs in his testimony, he knew that could all be erased by Janine Reeves, Tremont's main lawyer, who had walked to the podium, opened a folder, and was now looking at him.

"Mr. Worthy, I imagine that an appeal is a painful experience for any detective. Am I right?"

"I would agree."

"But of all the cases that you've solved in your career, this one must cause the most consternation and discomfort."

She waited, but Worthy, hearing her words as a statement, not a question, didn't respond.

"Am I right in thinking this case raises particularly unpleasant memories?"

"Every murder case is filled with unpleasant memories, especially for the families involved."

Reeves took a moment as if she were contemplating Worthy's words.

"Of course, Mr. Worthy, but I'm asking about the emotional effect on investigators like you. A solved homicide must bring a sense of satisfaction, of justice being done. And William Tremont's arrest and conviction, weren't his arrest and conviction what led to your being labelled Detroit's top homicide investigator? I'll share my research. Before Tremont's arrest, your photo wasn't in the newspapers, not once. But after that, you became the police department's poster boy."

"Other people made that decision."

"Granted, but you were given a commendation by the police commissioner, weren't you?"

"Yes, but again, other people determined that."

"So we agree that Renee Vickers' murder was the first of other homicide cases in which your achievements were celebrated. Now, you mentioned the pain experienced by the families of the victims. You obviously feel that your job is a service to those families. But would I be right in thinking that in giving closure to the families you also felt closure as a detective?"

"You can put it that way."

"Then here's my question. Did you feel that same sense of closure when William Tremont was arrested and convicted? As we both agree, you became the toast of the town."

"I don't pay too much attention to the media," Worthy said.

"But still on a personal level, you must have been pleased. This was your biggest win to that point. Do you remember what you did to celebrate, Mr. Worthy?"

"What do you mean?" Worthy asked, although he felt a tightening in his stomach as he realized where Reeves was headed.

"For example, did you take a vacation?"

"A vacation?"

"Yes, a vacation with the family. They must have been very proud of you."

Worthy felt sweat trickling down his spine. "I don't remember a vacation, no."

Howard Hullinger, the homicide department's head lawyer, rose to object. "What is the relevance of these questions, your honor?"

The chief judge nodded and addressed Tremont's lawyer. "That's a good question, Ms. Reeves. Where are you going with this?"

Reeves shuffled some papers until, in what seemed to Worthy a dramatic gesture, she selected one from the folder and raised it for the three justices to see.

"This should clarify my point. It's a housing agreement form, dated November third, 2010, listing Christopher Worthy as the new occupant, occupancy immediately. Can you explain to the court why you rented an apartment two days after William Tremont was arrested and just months before your divorce was finalized?"

Hullinger again rose. "Your honor, I object. Mr. Worthy's marital state has no bearing on the case. What Mr. Worthy did or did not do in terms of renting an apartment is irrelevant. Furthermore, these issues were never raised in the first trial and should therefore be inadmissible."

Reeves replied before the judge could rule. "We contend that the failure to probe Mr. Worthy's—then Lieutenant Worthy's—state of mind when he arrested Mr. Tremont is evidence that my client received, at his first trial, incompetent legal representation."

Hullinger did not give up, his voice louder. "Where is the evidence that my client's mental state was ever questioned, your honor? This is pure speculation thirteen years after the fact."

"Counselor, our hearing is just fine. Ms. Reeves, your questions are beginning to sound like a fishing expedition."

Worthy looked over at Nick, whose head was down. *He's praying, but I'm starting to think it's too late,* Worthy thought. He knew Tremont's team must have been alerted to his divorce from only one of two people: Phillip Sherrod or Kenna McCarty, and if Tremont's team had the divorce and apartment documents, he could only imagine what else they'd been given.

He didn't have long to wait. Reeves held up two sheets of paper. "If it please the court, I have evidence that establishes that Mr. Worthy's divorce was a pertinent indicator of his mental state as he was building a case against my client."

Hullinger rose to object. "Your honor, whatever evidence Ms. Reeves believes she has, the fact remains that she did not share this material with us. With today being Wednesday, I request that we be given until after the weekend to review this material."

The justices conferred for a few moments before the lead justice said, "Granted, Mr. Hullinger. Court will adjourn until Monday."

✝

EMPTY COURTROOM

NICK HAD INDEED BEEN PRAYING FOR HIS FRIEND, who looked exhausted after the attack by Tremont's lawyer. Now, after walking woodenly back to his seat, Worthy sat down, looking neither to the left nor right as the courtroom emptied.

"Give me a few minutes, Nick," he said. "I'm not ready to face the press outside, and they'll have smelled blood—mine."

"Of course, my friend," Nick said. "We can wait as long as you need."

"What I need is to be in Rome, with no thought of Detroit and my past here."

"I'm so sorry, my friend. I was watching your lawyer, Mr. Hullinger, and I could see that he was getting flustered. It seems the other lawyer's attacks were more personal than anyone anticipated."

"And I think we both know that the worst is yet to come." Worthy paused before saying, "What was going on with me thirteen years ago was a nightmare. I was lost, in freefall and drinking too much every night. I barely hung on to his job. A month before, I'd been just what Tremont's lawyer said—I was the toast of the city. Just months later, I was barely able to do my job. November 1, 2010, was for me year one, AD—after divorce."

"But you're not the same person you were back then, Christopher."

"True, but that makes this all the worse—for me, I mean. We assumed that the central focus of the appeal would be Doc Wallace's tox screening, but now it's clear that my mental state is going to be a major part of Tremont's appeal. They're going to paint me as a jilted husband, a father whose family wanted nothing to do with him, a cop obsessed with Renee Vickers' murder. And they'd be right, Nick."

Nick put his arm around Worthy's shoulder. "Tremont's lawyers still have to prove that your arrest of Tremont was a miscarriage of justice, don't they?"

"Yes and no. The confusion about the toxicology report gives Tremont's lawyers about forty percent of what they need to find reasonable doubt in his conviction. They need only another ten to fifteen percent of additional doubt to rule in Tremont's favor, and the mess in my life back then could give them that."

Nick didn't say anything, but offered another prayer, a simple one. *Give my friend the strength to endure, O Merciful God.* And then he knew what he had to do. He had to convince Lena to find some way to come to Detroit immediately.

CHAPTER THIRTY-TWO

———— ◆ ————

IN SAMIYAH'S CAR

SAMIYAH'S HANDS WERE STILL SHAKING AS SHE DROVE back from her meeting with Eldridge Loften. She was relieved that he hadn't recognized her as someone he'd met before as Connie.

When a teenager with shaved head led her into a small room in the back of an abandoned building, Samiyah had hardly recognized Loften from his mug shots. Gone was the afro, and he looked a good thirty pounds lighter. The dead look in his eyes was gone, replaced by a cold stare that unnerved her. Had the police not arrested Sophia Demetrios for King's shooting, she reasoned that they'd have considered Loften as a suspect. Drug lords had to expect that one of their lieutenants would be envious of the money and power that came with moving up the ladder.

She'd let Loften control the meeting, and he'd begun by asking where she'd come from. She described drifting for a few years, moving from Atlanta to Baton Rouge and finally Detroit, before she took the risk of telling him a bit of the truth, that Savreen wasn't her real name. "I use that name to confuse anyone in law enforcement who might be getting too curious," she said.

Loften's next demand was for the phone number where he could reach Francine to substantiate her story. Not for the first time, Samiyah realized that her life was in Francine's hands.

Samiyah was ready when Loften asked, "Why did Francine choose you?"

"Francine knows she can trust me, just like you trust those above you."

Loften's eyes narrowed at that. "What makes you think somebody's above me?"

Samiyah tried to settle her breathing as she looked Loften in the face. "Because Francine told me that King reported to someone."

"Did she? And who's that?"

Samiyah pretended to look puzzled. "The only thing she said was that the guy is high up in the DEA."

Loften paused for a long moment before saying, "The DEA. She told you that?"

"That's what King told her. Was he wrong?"

Loften looked down as he wrote something on a piece of paper. "That's on a 'need to know' basis, and you don't qualify. Here, take this."

Samiyah took the phone and the paper with four phone numbers written on it. "What are these?"

"Until the dust settles, I'm taking over distribution. My people will supply what your guppies need. When a guppy contacts you, you give him that first number. It's a burner phone, so it won't blow back on me or you. They'll be given an address for the pickup. When another guppy calls you, you give her the second number. She'll be sent to a different pickup spot. Never the same number to two in a row, never the same location."

Samiyah hoped that her relief didn't show on her face. She would have preferred to have nothing to do with passing drugs along, but at least she wouldn't have to hand drugs over personally. "I get it," she said. "That makes it harder for DEA to track us. Anything else I should know?"

Again, Loften stared at her before answering. "What are you thinking about?"

"Just what I'm hearing on the streets, that the cartels are coming into the city."

"That's just a rumor. But you know what to do if you see anything, right?"

"Of course." And that's when Samiyah realized that Loften had just given her the best chance of flushing out the dirty agent.

✠

OCTOBER 26, 2003, IN AN AIRPLANE OVER THE ALPS

LENA LOOKED OUT THE WINDOW OF the airplane, still amazed that she'd convinced her academic dean to let her end her semester early. He'd agreed to let her students write a research paper instead of taking a final exam, papers that they could email to her in the States.

Nick's words—"Christopher is lower than I've ever seen him"—echoed in her mind as she looked down on the snowcapped Alps. She'd be in Detroit in nine hours, but time seemed to have slowed down to a crawl. It didn't help that she couldn't stop asking herself what she could do for Worthy. Her entire career had been as a researcher, someone who sifted through writings, diaries, biographies, legends, and other evidence to bring a figure from the past into clearer focus. That's what she wanted to do for Worthy, but, for what seemed like the hundredth time, she failed to see where to begin.

She turned from the window to look down at a list of possible subjects. At the top were William Tremont, Renee Vickers, and Kerry Paulsen. But given that thirteen years had passed since Renee's death and her belief that Worthy had done everything required to locate and arrest Tremont, she saw nothing to pursue.

The next name on her list was Doctor Robin Wallace, the pathologist whose toxicology report was, according to Worthy, the basis for the appeal. Lena sensed that she might have an advantage over others who saw Wallace's death as a dead end, a brick wall, something solely in the defense lawyers' favor. The vast majority of her research had been to profile people—saints and charlatans—long dead. She knew that the dead were not silent as long as someone—someone like her—found a way to let them speak.

She sat back in her seat and looked down on the thick clouds settling over the French side of the Alps. Whatever Doctor Wallace had done or not done thirteen years before in William Tremont's case was hidden beneath its own cloud cover. The question was where to look. From everything Worthy had told her, Wallace kept no private records. Worthy had also told her that the pathologist's widow had dementia so severe that she had a hard time remembering that she'd ever been married to someone named Robin Wallace.

Yet Lena was convinced that Worthy's best chance in the appeal was for someone to find a way to let Doctor Wallace, though dead for over eight months, speak. *So this is what I will do. I'll dig and dig and dig until Wallace speaks, explaining the correction on Tremont's screening,* she thought.

CHAPTER THIRTY-THREE

---◆---

St. Simeon's

Brother Pachomius scanned the files on Kerry Paulsen's computer, trying to determine where the clue of "suomynona," now understood as "anonymous" spelt backwards, would lead. But Paulsen hadn't made the search any easier. Anonymous suggested vagueness or hiddenness, and that meant that the next clue would likely be even more cryptic. Remembering Father Nicholas' demand that he not neglect his prayers, he paused to dedicate his work to finding the truth.

It was soon after he opened his eyes that he saw the file labelled "Christmas—no tag." It was the "no tag" part of the label that made him think of anonymous, suggesting that the file's contents might contain information sent to Paulsen from an unnamed source.

He opened the file and read "Present #1—Look in media for pig's record in early 2011. Signed, A Friend." Pachomius remembered "pig" being used in another file for the police, and he speculated that the anonymous message was pointing him to newspaper accounts from early 2011 that were centered on Worthy.

After a half hour of digging, Pachomius came across two articles in *The Detroit Post*, each describing a case that Lieutenant Christopher Worthy had botched. Pachomius felt another domino falling over. An anonymous source, perhaps someone from the media, had led Paulsen to two damaging stories about Worthy from 2011. 2011 was just one year after Worthy's success in arresting Tremont. Pachomius had little doubt about what Paulsen did with the information. He'd have passed those stories on to Tremont who, in prison, was looking for grounds to launch an appeal. While neither newspaper story connected directly to Tremont's own case, they showed the chink in Worthy's reputation.

Pachomius wondered who the anonymous source could be and why he or she hadn't sent the damaging material directly to Tremont. Pachomius reasoned that the source had to be someone who remembered that Paulsen was Tremont's closest friend. Though it was possible that the source was someone in the prison who knew of Paulsen's regular visits to Tremont, Pachomius doubted it. He thought it more likely that the anonymous source was someone connected with Tremont's case in 2010, someone who'd been waiting for over a decade to play his or her hand. The only thing that Pachomius knew for certain was that the anonymous source was someone who wanted his or her identity to remain hidden, and Paulsen had accommodated the source by hiding the material in his coded filing system.

Pachomius felt energized, aware that he was the right person in the right place to crack Paulsen's code. With the "Christmas—no tag" and the "Present #1" clues, he searched for what might come next. He looked for a file with the number two in it but found none. He gave his eyes a five-minute break by looking out at the heavy foliage on the monastery's grounds before returning to the screen.

The brief break did him good, as he spotted almost immediately a file named "More Bacon Bits." Opening it, he read a brief message in quotation marks, "Still with me? Follow the yellow-brick road to the pig book from 2010. Look for what's odd there about a bird named 'robin.'"

On a hunch, Pachomius googled "Christopher Worthy Appeal 2023." The first listing that popped up was from a story posted the day before, one written by a reporter named Kenna McCarty. He skimmed the article until he found what he was looking for.

"William Tremont's appeal is based on the official 'murder book' associated with Renee Vickers' murder." McCarty's article then focused on an issue related to the toxicology report written by Dr. Robin Wallace, the pathologist on the case. The article concluded with the sentence, "Unfortunately, Dr. Wallace is recently deceased, thus unable to answer what appears to be the question at the center of the appeal. This confusion will likely favor William Tremont in the appeal and wound the reputation of Christopher Worthy."

Pachomius reread McCarty's article, understanding the significance of what he'd discovered in cracking Paulsen's code. Tremont's lawyers hadn't discovered the dating problem with the toxicology screening by accident. No, the lawyers had been alerted by Tremont who'd been given the information from Kerry Paulsen—and Paulsen had opened his email one day to find that an anonymous source had sent the clue that could free his only friend, William Tremont.

Pachomius shivered as he thought, *Someone really hates Worthy.*

Barminster Prison

"It turns out that Francine Nichols has been in and out of trouble since Sophia's trial," Henderson said as he drove with Nick to Barminster prison.

"Sorry, I'm a little distracted right now."

"I think we all are. But Worthy said he wants us to concentrate on Sophia right now."

"Yes, I know. But I wish I could do more for Christopher on the appeal."

"Same with me, and that's why I confronted Sherrod."

"Did he admit to anything?"

"If you mean his clueing Tremont and his lawyers in about Chris' personal issues in 2010, no. But he's enjoying Chris' pain."

"And you also think he looks like he's dying. Imagine knowing you're going to die and wasting your last months of life on seeking revenge," Nick said.

"It makes me wonder if hate can give a person cancer."

"I don't know, but anger and jealousy can't do anything good for a person. Someone should tell him to let go of his vendetta against Christopher."

"I did tell him that, but he wasn't having any of it. His obsession with Chris might kill him, but I got the feeling that Sherrod will die happy if Worthy loses the appeal."

Nick shook his head even as he made the sign of the cross.

"Anyway, Nick, I told you before that she was picked up again for dealing, but here is what's interesting. Given her record, she should have been given a jail sentence. Instead, she's in a rehab facility in Ohio, and not just any rehab center. This one is high-end, like a resort."

"So what you're saying is that she provided the only eye-witness testimony at Sophia's trial and now, after going back to dealing, she ends up in a posh rehab facility. Coincidence?"

"Or payoff," Henderson said. "We can't forget the Connie person."

"Ah-ha. Francine Nichol's friend who never testified at Sophia's trial. So what do we know or think we know? Connie might be an undercover DEA agent. The man calling himself Gus Cooper might be the same. Meanwhile, Francine Nichols is in a rehab center, and Sophia Demetrios is stuck in prison."

Henderson drove into the prison's parking lot and turned off the engine. "It's time for Sophia to start remembering what she knows about Connie."

After passing through security, Henderson and Nick were admitted to one of the prison's interview rooms instead of the visitors' room. As they waited, Nick was struck again at how miserable the American prison system is. The entire judicial system has forgotten that the word penitentiary derives from penance, a key element in the process of being forgiven. Nick thought the US prison system should admit that it is based on another word—punishment.

The worst part about the system, as Nick thought about it, is that many Americans believe prisoners are being coddled and vote for politicians who promise to increase the trauma of imprisonment.

Even with those thoughts, Nick was stunned when he saw the bruises on Sophia's face and arms when she was escorted into the room.

When the guards left Sophia with the two men, Henderson sat forward. "Who did this to you—a guard or another inmate?"

Sophia didn't even glance up. "Does it matter?"

"It does, Sophia," Henderson said.

No one said anything for a moment. "Why do you think this happened to you now?" Nick asked.

After sighing heavily, Sophia replied in little more than a whisper, "Let's just say that Reginald King has friends here."

"I thought your cellmate was looking out for you," Henderson said.

Sophia slowly shook her head. "She does, but she can't be with me all the time. Anyway, can we talk about something else?"

"Sure, but you need to know something. It's possible that what we're doing outside is making some people—the wrong people—mad."

Sophia raised her glance and stared at the two men. "Then maybe you should stop."

No one said anything until tears appeared in Sophia's eyes. Through the tears, she said, "I don't mean that. I want to get out of here."

"That's what we're working on, and we think that you can help us," Nick said. "We need you to tell us all that you remember about Connie."

"Connie? But she wasn't there the night King was killed."

"Let's leave that until later. First of all, have you remembered Connie's last name?" Henderson asked.

Sophia shook her head. "No, everything was always first names or nicknames. Mine was 'Mouse.' Francine told me I was Mouse because I was so quiet."

"Did Francine have a nickname?" Nick asked.

"No, she was just Francine. I didn't know her last name until the trial."

"Try to remember when you first met Connie," Henderson said. "Was she hanging around Francine when you first met Francine, or did she show up later?"

Sophia bit her lower lip. "I don't know. Connie was just there."

'Did you ever see her use drugs?" Henderson asked.

"I thought I told you that. She smoked weed."

"But nothing stronger?"

"Not when I was around. When Francine and I were doing lines of coke, Connie just watched us."

"So you never saw her pass out?" Nick asked.

Sophia paused. "I don't think so."

"But you saw Francine pass out?"

"Oh, yes, and I did too," Sophia said, tears running down her cheeks.

Nick handed a handkerchief to her, and Henderson waited until she'd wiped her face.

"Did Connie stay in Francine's apartment, or did she come and go?" Henderson asked.

Sophia shrugged. "I lived with Poppa and Marina, so I wasn't always at Francine's."

"Did you ever go with Francine to Connie's place?"

"Hmm. Maybe . . . no, never."

Nick had intentionally waited for Henderson to ask the big question, but he hoped it was soon, because Sophia looked exhausted.

Henderson sat forward, caught Sophia's eye, and said, "I'm going to share something about Connie. We think she might have been an undercover cop."

"A cop? No . . . really? But that . . ."

Henderson leaned forward and said, "I know it's hard to believe, but it's possible she was hanging around Francine to find out how Reginald King's operation worked."

"But that would mean . . . that would mean that she could have arrested Francine and me before . . . before that night." Sophia moaned softly. "I wish she'd done that. I wouldn't be here, would I?"

Henderson nodded. "That means she didn't want to arrest you or Francine. Francine was Connie's link to King. We think she wanted to get evidence on King and whoever was over King."

"If she was a cop, she wouldn't have been interested in me, a mouse," Sophia said as she put her head down on the table.

"No, Sophia, look at us," Henderson ordered. "You need to recall everything about Connie that you can. Now that you know she could have been a cop, is there anything that strikes you as odd?"

Teary-eyed, Sophia looked from Henderson to the barred window in the room.

"She watched me, staring sometimes. It was like she was sizing me up."

"I suspect that's exactly what she was doing," Henderson said. "If she were a DEA agent and was hanging around Francine before you came into the picture, she was trying to figure you out."

Sophia nodded. "Maybe it was Connie who called me Mouse. I guess that tells you what she thought of me."

"Anything else?" Nick asked.

"Like what?"

"We don't think Connie is her real name. Did you ever hear someone call her Connie, and she didn't answer?"

Sophia's eyes narrowed as if she were trying to focus on something. "I wanted her to change the TV channel and called her Connie. She ignored me until Francine said something like 'You hard of hearing, Connie?' And there was something else, but it probably doesn't mean anything."

"Tell us anyway," Henderson said.

"Did I tell you that Connie never ate pork? Francine liked pork barbeque and always had some of it in the fridge. I brought a plate out for Connie. She looked at it as if it were a pile of dog shit."

"You did tell us that. We think Connie might be Jewish or Muslim, but she could also be vegetarian," Nick said.

"No, she ate hamburgers." After a pause, she asked, "Can I go back to my cell now?"

Instead of getting up from his chair, Henderson said, "Give me a minute to jot down what I need you to do back in your cell. It could help you remember the night you were arrested. I said 'the night you were arrested,' not 'the night you shot King,' because we're not sure anymore what really happened that night. Will you do that?"

Sophia closed her eyes while Henderson was writing. When she opened them to look at Henderson and Nick, she asked in little more than a whisper, "Is it true that I might be innocent, or is all this bullshit?"

As Henderson handed the piece of paper to Sophia, he held her hand. "We believe you are innocent. Now, you have to start believing it."

CHAPTER THIRTY-FOUR

———◆———

OCTOBER 27, 2003, NEW LIFE REHABILITATION FACILITY

THE NEXT DAY, SATURDAY, NICK AND HENDERSON drove to northwest Ohio to where Francine Nichols was in rehab.

What first surprised Nick was that Nichols didn't seem surprised to see them. The other surprise was that Francine looked more like a young corporate executive than a drug dealer. She was dressed neatly in a color-coordinated outfit with her hair pulled back into a ponytail. Her eyes looked clear to Nick, and he hoped that this time Francine was serious about being clean.

After Henderson and Nick introduced themselves, Francine led them outside to a bench by a fountain.

In the car, Henderson shared that he planned to be blunt with Francine; consequently, Nick wasn't surprised when his first words were, "We're having a hard time believing someone like Sophia Demetrios shot Reginald King."

"Mouse," Francine said, meeting his eye.

"Mouse? That was Sophia's nickname, right?"

"We all called her Mouse. That's all the space she took up."

Henderson said, "That's my point. How could a mouse kill Reginald King?"

Francine shrugged, looking now at Nick. "But she did. It was like she was in a trance."

"But wasn't there another person there that night besides you, King, and Sophia? I'm talking about Connie," Henderson said.

"How many times do I have to say this? It was just the three of us. I was sitting with King at the table, looking at a map of the city. He was pissed, saying he'd heard that a cartel was moving in on his territory. He was ready to kill someone and was shouting when we heard something behind us, and there was Mouse with King's gun. Bam, bam."

"And she never said anything when she shot him?"

"Not a word. I was just glad that she didn't shoot me."

Nick thought about that point. "Did Sophia know King before the meeting?"

Francine gave a slight smile. "Why don't you ask her?"

"We're asking you," Henderson said. "Did they know each other?"

Francine gave another shrug. "Maybe she saw King once or twice when he stopped by my apartment."

"But you never saw them talking together or saw King make a move on her?"

Francine laughed. "Not likely. I mean, have you seen her? She's . . . well, she's a mouse."

"Maybe Mouse was King's type. You know, a timid shy girl," Nick said.

Francine yawned and stood up. "We'll never know now. Look, that other guy has already asked me all these questions."

"What other guy?" Henderson said, remaining seated.

"Muscle-man. Some sort of cop."

"When was this?"

"A couple of days ago."

"Why did you call him 'Muscle-man'?"

"Duh, he was buff. Why else?"

Nick sensed that Francine was closing down. "Did he go by the name of Gus Cooper?" he asked.

"No, I don't think so. You know this guy?"

"We plan to meet him soon," Henderson said. "My guess is that he also asked you about Connie."

When Francine rose and took a step toward the rehab center, Henderson held her arm. "One more question. Has Connie visited or called you?"

Nick noticed Francine glance down to the right. "Connie? No. For the last time, no. Connie wasn't there that night, she hasn't called, and she hasn't been here. Why should she? She's a junkie, man. You know where she is right now? She's off somewhere trying to score some weed. Lucky bitch. Can I go now?"

Henderson still didn't release his grip. "How did you end up in this cushy place? You should be in jail, rotting away like Sophia."

Francine's face reddened. "Go to hell."

They watched Francine walk back to the main building, not once turning around.

"You see what she did when I mentioned Connie?" Henderson asked.

"She looked down to the right. Christopher told me that that's a tell, a clue the person is lying."

"Bingo, Nick. She not only remembers Connie. Connie has been here to see her. Let's check something before we go. And I have to warn you, I'm going to cross the line on what's legal again."

Inside the main building, Nick followed Henderson to the reception desk where he flashed his old police ID and asked the receptionist to print off the list of Francine Nichols' visitors. The receptionist studied Henderson's invalid ID so long that Nick thought she'd seen through the ruse, but then she typed on her computer and sent the document to the printer. In a matter of minutes, Nick and Henderson were back in the car, looking down at a list with three names.

Nick's initial reaction was disappointment, as both visitors were all relatives of Francine. One was James Nichols, a second was Samantha Nichols, and the last one was Candace Nichols.

"Huh, I wonder," Henderson said, glancing back at the rehab center.

"What?"

"If I'm Connie and I need to visit Francine, wouldn't I pretend to be family?"

"So you're not the only one who fudged on the truth," Nick said.

Henderson laughed. "And maybe more than just Connie and me. If the DEA agent calling himself Gus Cooper is the muscular guy Francine described, he must have signed in as James Nichols. And that means that Connie signed in as either Samantha Nichols or Candace Nichols, which leaves us with an intriguing question. Did she pick those names at random, or is Connie's real first name Samantha or Candace?"

OCTOBER 29, 2023, HENDERSON'S HOME

FOR THE TEN-THOUSANDTH TIME, HENDERSON WAS grateful that he had such a compassionate life partner. Sulla had the gift of knowing just the right thing to say, the right decision to make. Now, with this being Sunday night and after leaving Worthy alone with Lena for the past two days, Sulla suggested that they invite both of them along with Nick over for a barbeque.

"I think you all could use a bit of normal, don't you, Carnell? You've been working non-stop on that poor girl's case. And from what you told me, Chris' appeal is draining him."

"Not to mention that Nick has been working on both those cases. But Chris and Lena might prefer being alone."

"Then we honor their request, but I have a feeling that they might be happy for a reprieve."

Sulla was right. Worthy initially sounded tired when Henderson called, but after a quick check with Lena, he thanked Henderson for the invitation.

Not surprisingly, Jamie wanted to be there. He wanted to ask Worthy if the clock he'd fixed was still working, and when he heard that Worthy's wife from Italy would be there as well, Jamie asked his father, "Does she make Mr. Worthy happy?"

"She does, although Mr. Worthy is under a lot of pressure right now."

Jamie didn't say anything for a moment. "Will Mr. Worthy be okay?"

"Sure, Jamie," Henderson said, hoping he was telling the truth.

Nevertheless, when Worthy and Lena entered Henderson's house, Jamie was waiting at the door and greeted them by saying, "Mr. Worthy, I hope you're okay."

Worthy managed a weak smile. "I always feel better when I see you, Jamie."

"Good. My Dad says that you'll be okay. My Mom said so too."

Jamie reached out his hand toward Lena. "Mrs. Worthy, I'm Jamie."

Lena took Jamie hand in both of hers. "Chris has told me all about you. You fixed his clock. I love the sound of the chime."

Jamie smiled. "Tell me if you need something fixed."

"I will, Jamie. That's so kind."

"Would you like to meet my mom?"

"Yes, I would."

"Here I am," Sulla said as she came into the room from the kitchen and gave Lena a hug. "We're so happy you could come early. And look who else is here, Jamie. It's Father Nick."

Nick followed Lena and Worthy into the front parlor. "Hello, everyone. I guess I don't need to say hello to Carnell; we've been together almost every day."

"No shop talk tonight," Henderson said. "And that goes for me as well. Let's all go out the patio. I'm ready to put some pork chops and burgers on the grill," he said.

Jamie, carrying a book from his room, said, "Mrs. Worthy, I found Italy in my atlas. Do people eat hamburgers in Italy?"

"We do, but I'll admit that American hamburgers taste better than any I've had in Italy."

Henderson was relieved that the evening was beginning with such a casual tone, but he could feel an undertone. Worthy was quiet, but Henderson was used to that. The relationship between Sulla and Lena was easy, Sulla talking about how she'd always wanted to visit Italy, Lena offering her apartment for Sulla and Henderson to stay in if they came.

Jamie was also not saying much, but he was clearly pleased to sit next to Worthy on the patio. The two of them seemed satisfied to remain silent for long minutes, and Henderson thought that this might be Jamie's gift to Worthy. On the way back from Barminster prison, Nick had updated Henderson on the appeal, especially Tremont's lawyers portraying Worthy as a cop obsessed with Tremont.

At the door, when Worthy, Lena, and Nick were about to leave, Jamie lunged toward Worthy and threw his arms around him. Henderson felt a lump in his throat, affection being something not easy for Jamie to give or receive.

"You'll be okay, Mr. Worthy. We all say so," Jamie said as he continued to hug Worthy.

Worthy wrapped his arms around Jamie and hugged him back.

"I look at the clock you fixed for me, Jamie, and I know things will be okay," he said.

Jamie let go of the embrace. "My Mom says that everything can be fixed, Mr. Worthy."

CHAPTER THIRTY-FIVE

ON MONDAY MORNING, LENA CAME INTO THE KITCHEN to find Worthy staring at his cup of coffee.

"Did you sleep well?" Worthy asked as Lena sat down next to him.

"It wasn't the greatest night's sleep I've ever had, but, judging by your tossing and turning, I know that I slept better than you."

"I can't argue with that." He took a sip of coffee before saying, "In the middle of the night, I thought about what you asked when you got off the plane, about you wanting to help me. I wasn't sure then, but I know the answer now. It's probably an answer you won't agree with, but it's the best answer I can give. I think you shouldn't come to court today, Lena."

Lena groaned. "Chris, please don't ask me that. Nick told me that the appeal has turned into a personal attack on you. I want to be there. I need to be there."

"But that's just it. Today is likely to be my last day on the stand. Then, depending on how that goes, there might be a ZOOM call to a cop who sat in on Tremont's initial interrogation. After that, the court is likely to give both lawyers a couple of days to prepare their final arguments. But I'm not saying you should stay away because I think you're not strong enough to hear the crap that Tremont's lawyers will throw at me."

"Then what is it?"

"It's me who's not strong enough. When his lawyers say all those things, it'll be hard to see you sitting there. It's been hard enough seeing Nick in the courtroom."

"Please, Chris, what you're asking is so unfair. I didn't come all this way to sit in this apartment."

Worthy nodded as he swirled the coffee in his cup. "I'm not asking that you sit here. I need you to do something more important than be in court today. It's what you already told me you were thinking about on the plane. I'm talking about you visiting Doc Wallace's widow. I know that the chance of her remembering anything is slim, but I have to hope. And trust me, you giving me hope is more important than sitting with me in court."

Lena didn't say anything for a moment. She knew that Worthy was right, that whatever was said in the courtroom today would be said whether she was sitting with Worthy or not. Lena remembered from her grandmother's own Alzheimer's that the afflicted person's memory could come and go. If there were even a tiny chance that Wallace's widow would remember the reason for the change of dating on Tremont's toxicology screening, Lena would do whatever she could to access that memory.

"Okay, Chris, I'll talk with the widow, but I have one request. I want to bring someone along, someone who might put her at ease."

Worthy looked puzzled. "If you're thinking of Nick, don't you think his size and appearance could have the opposite effect?"

"I'm not thinking of Nick. I want Jamie to come with me."

LOFTEN'S HEADQUARTERS

SAMIYAH HAD WAITED FIVE DAYS, DUTIFULLY HANDING out the phone numbers Loften had given her for users, before putting her plan into action. Now, as she drove to the abandoned building where she'd met Loften before, she prayed that her plan, what could be the endgame to her search, would work. "Inshallah," she whispered, and immediately felt the relief that came from the Arabic word that acknowledged that everything happened according to Allah's will.

The same teenager she'd seen before led her to the back of the building where Loften was leaning back in a recliner, a bottle of beer in his hand. The chair looked new, and Samiyah wondered if Loften was spending some of the new money he was taking in as King's replacement.

"You said this was important," he said in what sounded like a challenge.

"You told me to contact you if I heard anything about a cartel moving in."

Loften's brought the recliner forward to an upright position. "Spill it."

"Can I sit down?" Samiyah asked, feeling her knees begin to shake. If she didn't come across as convincing, she knew she might never leave the room alive.

"I had a visit from a guy with a Spanish accent. He said he was new to the city, up from Guadalajara. He didn't give me his name, but it's what he already knew that bothered me."

"What do you mean 'what he already knew'?" Loften asked.

"He knows that Francine is in rehab. He also knows that King is dead."

"Does he know me?"

Samiyah nodded. "Yeah, and he also knows that you work for—sorry, that you work with—a DEA agent."

As Samiyah had expected, the tension in the room increased.

"This Hispanic guy with all the info, he wants to meet?" Loften asked.

Samiyah knew this was the make-or-break moment. She offered another prayer before saying, "The guy's boss wants to meet not just you but the DEA agent. In person."

Loften uttered a string of obscenities as he looked down at his beer. Samiyah could see fear on his face and wondered if Loften suddenly realized that everything he enjoyed could disappear.

"Anything else from this muchacho?" he finally asked.

"He said you should pick the time for the meet, and he'll choose a safe location. I'm to communicate the details."

Samiyah felt dizzy as she felt Loften's stare boring into her. "Why you? You're what—more than a guppy yourself all of a sudden?" he said.

She shrugged. "I'm just telling you what he said. Believe me, I wish I weren't involved. He scared me."

Loften rose and came to stand in front of Samiyah. "Does he scare you more than me?"

Samiyah was happy to revert to telling a truth. "No, not more than you."

CHAPTER THIRTY-SIX

———————— ◆ ————————

REBECCA WILLISTON'S OFFICE

As Henderson sat in Rebecca Williston's office and waited for her to end a phone call, he remembered that Worthy held her in high regard. Henderson was in her office because Nick remembered that Williston had promised to look into the part the DEA might have played in Sophia's arrest.

"Lieutenant Henderson, I can guess why you're here, but in case I'm wrong, why don't you start," she said.

"It's just Hoops Henderson now, but yes, you probably know why I've come. Worthy is tied up in his appeal case, and so I'm helping the Demetrios family where I can. Chris told me that he mentioned our suspicion that someone using the name Connie was a DEA agent who infiltrated Francine Nichols' circle. We also think that another DEA agent has been following Sophia's sister, Marina."

Williston nodded. "As I remember, this Connie is African-American and could be Muslim or Jewish. But why another agent would be following Sophia's sister beats me. As we both know, the DEA works and lives in the shadows. Of course, given the work that they do, can you blame them?"

Henderson thought that he understood what Williston was implying. She'd didn't have much hope that anyone could breach the DEA's wall of secrecy.

"No, I don't blame them, but we're still trying to get some answers," he said, as he handed over photos that he'd taken in the DEA's parking lot. "We're ninety-nine percent certain this guy is the agent who's been following Marina Demetrios. I don't expect you to recognize him, but do you have contacts in the DEA who you could show this photo to?"

Williston studied the photos. "You're right. I don't know this guy. Still . . ."

"Yes?"

"What Worthy and Father Fortis shared with me about the DEA being involved in King's murder—my case—well, it bothers me. I don't like to be played, even by someone in law enforcement." Pausing to look again at the photos, she added, "I'll show these to a friend in the DEA. No guarantees, but I'll try. Anything more on this Connie person?"

Henderson grimaced. "Maybe I should plead the fifth on that."

"Let me guess. You visited Nichols over in Ohio."

"Was that really a guess, or have you kept track of her visitors?" Henderson asked.

"No, a pure guess. Did she tell you anything new, or maybe I should ask, 'Did she say anything that I don't already know?'"

"She admitted to Father Nick and me that a muscular guy had visited her. When I asked if he used the name Gus Cooper, she didn't think so. But she stonewalled us when we pressed her on Connie. Before we left, however, I stretched the truth a bit to get a printout of the visitors' log. All of Francine's visitors used her last name, Nichols."

"But you're thinking that was a ruse. Maybe from DEA agents?"

"Yes. She received visits from a Candace Nichols and a Samantha Nichols. Maybe Connie used one of those names when she visited her. It's a long shot, but maybe Connie's real name is Candace or Samantha."

Williston didn't respond immediately.

"We know you don't owe us anything, Lieutenant," Henderson said. "But we're hoping you want the whole story of King's death to come out as much as we do."

Williston finally nodded. "You're right. I don't owe you, Worthy, or his priest friend, but I do owe something to Sophia. Let me contact my friend in the DEA and see what she says. I'll let you know if—and I say 'if' because she'll probably refuse to answer—she gives me anything useful. Now, let me ask you something."

"Of course."

"How is Sophia holding up in prison?"

"She was beaten up a couple of days ago."

Williston exhaled slowly. "Friends of King?"

"Probably, but we both know punch-ups in prison come with the territory."

"Does she remember anything more about the night King was killed?"

"A bit, but not enough to make a difference to her sentence."

As Williston rose to shake Henderson's hand, she said, "But maybe she'll remember more, is that what you're saying?"

Henderson nodded. "That's our hope."

✝

APPELLATE COURT

FOR WORTHY, EACH DAY IN COURT FELT LIKE A LAYER of his skin was being torn off, exposing his nerves to acid. He'd felt the same thirteen years before when Susan asked for a divorce.

Tremont's arrest in 2010 hadn't been an ending to the case, being rather the beginning of his meetings with the prosecutor's office as the state prepared its case. When his personal life was in shambles, it had taken all his willpower to stay focused as he coordinated with the district attorney, the department's PR department, and the media.

When Susan asked him to leave the house, Worthy moved into a one-bedroom apartment where, every night, he tried to concentrate on the case's paperwork, even as his mind kept returning to the larger mystery in his life—why his wife of over eighteen years had asked for a divorce. For weeks, he'd awakened to stare at his apartment's blank walls, not remembering at first what had happened to him.

His first day on the witness stand in Tremont's appeal had nearly triggered a panic attack, as he realized how wrong he and Hullinger's team had been about the appeal. The basis of the trial was far more reaching than the disputed date on the toxicology report.

On that morning, he'd awakened with dread, feeling as alone as he had thirteen years before. Logically, he knew this wasn't true. Nick, Henderson, and Lena had all entered his life after 2010, but the appeal had forced him to return to the time when he lost the only support system—his family—that he thought he'd ever need.

All weekend, he had tried to anticipate what Janine Reeves, Tremont's chief lawyer, was planning to do to seal their case. Even before Hullinger said it on Friday, Worthy knew that Tremont's lawyers were building toward some climax, some surprise orchestrated by Tremont.

Only when he was sitting in the courtroom, waiting to be called back to the witness stand, did he stop trying to predict what would happen in the next hour. He was grateful that he'd convinced Lena to stay away even as he glanced at Nick, seated next to him with his head bowed in prayer. The others in the room, waiting for the judges to appear, seemed quieter than in previous days, as if they too sensed that the end was near.

He glanced briefly at Tremont, who smiled as he whispered something to Janine Reeves. *The two of them are the only ones who know what's coming,* he thought. Next to him, he heard Nick whisper, "Lord, have mercy."

After the judges entered and resumed their seats, Reeves rose. In a voice that sounded to Worthy like ice cracking, she said, "Your honors, I have a few more questions for Mr. Worthy, which I will assure the court remain within the bounds of the original trial."

"You may proceed, but know that we'll hold you to that."

After Worthy was sworn in, Reeves put on her glasses and took a moment to stare at him. Worthy knew the trick. Her staring at him led everyone in the courtroom to follow her lead, and the purpose of that was to make him uncomfortable. He held her gaze and took several deep breaths.

"Mr. Worthy, on how many of your cases did Dr. Wallace serve as chief pathologist?"

"Toxicology screenings or port-mortems?"

"Either."

"I can't say off-hand, but quite a few."

"Would you say that you and Doctor Wallace were friends?"

Worthy paused before responding. "If you're insinuating that Dr. Wallace would falsify a report because we were friends, you obviously haven't learned anything about the man. Wallace was a giant in his field."

To Worthy's surprise, the lawyer smiled as if Worthy had just given her a gift. "No, I'm far from questioning Dr. Wallace's integrity. So let me rephrase the question. Do you think that you knew Dr. Wallace well?"

"Yes, I do."

"Good. In all the cases where Dr. Wallace assisted you as a pathologist, did he ever make a mistake in dating a toxicology report?"

The atmosphere in the room, already tense, seemed to ratchet up another degree.

"No, but Dr. Wallace would be the first to admit that he was human."

"Ah, how unfortunate that he can't say that for himself. But on cases you led, Doctor Wallace never to your knowledge made a mistake on dating a document. Mr. Worthy, would you like to know how many mistakes in dating that Doctor Wallace made in his entire career?"

Worthy didn't say anything.

"The answer is that is never. Never, that is, according to you, until the case involving Mr. Tremont."

"No, not according to me; according to the record," Worthy shot back.

"Let's consider another option that better accounts for this rare occurrence, this anomaly. Mr. Tremont asserts under oath that he was high on Ecstasy at the time you solicited his confession. And in the recording of the interview that we've all had a chance to hear, Mr. Tremont certainly seems excited."

Worthy nodded. "Your client was excited. He was thrilled because he'd not only killed someone, but had fooled the police for so long. But he wasn't high, as the tox—"

"Let me stop you there. What you just said is only your interpretation of my client's excitement at that initial interview. But Mr. Tremont's conviction is under appeal because the court recognizes the need to reconsider the other option. That option is that Mr. Tremont was in fact high on Ecstasy on November 1, 2010."

"But—"

"Please let me finish, Mr. Worthy. The option the court has agreed to consider is that Mr. Tremont's toxicology screening wasn't administered by Dr. Wallace until the following morning, November 2, 2010. If that was the case, then Mr. Tremont spent an afternoon and night in a cell when Ecstasy could largely pass out of his system."

Hullinger rose again to object. "Is the defense suggesting that there'd have been no evidence of Ecstasy in his system fifteen or twenty hours later?"

Reeves looked only at the chief judge. "If it please the court, what we're suggesting is that my client wasn't familiar with Ecstasy. A small amount ingested by someone like Mr. Tremont, someone unused to the drug could produce bizarre behavior, and a small amount would not be found in a person's bloodstream a day later."

"You may proceed, counselor, but the court acknowledges that you are speculating."

"Do you admit, Mr. Worthy, that Mr. Tremont didn't confess to killing Renee Vickers after your initial interview with him on November 1, 2010?"

"Yes, but that isn't unusual. Lawyers like you would have advised him to not incriminate himself any further."

"Ah, yes, the advice from Mr. Tremont's lawyer at his first trial is pertinent, isn't it? Bearing that in mind, we ask the court and you, Mr. Worthy, to consider another explanation, a better explanation, for the crossed-out date on the toxicology report. This better explanation is one that Mr. Tremont's lawyer at his first trial failed to raise—as they should have."

Worthy didn't comment, waiting with everyone else in the room for Reeves to spring the final surprise.

"We suggest that Dr. Wallace conducted the toxicology screening on the morning of November 2, 2010, the day after you interviewed and arrested Mr. Tremont. That would mean that the original date on the report, November 2, is correct. That leads us to suggest the following."

Reeves paused, and Worthy wondered if she expected him to panic. He felt cold throughout his body, but not panic.

"We ask the court to consider the possibility that it wasn't Dr. Wallace who altered the date on the document. It was you, Mr. Worthy, then Lieutenant Worthy, who did that. You were the one obsessed with Renee Vickers' murder and under pressure from the media and the police to make an arrest. You were the one, in those very days, who was reeling from your marriage disintegrating. You altered the date on the toxicology report, Mr. Worthy."

The room was deathly quiet until Worthy simply said, "No, I didn't change the date."

Reeves turned to point at Tremont. "My client was so high on Ecstasy that he'd have confessed to anything in that first interview. In subsequent interviews, he never repeated his confession. Yes, his lawyer at the time owed him better representation, but that lawyer was another person who was clearly intimidated by you, Mr. Worthy."

She turned back to the judges. "Your honors, we submit that what I've just outlined offer a simpler and therefore better explanation for the correction page not being found. The correction page with Doctor Wallace's admission of a mistake will never be found because it . . . never . . . existed. The toxicology screening was changed by Lieutenant Worthy."

After another pause, Reeves said, "We have no further questions for Mr. Worthy, your honors."

Worthy remained in the witness box, praying that Hullinger wouldn't let Reeves have the last word. Hullinger obliged, rising slowly and facing him.

"Quite a fiction, wouldn't you say, Mr. Worthy?"

Before Worthy could answer, Reeves rose. "Objection, your honor."

"Sustained. Mr. Hullinger, I'm sure you remember the first rule of law school. Show respect to the court."

"I do, your honor, and I apologize. Mr. Worthy, let's return to the facts of the case. and that means let us return to focusing on William Tremont. We know that you interrogated William Tremont five times after the initial one. In those five subsequent interrogations, did William Tremont ever mention being high on Ecstasy on November 1, 2010, during your first interrogation?"

Worthy shook his head. "Every one of those interrogations was videotaped. But for the record, no, Mr. Tremont never mentioned Ecstasy or any other drug."

"And until six months ago, has Mr. Tremont ever claimed—in his twelve and a half years of imprisonment—that he was under the influence of drugs when he confessed?"

Reeves rose. "Objection, your honor. Mr. Worthy can't possibly know what my client was thinking about and regretting in those years in prison."

Hullinger said, "I will rephrase, your honor. Mr. Worthy, prior to six months ago, were you aware of any legal steps taken by William Tremont to void his initial conviction?"

"None to my knowledge."

"On that other matter. The judges will answer for themselves this question, but I will ask you. Did you ever try to intimidate William Tremont or his lawyer at the time?"

Reeves rose again to object. "Mr. Worthy is hardly likely to admit intimidation, your honor."

"Overruled. As Mr. Hullinger admitted, we will make that decision, but Mr. Worthy's view on the matter is pertinent."

When Hullinger nodded in his direction, Worthy said, "No, I've never knowingly intimidated anyone, neither a witness nor a suspect."

"Mr. Worthy, you're now a retired homicide detective who was given numerous citations for your effectiveness in solving murders. I look at you as an expert in the field of homicide detection. Why do you think William Tremont's claim that he was high on Ecstasy on November 1, 2010, has surfaced so recently?"

Worthy kept his eyes solely on Hullinger, willing himself not to look at Tremont.

"We'll never know who first noticed the dating correction on Mr. Tremont's toxicology screening or when that person noticed the correction. But it wasn't until Dr. Wallace died that someone saw the chance to exploit the correction."

Hullinger's next words were drowned out by Tremont rising from his chair and pointing at Worthy. "Then where's the correction page? Where's the damn page?" he shouted, with the sound of crying coming from Tremont's mother being heard over the buzzing of the gallery.

The center judge slammed the gavel down. "Sit down, Mr. Tremont. And Ms. Reeves, advise your client to be silent. He's only jeopardizing his own case. And I will clear the court of anyone else who is out of order."

Hullinger waited until the room was silent, pausing another moment before speaking. "Before the interruption, Mr. Worthy, I was going to ask you the same question. Why do you think there's no correction page in William Tremont's case file?"

"I honestly don't know. But the Dr. Wallace who I knew would have owned up to and explained any correction he'd made to an official document."

"Does that mean that you believe that such a page was once in the case file?"

"Yes, it must have been."

"Do you think the correction page has been misplaced or was deliberately removed by someone?"

Worthy was surprised at Hullinger's question, and he was quite certain that, later, the police department would rake Hullinger over the coals for suggesting that someone in the police had deliberately removed crucial evidence. It was then he realized that Hullinger had also made a decision, that decision being to represent Worthy, not just the police department. He also knew, in answering Hullinger's question, that he could throw doubt onto the two people whose signatures proved, in the months before the appeal, that they'd checked out the case file—Captain Walker and Phillip Sherrod.

Worthy looked from Hullinger to Nick and saw Nick slowly shake his head. Worthy knew that Nick was right.

"My opinion? I believe the correction page has been misfiled and will surface someday."

CHAPTER THIRTY-SEVEN

———◆———

BARMINSTER PRISON

SOPHIA WAITED UNTIL LIGHTS WERE OUT and she heard her cellmate, Deidra, snoring before unfolding the piece of paper that Henderson had left. Having survived in Barminster by being numb, she hadn't found the energy to look at what he'd written until that evening. Even now, she heard the voice in her head, *Why bother? You're stuck here no matter what he wrote.*

But that afternoon, she'd remembered her life before her mother was diagnosed with cancer. At first, the memories made her feel guilty as she thought how disappointed her mother would be if she could see her now, but the strongest memory wasn't of her mother scolding her, but of her mother laughing with her as they indulged in their favorite pastime after-school treat—milk and cookies while playing their favorite game of *Sorry*.

The memory of her mother's smile had been enough to encourage her to unfold the sheet of paper and read what was written on the first line: "Do the following things in order and do them slowly."

From the meager light in the corridor outside her cell, she could make out numbered steps on both sides of the paper. Curiosity more than anything else led her to read the first step: "Try to believe that these steps will help you remember what happened the night you were arrested."

She looked up from the page to the cement-block walls of her cell. She thought about crumpling up the paper, for hadn't she already tried to remember that night, only each time to face a dark emptiness? Yet she couldn't seem to stop her eyes from reading down the list. Step number two was, "You haven't remembered what happened that night because you're afraid of what you'll remember." She felt as if she'd been slapped. What gave this ex-cop, a man who knew nothing about her, the right to say that she was afraid to remember? But she'd already begun to read what was written on the third line: "Don't force yourself to remember. Just close your eyes and wait for whatever will come into your mind."

For what seemed like five minutes, nothing happened. Then she was startled by a loud bang from another cell farther down her wing. Loud noises at all hours of the day and night were common in Barminster, but this loud bang brought back a memory of another bang, the sound of a gun going off. At the same instant, she remembered what Lieutenant Williston told her that night: "You shot Reginald King." *So it's true. I did shoot him,* she thought as she began to sob silently.

Somehow, however, she read what was written next: "Don't trust your first memories. Your mind has been contaminated by what you were told by the police and what you heard at your trial. Go back to that night." Sophia stopped crying, aware that Henderson was right. All she remembered from that night was the sound of a gunshot.

She replayed that sound in her head until an image surfaced out of the fog. With the bang was an image of a gun in her hand.

The image seemed more damning to her than the sound of the gun. Wasn't the image proof that she'd shot King? But then something else cleared in her mind that confused her. Why had she heard the gunshot before she felt the gun being put into her hand?

She opened her eyes to read what was next on the sheet of paper. "If you remember something clearly, ask what had happened before that memory."

She felt more awake than she'd been since her mother was alive. *Perhaps Mama wants me to do this,* she thought. She closed her eyes again and returned to the sound of the gun and then the gun being put in her hand. The words "What came before? What came before?" spun like a bicycle wheel in her mind. As if in answer, she sensed more than heard another question: "Where did the gun come from?"

For several moments, she received no answer. In Lieutenant Williston's interrogation of her that night, she'd been told that she'd taken King's gun out of his jacket pocket—but now everything in her shouted, *No, someone handed the gun to me after the first loud bang.*

She could feel her heart beating rapidly. What did she mean by "the first loud bang?" *Did I hear another gun shot?* she asked herself.

She felt her eyes burning as she tried to remember. She recalled what Henderson had written above, that she should force nothing, but how could she stop herself? A night totally blank in her memory was suddenly full of images and sounds, and she wanted more than anything to make sense of it all. Yes, there had been a loud bang. She could hear it now, but she also realized that this gunshot was different from the first explosion.

She opened her eyes, turned the paper over to read the fifth and final instruction. "What you remember might be confusing and even painful. Don't look away. Stay with the confusion and pain." Sophia didn't need the encouragement. Her right hand was tingling as she read further. "If it helps, picture a train. Notice how one train car hooks on to another car from the front of the train to the caboose."

Sophia saw the train in her mind, even as she saw the engine enter a dark tunnel. Panic seized her as she knew, without knowing why, that Henderson's directions were taking her to something very dark. She felt a flicker of temptation to return to numbness. She breathed slowly, and for the first time since her mother's funeral, she said a prayer. "Show me the truth of that night. I have to know."

The tingling in her right hand had now morphed into a sharp pain. Her hand hurt, as if it were being squeezed tightly. In her mind, she saw the train emerging from the tunnel into the light. The lead car was the first gunshot. The second car was her being handed a gun. The third car was surprisingly empty, even as the fourth car was a second gunshot.

She willed the train to stop as she thought, *Why is that third car empty? Am I afraid to admit that I shot King?* Somehow, that just didn't seem right. Without willing it, she looked down to see her left hand cupped around her right hand. She squeezed the hand harder and harder until the pain seemed nearly unendurable.

Her cell was nearly dark, yet the previously empty train car in her mind was floodlit. "I remember now. Someone in a yellow sweatshirt was squeezing my hand, and that's why this finger," she whispered as she raised her index finger, "is so sore. God, oh God. Yes, yes, yes, someone forced me to pull the trigger."

She heard a voice from the bottom bunk, "What's going on up there?" Deidra asked.

"Did I wake you?"

"You sure as hell did. What gives?"

"It's nothing. Go back to sleep."

Instead, she heard Deidra get out of bed. In a moment, she was looking at Sophia. "No, as long as I'm awake, tell me. Are you sick?"

Sophia was holding her head in her hands. "Sick? No. I just realized that I didn't shoot Reginald King. I mean, I pulled the trigger, but someone else squeezed my hand until the gun went off."

"Girl, are you dreaming? What do you mean you didn't kill King? You must have. Else, why are you here?"

"I didn't kill him! I didn't kill him! I remember it all, Deidra. It wasn't me."

"Then who the hell shot him?"

"Connie. Connie shot him."

CHAPTER THIRTY-EIGHT

——— ◆ ———

OCTOBER 31, 2023, SUNNY HORIZON ASSISTED LIVING FACILITY

LENA WAS GRATEFUL THAT HENDERSON HAD AGREED that Jamie could accompany her when she visited Doctor Wallace's widow, but she could tell that Henderson was perturbed when she asked him to remain in the car.

"I remember my grandmother being easily upset in her last years. If it makes you feel better, Carnell, I'd ask Nick to stay in the car too. You're both big men physically. Jamie and I won't be so intimidating."

As Jamie accompanied Lena into the assisted living facility, Jamie smiled broadly, leading Lena to conclude that he felt special. *And you are,* Lena thought.

A staff member escorted them into a sunroom where a woman sat staring out a window. Lena had pictured Barbara Wallace looking frail, as Lena's grandmother had been, but this woman looked physically healthy, sitting up straight in her chair, as if she were as visitor to the facility instead of a resident. Lena had to remind herself that dementia often attacked the mind before it affected the body.

"Barbara, two visitors have come to see you," the staff member said in a louder-than- normal voice. Mrs. Wallace gave no sign of having heard, her gaze remaining on the view outside.

"I suggest that you sit facing Barbara and talk slowly to her," the caregiver said. "But I wouldn't be too hopeful."

For the first few minutes, Barbara Wallace seemed oblivious as Lena explained who Jamie and she were, adding that her husband, Christopher Worthy, had worked with Robin Wallace. She brought out a photo of the pathologist and placed it on a tray, but the woman didn't even glance at it.

Lena reminded herself to be patient, remembering how quickly her grandmother could drift in and out of reality. She tried commenting on the beautiful grounds outside the window, thinking that if Barbara Wallace wasn't able to enter Lena's reality, maybe she could share Barbara Wallace's. Again, there was no sign that the woman even noticed that two strangers were sitting with her.

It was just when Lena was thinking that the trip was wasted that Jamie touched her arm. "Can I try?"

"Of course."

Slowly, he took from his pants pocket a jumble of small wooden pieces. Turning to Lena, Jamie said, "When someone new comes to the halfway house, they can be frightened. I show them how to solve this puzzle. Sometimes, it calms them."

Lena nodded. "Go ahead, Jamie."

Jamie slowly selected one piece of the puzzle and raised it so that it was in the direct line of Barbara Wallace's vision. Lena saw no response, but Jamie continued, raising a second piece, then a third before fitting the pieces together.

With the fourth piece, Lena noticed that Barbara Wallace's eyes followed the piece as Jamie fitted it into place. When the same occurred with the fifth, sixth, and seventh piece, Lena was about to speak again to Barbara Wallace when Jamie whispered, "Shh."

There were three pieces left to complete the puzzle, and Lena noticed that Jamie never deviated from slowly showing the piece before fitting it into place. With the eighth and ninth piece, Lena could see that Barbara Wallace's fingers were beginning to move.

Then, just when Lena expected Jamie to finish the puzzle with the one remaining piece, he changed his routine. After holding up the tenth piece for Mrs. Wallace to see, he reached out and put it into her hand. Then he held up the puzzle, showing the slot where the final piece should be inserted.

Nothing moved for a moment, not Jamie's hand, not Barbara Wallace's hand, not Lena's breathing. And then, as if in slow motion, the woman raised the tenth piece of the puzzle and slid it into the opening. As Jamie smiled and nodded, Barbara Wallace did the same.

"My name is Jamie," he said. "What's yours?"

In little more than a whisper, the woman said, "Bar . . . Barbara. Did you bring that puzzle for me?"

"I did."

She smiled again and seemed to notice Lena for the first time. "Who are you?"

"My name is Lena. My husband was a friend of your husband, Robin."

"Robin. Robin was a good man."

"That's what everyone says about him," Lena said. "Do you remember what Robin did for a living?"

Barbara Wallace looked down at the puzzle in her hand. "He worked on dead people."

Lena felt her heart quicken, remembering how her grandmother, on a good day, could connect with reality for ten minutes or more before drifting away.

"He was a pathologist?" Lena asked.

Barbara Wallace nodded, then looked at Jamie and handed back the puzzle. "Show me again."

Slowly, Jamie took the puzzle apart and laid the pieces on the tray before picking one up. "Start with this one, Mrs. Wallace."

She picked up the piece but looked confused. Jamie picked up a second and putting it in her other hand, guided her hands until the two pieces fit together.

Barbara Wallace picked up a third piece. "Does this one come next?"

"You tell me," Jamie said with a smile.

She tried to fit the third piece to the other two, but without success.

"Here, try this one," Jamie said, handing her a different one.

With hardly a hesitation, she found how the piece fit. "Now what?" she asked.

"You tell me," Jamie repeated.

She tried two pieces from the tray, but failed until she picked up another. When she found where it fit and then did the same with a fifth piece, she smiled toward both Jamie and Lena.

"We're halfway there," Jamie said. Turning to Lena, he nodded.

"Barbara, did your husband, Robin, like puzzles?" she asked.

For the first time, Barbara laughed, even as she reached for another piece on the tray. "No, no. Robin was a perfectionist. 'No mistakes, no mistakes in my business,' he used to say. That's why he wouldn't work with anybody."

Lena reminded herself to proceed slowly. "Yet he worked with students, didn't he, Barbara? Surely, students made mistakes."

Barbara didn't say anything for a moment as she fitted the sixth and seventh pieces into the puzzle. Then she shook her head as she said, "Students could only observe."

"He wouldn't even let students fill out forms?" she asked.

Barbara had lifted the eighth piece and was about to fit it into the correct slot when her hand stopped. "'Never again, Barbara, never again,'" she said in a low, gruff voice.

Understanding that Barbara Wallace was imitating her husband's voice, she asked, "What did Robin mean?"

Barbara fit the eighth piece but then was silent.

"Just two more pieces, Mrs. Wallace," Jamie said.

"Some doctor's nephew wasn't satisfied to just watch." Barbara Wallace lowered her voice and repeated, "Never again, Barbara, never again."

Lena took a deep breath and counted to five. "So, there was one student who did something wrong? What was that, Barbara?"

Moving more slowly, Barbara Wallace picked up the ninth puzzle piece, then the tenth, and completed the puzzle. Her hands then went slack, and her head dropped to her chest. After that, she was silent.

Taking the completed puzzle from the tray, Jamie placed it in Barbara's right hand and cupped her fingers around it. "This is for you, Mrs. Wallace. The next time, you'll do it on your own."

Back in the car, Henderson said, "By the smile on your faces, it looks like you succeeded."

Jamie looked over at his Dad. "I gave her one of my wooden puzzles."

Henderson turned to catch Lena's eye in the backseat.

Lena leaned forward and patted Jamie's shoulder. "It was all Jamie, and he might have just saved Chris."

NOVEMBER 1, 2023, BARMINSTER PRISON

NICK HAD HEARD MANY CONFESSIONS, BUT he would never forget Sophia's. She looked years younger than when he'd first visited, her face open, her eyes clear as she sat next to him in Barminster's small chapel. She told him how Henderson's list of directions had been the catalyst, leading her to remember how Connie had forced her to pull the trigger and shoot Reginald King.

"Your friend Henderson and you saved my life, Father."

"You were always innocent, my dear. I'm so grateful that you found the strength to believe in yourself."

"No, Father, I haven't believed in myself for a long time. That's why I asked you to visit. I want you to know what I remembered, but I also need you to hear my confession. If I hadn't given up after Momma died, I wouldn't have met Francine and gotten into drugs. All the suffering that I caused my family would never have happened if I'd been stronger and had listened to Marina."

When he gave her Holy Communion, Sophia's face had glowed. As he dropped the morsel of bread mixed with wine in her mouth, he'd felt that he was feeding a child, someone reborn.

Afterwards, they sat together and talked about the next steps that Henderson and he would take. Nick knew that Sophia's remembering what happened the night of King's death wouldn't prove her innocence to the police or court. Sophia's exoneration would depend on finding Connie, and that was why, the following morning, Nick and Henderson were walking into Detroit's homicide division to meet with Rebecca Williston again.

In his morning prayers, Nick had asked that Williston would hear them out and not become defensive, not taking Sophia's memory as an indictment of her mishandling the case. Now, as they entered her office, he remembered that Worthy held her in high regard. *May she be worthy of Christopher's praise,* he thought.

"I assume that you have some news," she said as she motioned them to sit in chairs on the other side of her desk.

"We do, but I'd like Father Nick to begin," Henderson said.

May Your will be done, he prayed silently before saying, "Sophia's memory has come back. About the night of King's death, I mean." Williston's expression didn't change, and Nick understood she would need a lot more to be convinced.

"What Sophia has remembered is Connie cupping her hand around hers," he said, demonstrating what he meant with his own hands, "and pulling the trigger the second time. That's why you found gunshot residue on Sophia's hand and sleeve."

Even to Nick's own ears, what he was saying sounded farfetched. It also sounded all too much like Tremont's fabricated story of his confession. Nick expected Williston, who still hadn't changed her expression, to dismiss outright what he'd said and tell them to leave.

Finally, Williston spoke. "If you'd come with this story last week, I'd have sent you packing." Rustling through some papers on her desk, she chose one and looked up after studying it. "Last time we met, Henderson, you wanted my friend in the DEA to ask about a female African-American agent, possibly Muslim or Jewish, someone who worked undercover within Francine Nichols' circle. You also suggested her real first name could be Candace or Samantha. That narrowed it down, but I expected to be shut out."

"You weren't?" Henderson asked.

"I received this reply just this morning," Williston said, as she handed the printed across the desk to Henderson who held it so that Nick could also read it. On it, Nick read, "Just as I predicted, the colleague who I asked told me where I could get off. But this morning, out of the blue, she called me into her office. She said I shouldn't ask any questions, but she'd been given a name. The name is Samiyah Aisha. All I know is that she is DEA here in Detroit, African-American, and Muslim."

"I've never known the DEA to offer this kind of information," Williston admitted. "Someone decided to break the rules, and I don't know why."

Nick was too shocked to say anything, and Henderson was also silent. Williston leaned across her desk. "You'll notice that the note isn't signed. You'll never know who my contact is or who gave my contact this name. This is where my help ends. It's up to you to find out if Sophia's new story is on the level, and if this Connie, maybe Samiyah Aisha or maybe not, was involved in King's death. Now, if you'll hand back that piece of paper, I'll destroy it, and no one will ever know the note existed."

✝

HENDERSON'S DEN

ALTHOUGH THERE WERE MOMENTS WHEN NICK had felt torn between helping the Demetrios family and supporting Worthy, working both cases had helped him understand the similarity between the cases. To Nick, the most obvious similarity was that Sophia and Worthy were both innocent victims of the machinations of others. *Like lambs led to the slaughter,* he thought.

A more troublesome similarity between Sophia and Worthy was that time was running out for both of them to prove their innocence. Yes, Sophia's memory had returned, but her concussion and bruises were reminders that she remained in danger as long as she was in Barminster.

In its own way, Worthy's plight was as emotionally fraught as Sophia's had been. Until two years ago, Worthy had described his spiritual condition as bankrupt. Susan's demand for a divorce, his older daughter running away, and his struggle to keep his job had convinced him that God had also abandoned him. But at the end of a difficult case in Canada's north in 2021, Worthy had experienced something, a "presence," as he'd described it to Nick. Nick hadn't said anything at the time, but he understood that his friend had felt—no, had known in some way—that God had not left him. Now, Tremont's appeal could erase that awareness, the trial forcing Worthy to return to who he'd been in 2010—a man alone, a man whose life was in freefall.

Nick's thoughts were interrupted by Lena sharing what Jamie and she had gleaned from their time with Barbara Wallace. "Because of what Jamie did, we know that Doctor Wallace allowed a student—maybe just once—to assist on a procedure," Lena said. "And it seems this student made a mistake, a mistake serious enough for Doctor Wallace to never let another student assist him."

Nick glanced at Worthy and thought he could guess what his friend was thinking. Jamie's and Lena's achievement was very likely too little and too late. Tracking down the guilty student after thirteen years would be hard enough, but surely impossible with closing arguments in Tremont's appeal scheduled to begin in two days.

Then he noticed Jamie rising from the couch and walking over to Lena to whisper in her ear.

"Oh, Jamie's right. I forget to tell you about the uncle-nephew thing," she said. "The student we're looking for was the nephew of a some big-shot surgeon in Detroit. That should help us narrow the search, don't you think, Chris?"

Worthy seemed to weigh the question and said nothing before giving an unconvincing nod. Henderson spoke instead. "Lena, let me run that down. I'll ask around at the local med schools. There can't be that many med students from 2010 with uncles who are well-known doctors."

The room grew quiet as everyone seemed to be waiting for Worthy to say something. Finally, clearing his throat, he said in little more than a whisper, "I want to thank everyone, especially you, Jamie, for everything you've done for me. I'll never forget this, never."

CHAPTER THIRTY-NINE

---◆---

NOVEMBER 2, 2023, CITY PATHOLOGY LAB

HENDERSON KNOCKED ON THE DOOR OF THE pathology lab that during Henderson's entire time on the force was Doc Wallace's private fiefdom. But instead of seeing the crusty old Scotsman, he was welcomed by a young woman who looked no more than thirty.

"I don't think we've met," he said. "I'm Carnell Henderson. I was in homicide until I retired last year."

"I recognize your name from the files. "I'm Dr. Burgo," she said, offering her hand, "but please call me Brenda and have a seat. Would you like coffee?"

Henderson thought about joking about the precinct's lousy coffee but then saw that Dr. Burgo had her own coffeemaker.

"If you're going to have some, I'll join you."

"I was about to take a break," Dr. Burgo said.

As she poured two cups, Henderson asked, "Are you new to Detroit?"

She turned and smiled. "Is that your way of saying that I look too young to have this job?"

"You got me," he replied, wondering why someone so outgoing would want to spend her working life in scrubs and a mask while leaning over corpses.

Handing a cup to Henderson, she said, "I'm thirty, and I worked three years in Kalamazoo before I came here two months ago."

"Did you always want to be a pathologist?"

"I won't say 'always,' but I became interested in my first year of med school. People think pathologists must be extreme introverts who prefer working on bodies that can't talk back. But I see what I do as a way of giving the dead the final say."

"Then you'd like my boss, Chris Worthy. His pattern—maybe I should say his genius—was to approach homicide cases by finding out all he could about the victims. He was never the type to start an investigation by running after potential suspects."

"Worthy. Now there's a name that I've heard around here quite a bit."

Henderson had steeled himself, expecting to meet someone like Doc Wallace, but Dr. Burgo's demeanor couldn't have been more different. He wondered if the cantankerous Doc Wallace had ever been this friendly.

"Maybe you've also seen his name or photo in the news about the Tremont appeal," he said.

She leaned forward and whispered, "Would you be surprised that there are folks here who hope that Tremont gets off?"

Henderson took a sip of coffee. "Hmm, this coffee isn't what Doc Wallace would serve. "Maybe they don't want Tremont to get off as much as they hope that Worthy will look bad."

Dr. Burgo nodded. "You're probably right. I'm a newbie, so I've avoided saying anything. But it seems odd that some folks in this building have turned on one of their own. Because he's your boss, you must know why Lieutenant Worthy is so unpopular."

"I'm pretty sure I do, but you have to know that Worthy is more than my boss. He's a friend. Worthy has a knack for solving cold cases, cases that others couldn't close, so that's a big part of why he was resented. But another reason is that the media doted on him—when he succeeded, I mean."

"So, it's jealousy?"

"I'd say that's about ninety percent of it. But Worthy is also an introvert and would be the first to admit that he preferred working cases alone."

"Was that how he handled the Tremont case?"

"Tremont's trial came before I knew Chris, but that's what Tremont's lawyers are trying to sell to the judges. Their version is that Chris was obsessed with Tremont, so much so that he played fast and loose with procedures."

Dr. Burgo looked puzzled. "Isn't the main issue in the appeal some problem related to Doctor Wallace?"

"That's why I'm here. If Tremont gets off, it'll likely be because the date on Tremont's tox screening was crossed out and changed. It sounds minor, but the problem is that there's no corrections page in the case file."

"So there's no explanation for the change and Doctor Wallace isn't alive to explain. From what I can gather, my predecessor was like your friend Worthy. He preferred working alone."

"Students could observe Doc Wallace, but they weren't allowed to handle official forms."

"Then he was 'old school,' doing things he couldn't get away with now. Every procedure now must have a lead pathologist and a second one present." She paused before adding, "So, given what you've told me, is there anything I can do to help?"

"There's a chance, but it's a slim one. Doc Wallace's widow has dementia, but a friend and my son caught her in one of her more lucid periods. Apparently her husband doubled down on his 'going it alone rule' after he was pressured into letting a student assist him. Apparently, that student made a mistake."

Dr. Burgo nodded. "So, you're hoping that the change of date on Tremont's tox screening was this student's fault. Even if that's the case, there must be scores of med students who observed Doctor Wallace in the fall of 2010."

"There is something that might help narrow the list. The student who made the mistake had an uncle who was a big-name surgeon in Detroit."

"Have you tried the med schools in the area?"

"I called two earlier this morning, but they told me that students' right to privacy prevented them even looking into their records. That's when I thought of you."

Dr. Burgo didn't say anything for a moment. "I don't mind taking a look in our records, but you must have considered that the uncle, if he was on the mother's side, had a different last name."

"Oh, shit. No, I didn't think of that."

Dr. Burgo turned to open a laptop. "Don't give up yet. There's a fifty-fifty chance that uncle and nephew have the same last name, so . . ." She tapped a few keys on her computer. "What are the disputed dates from the tox screening?"

"November 1 and 2, 2010."

"Okay, you're just assuming—hoping, really—that the crossed-out date on the tox screening is the mistake made by the student. I mean, they could be two different incidents."

Henderson groaned. "Sounds like I violated the first rule of detection: never assume."

"Don't be too hard on yourself, and keep a good thought." After a few minutes of studying her computer screen, the pathologist said, "I'm looking at the three main med schools in Detroit that had pathology rotations with Doctor Wallace in the fall semester, 2010. Here, take a look."

Henderson stood behind Burgo and looked at a long list of names.

"Here's what I'll do now. I'll cross-reference the surnames of students with all the surgeons licensed to practice in Michigan in 2010. And you're permitted to cross your fingers," she added.

"I have a friend, a monk, who's doing more than crossing his fingers. He's praying."

"All the better," Dr. Burgo said, as she hit a few more keys. The screen remained blank until two pairs of names appeared. "It looks like there was a Dr. Nolan Schmidt and a med student named Mason Schmidt. And here's a Dr. Oscar Johnson and a med student named Peter Johnson. What do you think?" she said. "It could be what you're looking for or . . .'

Henderson nodded. "Or it could be nothing. But I won't know until I run them down."

"And there's one more thing I can do," she said. "Let's hope they both graduated from med schools, because if they did, their med schools should list where they are now."

After another moment, a page with a photo appeared on the screen. "Mason Schmidt, graduated from Allgemein University's Medical School in 2012 before having a residency in psychiatry in Chicago. He currently practices in the Malmgren Mental Health Center in Lansing."

Henderson jotted down the information before nodding for Burgo to proceed. After she hit another key, a similar page appeared with Peter

Johnson's name and photo at the top. Below, was written "Peter Johnson graduated from Loyola University's Medical School in 2013 with a specialty in hematology. Dr. Peter Johnson is currently on staff at Wayne County's South Blood Center."

Henderson closed his notebook. "Whoa, I can't tell you what a big help you've been. I mean, you've been a really big help. Chris and I owe you," he said as headed for the door.

Brenda Burgo glanced up from her computer and smiled. "I could see that Doc Wallace's reputation is at stake, which means my office's reputation is also at stake. I'd love to think you'll clear his name as well."

"I'll give you a call with whatever we find out."

As he was on his way out of her office, the young pathologist added, "Tell your friend the monk that his prayers seem to have helped, at least for now."

✝

RONALD FITHIAN'S OFFICE

SAMIYAH AND RONALD FITHIAN HAD HARDLY SPOKEN since she'd returned to routine street undercover work after King's death. At the time, Fithian had thanked her for her work, but he couldn't hide his frustration that of all nights for Samiyah to be with her father at the hospital instead of with Francine Nichols, it had been the night King was killed.

She had never told Fithian that she continued to look for the dirty agent. Fithian would have nixed the idea and would have made sure that she obeyed. Being called to his office, however, made her wonder if Fithian had discovered her secret anyway.

While she waited for Fithian to appear, she glanced around his office. Mounted on the walls were sports photos, one the team photo of the Detroit Lions, another of the Detroit Pistons, and taking center place on the wall was a photo of Fithian standing next to Isiah Thomas. Fithian was taller than Thomas, so someone who was ignorant of professional sports might have assumed that the photo was of two athletes, not one athlete and an admirer.

After Fithian entered and closed the door, he said, "I want to bring you up to date, Samiyah. When you were undercover last year, I asked you to keep your eyes and ears open for any mention of someone named Lamar Wilson."

Samiyah nodded. "I remember. That was before we found out the dirty agent was someone in our own agency."

"Right. Wilson is in burglary, not DEA. So, we dismissed the idea that Wilson was involved." He leaned across the desk and smiled knowingly as he whispered, "But things have changed."

Samiyah's jaw dropped. "How so, sir?"

"I dig some digging and found out Lamar Wilson has a cousin in our agency, one Leonard D'Poussaint. Quite a name, right? No, you don't know him because he's in the Lansing office. I'm just wondering if you heard that name when you were undercover."

"No, and I'd remember a name like that. Are you saying two cousins are working together?"

Fithian looked out his office windows before whispering, "That's exactly what I think. Come around here and look at these photos."

She could feel Fithian's excitement even as she felt the opposite as she looked at the photos of two Black men. "Does either of them look familiar?" Fithian asked.

"I'm not sure." Pointing at the face on the left, she said, "It's possible I saw him when I dropped money off at King's place."

"That's D'Poussaint, the DEA agent in Lansing."

Samiyah tried to keep her voice even as she thought back to all the hiding and lying that she'd done the past eight months, all the nights she'd neglected her father—all wasted. She hadn't found the dirty agent; Fithian had. When she admitted that to herself, the face of someone who'd sacrificed the most came to mind, and she was filled with shame.

She became aware of Fithian gazing up at her. "I thought you'd be happy, Samiyah. We flushed out Lamar Wilson."

"I'm just surprised," Samiyah said, forcing a smile. "Have you arrested him?"

"Not yet. We're tailing him, just waiting to catch him with one of his dealers."

Samiyah felt as if she were looking down on Fithian and herself from a far height. "So he doesn't know you suspect him?"

"Absolutely not, and technically I shouldn't have said anything until we have him in custody. But given the hard work you put in last year, I wanted you to know. I also want you to know that after the arrest, I'm going to put your name forward for a commendation. With King dead and Wilson in prison, the drug trade here in Detroit will take a big hit. So, smile, will you?"

"It's just so unexpected. I didn't know you were still working the case."

"I wanted to tell you, especially after I pulled you out of working undercover after King was killed. Samiyah, take a week off, full pay. Unplug and unwind. Celebrate with your friends and your father, okay? It's over. We got them."

CHAPTER FORTY

---◆---

St. Simeon's

Cracking Kerry Paulsen's code made Pachomius feel more alive than he had since his first days at St. Simeon's, but that meant returning to the routine of monastic life had left him feeling flat. After watching him play video games well into the early morning, his college roommate had described him as an adrenalin junkie. Now, after helping Father Nick for the past few weeks, he knew that the feeling of discovery still hooked him.

That was why he was again sitting in the security office and poring over Kerry Paulsen's computer files. He wasn't looking for additional cryptic clues to William Tremont's appeal. Instead, he was hoping to find the answer to the one question that still nagged at him. Why had Kerry Paulsen committed suicide?

He suspected that if Paulsen had left a suicide note, it would be hidden behind another code. Instead of looking for a subtle file name, he narrowed his search by looking for files written between June 17, Paulsen's last visit to Tremont in prison, and June 30, the date of his death.

It took him only ten minutes by scanning within those perimeters to isolate a file labelled "Star Trek." He wasn't surprised that a loner like Paulsen would be a "Trekkie." After all, Pachomius admitted, he was one as well. Opening the file, he was initially puzzled to find three scripts featuring Captain Kirk and Spock. He was halfway through the first script when he realized that what he was reading wasn't from the Star Trek TV show or any of the Star Trek movies. The plots were clearly Paulsen's own inventions, thinly-veiled fantasies featuring Tremont as Captain Kirk and Paulsen as Spock. In the first story line, Spock rescues Kirk from a trap set by the Romulans. In the second script, Kirk is held in a suspended state by another alien race until Spock saves him, an outcome that Pachomius thought was Paulsen shamelessly borrowing from Star Wars. In the third, Kirk and Spock fight back-to-back, hacking away at vines with snake heads that are encircling their legs. The third script, dated just days before his last visit to Tremont in prison, ended with Captain Kirk turning to Spock and saying, "We're friends for life, Spock."

Pachomius could imagine Paulsen writing those words. By the end of June, Paulsen had done everything he could to save Tremont, passing along everything he'd received from the anonymous source. Pachomius imagined Paulsen visiting Tremont that last time, expecting Tremont to thank him for winning his release, maybe even using the words from Paulsen's fantasy, "We're friends for life, Kerry."

But within days of that final visit, Paulsen committed suicide. Pachomius understood that something soul-crushing for Paulsen happened on that last visit. Had Tremont laughed at him? Had he sneered at the one person who'd remained faithful to him for the past thirteen years, the one person who fed him the news of Worthy's divorce, supplied the list of cases in 2011 and 2012 that Worthy fumbled, and most important, provided the key information about the dating confusion on Tremont's toxicology screening?

Pachomius looked away from the pitiful Star Trek scripts, sensing what Tremont most likely said to Paulsen on that last visit. "You think you matter to me? You don't matter to anybody. When I'm released . . ."

And in that moment, Captain Kirk jettisoned Spock out into a cold and uncaring universe.

Closing his computer, Pachomius said a prayer for the soul of Kerry Paulsen. Tremont had killed Paulsen as surely as he had killed Renee Vickers, and Pachomius knew that if his appeal were granted, Tremont would kill again.

NOVEMBER 3, 2023, DR. PETER JOHNSON'S OFFICE

WITH HENDERSON AND NICK ABSORBED WITH locating Samiyah Aisha, Lena and Sulla were only too happy to drive to Dr. Peter Johnson's office at the Blood Center in South Detroit. If Peter Johnson wasn't the med student thirty years before who'd convinced Doc Wallace to let him assist, then they'd have no choice but to drive to Dr. Mason Schmidt's office in Lansing. With final arguments in Tremont's appeal scheduled for Monday, they knew that what they found—or didn't find this day—would likely determine the judges' ruling, one way or another.

Even though Lena and Sulla had formed a quick bond over the past few days, Lena could feel the tension in the car. They'd said little until Sulla said, "I don't know if you remember what Jamie said the other night, that Chris would be cleared in the appeal because I'd said so. I pray he's right," Sulla said.

"I do remember him saying that. I know that meant a lot to Chris."

"We all know Jamie has limitations, but sometimes Jamie grasps things that the rest of us miss. What I mean is that no matter what happened when Tremont was arrested, Jamie knows that Chris is incapable of doing what he's being accused of."

Lena felt a lump in her throat. "I try not to think about how Chris will take it if Tremont gets off. So, I'm going to hang on to Jamie's faith."

At the blood center, once the receptionist understood that they hadn't come to donate blood, she asked the reason for their visit.

"We'd here to talk with Dr. Peter Johnson, if he's available," Lena said.

"May I ask what this is about?"

"It's about a court case," Lena explained.

The receptionist's eyebrows shot up as she dialed a number and repeated what Lena had said. Ending the call, she said, "Dr. Johnson can see you now. His office is the third on the left."

Lena's first impression of Peter Johnson was that he seemed a perfect match for his office. Stacks of folders and papers covered the shelves and the desk behind which sat a man in his late thirties. Johnson's tie was askew, and an ink stain had bled from his shirt pocket. On the wall was a framed *Mad Magazine* cover, featuring Alfred E. Neuman in a doctor's garb.

If there ever was someone who looked like he could have made a careless mistake as a med student, this is the guy, Lena thought.

"Peter Johnson," he said as she rose from his chair. After Lena and Sulla introduced themselves, he added, "Sit, sit, please. I understand you're here on a court case." He laughed nervously, saying, "Don't tell me there's a malpractice case against me."

"No, nothing like that," Lena said. "We understand you had a rotation in pathology in your second year of med school."

"Did I? Well, if you say so. I can't say I remember much about that, other than how scared we all were of Doc Wallace. You've heard of him?"

"Yes, and that's what we want to ask you about. Can you tell us your memories of Dr. Wallace?"

Peter Johnson made a face like he had tasted something sour. "He looked like Gandalf from *Lord of the Rings*. In fact, that's what we called him—Gandalf. When he looked at you, you could feel him boring a hole through your brain." He shivered. "Just the thought of the man . . ."

"Did you ever assist in his lab? We're primarily interested in a toxicology screening for a William Tremont."

"You got to be kidding. We had to watch the great Doc Wallace from afar. Nobody was allowed in Doc Wallace's domain."

"So your father didn't convince Dr. Wallace to make an exception for you? You never filled out court documents for him?"

"You mean because my old man, Dr. Oscar 'Gus' Johnson, was president of Detroit's AMA at the time? That's the last thing I wanted my old man to do. I wanted to be as far away from Gandalf as I could."

Lena's whole body went limp, aware that they had nothing more to ask Peter Johnson. He looked the part, but he was clearly not a med student who'd have put himself forward. She was getting ready to stand when Sulla spoke.

"Did you happen to know another med student at the time named Mason Schmidt?"

Peter Johnson's head shot back in his chair even as his palm hit his desk, unbalancing a column of papers. "Ha, old Schmidty! God bless him, yes, now I remember. Yeah, Schmidty was a legend. Of course, with a name like that, you can guess what his nickname was—'Shitty.' Schmidty and I weren't at the same med school, but his school's rotation in pathology was right before ours. His old man was even more powerful than mine, and Schmidty was happy to ride his daddy's coattails. I hear Mason is some hotshot psychiatrist now. God knows, he would have needed counseling after what Doc Wallace did to him."

Lena felt a wave of dizziness, Peter Johnson's comments sending her emotions on a rollercoaster ride.

"Can you be specific about what Dr. Wallace did to him?" Lena asked.

"Happy to do so. Mason was the golden boy; his old man made sure of that. The first day we showed up for our pathology rotation, we heard what had happened to the golden boy. His old man had twisted Doc Wallace's arm, and after badgering him for days, Gandalf let Mason down on the lab floor while he was running some tests. But that wasn't enough for Mason. The rumor was that Mason turned to Doc at some point and asked—he probably dropped his old man's name—to make his specialness official by allowing him to fill out the paper work of whatever test Wallace was running. Schmidty had balls, I give him that."

Feeling close to screaming, Lena found the only words that came to mind were in Italian. She looked at Sulla with a pleading gaze.

"Dr. Johnson, are you saying that something went wrong?" Sulla asked.

"Oh, yes. Another rumor was that Mason had been out drinking with some of his buddies the night before the shit hit the fan. Ha, 'The shit hit the fan for Shitty.' It sounds like the beginning of a poem, like 'Casey at Bat.' Anyway, maybe the booze gave him the nerve to push his luck. Old Doc Wallace let Schmidty fill out the official forms, but here's where this gets fuzzy for me. Schmidty made some mistake. It was probably something minor, no big deal, but with Doc Wallace any mistake was unacceptable. We were told that everyone in the building heard him yelling."

"Did you ever hear what kind of mistake Mason Schmidt made?" Lena asked.

"No, all I remember is that on our first day with Doc Wallace, he lit into us as if all we'd made the mistake. He went on and on about doctors who thought they were gods. I remember him calling the floor of his lab the 'holy of holies,' and never again would his sacred space be violated."

Lena didn't try to hide the tears welling up in her eyes, but Peter Johnson didn't seem to notice.

"I got a question for you," he said, sitting forward. "This trip down memory lane has been fun, but all this happened, what, twelve or thirteen years ago? Whatever mistake Schmidty made, it was minor. Only someone like Gandalf would have made a big deal about it. But if I remember it, Schmidty has to remember it as well. I should warn you, though. If Schmidty is anything like he was back then, he won't want to talk about it." Peter Johnson smiled. "But you're going to make my day if you tell me there's a court case where his mistake is important."

Through her tears, Lena laughed, rising from the chair. "Then, I guess we've made your day."

Sulla also rose. "And you've made more than our day. My friend and I, well, we think you might have saved a good man's reputation."

CHAPTER FORTY-ONE

———◆———

HENDERSON'S DEN

HENDERSON, NICK, AND WORTHY SAT TOGETHER in Henderson's den, unaware of what Sulla and Lena had learned from Dr. Johnson. The men's challenge was to lure Samiyah Aisha into the open. They agreed that the DEA agent would retreat into the shadows if they confronted her directly.

"I'm convinced," Henderson said, "that the man calling himself Gus Cooper and Samiyah Aisha have been partners all along. We all know that the DEA is secretive, and for some reason the agency doesn't want the truth about King's death coming out. The guy's been following Marina because he believes that Sophia will tell Marina first if she remembered what really happened the night King was shot. And he's right. Sophia has remembered."

Worthy started to say something but then stopped.

"Go ahead, Christopher," Nick said.

"Look, I'm an outsider on this case, so maybe I shouldn't say anything."

"Geez, Chris, you're hardly an outsider. We've shared everything we know about Sophia with you. Besides, you're still Lieutenant Christopher Worthy at heart, remember?"

Worthy grimaced. "We'll see on Monday if my reputation is still intact, but let's not think about that. What I'm wondering about is what you just said, Hoops. You said that the DEA for some reason doesn't want the truth of King's murder coming out. But we know that Samiyah Aisha, if she's Connie, was the one who killed King. Why would the DEA cover up one of their agents taking King out? Maybe the DEA thinks that King's killing looked like an assassination, which wouldn't be a good image for the agency, but I can't see that leading to my main problem with your theory. You're saying that the DEA knowingly let Sophia, an innocent woman barely more than a teenager, go to prison for thirty years for a crime she didn't commit. That's pretty cold, even by DEA standards."

No one said anything until Nick asked, "Is it possible that Samiyah Aisha is too valuable to the DEA to be named? Or maybe the DEA thinks she could be targeted by others in the drug trade if her identity came out. But I agree. Letting Sophia take the fall for what this agent did is inhuman."

Henderson sat back and looked up at the ceiling. "What we can all agree on is that we need to find Samiyah Aisha. So, how do we do that, and how do we get her to talk?"

"I have a suggestion," Nick said, "but it involves other people, people I'm not sure will agree to help."

"Let's hear it," Henderson said.

"I think what we lack, even if we find Aisha, is leverage. She doesn't owe us anything. The one person who might be able to drag her out of the shadows is Marina. Wouldn't the agent be desperate to know what Sophia has remembered?"

"You're right, Nick. We should approach her through Marina," Henderson said. "But what would that approach look like?"

Worthy smiled. "I've worked with you long enough, Nick, to know from your expression that you have something in mind. You said that we'd need the help of other people. Marina is only one person. So who else?"

"It's a group of people who'll be harder to convince than Marina. I'm thinking of my community at St. Simeon's. This Samiyah Aisha must know from working with Cooper that Marina has gone to St. Simeon's not once, but twice. Samiyah would know that Marina sees St. Simeon's as a safe place to meet."

"That could work, Nick, except for one problem," Worthy said.

"I know, I know. The problem is getting my abbot's permission. If there's even the smallest chance of danger or violence, he'll say no. But

St. Simeon's is where this whole thing started. I first saw Marina at the far end of our lake. The lake is over a mile from the main buildings."

"Won't Aisha have to come through the main gate and identify herself?" Henderson asked.

"That's no problem. Brother Pachomius, the one who's decoded Kerry Paulsen's files, also works security. I'll alert him to let her in and direct her to the lake." Nick saw that Worthy had started writing. "What are you doing, Christopher?"

Worthy said, "Give me a minute." After a few moments of writing, he handed a note to Nick.

"It's something we could send by email," Worthy said.

Nick read the note out loud. "My sister Sophia's memory has cleared. That is bad news for you. I know that you might not believe me. When we meet, I can prove it. Meet me tomorrow night, Saturday, at six-thirty at St. Simeon's monastery outside Tiffin, Ohio. I'll be sitting on a bench at the far end of the monastery's lake. If you think I'm bluffing and decide not to come, I go to the police. If anything happens to Sophia in Barminster, I go to the police."

CHAPTER FORTY-TWO

———◆———

SAMIYAH AISHA'S APARTMENT

SAMIYAH STARED AT HER PHONE, WAITING FOR LOFTEN to call with the time for the meet that would bring the search for the dirty agent—now agents—to an end. When Fithian had shared the news about Wilson and D'Poussaint, she'd almost told him the truth, but shame and feeling a failure had prevented her confessing. She was about to call Fithian at home when her computer dinged, indicating an email.

Her first thought was that Loften had sent the message by email until she remembered that he didn't know her email address. As she read the message from Marina Demetrios, panic rose from her stomach into her throat.

"My sister Sophia's memory has cleared. That is bad news for you. I know that you might not believe me. When we meet, I can prove it. Meet me tomorrow night, Saturday, at six-thirty at St. Simeon's monastery outside Tiffin, Ohio. I'll be sitting on a bench at the far end of the monastery's lake. If you think I'm bluffing and decide not to come, I go to the police. If anything happens to Sophia in Barminster, I go to the police."

Samiyah had heard from her contact in Barminster that Sophia's memory had returned, but she'd hoped for one more day, two at the most, to complete her plan. Once Fithian had incriminating photos of Wilson or D'Poussaint, she'd be only too happy to break her silence about the night King was killed. Letting Sophia take the blame had seemed the only way to remain in the shadows as she continued her search for the dirty agent. The email from Marina Demetrios, however, threatening that she'd go to the police, would alert Wilson and D'Poussaint within hours, and they'd go to ground for years if not forever.

Just as she was about to telephone Fithian, her phone rang.

"Tell your cartel contact that the meet is on for six tomorrow night," Loften said. "Call me when you hear the location."

Samiyah felt as if she were at the bottom of a hole, one she'd dug for herself, but now the sides were falling as in on her. The plan to force the dirty agents out into the open was about to succeed, but the time set by Marina Demetrios for a meeting was on the same night and miles away in northwest Ohio.

"The guy from the cartel needs more time," she said. "He now says Sunday."

Loften swore on the other end of the phone before saying, "Are you playing me, Savreen?"

For a moment, Samiyah forgot that was using the name Savreen, not Connie, with Loften. "No, he wants to meet, but it has to be Sunday."

When Loften didn't reply, Samiyah asked, "Should I tell him Sunday is okay?"

"Yeah, but call me as soon as he tells you the location."

"Right." Disconnecting, she sat frozen on her couch. Fifteen minutes before, she would have been relieved to hear from Loften and know that she was hours away from flushing out Wilson or D'Poussaint, but Marina Demetrios' email had forced a change of plans. Samiyah's only hope was to meet with Marina and convince her to give her another twenty-four hours.

✠

NOVEMBER 4, 2023, ST. SIMEON'S LAKE

SAMIYAH WAS RELIEVED THAT THE MONK MANNING the entrance to the monastery hadn't seemed surprised when she asked directions to the lake. She could have never predicted that her work over the last year and half would led her to a monastery, but here she was. Following the signs to the lake, she found three people waiting for her.

She parked and walked toward a bench where a young woman, whom she assumed was Marina Demetrios, was sitting. She could see that Marina had been crying, and Samiyah knew that she was the cause of those tears.

A tall Black man greeted her by asking, "Where's your partner?"

"Who are you two?" she asked looking from the tall man to someone she assumed was a monk.

"I'm Father Nicholas Fortis, a friend of the Demetrios family."

"All you need to know about me is that I'm a retired policeman," the other man said. I asked you a question. Where's your partner?"

"I don't know what you're talking about. I don't have a partner."

Samiyah waited for Marina to say something but it was the retired policeman who spoke. "We know about the other agent, the guy calling himself Gus Cooper. And we know that the two of you have been tag-teaming all along. You were the inside agent, planted inside Francine Nichols' circle, and he's the one who's been stalking Marina."

"I swear I don't know any Gus Cooper. There is no other agent; just me. Why would anyone be stalking you?" she asked, looking at Marina. But Marina's expression gave nothing away.

"Lying won't help you now, Samiyah. It's too late," the monk said. "Your partner has been here twice, both times when Marina came to St. Simeon's on retreat."

Samiyah tried to make sense of what she was hearing. Who were these people talking about? "I still don't understand why anyone would be following you, Marina," she said.

"And I don't understand why you're lying," the ex-cop said. "When Sophia's memory cleared, your partner knew that she'd tell Marina that it was you who killed King, not her."

"It's not what you think," Samiyah began, fearing that she wouldn't be able to explain the tangled story that led them to be standing beside the lake.

"Just tell us the truth," the monk said.

"The truth? Will you believe me if I do?"

"The truth is all that matters now, my dear."

The unexpected term of endearment gave her courage. "I was just what you said, an undercover DEA agent planted inside Francine

Nichols' circle. My mission was to find out who Reginald King reported to. We'd discovered that this person was in law enforcement, a bent cop. And yes, I admit that I knew Sophia. I pitied her. She was so trusting, so vulnerable. So many times, I wished I could rescue her, save her from getting into drugs too deep."

For the first time, Marina spoke. "Instead, you let her take the blame for what you did." .

"I don't deny that, but I need you to understand why I did that. I'd discovered that the dirty agent was in my own agency, the DEA. That made everything harder. I had to find out his identity before he found out about who I really was. But it turns out I failed somehow. That's why King came that night to kill me that night."

"Tell us everything that happened," the monk said.

"I knew something was up by the way that Francine was acting. I'd catch her looking at me, and then she'd look away. She was hitting the coke harder than usual. Anyway, Francine was distracted and wasn't paying attention to Sophia." She turned toward Marina. "Maybe Sophia was so high that night because she picked up how tense everything seemed at Francine's place. But I remember Sophia saying she'd had a fight with you that day," she said, looking at Marina.

Marina gasped. "O God, I forgot about that. The anniversary of Momma's death was coming up, and I tried to shame Sophia into going to the cemetery with the rest of us. But she wasn't having any of it."

No one said anything until the ex-cop spoke. "Father Nick and I have read the transcript of the case. I never understood how Sophia could have shot Reginald King with his own gun, but the same is true of you. You say that he'd discovered you were DEA and had come to kill you. What really happened that night?"

Samiyah shook her head. "You're wondering how I managed to survive. I'd be dead now if Francine hadn't had a panic attack on the way to the motel and had to pull over. She was hyperventilating, and it took me a few minutes to calm her down. Finally, she managed to say, 'Drugs are one thing, but I can't do this.' I asked her what she meant, and for a moment she didn't answer. I kept at her, and eventually she said 'I can't do murder.'"

"In the trial, Francine said my sister was lying down in the backseat. Did she hear Francine say that?" Marina asked.

"No, Mouse—that was your sister's nickname—was out of it. The whole time Francine was freaking out, Sophia didn't even stir. I'm sure she didn't overhear. But that was when I realized why Francine had been so nervous all day. My cover had been blown. Francine finally told me King's plan. She was supposed to bring me to the meeting place, a cheap motel room in the city. King would confront me, get everything he could out of me one way or another, and then kill me."

"So my sister had no reason to be there?"

Samiyah thought for a moment. "I guess that's right, but she tended to tag along with Francine."

Marina was now staring at her. "But if she'd stayed in the car when you got to the motel, she couldn't have been charged with King's murder."

Until that moment, Samiyah hadn't considered that Sophia was a perfect example of someone being in the wrong place at the wrong time. "Yes, I see that now."

The ex-cop said, "Finish the story. With what Francine told you, why didn't you refuse to go to the meet with King?"

"In the car, all I could think was that with my cover blown, my only chance of finding out the identity of the dirty DEA agent was to go to the meet and somehow turn the tables on King. This would be my only change to find out the name of the Judas. But to do that, I had to get King's gun, and that meant Francine had to help me. I told Francine if she helped, I, as a DEA agent, could guarantee that she'd be granted immunity." Samiyah paused before adding, "I never intended to shoot King."

"So you walked into this motel room, and then what happened?" the ex-cop asked.

"I knew King would be waiting, but I expected him to ease into things and try to catch me off guard. And that's where Sophia played a role, even though she wasn't conscious enough to know it. Francine and I carried her into the motel room, and Francine did as I asked. She acted all panicky, telling King she didn't know what to do. She said she was sure your sister had OD'ed and yelled, 'Do something, Reggie?' So King started cussing as he jumped up from his chair and grabbed your sister. He threw Sophia down on the couch and began slapping her face."

"A distraction, then," the ex-cop said.

"And it worked. I could see that King didn't have a gun on him, so I thought his weapon must be in his coat that was draped over the back of a chair. I had just seconds to rummage through the coat, but I found the gun, a Sig Sauer with a silencer. I told him to raise his arms and sit down in the chair. My plan was to tie him to the chair and give him a chance to cut his jail time by telling me the name of the bent agent. But . . ."

"Instead, he charged you, right?" the monk asked.

"Like one of those bulls you see in a rodeo. I didn't even know I'd pulled the trigger until I saw him fall, blood spurting out of his upper chest. All I could think about was that I'd failed. I'd killed the one person who could give me the name of the bent agent."

"What did my sister do?" Marina asked.

"She sort of came to. I remember she sat up, but she clearly didn't know where she was. Francine meanwhile didn't have to pretend to be freaking out. She kept saying 'They're going to kill me. When they find out what you did, they'll kill me.' Somehow, her saying that made me snap out of it. I saw what I needed to do if I were to keep looking for the bent agent. Francine had opened the door to the room, and I hadn't touched anything except King's coat and the gun. But when I started to tell Francine my plan, she said, 'You're not going to pin this on me.' That's when I told her the rest of the plan, which you figured out."

"No, which my sister remembered."

No one said anything until Samiyah added, "I convinced myself at the beginning that your sister would get off light by being so young. Even when I heard that she was arraigned as an adult, I was told that the prosecution had agreed to the lesser charge of manslaughter. No one expected the judge to come down so hard on your sister. But I didn't stop there. Has Sophia ever mentioned her second cellmate, Deidra?"

When Marina nodded, Samiyah continued. "I arrested Deidra for possession six months before. I promised that I'd speak on her behalf at her next parole hearing if she'd move in with your sister and protect her."

"Don't expect me to absolve you," Marina said. "My sister was nearly killed in prison, and her blood would have been on you."

Samiyah accepted Marina's anger without protest, knowing that she'd react the same way if she were Sophia's sister. But Samiyah also realized that her confession, which she knew was what Marina, the monk, and the ex-cop had come for, was for her just a prelude to what she'd say next.

"I've told you the truth about what happened the night King died, and you have every right to hate me, Marina." Looking at all of them, she said, "But I'm begging you. I need twenty-four hours to finish what I started almost two years ago. We're that close to uncovering the dirty agents, two men who've betrayed their oaths and taken in hundreds of thousands of dollars, all from people like Sophia. Can you give me that?"

CHAPTER FORTY-THREE

---❖---

St. Simeon's Entrance Gate

Brother Pachomius smarted under Father Nick's direction—no, order—that he'd given him that afternoon. Father Nick had seemed preoccupied, tense even. "You have to stay at the entrance gate tonight, Pachomius. Given that it's Saturday and most of the weekend retreatants arrived yesterday, there shouldn't be much traffic. But I expect a young woman to drive in and ask how to find the lake."

"Who is she?" he'd asked.

"She's a drug enforcement agent from Detroit, but don't ask her to identify herself. I don't what to alarm her, and any hint that you were expecting her could ruin everything."

Ruin everything. Father Nick is remembering how I disobeyed orders before, but what is "everything?" he thought. *Haven't I helped enough to be told what's going on?*

As he sat by the entrance gate, he wished the monastery had cameras aimed toward the lake. But if Father Nick wanted him to know what happened, he'd hear that after the event. With every half-hour bring no one to the gate, Pachomius felt more and more devalued.

No, worse than devalued. I feel used, he thought. *When Father Nick needs a computer geek, he calls on me. And now he needs a watchdog, telling him when a drug enforcement officer arrives. So I'm now a watchdog. But other than that, you're not in the picture, Pachomius.*

He thought back to Father Nick and Marina Demetrios arriving that morning, the car driven by a large man who glared at him through the windshield. He hadn't recognized the man but knew from photos online that the man wasn't Christopher Worthy.

After that car arrived, the only vehicles coming through the entrance gate had been a garbage truck and a car full of priests. He yawned as he looked at his watch and saw that if nothing happened soon, he'd miss dinner and have to settle for leftovers in the kitchen. His stomach growled in protest, and, as he focused on the stick of gum he was unwrapping, he didn't see the car approaching the gate until a woman looked out the driver's window and said, "Which way to the lake?"

"Just follow the signs. You can't miss it," he said even as he was tempted to ask if she needed him to escort her.

As the car drove through the gate and headed toward the fork in the road, Pachomius thought of all the reasons to follow her on foot. What if the woman misread the signs and went the wrong way? Wouldn't Father Nick want him to make sure the woman didn't get lost?

No, if I do that, Father Nick will know that I've disobeyed once again, he thought, as he sat by the computer screens in the security office. That was when, to his surprise, he saw a car on the screen that covered the road running perpendicular to St. Simeon's entrance gate. The car moved slowly past the monastery gate until it came to the end of St. Simeon's grounds and turned right. The scene brought back the memory of sitting in the security office with Father Nick weeks before and seeing something similar.

He couldn't keep his mind from jumping. There had been no traffic for hours, and then two cars not more than three or four minutes apart had appeared.

He stood, grabbed the security cellphone, and left the office. "Forgive me, Lord, if I'm breaking my vow of obedience, but I have to find out."

✝

St. Simeon's Lake

SAMIYAH COULD SEE FROM THE LOOK on Marina's face that her request for twenty-four hours to flush out the dirty agents would be rejected.

The monk and the ex-cop with Marina would undoubtedly leave the decision to her.

"I know your sister has suffered because I put my job over her right to be free. And what Sophia has gone through, and what you too, Marina, have gone through, is a huge sacrifice. Worse yet, I forced that sacrifice on you without giving you a choice. All I can do is repeat what I said. The dirty agents who we'll catch tomorrow are responsible for the deaths and the ruined lives of hundreds of others. If you force me to go to the police now, those agents will disappear from sight. But that won't stop what they've been doing. They'll just be cleverer about doing it."

As she finished her plea, she heard a commotion from the edge of the woods.

The man named Henderson looked from the sound to stare at Samiyah. "So you did bring your partner, which means everything you've said is just a lie."

Confused, Samiyah turned and saw two figures coming toward them, the first someone who brought her a wave of relief. This man would vouch for her, and she would no longer be holding her secret alone. She'd get those twenty-four hours and complete her mission.

Everything changed when she saw a second figure, Eldridge Loften, gun in hand, to the right of Ronald Fithian.

Samiyah slumped down on the bench as the nightmare that began with Marina's email the previous afternoon took an even darker turn. The scene would have made sense if Loften's gun had been trained on Fithian. Instead, Fithian had brought out his own gun from a shoulder holster.

"What the hell are you doing here, Savreen?" Loften said.

"Savreen? Don't you mean—oh, now I see," Fithian said, continuing to step toward them. "Savreen, Connie, and Samiyah. All the same person. I should have guessed."

The monk, edging closer to Marina, said, "And my guess is that Gus Cooper isn't your real name."

"You're the man who's been stalking me?" Marina asked.

Samiyah, head in her hands, said, "His real name is Ronald Fithian. He's my supervisor, someone high up in the DEA. He's the one who hired me to find the traitor in our agency, and the man next to him is Eldridge Loften, the dealer who's taken Reginald King's place." She stared at Fithian. "You were using me all along, weren't you? I was never meant to find the dirty agent. I was supposed to let you know how safe your secret is."

"Now that we've made introductions and we've all heard Samiyah's heart-wrenching story—yes, we heard it all from back there in the trees," Fithian said, "I'd like the three of you to join Marina by the bench. I don't suspect that you, Father Fortis, are armed, but my guess is that you are," he said, looking at Henderson. "So take your gun out slowly and put it on the ground."

As Henderson complied, Samiyah said, "You followed me from Detroit?"

"Not so difficult. I put a tracker on your car the day I got an email from Rebecca Williston. You remember Williston, Marina. She's the one who arrested your sister. The email was my wake-up call, although it never made sense to me that a doped-up community college dropout like Sophia Demetrios killed Reginald King, a street-smart drug lord, with his own gun. But my bigger mistake was buying your story, Samiyah, that you were with your father at the hospital the night King was killed. How did you get nurse hospital to lie for you?"

"She didn't lie. I got the call from the E.R. right after I left the motel room."

"So you were clear-headed even after killing King. I'm impressed, Samiyah, and I admit you fooled me. I didn't realize that I trusted the wrong rookie agent until I saw Williston's request, asking about an African-American female agent who was either Jewish or Muslim. Williston knew or suspected something, something about King's death, and you were somehow involved. That's why I gave Williston your name and contact information. I had to find out what you knew or thought you knew, and I thought Williston would find that out for me. How am I doing so far, Samiyah?"

Samiyah, her head still in her hands, didn't reply.

Fithian said, "Oh, well, you deserve to know how badly you failed. Williston could have gotten your name from only two people: Francine or Sophia. When I followed you here the first time, Marina, and saw you talking with Father Fortis, I knew that Sophia's memory must be returning."

"Except it wasn't," Nick said. "Marina came here because Sophia had given up hope."

"I stand corrected, Father," Fithian said with a smile. "But settle one thing for me, Samiyah. Did I fool you with my story about Lamar Wilson and Leonard D'Poussaint? Was that why you were begging for another twenty-four hours?"

In little more than a whisper, Samiyah said, "We all trusted you and looked up to you. I looked up to you."

"Did you trust me, really? As your supervisor, your mentor, shouldn't you have cleared with me what you've been doing under your new name, Savreen?"

"I almost told you everything in your office yesterday. I was going to ask you to be the second witness when Wilson and D'Poussaint showed up."

"Then that's something we can all wish you'd done. If you'd cleared your plan with me, Loften and I obviously wouldn't be here tonight. You'd have been able to ask Marina for her forgiveness—fat chance of that, I bet—and I wouldn't be asking myself what I'm going to do with the four of you. I can't let you leave knowing what you know."

"You're prepared to kill all of us?" Nick asked.

"Father, really. It's more accurate to ask if I'm prepared to kill four more people."

"How many others have you killed?" Samiyah asked.

"That's good, Samiyah. Try to activate my conscience, tell me it's not too late for me to do the right thing. The truth is, I don't remember how many others I've had to kill."

"Tell me, were you ever a good agent?"

"Do I remember the first time I stumbled? Do you remember yours, Samiyah? Oh, yes, Reggie figured out that you were skimming off the take. And now I understand why you kept looking for your 'dirty agent.' And Father, you'll appreciate this. Samiyah needed to find me to atone for skimming money."

"I was going to pay the money back."

"We all make promises, but how many do we keep? Anyway, once King found out about your skimming, he wanted to kill you. I told him to wait, because you were still unknowingly feeding me info on how safe

I was. But when I told him you were DEA and working undercover, he lost it. That's why he went for you that night. He lost perspective; that's something I've tried never to do. But where was I? Oh, yes, how it all started for me. Like you, I started by skimming off a few hundred here or there, then a thousand."

"Are you saying you have a sick father like me?"

"No, nothing so noble. All that money lying around in boxes and bags, Samiyah, and what, we're pulling down forty-five to sixty thousand a year before taxes? It made no sense."

"So it was just greed," Nick said. "Simple greed."

"I prefer to think of it as accepting reality. There is no war on drugs, Father. Drugs won that war long ago. Oh, sure, the DEA gets pumped up when we—when they intercept—a big shipment. And God, how we gloated when we extradited El Chapo. But the DEA is a mosquito. It buzzes around, and once in a blue moon it manages to bite, but it leaves only a temporary itch, nothing more."

✝

IN ST. SIMEON'S WOODS

PACHOMIUS RAN DOWN THE ROAD TAKEN by the second car. What he planned to do depended on what he saw when he rounded the corner. If he didn't see the car that had appeared on the monitor, he'd know that he'd overreacted and would return to the monastery for dinner and prayers. But if he found an empty car parked there, he'd scale the stone wall and use one of the paths to reach the lake.

Turning the corner, he realized with the growing darkness that he couldn't see if a car was parked farther down the road. He walked along the verge for a few minutes before he spotted a car pulled off the road into the grass. He hid behind a tree and waited until he felt certain that the car was empty. Approaching it quietly, he saw that it was a Ford sedan with a spotlight on the driver's side. *A cop car,* he thought as he peeked inside. The only thing he could make out was a red dot flashing on the dash, the indication that the car alarm was set. He stepped back, fearful that even touching the car would set off the alarm.

Now what? he asked himself, wondering if continuing on to the lake would bring him to a scene where he was neither needed nor wanted. Father Nick might have any one of many reasons for calling the police for help. *But if the police had been called, why hadn't they come through the front gate?* he thought.

In the process of scaling the wall, Pachomius dropped the cellphone, and in the growing gloom it took him a few minutes to find it in the heavy leaf cover. He turned on the phone's light briefly and found a path that he hoped would take him to the lake.

Two hundred yards farther along the path, he slowed as he heard voices. Removing his shoes, he moved from one tree to another until he saw what looked like four people by the bench and two men standing ten yards away. He inched forward, hoping to hear what was being said, but he was able to make out only a few words from one of the men whose back was to him.

He squinted into the darkness hoping to see Father Nick. At the same moment that he picked out Father Nick's large frame as he sat with the other three, he heard the words "Father, really. It's more accurate to ask if I'm prepared to kill four more people."

In that instant, Pachomius recognized the man's voice as the man who used the name Gus Cooper and followed Marina to the monastery twice before. He also realized how useless he was. The two men had guns, and what did he have? A cell phone. The realization triggered a memory from high school when he'd been cornered in the boys' bathroom by two bullies, just an hour after the bigger one had been given detention for tripping Pachomius as he walked to his desk. At the moment of being caught by the observant teacher, the bully had stared at Pachomius, as if he'd forced the bully to pick on him just by existing and being the smartest kid in the class.

In that high school bathroom, he hadn't even had a cell phone, and yet he'd managed to leave without a scratch. The only weapon he'd had was what he had now—his quick-thinking mind. As he studied the scene in front of him, the two armed men having their backs to him, he imagined himself charging them. But his first thought was rarely a workable one. He wasn't Bruce Lee, despite his childhood fantasies. Even if he managed to knock one of them over, the imbalance of the situation would remain. The other man would still hold his gun, and

Pachomius would be forced to join the four others. That is, unless he was shot first.

First things first. I have to figure out what my goal is, he thought. *I have to force the two armed men, if not to surrender, to leave without hurting anyone. So how do I do that?*

In the high school bathroom, he'd moved to the far wall and put his hand on the fire alarm.

"You wouldn't dare," the bigger bully had said.

"Not only will I pull it, but I'll say you did it. Dwayne, who do you think they'll believe? You, who're repeating your junior year or me, one of Cortland's top ten students?"

Even as Dwayne had taken a step toward the door, he whispered, "Expect to see me in the parking lot after school."

That was the advantage Pachomius had over the Dwaynes of the world. Dwayne hadn't expected him to do anything but cower; whereas, he'd anticipated that Dwayne would have no response but to threaten him.

"Actually, Dwayne, you won't be waiting for me in the parking lot, not today, not ever," he'd said.

"What are going to do, hit me over the head with your computer?"

"Wow, Dwayne, you almost got it. You wouldn't have any way of knowing this, but I've managed to break into the school's network. I know your confidential ID number—it's 715478898, but as you now know, it's no longer confidential. I can send out anything I want under your name. Even if you get your ID number changed, I'll know that number before you do. You tripped me today in class Dwayne, but that's nothing compared to the hundred different ways I can trip you up. So if you ever threaten me again, I'll ruin you here at Cortland."

And Dwayne had bought it all. Yes, he'd managed when in high school to find out Dwayne's ID number, but the rest had been pure bluff. And creating a convincing bluff was exactly what he needed to do now.

He hid behind a tree, turned on the phone, and immediately silenced it as he thought, *Let's hope you're a smart phone, a really smart phone.*

He pushed the menu button and scanned the options, hoping one would offer a glimmer of hope. He first saw the emergency button that would connect him with the Tifton, Ohio, police department. Tifton was a good ten miles away, and he knew he'd have to be out of the hearing range of the men to make that call. Besides that, he doubted if Father Nick and the others had that much time left.

Hearing the panicky voice within him saying over and over again, *Do something,* he suddenly realized that he hadn't once thought of praying. *Some monk I am,* he thought. *Holy God, Holy Mighty, Holy Immortal, have mercy on us—have mercy on me. I believe you want to spare the lives of Father Nick and the others. I pray that you will open my mind.*

Even as he repeated the prayer to himself, his eye saw the option on the phone for "Fire Emergency." Since he'd been at St. Simeon's, there had been no such emergency, and he had no idea what would happen if he pushed that button. Would sirens go off throughout the monastery, or would the number of the Tifton Fire Department appear on the screen?

Scrolling through the other options listed, he saw that he had no choice. But a plan had formed in his mind, and hoping the plan was an answer to his prayer, he started to put it in place.

The first part of the plan was the most problematic. He had to step out from behind the tree and hope that Father Nick or one of the others standing with him would see him, despite the growing darkness, signaling from behind the two men.

After taking a deep breath, he stepped out to where he could see Father Nick clearly. Everything depended on Father Nick seeing him.

Father Nick's face, however, was turned to one of the women. But Pachomius saw the man with Father Nick looking directly at him and nodding slowly. Pachomius held up five fingers and with his other hand made a circular motion. He prayed that his signal made sense to the man—keep the two men talking for five minutes.

He turned to begin the second part of the plan, to retrace his steps to St. Simeon's boundary line. After the first thirty yards, with his stockinged feet complaining of the sharp sticks and roots, he jogged, then ran, toward the wall. Scaling it, he was relieved to see that he'd come out only fifteen yards from the car.

Moving to the driver's door, he initiated with more prayer the last part of the plan that he hoped had been given to him with God's blessing. At the same moment he hit the button on the phone for "Fire Emergency," he yanked with all his strength on the car's driver's door handle. What

followed was the most beautiful sounds he'd ever heard, fire alarms going off from throughout the monastery, including on the path to the
lake, and, at the same time, the car's alarm emitting a loud and pulsating
shriek. Even better, he didn't hear what he most feared—the sound of
guns going off.

He was so grateful that the plan worked that he'd forgotten about the
gunmen returning to the car until he heard the sounds of cursing and
running. He dove into the ditch next to the road and prayed that he'd be
invisible in the darkness.

"Dammit, where is he?" the voice he recognized as Gus Cooper's
asked.

"Who you talking about, and who the hell cares? We got to get out of
here," the other man said.

"Somebody set off the car alarm, that's who," Gus Cooper answered,
and from the bottom of the ditch Pachomius saw the beam of a flashlight
playing over the nearby trees. Then, just as he felt certain he would be
discovered, the same voice said, "What the hell are you doing pointing
that at me?"

"What the gun and I are saying is simple, Fithian. Get in and drive."

"And go where? They know who I am."

"That's your problem, not mine. I said, get in and drive."

Doors slammed, and in a matter of seconds, the car spat pebbles
and dirt as it made a U-turn and sped away. Only then did Pachomius
hear the footsteps of another person approaching where he lay. He
panicked, believing he'd missed a third person standing with the gunmen by the lake.

But then he saw the face of someone who looked familiar, finally
recognizing the tall man who'd sat with Father Nick and the women by
the lake.

"I guess you're the one we need to thank," the man said as he grabbed
Pachomius' hand and lifted him from the ditch.

CHAPTER FORTY-FOUR

------- ◆ -------

St. Simeon's Church

ONCE THE REPRESENTATIVES OF TIFTON'S fire department left St. Simeon's and the police had taken down the names and descriptions of Ronald Fithian and Eldridge Loften, Nick felt the blessed silence of St. Simeon's returning. He sat in the back of the monastery's church with Marina, Henderson, Samiyah, and Brother Pachomius. Earlier that day, he'd promised Abbot Lucas, erroneously as it turned out, that there'd be no threat to the community when he met with the DEA agent, Samiyah. Now, he had to explain all that happened by the lake, how Connie had been Savreen but really Samiyah, and how Gus Cooper was really Ronald Fithian, but all that seemed minor compared to realizing that Sophia's ordeal, and indeed the ordeal of the entire Demetrios family, was over.

Samiyah looked down at the floor as she said, "Marina, I want you to know that I didn't put the blame for killing King on your sister just to protect myself. I couldn't think of another way to continue my search for the dirty agent. If I admitted to shooting King, then that agent would go quiet but not stop what he was doing. I thought of all the kids like your sister who'd gotten into drugs to block out their pain and all the people who had doctors who wrote too many prescriptions for painkillers and got them addicted to opioids."

She paused and looked up to meet Nick's eye. "Fithian might have been partially right, about my wanting to atone for stealing the money.

But something else kept me up at night. I knew that if the dirty agent wasn't stopped, he'd go on protecting the drug lords, alerting them when a raid or crackdown was planned. He'd do what he could to disrupt the Mexican cartels moving into the city, but Loften and others would never have to worry."

Marina wiped tears from her cheeks. "All I can think about right now is that Sophia's nightmare is over. But I want to thank you for trying to protect my sister in prison. Sophia was beaten up once, but who knows what would have happened if her cellmate hadn't been there."

"How did you arrange that without Fithian finding out?" Henderson asked.

"A member of our mosque works at Barminster, and she arranged it. I think Deidra, Sophia's cellmate, protected Sophia when she could for more than just my promise to speak in her favor at her parole hearing. I think she was happy to be doing something good. And I was hoping that that's what I was doing—something good."

They were all silent until Nick said, "Marina, tomorrow morning, after Divine Liturgy, I'll drive you back to Detroit. We'll go right to the prison and give Sophia the good news."

Marina sobbed quietly for a moment. "Can we pick up Poppa before that?"

"Of course," Nick said. He knew that Sophia would now be free, no longer a lamb being marked for slaughter, and he hoped that Sophia would be free in other ways as well.

Samiyah cleared her throat and looked up at the ex-cop. "What are the chances that Fithian and Loften will get away?"

He didn't say anything for a moment. "My guess is that Fithian had an escape plan in place in case he was ever uncovered. He probably has offshore accounts and a few false passports. If his plan is to leave the country, he might already be on the road, or he could lying low, waiting a few days before making a move. If he does get away, and it's a big if, I suspect his first stop will be to a plastic surgeon who'll give him a new face."

"Which means he could come back sometime in the future to settle up with me," Samiyah said.

"Carnell, you said 'if' Fithian gets away," Nick said. "What did you mean? You think the police will catch him?"

"No, not likely. My bet is that Loften is realizing about now that a dirty DEA agent whose cover is blown is of no more use to him. Loften might take Fithian out himself, but he might trade Fithian to the Mexican cartels in exchange for their letting him stay in business. I think Ronald Fithian is already dead or will be before the sun rises tomorrow. And I don't see Loften coming for you, Samiyah."

"Which leaves the three of you to decide what you'll do, now that you know that I stole money from King," Samiyah said in little more than a whisper.

The ex-cop said, "I'm not on the force anymore, so I'm not obliged to tell anyone about the money you took. Another reason I won't report you is that I believe you intend to pay it back." He smiled at her. "Of course, you don't have to give that money to Loften. I suggest you give the money to a good cause, like better conditions for inmates at Barminster."

CHAPTER FORTY-FIVE

November 5, 2023 Barminster Prison

Sophia looked around the new cell—no, the space in Barminster reserved for inmates soon to be released was more like a hotel room. After months of numbness, broken only after she remembered what happened the night King was killed, Sophia was once again numb.

This wasn't the numbness that she'd felt before, the numbness of a dead soul, but the numbness of someone who'd been told what to say and think for the past eight months. She'd been told that she was a killer. She'd been told that it was in her best interests to confess. In Barminster, she'd been told when to get up, when to eat, when to exercise, and when to try to sleep. But now Samiyah Aisha, who'd gone by the name Connie, had changed all that by giving Sophia a choice.

That morning, when Samiyah asked for her understanding and forgiveness, Sophia felt her mind freeze. That was why she'd asked Father Nick to stay after Marina, her father, and Samiyah left. But Father Nick had disappointed her. When she asked what she should do, his only advice was to think about what would free her the most.

Sophia was used to inmates in Barminster claiming that they'd been brutalized by the police or arrested falsely. Those claims had always seemed like bluster to her, but now she realized that she could seek revenge. She looked at Nick and said, "What's to stop me suing the DEA and getting a big settlement?"

"You can do it, Sophia, if that's what you truly need. No one doubts that months of your life were taken from you."

"But that's not what you're suggesting, right?"

Nick didn't say anything for a moment. Finally, he said, "Have you thought about who'd you be now if Samiyah had admitted to shooting King that night?"

She looked down at her hands. "I suppose I could be working and having my own apartment. No, who am I kidding? I'd probably be a full-blown heroin addict. I'd probably be on the streets now, maybe even selling my body for a fix." Tears came to her eyes. "I might even be dead, but does that mean I have to thank the system for getting me clean?"

"I'm not saying you should, but it's important that you know why that wouldn't be enough."

"That's easy to answer. These last months have been hell. No one gives a shit about you in prison. I was lucky that I had Deidra for a cellmate, but inmates mainly prey on each other. I mean, there's no privacy. When you go to the bathroom, your cellmate and any guard that wants can watch you. The guards watch on cameras when you take a shower."

Pausing, she looked around the room. "Every time I see a prison in a movie or read about somebody getting arrested with drugs, I'll be right back here. You asked what freedom I most want, Father. I want to be free of all the memories I have of this place, but they're tattooed in here," she said, pointing to her head. "I can't erase them, you can't, and even God can't."

"Sophia, you're right. Nobody can erase these last eight months. There's only one way to be free, and that's for you to be free not *from* these memories, but free *with* them. To be free, you have to find some meaning in what you've gone through."

"Meaning?" Sophia shook her head. "Father, these months have zero meaning for me. And they never will."

Nick took her hands in his. "But these months have meaning—immense meaning—for others. If Samiyah had confessed to killing King on that night, what would that have meant for Ronald Fithian?"

"I don't understand what you're asking."

"I'll put it this way. If Samiyah had told the truth, what do you think would have happened to Fithian?"

"Nothing, I suppose."

"Wouldn't he have been warned? Wouldn't he have retreated further back into the shadows where he'd still be free to oversee the drug traffic of the city?"

Sophia felt something shift, a door in her mind crack open. "You're right," she said.

"The night King was killed, you weren't given a choice, Sophia. You weren't asked if you were willing to suffer so that Fithian could be stopped and no longer lure young people like you into his net. What happened to you—addiction and even worse—would continue to happen to hundreds, maybe even thousands of others. You didn't have a choice then, but you have a choice now. Instead of these months being taken from you, they can be months of your life that you gave to save others."

ABBOT'S OFFICE, ST. SIMEON'S

BROTHER PACHOMIUS COULDN'T CONTROL THE TREMOR in his legs as he waited for Abbot Lucas to finish typing on his computer.

The abbot finally looked up. "Brother, I met with Father Nicholas last night about what happened by the lake. But as you were also closely involved, I want your thoughts as well."

"Of course, Reverend Father."

Frowning, Abbot Lucas said, "Yesterday afternoon, life here at St. Simeon's was peaceful as it usually is. Father Nicholas assured me then that there'd be no disruption to the community, that what would transpire by the lake would be simply a conversation, a meeting. I think we all agree that this isn't close to what happened. First there were the fire alarms going off, then the police sirens. That was nothing compared to what was happening down by the lake. Men showed up with guns, and people could have been killed. Have I left anything out?"

"No, Reverend Father, that about sums it up. But Father Nicholas shouldn't be blamed. He never—"

Abbot Lucas raised his hand. "Yes, I know. The men with the guns weren't invited, and they didn't come in through our gate. But had people been killed, such a tragedy might have spelled the end of St. Simeon's.

Pachomius could think of nothing to say so remained silent.

"I'm sure Father Nicholas has told you that after I became Abbot, I initially opposed his work with the police. I relented, but with what happened last night, I expect some of the brothers to demand that I withdraw my permission." He paused before he said, "I'd like your opinion on that, Brother."

"Oh, Reverend Father, I beg you not to do that."

"I appreciate your loyalty to Father Nicholas, but it's one thing for him to be drawn into the violence of the outside world and another for that violence to find its way into our life here. Our community has been traumatized and shaken to its core."

"Maybe it's partially loyalty," Pachomius said, "but it's more than that. Father Nicholas' work has saved lives over the past weeks."

"Yes, yes. Well, I will be talking with Father Nicholas about his future work with the police. But there is something else I want to talk with you about, Brother."

Pachomius nodded, "I suppose you mean my future."

"Exactly. In your work for Father Nicholas, you managed to violate almost every restriction our community gave you. To put it another way, you broke your vow of obedience over and over again. That doesn't bode well for the future, does it, Brother?"

"No, Father, it doesn't."

After a pause, Abbot Lucas said, "I see three options, paths leading into the future—your future. One is for us to agree that you don't have a monastic vocation. I don't say that to shame you. It's strictly a matter of fitting in. I hope you can see that, Brother."

As hard as it was to hear that, Brother Pachomius took solace in knowing that leaving was only one of three possibilities.

"The second option is to concede that we, and especially Father Nicholas, have failed you these past weeks. In the Lord's Prayer, we say 'lead us not into temptation,' but this, I believe, is precisely what we did to you. Father Nicholas' lack of computer skills put you into tempting situations. Can we not agree that if he hadn't solicited your help, you would never have been tempted to contact a female retreatant after dark or leave your post in the security office?"

"Reverend Father, these are decisions I made. Please don't blame Father Nicholas."

"Putting aside who is to blame, this second option leads to a less drastic response. In the future, you would return to normal life as a novice. There will be no computer work, no work in the security office, no deviation from the daily pattern of life at St. Simeon's, and especially no special assignments for Father Nicholas."

In other words, I'd be on a leash, Pachomius thought, but said, "I understand."

"The two paths that I've outlined, leaving the community or returning to the normal duties of a novice, are options tested and found effective in nearly two thousand years of monastic life. And, I'm confident that most of the brothers in the community expect me to choose one of those options."

Pachomius nodded even as he thought, *What then is the third path?*

"The third option is risky for you and for our community, Brother. It has fewer precedents in monastic life. But as I listened last night to Father Nicholas' account of what happened at the lake, I realized that I had to consider if these two options are the will of God in this case."

Pachomius had anticipated the first two options outlined by the abbot, but now he felt lost, unable to guess where the abbot was leading.

"Father Nicholas asked me to take into consideration that your assistance contributed to innocent people being cleared. In addition, your work helped end the evil work of a drug dealer. Do you agree?"

Pachomius felt his face redden. "I'm not sure I did anything special. Another person with computer skills, someone from outside our community, could have figured out what I did."

He thought he detected a softening on the abbot's face.

"Nothing special. Well, that might be true about much of what you contributed, but not about what you did last night."

"Sorry, Reverend Father, I don't follow."

"You disobeyed Father Nicholas' clear instruction that you stay in the security office."

The accusation hung over Pachomius like a cloud. "Yes, I confess that I disobeyed."

"And if you hadn't, four people would likely be dead now."

"What?"

"Obedience is clearly a challenge for you, Brother, yet I must acknowledge that God used your disobedience to save the lives of two young women, an ex-police officer, and Father Nicholas. Mysterious indeed are the ways of God, my son."

Not bothering to fight back tears, Pachomius asked, "I can stay?"

Abbot Lucas came around his desk and rested his hand on Pachomius' head. "Yes, Brother, you can stay. But know that the God who used your disobedience in this case is the same God who gave us the vow of obedience."

"Yes, Reverend Father, I understand."

Smiling, Abbot Lucas said, "Then pray for me as I try to explain this to the community."

CHAPTER FORTY-SIX

❖

NOVEMBER 6, 2023, APPELLATE COURT

THE DAY BEGAN WITH WORTHY ENTERING THE COURTROOM, feeling calm for the first time since returning to Detroit. William Tremont had leered at him, as if he were already celebrating his imminent release. Worthy sat stoically, not letting on that Tremont's appeal could be in jeopardy.

Worthy wondered what Kenna McCarty and Phillip Sherrod, sitting across the courtroom, were making of Lena, Henderson, Sulla, and Nick in the seats beside him. Did the two of them assume that his friends had come to support him when the judges ruled in Tremont's favor? If so, they must be surprised, Worthy assumed, that none of his supporters looked downcast or anxious.

After the center judge called the court to order, Howard Hullinger rose and asked permission to address the bench.

Nodding, the lead judge said, "You may proceed."

"If it please the court, I request that final arguments be delayed until I call a final witness, one who can resolve the central question of the case, the dating confusion on William Tremont's toxicology report."

He'd barely finished speaking before Janine Reeves, Tremont's lawyer, objected. "Your honors, Mr. Worthy's lawyers have known for the past five days that final arguments are scheduled for today. It's too late to present new evidence, and I ask the court to treat this as just a stalling tactic."

"Not true, your honors. The evidence that the witness, a noted medical doctor, will present didn't surface until this weekend. I ask that he be allowed to testify. If the court deems his testimony irrelevant, you can always strike it from the record. But once you hear his testimony, I am convinced you will accept that it is more than relevant. His testimony is conclusive."

A murmuring spread through the room as the judges conferred. Finally, the lead judge used the gavel to restore order. "We will hear the new evidence, but counsel is advised that if the testimony presented is judged to be a delaying tactic, we will proceed with final arguments immediately."

"Agreed, your honors," Hullinger said. "I call Dr. Mason Schmidt to the stand."

Lena squeezed Worthy's hand, which reminded Worthy that his fate was in the hands of a man he'd never seen before. Worthy knew that Hullinger wouldn't have subpoenaed Dr. Schmidt to testify if he thought the psychiatrist would be uncooperative, but he wondered if the psychiatrist would nevertheless downplay his mistake to protect his reputation.

Dr. Schmidt, dressed smartly in a double-breasted suit and matching dark blue glasses, took the oath in a monotone voice. *He's used to giving testimony, but is he used to telling the complete truth?* Worthy thought.

"Dr. Schmidt, let's clarify your credentials as we begin," Hullinger said. "You are a psychiatrist and already the head of a practice in Lansing, is that right?"

"Correct."

"I assume that you've been called on before to offer testimony."

"Again, that's correct."

"While your practice is in Lansing, your medical school training was here in Detroit," Hullinger said,

"Yes."

"Dr. Schmidt, do you remember where you were on November 2, 2010?"

"I do. I had a pathology rotation and was observing Dr. Robin Wallace."

"But isn't it true that you were involved in more than an observing capacity on that day? Did you not fill out some forms for Dr. Wallace?"

"That I did, sorry to say."

"Do you remember what forms these were?"

"They dealt with the toxicology screening of William Tremont."

Worthy saw Tremont grab his lawyer's arm as if to force her to her feet, but Reeves brushed his arm away.

"Some people would say that you must have an extraordinary memory, Dr. Schmidt."

"In psychiatry, we know that humiliating memories are often the strongest."

"And this was a humiliating memory, then."

"Dr. Wallace had a sharp tongue and a short temper. He laid into me in front of my peers for misdating the toxicology screening."

"What was the wrong date that you wrote on the form?"

"November 2, 2010."

"And the correct date of Mr. Tremont's screening was what?"

"November 1."

"Did Dr. Wallace explain how he would handle the error?"

"Yes, he used my mistake to show the class the correction page that would be placed in the case file."

"So, you actually saw the correction page. Had he filled it out?"

"Yes, he had."

"No further questions, your honors," Hullinger said, sitting down.

It wasn't until Lena's hand relaxed on Worthy's arm that he realized how tightly she'd held onto him.

Tremont's face was red, his hands in fists, as Reeves rose.

"Dr. Schmidt, just a few questions. Your testimony is nothing short of amazing and timely. You come here at the exact end of this trial and ask us to believe that you remember an event from thirteen years ago."

Dr. Schmidt looked over the top of his glasses at Reeves. "That's a statement. You said you had questions."

"My questions are obvious. Why come forward now? And despite your psychiatric assessment of the persistence of humiliating memories, is it really believable that you remember the event you described in such detail?"

"Pardon, but I never caught your name," Schmidt said.

"I'm sorry, are you asking me my name?"

"Yes."

"It's Ms. Reeves."

"Well, Ms. Reeves, I didn't exactly come forward. I was subpoenaed. Now, about my memory of the dates. If you ask my colleagues in my practice, they will tell you that everyone is invited to a particular bar in Lansing every year on November 1. The occasion is not just free drinks, but a micro-lecture delivered by me on the importance of accuracy in all matters, written and otherwise, related to our clients. Every November 1, whether they are new to the practice or have been with me for years, my colleagues hear the story of Dr. Robin Wallace and my error. I spare none of the details. I hope that answers your question."

Everyone in the courtroom seemed to be holding their breath. Worthy looked over at Kenna McCarty, her mouth gaping open. Next to her, Phillip Sherrod let his head drop to his chest.

The spell was broken by Tremont's mother beginning to wail. Tremont sat frozen, his hands now gripping the armrests, while the lead judge used her gavel to bring order to the room before saying, "Ms. Reeves, do have any further questions for the witness?"

Worthy understood why Reeves sat down without saying anything. Asking Schmidt further questions would only give the psychiatrist a chance to further establish his credibility.

"Hearing none, closing arguments will begin on Wednesday, nine o'clock," the lead judge announced before rising with her fellow judges and departing the courtroom.

Worthy heard Lena say something, but it was as if she were speaking from the end of a long hallway. "What did you say?" he asked, as Hullinger turned and gave him a thumbs up.

"Is it over, Chris? Is it really over?" Lena asked.

Even as he heard himself say "We'll know on Wednesday," he tried to imagine how Tremont's lawyers could counter Dr. Schmidt's devastating testimony in their final arguments. But he could think of nothing—absolutely nothing.

✝

NOVEMBER 7, 2023 HOMICIDE HEADQUARTERS

NICK FOUND PHILLIP SHERROD IN THE homicide division's break room where he was sitting with a glass of water and a bottle of pills.

Looking up, Sherrod said, "Ah, I see that Worthy didn't even come in person to gloat."

"No, Christopher doesn't know I'm here."

"And you expect me to believe that?"

"People believe what they want—or need. Do you need to believe that Worthy is gloating right now?"

Sherrod grimaced as he tipped out a pill from the bottle and swallowed it. Pointing to the door, he said, "Just go."

"Is the pain bad?" Nick asked.

"Christ Almighty, what does it look like?"

"Can I sit down?"

Sherrod exhaled slowly. "I'm not in a position to stop you. Six months ago, I'd have thrown you out, I don't care how big you are."

"I believe you." Pausing for a moment, Nick added, "It's the timing of all of this, Lieutenant, don't you think?"

"Cancer has its own timetable, Padre."

"How much time do the doctors give you?"

"Four to five months—if I'm lucky. Your buddy Worthy will be glad. No, that's not quite right. Worthy won't care."

"I could say that you're wrong, that Christopher has never thought the two of you were competing, but that might just prove your point. That he doesn't care, I mean."

"I'd hoped that Tremont would bring the golden boy down, but no, Worthy still ends up shining."

Nick felt the urge to tell Sherrod that Worthy had experienced numerous setbacks, but instead said, "You've wanted to see Christopher humiliated for a long time, haven't you?"

"If you're asking if seeing golden boy fall face-down in his own shit is on my bucket list, you're right."

"I'm wondering how far you would take that wish. Or maybe I should ask, how far did you take it?"

Sherrod glared at Nick. "So that's why you've come. Worthy sent you to find out if I was the one who removed the correction page. He tried that before with Henderson."

"No, it's me who wants to know if you did that."

"Why? So that you can have me charged with obstruction of justice?"

Nick shook his head. "As a priest, I can't share anything you choose to tell me."

Sherrod leaned back and looked up at the ceiling. "Who says I want to tell you anything?"

"It's what I believe as a priest. You're going to die. I'm going to die. That's a given, but we have a choice about how we die. There are good deaths and not so good deaths."

"No, I know how I'm going to die. I'm going to die in a morphine haze."

"But with these regrets on your mind."

"You think I'll have a 'good death' if I tell you that I removed the correction page from the file?"

"Only if you did do that and now want to die free."

"Free? What the hell are you talking about?"

"I'm talking about your regret that you haven't seen Christopher humiliated. Those regrets aren't weighing Christopher down. They're weighing you down. What I'm saying is that a good death is a light death."

Sherrod didn't say anything as he stared down the table. "And if I say I'm happy the way I am? Maybe you're just one of those priests who tries to scare people into telling their secrets."

"Do you believe that's why I came?"

With his eyes still averted, he said, "It's like you said before. We believe what we want to believe."

Nick rose as he passed a piece of paper across the table. "That's my cellphone number. You can leave a message anytime you want. I promise I'll get back to you. But before I go, I ask you to forgive me."

Sherrod started to take a sip of water but then stopped. "What kind of trick is this?"

"No trick. It's something I've realized for a long time but didn't do anything about. I've known that you've hated Christopher for years, going back to the priest who was strangled."

"So what if I have."

"I should have come to see you then. I knew how you felt, but I did nothing."

Sherrod shook his head. "Dream on. You think you could have said something and Worthy and I would have become pals? You have some crazy sort of savior complex, and it's pathetic."

"I'm not saying I would have changed anything. I'm not a therapist, and I'm certainly no healer. But a priest should be like a weather forecaster. I saw a storm brewing between the two of you, but I just let the storm build until . . . well, until you might have opened Tremont's case file and seen a chance to take Christopher down. So forgive me for being silent, for not warning you."

After some silence, Sherrod said in little more than a whisper, "It sounds like you're the one who wants to die free. "Please Father, just go."

CHAPTER FORTY-SEVEN

O VER THE PAST TWO DAYS OF WAITING, Worthy's friends tempered their relief at hearing Dr. Schmidt's testimony with caution. As Worthy explained, Tremont's lawyers had one more chance to attack Tremont's conviction with their closing arguments.

But now, as Worthy sat in the courtroom flanked by Lena, Nick, Henderson, Sulla, and even Jamie, he saw Hullinger smiling at Courtney, his assistant. Across from them sat a silent Tremont next to an equally silent Janine Reeves. Sitting in the press section was Kenna McCarty, but not Phillip Sherrod.

The room seemed eerily quiet to Worthy as the judges filed in. After adjusting the microphone in front of her, the lead judge said, "This morning, I received a message from Ms. Reeves that the appeal of Mr. Tremont's conviction has been withdrawn. Ms. Reeves, please ask your client to stand."

After Reeves and Tremont rose, the lead judge asked, "Mr. Tremont, is it your desire to withdraw your appeal?"

Tremont rested his clenched fists on the table in front of him but said nothing. He turned to look at his mother and sister before staring at Worthy. Finally, he faced the judge and nodded.

"Mr. Tremont, the court needs to hear you respond orally. Is it your desire to withdraw your appeal?"

In little more than a whisper, Tremont said, "Is it my desire? No, but yes, I withdraw my appeal."

The words triggered a loud buzzing throughout the courtroom. Using her gavel to silence the room, she said, "Then it is the decision of this appellate court that Mr. Tremont be returned to prison to complete the remaining portion of his sentence. Mr. Worthy, would you stand?"

Worthy's whole body felt weak as he rose.

"Mr. Worthy, all accusations made against you and your handling of Mr. Tremont's case will remain in the record of the case but will have the word 'Unproven' appended. To the degree that this is possible, you can forget that this appeal ever happened. Case dismissed."

Worthy wobbled as he was surrounded and hugged by his friends. Howard Hullinger worked his way into the circle to shake Worthy's hand and say, "The judge is right. Forget this appeal ever happened."

Henderson put his arm around Worthy and said, "The party is at our house. No argument, Chris."

"I won't argue, but you all should go on ahead. I need to check something with Hullinger."

That was a lie, but the last thing Worthy wanted was to face the press outside.

Lena kissed him before saying, "Sulla asked me to help with the party."

"Of course. I'll only be a few minutes."

After the room emptied, Nick came back in and asked, "Do you need to be alone, my friend?"

Worthy started to nod, then stopped. *Alone.* That was the one word that had dogged him throughout the appeal. Tremont's appeal had brought him back to the darkest days and months of his life when he'd been a loner, a divorcee, a father estranged from his daughters, a man without a friend to his name.

"If you don't mind, Nick, I'd appreciate you staying a bit. If this case has taught me anything, it's that I've been alone too much in my life."

Nick sat down. "These last weeks have been painful."

"They've been a nightmare, and I don't care what the judge and Hullinger said. I'll never forget the appeal. The case didn't just bring me back to the person I was thirteen years ago. I realized that if I'd remained that same person, Tremont would have won the appeal and who knows what he'd do back in society."

Nick said nothing, for which Worthy was grateful.

"You didn't know me thirteen years ago, Nick. I was living in a one-room apartment, my clothes still in boxes, and at least one bottle of whiskey next to my bed. That could still be me. No, that would still be me if I hadn't met you. After we worked together, Henderson was assigned as my partner on a case. He brought his own troubles, but we managed to rescue one another, thanks to you being there. And then three years ago, I met Lena, thanks to you bringing me to Rome on that case."

"You're giving me far too much credit, Christopher."

"I knew you'd say that, but I'm sitting here vindicated because of you, but also because of Lena, Henderson, Sulla, Jamie, and Brother Pachomius."

"That's what is true for all of us. We're saved by others."

"I remember you saying that before, but that's not how loners see the world."

Worthy glanced around the courtroom, a room that had been filled with so much tension, anger, lies, and grief over the past weeks. "You're the glue who helped me put my life back together, Nick."

"Not me, my friend. I always knew that God hadn't given up on you."

Worthy wiped away tears. "Do you remember my reaction when you said that the first time? I yelled at you, 'No, Nick, God has forgotten that I exist. It's you who believes in me.'"

"I do have a habit of putting my foot in my mouth, Christopher."

"Actually, I now see that you were right. We both know something happened two years ago, something I can't explain, when I held that priest as he died. Whatever that something was, it didn't last long, but I felt it again last year in Rome when I thought you could be killed. Whatever that something is, it doesn't seem to hang around."

Out of the corner of his eye, Worthy saw Nick clutch at the cross around his neck.

"But here's what I realized this morning when I looked down the row and saw you, Lena, Henderson, Sulla, Jamie, and Brother Pachomius. Nothing good in my life over the past decade has been an accident, has it?"

"No, not an accident," Nick said in little more than a whisper.

"Whatever that something was that I felt two years ago and then again last year, I now see that it was there all along in you, Lena, Henderson, and the others."

The two friends looked to the front of the empty courtroom. Finally, Worthy said, "I thought I was alone, but I see now that I never was. Does that qualify as a prayer, Nick?"

Nick nodded. "One of the best prayers I've ever heard, my friend."

For the past forty-five years, Franklin College has been David's home. During his career, David was attracted to the topics of faith development, Catholic-Orthodox relations, and Muslim-Christian dialogue. In the last twenty years, religious terrorism has become David's area of specialty. He frequently gave talks and was interviewed on radio and TV about ISIS, Al-Qaeda, and US terrorist groups. More recently, David has offered talks on the causes and potential outcomes of the Hamas-Israeli conflict.

Now retired, David enjoys writing non-fiction related to interfaith efforts and the Christopher Worthy/Father Fortis detective series.

His wife, Kathy, is a retired English professor, an award-winning artist, and his best editor. Their two sons took parental advice to follow their passions. The older, Leif, is a photographer, and the younger, Marten, is a filmmaker.

www.ingramcontent.com/pod-product-compliance
Lightning Source LLC
Chambersburg PA
CBHW010733130726
47899CB00015B/3234